Praise for **Barry Swanson** and *Still Points*

"*Still Points* is a novel of spectacular, untarnished beauty. A lovely, lyrical book that is both profound and honest, entertaining and real. Inspired by a true story, Swanson's literary debut is heartfelt, heartbreaking, and utterly heart-filling."

—Jennifer Niven, #1 *New York Times* bestselling author of *All the Bright Places*

"Barry Swanson's immersive debut is at once a tender romance, an insightful coming-of-age story, and an unflinching look at the realities of war. Swanson grabs the reader from the first page and keeps them in his thrall as he brings the characters and settings to vivid life. Both uplifting and heartbreaking, *Still Points* is a book you won't soon forget."

—Kathleen Barber, author of *Truth Be Told* (now an Apple TV+ series) and *Follow Me*

"In 1943, Philip Zumwalt, a radio gunner in the Army Air Corps, gazes up at the New Guinea sky, 'long(ing) for El or for anyone who love(s) him.' Based on the author's family history, this heartbreaking and compelling novel has the energy and passion of a story that must be told. It is a sweeping tale of love and war, a novel that shines a light on the 'still point' at the heart of all human longing."

—Abigail DeWitt, author of *News of Our Loved Ones*

"Barry Swanson's *Still Points* was inspired by diaries and papers left behind by his wife's Uncle Philip, a poet and musician who served in the U.S. Army during World War II. Swanson had promised to 'make something' of the story he was given. In fact, he did much more than that. He created totally engaging characters who face daunting battles, both in war and of the heart. This large, captivating tale illuminates how love and war—in very different ways—change everything. *Still Points* is heartbreaking. And, at the same time, it is filled with the energy of life."

—Judy Goldman, author of *Together: A Memoir of a Marriage and a Medical Mishap*

STILL POINTS

A NOVEL

Even in the midst of tragedy, there is hope.
Even in the midst of war, there is love.

BARRY LEE SWANSON

Published by:
Boat House Productions

STATESVILLE, NC
boathouseproductionsnc.com
boathouseproductionsnc@gmail.com

Library of Congress Control Number: 2021910758

ISBNs: 978-1-7372855-0-2 (hardcover)
978-1-7372855-1-9 (paperback)
978-1-7372855-2-6 (ebook)

Editing: Carol Killman Rosenberg

Interior & cover design: Gary A. Rosenberg

Photography: Rebecca McNeely and Tom Foley

Cover art "Overlooking the Coral Sea": Lara Swanson Wilson

For Gail Zumwalt Swanson,
our children and grandchildren

"Sometime they'll give a war and nobody will come."

—Carl Sandburg, *The People Yes*

"I only know there ain't no love at all
Without a song."

—Billy Rose, Edward Eliscu, and Vincent Youmans,
"Without a Song"

"Love does not begin and end the way we seem to think it does.
Love is a battle, love is war; love is growing up."

—James Baldwin, *Nobody Knows My Name:*
More Notes of a Native Son

The universe was not conceived in beauty. It was conceived in tragedy and travail. It evolved and continues to be only in the throes of desperate struggle. Pain and ugliness and brute force rule it.

In the midst of that continuous hurricane of destruction and death, there are born from time to time men who resolve this disorder. They create another vision from the fire and dust of disaster. They are poets and musicians and artists. That is their answer to the ugliness of the world. They do not ask to be understood. They do not even ask to be liked. But without them, we should find the universe an intolerable habitation. They lessen its terrors and ameliorate the eternal torture of its unanswered and unanswerable questions. They are a gallant company. They go singing down the highways of the world, and the echoes of their words comfort us when they have passed.

From Philip Zumwalt's diary
Port Moresby, New Guinea
June 28, 1942

Contents

PART FOUR

PRELUDE

Lake Norman, North Carolina
Summer 2020

THERE IS A CERTAIN RHYTHM TO IT ALL. The cool, moss-green lake water flows by, rushing up to the end of the cove. The setting sun reflecting on water displays an array of water bugs dancing. They sparkle in the sunlight like small Christmas tree bulbs. The dragonflies, butterflies, and bees flutter over the water—a squadron of nature at its finest. Free, unencumbered. The blue heron swoops down on a neighboring dock. It awaits its victim. A small crappie swims by. Stealth and focused, the heron dives. It doesn't kill for any reason other than survival. Most fishermen are more kind. Catch and release.

A south wind pushes the current north. Summer hangs around, spreading its heat and humidity wherever a breeze or air conditioning fail. The flag on our dock unfurls. Fifty white stars on a dark blue background, thirteen horizontal stripes alternating red, white, red. Flapping, it proclaims *my* freedom—completely taken for granted. I sit here—lazy, carefree, mesmerized by nature, breathing the fresh air in and out, in and out. The rhythm of existence. Grateful and content to just be, I ponder the promise I made so many years ago.

I trudge up the sloped lawn to the boathouse, which houses my study. A box sits nestled in a bookcase among World War II books, medals, and photographs of veterans—my grandfathers, my father, father-in-law, their brothers, Lucky Stevens, and me.

First presented to me on a snowy Christmas morning years ago, a gift from my father-in-law, Homer Zumwalt, the box was wrapped with metallic silver paper, gold ribbon, and a gold bow. After ripping open the paper, I was disappointed to find a plain gray-and-white cardboard box. Its lid was bound together with duct tape. The name PHILIP was written in blue ink over Wite-Out on the coffee-stained surface of the lid.

Opening the box, I discovered an assortment of artifacts: letters, yellowed newspaper clippings, black-and-white photographs, a stapled collection of poems, and three diaries with Philip Zumwalt's words in his own distinctive penmanship. Under the papers and photos lay gold, silver, and bronze medals representing and honoring his bravery, courage, and sacrifice.

Never a man who minced words, Homer had presented me with the simple box that contained the saga of his brother. "Thought maybe you could do something with these things of Philip's," he said.

I nodded, hoping I could, not beginning to imagine the burden I had placed upon myself and the fact that my affirmation to my father-in-law was a promise I was bound to honor.

My wife's relatives had told and retold, with an almost mythical reverence, the tales of her uncle Philip, a young, daring hero, a true Renaissance man who, after falling in love, sought an adventure that took him halfway around the world and landed him in the maelstrom of war.

On that Christmas afternoon, I cloistered myself in my study, opened the box, and leafed through the materials. I read with a sense of awe Philip's detailed accounts of his extraordinary adventures. This story emerged from those diaries and collection of papers and was inspired by actual events.

—Barry Swanson

PART ONE

CHAPTER 1

Of Fear and Feeble Prayers

Port Moresby, New Guinea
March 28, 1943

THE SOLDIER AWOKE FROM HIS AFTERNOON NAP. The Sundays he remembered were mostly filled with prayers, hymns, scripture. He had long ago rationalized all of that, his bargain with God—Pascal's wager. The clouds had passed over. No rain for a change. He wondered if Burnsy and Ruth had ended up in the woods next to their tent. He longed for such moments. Evening came, and he was left alone with his thoughts. Thinking had become an occupational hazard for him—overthink, overreact. What madness had landed him here? Mud, insects, bombs—death. Wilson's warning made sense now. Weapons existed for a single reason: to kill. No sugarcoating that.

After rereading his letter to El, he sealed it in an envelope, rose from his desk, and slipped through the tent's makeshift door. It was all makeshift here: his desk, his chair, the crude wood-burning stove, his mosquito-netting-draped cot, even the Flying Fortresses. They needed a gun in the nose. Hell, they needed a gun on every inch of every stinkin' plane. To its credit, or to the pilots', who made it a point to survive, the Fortress had earned its name.

Stepping outside, he gazed up into the clear night sky, preening for all who took in its spectacular, untarnished beauty. He longed for El or for anyone who loved him. He cursed his hubris, his naivete. What if all men said, "No!" to war, dropped their weapons, and just went home to those they loved—no more medals, no more citations of valor, no more letters or telegrams that begin, "We regret to inform you . . ."? How would those words be translated in Japanese, German, Italian, French, Russian? Weren't the tears the same in any language? Didn't all mothers and fathers feel the same ache? Do souls speak different languages?

It mattered not. This was his destiny. He had chosen and had no one to blame but himself. It was his decision to leave her behind, and she had every right to do what she had to do to find some joy in this sorrowful world. The stars held no alternative answers, nor did the God he felt had ignored his feeble prayers.

The soldier returned to his tent, threw back the mosquito netting, and climbed onto his cot. The inane conversation, slapstick humor, and redundant profanity had become his daily reality, men making the best of it, sidestepping the topic they feared the most while a mystery hung like a sacred, silken shroud over each tent: Who was next? For now, he tuned it out as his mind raced back to her and the day it all began.

CHAPTER 2

Delusions of Grandeur

Nebo, Illinois
August 31, 1940

THE MORNING STORM HAD NEARLY GIVEN UP. Remnants of August's last gasp to saturate the Illinois prairie dripped from the six-paned window. Philip Zumwalt gazed through the glass and surveyed the mud-soaked terrain below. Turning wistfully, he took in the totality of the room he shared with his two younger brothers. He would miss them. Three single, wooden beds draped with multicolored quilts stood silent. Upon the faded whitewashed walls hung crooked framed certificates heralding the academic, musical, and athletic accomplishments of the boys. A three-drawer oak dresser stood centered on the west wall. Medals hung over a display of trophies. Beside the dresser was a crude four-shelved pine bookcase crammed with an array of classic works of literature, dime novels, and Penguin paperbacks.

A wooden storage trunk sat at the foot of each bed. Opening his trunk, he retrieved a small leather and canvas satchel, tugged open the top drawer of the dresser, and gathered up his underwear and socks. Meticulously, he placed the items in the satchel, leaving room for the toiletries he would add later. After filling a leather suitcase with shirts, pants, two sweaters, and two ties, one red and one blue, he removed two of his favorite books from the shelf, *Winged Victory* and *Air, Men and Wings*. Being an airplane pilot had been a dream of his since first hearing of the legend of the Vin Fiz as a young boy. He realized such a fantasy was far-fetched, but it remained a goal nonetheless.

His long, thin fingers caressed the books, one in each hand. He shook his head. *Another delusion of grandeur,* he thought. He slammed the books together and, bending his elongated frame at the waist, carefully placed them atop a stack of sheet music and the other dozen or so books in his temporary library—all neatly nestled together in two wooden Blue Goose fruit crates. He left the majority of the books for his brothers.

A familiar voice echoed up the narrow stairs from below, "Philip? Philip, are you in your room?"

"Yes, Mother," the eldest brother replied. "Just finishing up with some packing."

"Are you still headed out to Boren's this morning?"

"Yes, ma'am. Soon as the rain lets up."

"Would you please pick up a loaf of Wonder Bread while you're there? There's a dime on the table next to the umbrella stand."

"Glad to, Mother."

In a few days, the twenty-year-old college graduate would leave home. He would never admit to his parents, family, or friends that it was time to move on and begin his own journey—to leave Nebo's dirt roads and no-nonsense folks behind. He doubted they would understand his wanderlust, his need for adventure. Even his new teaching position in Payson was simply a stopgap. Someday, he planned on being a great songwriter, like Gershwin, and perhaps fly himself from one metropolis to another to entertain throngs of adoring fans. His best friend, Billy Epperson, continually accused him of being an unrealistic dreamer, but Philip Zumwalt believed in himself, his talent, his destiny.

He descended the steps from his bedroom, and passing by the Zumwalt spinet piano, he struck middle C on the keyboard. "Still in tune, Mother."

"Still in tune, dear," his mother replied.

"Headed out to Boren's!" he shouted.

Grabbing an umbrella from the stand next to the front door, he reached back, snatched the dime from the table, swung open the screen door, and stepped off the front porch into the diminishing sweet, fresh rain. It dripped from his umbrella as he headed down Pine Street, turned left at Smith's Alley, darted onto Union Street, and headed to Boren's Grocery and Meat Market.

Philip chatted with Homer Boren and paid for the bread and a few necessities for himself—a tube of toothpaste, two bars of soap, a jar of Brylcreem, and a bottle of Old Spice aftershave. The rain refused to surrender. Umbrella in one hand and paper sack in the other, he hummed a tune as he strolled home.

"Hey, Nelly!" Billy Epperson yelled as he sprinted toward Philip— a man on a mission. Soaking wet and breathing hard, he ducked under Philip's umbrella. By the time they reached the Zumwalt front porch, Billy had caught his breath. "Can't wait to hear Dorsey tonight."

As the self-appointed social chair of "The Pike County Posse," Billy had big plans on this last Saturday night of August. One final hurrah before he and his buddies went their separate ways. One last fling—music, dancing, and liquor. Live for the moment.

"I think I'm gonna pass. I'm a little short on cash. Besides, we'll be jammed into the Casino like sardines in a can. The only band I'd pay two bucks to hear is Glenn Miller's." Philip could barely restrain a grin.

"You're kidding, right? You said you'd drive. You can't back out now. Ah, you're messing with me, aren't you? I know you wouldn't pass up a chance to see Sinatra."

Philip continued the charade. "Sorry, pal. I'm just not in the mood . . ." Philip could no longer contain himself and began to laugh at his friend's pitiful look of disappointment. "Of course I'm ready. Who's better than Dorsey and Sinatra? Nobody."

"Well, you're right about that!" Billy exclaimed. "And who knows? Now that we're both single, maybe we'll get lucky. The girl of our dreams just might be waiting for us right out there on the Casino's dance floor. You gotta get your head out of the clouds. Kate's moved on and so should you."

"Agree. We both need to move on," Philip replied.

Billy and Pat Carpenter, a couple since their sophomore year, had called it quits after their graduation from Western Teachers' College. Philip understood his best friend's heartache. He and Kate Uphouser had also been a couple for the past two years. But a month or so after graduation, following her best friend Pat's lead, Kate, too, had called the whole thing off.

"Posse forever, right?" Billy said.

"Posse forever," Philip replied. "I'll pick you guys up at Boren's gas station."

Billy "The Kid" could barely contain himself. "This just might be our lucky night! Yahoo! Dorsey and Sinatra. I'm gonna be dancin' to Sinatra and Dorsey! I can't believe it!" He leaped off the porch into the still drizzling rain, turned 180 degrees in the air, and gave Philip the Posse salute—two fingers up to the forehead—and then swung his hand to his side. Philip smiled and returned the gesture.

As Billy dashed home, Philip laughed. *Not enough sense to come in out of the rain*, he thought. Deep down, he had immense respect for his best friend. Billy was a truth-teller. Philip listened to Billy's advice, even when he didn't completely agree with it. Billy and Philip had been best pals since grade school—founding members of the Pike County Posse. Over the years they'd shared their most intimate secrets. Billy appreciated Philip's musical talents and Philip was Billy's biggest fan. Whether on the football field or basketball court, Billy was an elite athlete, lettering in both sports at Western. What Philip respected most about Billy though was that he was a stand-up guy, as honest as the day was long. Above all, he was loyal to his pals, especially Philip.

Billy was a true friend, always willing to offer his counsel, so it was no surprise in the spring, following Philip's breakup with Kate, that he'd shared his wisdom. "You know what your problem is, Nelly?

Your head's full of delusions of grandeur. You're not going to get Kate back, and most likely, you're never gonna be famous. How many folks do you know from Nebo who became famous? Now, I gotta admit you're a helluva piano player, but only a few musicians make it in the big time. You know, Carnegie Hall or Broadway. And your chances of becoming a famous songwriter? C'mon, pal, get real! Gettin' a gig like that's nearly impossible."

"Maybe so," Philip had responded, "but I'm gonna hang on to what you just said, *most likely* and *nearly impossible*. It might take some time, but I'm gonna make it, just you watch."

"Dream all you want about that, buddy, but the reality right now is you're gonna be a schoolteacher. You can't change what you're gonna be, for a year at least. You already signed a contract. And we both know Kate's history."

Billy was right and Philip knew it. *But what if he's right about tonight, too?* he thought. Maybe Sinatra will bring him luck. And what if his dream girl did magically appear out of the shadows? *Of course,* he thought, *that, too, is probably just another delusion of grandeur!*

The Posse gathered at Boren's gas station and piled into Philip's decade-old dark-blue Chevy Coach. Adorned with blue-and-silver steel disk wheels, it shined inside and out. Philip guarded and protected his vehicle like a sentry at Buckingham Palace. The Posse was present and accounted for. Steve "Big Fish" Trout, Charlie "Hawkeye" Harkness, and Billy "The Kid" Epperson settled into the backseat. Philip slipped into the driver's seat. Jerry "The Giant" Inness rode shotgun. Fantasizing he was riding on a stagecoach in one of his beloved western movies, he assured Philip, "You're safe with me up here, Nelly."

Philip put the car in gear and pointed it due north on the Pittsfield Road.

"Gem City or bust!" Epperson yelled.

Harkness laughed. "I wonder if any of us will hit the jackpot at the Casino."

Trout passed around his silver-coated flask of Jack Daniel's whiskey and a pack of Camel cigarettes. As hooch was sipped and Camels smoked, conversation of alleged carnal knowledge drifted from the backseat toward Philip.

Philip concentrated on the road but couldn't get Kate out of his mind. Maybe this one time, fate would be on his side. He turned the Chevy northwest into the setting summer sun as the tepid breeze blew through the open windows, offering minimal relief from the oppressive August heat. The backseat conversation turned to baseball—Johnny Mize's home runs, the New York Yankees, and Joe DiMaggio.

Philip had been a fool for Kate. That wasn't about to happen again. He tuned out the chatter and hummed to himself, the words repeating in his head:

"Fools rush in,
Where wise men never go,
But wise men never fall in love,
So how are they to know?"

I'll be wise tonight. Dance—yes! Fall in love—no! As he pushed his foot down on the accelerator, the last of the August rain began again.

"Hey, Nelly, whaddya hummin'?" Harkness asked from the backseat.

"Ah, it's a new one Sinatra sings called 'Fools Rush In,'" Philip said.

"Sing it for us, Nelly," Epperson urged.

"Naw, I bet he'll sing it tonight. He's a lot better crooner than me, for sure." Philip stopped humming, but he couldn't get the word *fool* out of his mind.

CHAPTER 3

The Casino

THE PARKING LOT AT THE CASINO dance club in Quincy's Highland Park was packed with blue and black Chevys and Fords and a single lipstick-red Ford Deluxe convertible with a tan ragtop. The early evening sprinkles turned to a downpour and drenched the Posse as they sprinted onto the dance club's front porch, a grand stone edifice supported by Greek Corinthian columns. A black rectangular sign hung over the entrance. White block letters announced, THE CASINO. They were in the right place. The Posse raced up a flight of stairs flanked by oval windows hijacked from an ocean liner. Busting through the leather-covered doors decorated with imitation jewels, the Posse had arrived.

"Two dollars each, please," said the young blond woman at the card table.

I hope Sinatra's worth it, Philip thought. He forked over two one-dollar bills and entered the hall with the others.

A black, four-foot plaster wall surrounded the dance floor. Sparkling light shimmered from overhead chandeliers and bounced off the floor where a crowd danced to the sounds of the Dorsey Band. Stretching along one end of the floor, the band wore white tuxedo jackets, black pants, white shirts, and black bow ties. Their instruments glimmered, golds and silvers reflecting the light from the chandeliers.

Conversations and laughter rose from the tables surrounding the dance floor. Drinks flowed as misty smoke swirled above the patrons.

As the Posse entered the ballroom, a thin, dark-haired soloist stepped up to the microphone.

"That's Sinatra, Nelly!" Epperson's dream had come true. "The gals call him Ol' Blue Eyes."

Ol' Blue Eyes sang:

> "Fools rush in where angels fear to tread . . ."

"Looks to me like there's plenty of ladies to choose from out there. You just gotta have a few moves. Observe." Trout strolled onto the floor looking like an octopus, arms and legs flailing all over.

"That's what he calls moves?" joked Harkness.

"Yeh, real smooth," added Epperson.

Sinatra concluded:

> "When we met, I felt my life begin,
> So open up your heart and let this fool rush in."

The dance floor erupted with spontaneous applause for the young crooner. Dorsey revved up the band and the first few rhythmically displaced notes of "In the Mood" sent the dance floor into a frenzy. The Posse members shook their heads in disbelief. Trout was dancing and swinging with a pretty redhead.

"Maybe he does have a few moves," Inness said. "We better get out there or all the gals'll be taken."

Harkness, Inness, and Epperson sauntered onto the dance floor and joined Trout. Philip brought up the rear. Trout's partner introduced a few of her friends, but by the time Philip joined his friends, all the available dance partners were taken.

Next dance, he thought. After retreating to a table at the edge of the floor, he noticed a young woman smoking a cigarette emerging from the shadows. The light of the candle on Philip's table exposed the intruder.

"May I?" she asked, pointing to the ashtray on his table.

Philip grinned. "Help yourself."

She crushed her cigarette into the ashtray. "Can't dance or just don't want to?"

"Oh, I can. Just haven't seen anyone who can keep up with me," he said half laughing. He was doing his best to mimic suave Cary Grant, but his hair, suit, and shirt were still damp. He imagined he looked more like a drowned rat than the dashing movie star.

The interloper was certainly worthy of a spin. With lips full and as crimson as the posh red convertible in the parking lot, she stood only a few inches shorter than Philip. Her perfectly coiffed auburn hair accentuated her champagne-colored cocktail dress. The dress, draped just below her shoulders exposed her smooth, bronze skin. "Bet I can keep up with you," she said.

"Okay, you're on!" Philip hopped up and took her hand.

Gliding onto the dance floor, they executed a perfect 360-degree twirl, catching nearby dancers by surprise. Philip had won the last two homecoming dance competitions with Kate at Western. His new partner knew her way around the dance floor. The pair floated across the floor, spinning right and left, and back to the right again. "In the Mood" was the perfect song for the couple to display their synchronicity. She responded to each of Philip's steps with her own graceful moves. *This gal can dance!*

Trumpets flourished through the final notes as the band segued into a slow dance, "Cheek to Cheek." Sinatra was back. He crooned:

"Heaven, I'm in Heaven,
And my heart beats so that I can hardly speak—"

"So, can you slow it down, too?" she asked.

He took her hand once again. A foxtrot. He didn't take the song literally, even though her cheeks looked inviting. The song ended. Mr. Dorsey announced an intermission. The dancers exited the dance floor dripping with sweat. The young woman walked ahead of Philip, moisture glistening on her soft shoulders. He hung his suit coat over a chair, rolled up his shirtsleeves, loosened his tie, and unbuttoned the neck of his shirt, now even more soaked.

"Cocktail?" he asked.

"That'd be swell. A sloe gin fizz, please."

She accompanied him to the bar. He ordered the drink, paid the bartender, and handed it to her.

"Thank you. My name's Elinor Robinson, by the way, but my friends call me El." Her voice was deep, soft. She sipped the cocktail with the same elegance she had displayed on the dance floor.

"A pleasure to meet you, El. You're quite a dancer." Philip retrieved his coat from the chair. They moved to one of the tables along the dance floor. He took a sip of his cocktail, and the old-fashioned burned all the way down. Outside the rain had stopped, but humidity saturated the air. "Are you from Quincy?"

"No, just tagged along with my cousin who lives here. I'm from a small town just a few miles from here called Payson. Doubt you've heard of it."

What? This young beauty lives in Payson? Too good to be true!

The band returned and revved up again. The piano began tinkling the first few notes of "Take the A Train." The entire brass section joined in and began blasting out the popular tune. Couples raced to the dance floor and began to swing.

"Actually, I have," Philip responded with enthusiasm. Ignoring the din and commotion erupting on the floor next to their table, he was far more interested in introducing himself to his new dance partner. "My name's Philip, Philip Zumwalt. Believe it or not, I'm going to be a teacher in Payson."

The deafening music made it difficult for El to hear. "A preacher? Which church?"

Thinking she had said *teacher*, Philip said, "Yes," and then politely responded to the second part of her inquiry, "First Christian. What about you?"

"Oh, Congregationalist, Bluff Hall. But Payson's a small place. I'm certain we'll see each other around town other than on a Sunday. It's sure loud in here, isn't it? You did say your name was Philip, right?"

"Yes, *Philip*," he half shouted.

"Well, a pleasure to meet you, Philip." She stuck out her hand, and he took it once again. Somewhat puzzled by the handsome young man, she thought, *Awfully young to be a preacher. Where in the world did he learn to dance like that? Maybe the First Christians don't care if their preachers drink or frequent nightclubs.* A yell from across the room interrupted her thoughts.

"Hey, Nelly! You still got it, boy!" It was Trout. "Ya cut a mean rug out there." He made his way over to their table, a stunning redhaired woman on his arm. "Meet Miss DeAnne Eubanks, the Queen of Quincy."

Philip rose from his chair. Elinor smiled. Both nodded their heads at the Queen of Quincy, but before Philip could respond with his own introduction, Trout and the queen were back on the dance floor.

The music died down as their conversation resumed. "Nelly? So, are you trying to deceive me? Any more aliases?" El laughed, reached for her purse, and pulled out a pack of Lucky Strikes. She slipped one from its carton along with her lighter.

Philip picked up the lighter and lit her cigarette as he'd done hundreds of times for Kate. El obliged. "Would you like one?" she asked.

"Oh, no thank you. I don't smoke," he replied.

Of course not, she thought. *One vice is probably all the preacher is allowed.* "I just love how it makes me feel so euphoric!" She took a long, elegant drag and exhaled seductively over her shoulder. "So, what's with the nickname? Nelly, is it?"

"That's my nickname—at least to these guys. But I had no intention of deceiving you, Miss Robinson." He smiled at her, spellbound by his new dance partner.

She continued, "Why don't we shorten your cute little nickname to Nell. Get it? El and Nell." She giggled. "Don't get me wrong. I just meant like, you know, a dancing duo—Ginger and Fred. Of course, they don't rhyme."

Her euphoria made Philip laugh, too. "Well, Ginger, shall we dance?"

"Why, yes, Fred, I thought you'd never ask."

They danced as the band played. Romance and humidity drenched the Casino. Dreamy-eyed couples floated by, propelled by boundless, youthful energy. The sight of stylish twosomes gliding across the floor was exhilarating. *Best two bucks I ever spent!* Philip thought.

The evening wore down, and Sinatra returned to the microphone.

> "I'm in the mood for love
> Simply because you're near me . . ."

The singer's voice was soft, sensual. As they danced, their bodies brushed against each other. Moving to the music as if in a trance, Philip lost himself in his own version of fantasia. He did his best to dismiss the feelings rising up inside him. As the song ended, Philip dipped El. She lingered in his arms. It seemed to him she was almost begging to be kissed. Instead, she popped up with a proposition, "How about we take a stroll? There's a room in the lower level where we can talk and actually hear each other."

"Sure," he replied.

Venturing down to the lower level of the Casino, they arrived at a doorway draped with blue tapestries: THE BLUE ROOM, a sign advertised. Separating the drapes, they entered the room and discovered couples entangled on couches and loveseats, lost in romantic interludes. El and Philip claimed a blue brocade loveseat as their own. Sitting next to each other, they talked. Their conversation was easy and comfortable.

"Payson's a pretty boring place, you know," El warned.

"Really? Not according to Ralph Guthrie, a friend of mine from Western. He's now a teacher at the high school. Apparently, there was a scandal involving the music teacher and a married woman in town. The teacher was fired, and the woman left town in disgrace. Pretty juicy gossip if you ask me," Philip replied.

"I do remember that. Not a good thing for a teacher to be having an affair in a small town, I suppose."

"I imagine that's the case in a big town, too." Philip laughed.

"Like I said, Payson's awfully small, not a very exciting place."

It's becoming more exciting by the moment, Philip mused. "Oh, I don't know. I drove around after my interview, and it seemed mighty nice to me. Small but quaint. And the folks at the diner were sure friendly."

"People are plenty nice, just kinda boring," El said, smiling and shrugging. "I'm sure it'll be great. Folks at First Christian are really friendly." She sipped on her drink.

Her church reference puzzled Philip, but he dismissed it and worked on his second old-fashioned, wanting to know more about his newest dance partner. "What about you? What are you interested in?"

"Lots of things. I love music and dancing. My dogs, Stella and Moose—they're only a couple of years old. We kept them together when their mother, our beloved Muffin, died. I suppose you can tell my family is the most important thing to me. And I do love to read and ride our horses. Oh, and going to church, of course."

"Of course. Do you work in Payson?"

"Yes, I'm a pharmacist's assistant at Harris's, the local drugstore, which is also a diner and a soda fountain. We take care of what ails you, feed you, and then top it all off with a chocolate malt."

Philip laughed. "Dating anyone special?"

"Oh, goodness, no. Had a few dates with the same fella, but nothing serious. He's passed out drunk in his car as we speak." She knew Randall Yarborough considered her his girlfriend, but that was not how she viewed it. She had never even kissed him. "You?"

"Dated a girl in college for a couple of years. We were students at Western. Kate was her name. She moved to Chicago after graduation.

Her parents bankrolled her so she could take a crack at acting. I guess she's doing okay. Got a minor role on a new radio show called *Chicago Theater of the Air*."

"So, why didn't you go to Chicago?"

"Couldn't afford it. Decided to save up some money and head up there later. I'd like to think of myself as a musician and a songwriter. It would be my dream come true if some of my songs were published. If I ever got the chance to perform them onstage, that would be almost more than I could ever imagine. Like I said, it's a dream. But who knows?"

"I bet you're terrific." El's haunting, emerald-green eyes locked with his. *Wow!* she thought, *a singing preacher*. "That's quite a plan—sure sounds exciting."

Philip wondered how he'd gotten so lucky to end up with such a beautiful, sophisticated woman. His heart raced, and he looked deeply into her viridescent eyes. "It's not that I think I won't love being in Payson. I'm sure I will. No offense to small towns, but I don't plan on being stuck in one place all my life. I have a lot of dreams. I'd even like to be a pilot someday. Fly around the world and see firsthand all of its wonder."

"I feel the same way. There are a million places I would love to see. Exotic places I've only read about in books or seen in movies."

Conversation continued. Family—her two sisters, his two brothers. Literature—Austen and Brontë for her, Dickens and Twain for him. They engaged in a new dance, the two-step of intimacy, sharing the details of their lives like a malt at Harris's. Almost instinctively, they trusted each other, exchanging confidences, personal and private.

Near closing time, Philip gently cupped El's face. Feeling a rush of exhilaration, he whispered, "May I kiss you?" He leaned in.

Her eyes locked on his as she met his lips with hers. A mixture of gin, lemons, bourbon, vermouth, and bitters with a hint of tobacco mingled together in sweet ecstasy. She wrapped her arms around his neck. They kissed again. An electric current surged through every nerve ending in his body. He sensed it in hers, too. Time stood still. It was as though their souls had melded together.

Billy descended the stairs to the Casino's lower level. It was nearly midnight as he entered the darkened cobalt-hued room in search of his pal. Spotting Philip on the couch with a young woman, he hesitated to interrupt, but the Casino was closing, and the Posse needed a ride back to Nebo. "Hey, Nelly, it's time to hit the road."

Philip stood and offered El his hand. She bounced out of the love seat, smiling at the young man standing before her.

"Elinor Robinson, meet my best friend, Billy Epperson!" Philip said.

Billy nodded and shook El's hand. "Pleased to meet you, Elinor Robinson."

"My pleasure," El replied.

"Well, I guess bewitching hour's come," Philip said regretfully.

"Yeh, the joint's shuttin' down. You sure you can drive home, Nelly?" asked Billy.

Philip replied, "Absolutely." He turned toward El. "It was a real pleasure meeting you, Miss Elinor Robinson."

"Likewise," she said.

"Perhaps you could find some time to show me around Payson next week?"

"Perhaps . . ." She gathered up her evening clutch and sashayed toward the curtained doorway. "I need to find my cousin. She's my ride home, but knowing her, she's probably out in the backseat of her boyfriend's jalopy. Well, until we meet again." She bowed coyly. "Good night . . . Nell."

El glided toward the blue curtains and hesitated. She tossed her head over her shoulder, giving Philip one last chance to observe her elegant exit. Her chic dress caressed her body as she turned around, smiled, and waved.

Philip stood enthralled and grinned back. Putting his index and middle fingers together, he flashed the Posse semi-salute and repeated through his near-drunken haze, "Until we meet again." His heart pounded. Maybe it was the girl, maybe it was the bourbon, but to say he was now looking forward to living in Payson was an understatement. Hopefully, their next meeting would be sooner, not later.

CHAPTER 4

Front Porch Wars

September 1–3, 1940

NEBO, ILLINOIS, WAS A SLEEPY, DUSTY VILLAGE named for the mount that overlooked the Holy Land and the River Jordan, where Moses got his first glimpse of the Promised Land. Scripture reported God buried Moses there, and the prophet Jeremiah hid both the Tabernacle and the Ark of the Covenant on the same mount. The founding fathers of the fair village did, however, realize that their elevation level was much lower than the summit described in the Book of Deuteronomy. Hence, they were humble enough to drop the *mount.*

Paying homage to their village's name, the majority of Nebo's citizens faithfully attended an eleven o'clock church service every Sunday. The Zumwalt family was no exception. Following breakfast on this first Sunday in September, the family filed down the street to the First Christian Church of Nebo. Ruby, the mother of the family, had promised Pastor Harrison that her sons would provide worship music and piano accompaniment for the singing of hymns every other Sunday. Unfortunately for Philip, this was one of those Sundays.

Philip, hangover notwithstanding, and his brothers carried their instruments and sheet music into the sanctuary. It was out of the question for a Zumwalt to ever go back on their word. As he accompanied the congregation's singing of the somber sacred hymns, the upbeat, sultry swing music of Sinatra and the Dorsey Band lingered in his mind. The image of his beautiful dance partner did the same.

Labor Day passed without much fanfare in the village—a simple parade, a few family picnics. On a rainy Tuesday morning, Philip joined his parents and brothers, Homer and Wayne, eighteen and seventeen years old respectively, at the breakfast table.

"How would you boys like to come with me to Boren's this morning?" Alonzo Zumwalt said. "Give your mother a little peace and quiet. Thought you might even like to tell the fellas goodbye, Philip."

Alonzo Zumwalt, known as "Lonnie," had settled in Nebo around 1917 and quickly established himself as a first-rate carpenter. Standing nearly six feet tall with a full head of thick brown hair, wide shoulders, and clear blue eyes, he was an imposing figure. Philip admired his father's skills. He turned pieces of wood into kitchen cabinets to store supplies or tables and chairs upon which a family could eat those same provisions. He had helped to construct houses, garages, and many of the buildings in the merchant's block, including Boren's and Franklin's Hardware Store.

"Sure, Dad. That's a great idea," Philip replied, as his brothers nodded in agreement.

Philip had always enjoyed the lazy Saturday mornings when he and his brothers would tag along with their father and join the regulars who lounged on the front porch of Boren's—a combination grocery store, meat market, and drugstore his father helped build in the early 1920s. The three boys would sprawl out on the solid, splinter-laden floorboards and give their silent but full attention to tales spun, legends remembered, and the purported wisdom being dispensed—free of charge.

With breakfast finished, Lonnie Zumwalt and his three sons grabbed umbrellas and walked together to Boren's. An expansive tin roof stretched across the entire width of the red brick building, sheltering Nebo's elder statesmen from the rain. Philip could smell the scent of the clean morning air surrendering to the heavy aroma of burning tobacco mingled with the musty odor of wet dust.

Smoking corncob pipes, cigars, and cigarettes, the venerable group of men inhaled and exhaled plumes of smoke and smoke rings. Some chewed and spit tobacco, frequently missing their spittoons. Shaving on pieces of wood or just sitting in a collection of castoff chairs, whittling benches, and rockers, the locals discussed the weather, the condition of the crops, politics, and sports. Most mornings, they left the latest gossip to their wives but would, on occasion, repeat a salacious tidbit. Philip was always amused by the chatter.

Lonnie and his boys shook the rain from their umbrellas, found available chairs near three of the old-timers, and exchanged greetings with the other half-dozen men who regularly frequented Boren's. There was always talk of war on the front porch. Those who returned from "the war to end all wars" had hoped it would do just that. Glorified tales of battlefield gallantry and the heroic deeds of the men who did not return dominated most discussions. This morning was no exception.

Lloyd Newman was in the middle of one of his infamous diatribes. "The key to winning a war nowadays, boys, is the air. If FDR gets us into this war, which I hope he don't, we better damn well have a slew of airplanes ready to go." Newman was fervent in his pronouncement.

Colonel "Frankie" Franklin adjusted his blue wool Union Army kepi, took a puff on his corncob pipe, and leaned back in his rocking chair to repeat an oft-told tale. "I remember the day I first saw one a those flyin' machines. They called her 'The Vin Fiz.' A fella named Cal Rodgers flew her in here. It was 1911, as I recall. Landed over there by the cemetery in a hayfield. The whole town turned out to see that plane. The Wright brothers built it, and a special train with spare parts had to come along with her so's they could fix her if need be. Brought Rodgers's wife along, too."

Wayne, ever curious, asked, "What in the world is a 'Vin Fiz'? That was an odd name, wasn't it?"

Newman responded, "Well, sir, Armour and Company from Chicago sponsored the plane. Named it after a new five-cents-a-bottle, grape-flavored soft drink the company hoped to market. Offered to pay Rodgers around five dollars a mile to fly the plane west. Helluva an advertisement. On top of that, Rodgers was hoping to collect the fifty thousand that William Randolph Hearst was offering the first aviator to cross the United States in under thirty days."

"Did he make it?" Homer asked the question this time.

"Naw, took him almost forty-nine days to reach California," Newman answered.

"Damn shame, too," Franklin added. "He was a daredevil! Finally finished up the last twenty miles to complete the flight from the Atlantic to the Pacific but met his Maker after a stinkin' seagull flew into his plane. Jammed the steering mechanism and Rodgers crashed. Broke his neck. He flew all that way and then crashed on the last leg of the flight. Damn shame."

"Old Cal was a hero, though, a real pioneer," Newman said. "Without men like him we'd never be flyin airplanes today. I'm telling you, fellas, if we go to war, we better have thousands of 'em."

Colonel Franklin, with his white beard hanging from his wizened face, pierced the September morning air with his high-pitched voice. "Of course, we wouldn't need no airplanes if Ulysses S. Grant was still alive. The greatest American of all time. I'd still run through a wall of gunfire for old 'Unconditional Surrender' Grant."

"No disrespect, sir, but that would be if you could still run," Newman said with a mocking grin.

"Maybe not, but I'd follow Grant all the way into hell. Matter of fact, I did!"

Franklin's legend had flourished with the years, and his stories never grew old. At the age of twenty-one as a private in Grant's army, he'd fought in the Battle of Appomattox Court House and was a witness to Robert E. Lee's surrender. When Franklin turned eighty years old, a state senator from Pittsfield proposed the aging Union private be promoted. The state legislature approved, and Franklin was awarded the honorary rank of colonel in the Illinois State Militia.

Philip's high school English teacher, Edward Meacham, and Newman had returned from France more than twenty years before. Newman once told his friends that he walked down the streets of Paris, France, before he ever set foot in Pittsfield, Illinois. War talk rarely included vivid details. The veterans didn't mention poisonous gas, hand-to-hand combat, or mud-filled, rat-infested trenches. Or wounds. An explosion had left Newman with a mangled left ear. Meacham bore the proof of his combat on his right cheek; a piece of metal shrapnel had sliced the side of his face, leaving a scar that looked like an arrow pointing due north. He was only a member of the front porch gathering in the summertime. Reserved, quiet, gentle, and dignified, the man's professorial demeanor made it difficult for Philip to imagine that he had ever killed anyone.

Newman was never shy to offer his opinion on any matter, and he vehemently believed the United States of America should avoid war at all costs. Some folks in Nebo called the three front-porch veterans heroes. The trio dismissed the term, saying that the only heroes were the soldiers who didn't come home. All the men who frequented Boren's front porch, veteran or not, agreed on one thing—there was no such thing as a good war.

Newman said, "Well, Colonel, you're sure right about one thing. War is hell. You, Ed, and I all know that firsthand. I, for one, have had enough of war, and I sure as hell hope FDR don't get us into another one. The Nazis ain't gonna hurt us. Let 'em have Poland."

Meacham took issue. "After all we went through together over there, Lloyd, I think you'd agree you can't trust the Germans. I know you value freedom. You were willing to die to defend it. So now, should we turn our backs on the folks in Europe who want to keep their freedom? Too many of our buddies are buried over there. I'd hate to think that was all in vain."

Newman nodded in agreement but wasn't totally convinced.

"What about what Lucky Lindy said? Most Americans agree with him, and so do I. We have no business goin' over there again to Europe, no business at all. They can fight their own damned battles. I mean, how much good did it do for us to fight the war to end all wars, Ed? There's always another war."

Philip knew Newman had a point, and he and his friends had no interest in going to war. But what if the news reports were accurate about innocent European citizens being arrested and murdered simply because they were Jewish? Wouldn't that make a war necessary? Newman had another thing right. The citizens of the United States wanted nothing to do with war again. They, like Newman, no longer had the stomach for war. The last thing they desired was to send their boys off to be killed halfway across the world.

Philip daydreamed as he walked home in the rain with his father and brothers. Heading to Chicago was a pipe dream. Billy was right. Folks from Nebo just didn't become famous overnight. In fact, no one from Nebo had ever become even remotely famous to the best of his knowledge. His parents had other obligations, like sending their two younger sons to college.

He felt conflicted. On one hand, he was sure, at least in his fantasies, that he really could be the next Gershwin, but if war was on the horizon and Newman was right about the need for air superiority, perhaps he should put Chicago on hold and save up for pilot lessons instead. Both were equally valid dreams. Setting his conflict aside, he decided it was prudent to save for both and let fate decide his future path.

The front porch conversation continued to linger in his mind. *Why are men so intrigued by war?* He had been curious about war ever since he was a young boy. Even though the veterans all hated war, they never seemed to stop talking about it, like when folks talked about a terrible accident or a divorce. Everyone said how awful it was, but they'd still discuss it for days on end.

Questions raced through his mind. *Does a man fight for the love of his country, or is it out of fear of being called a coward? What would America look like if it was defeated in a war?*

Could it be what Mr. Meacham said? Fighting for freedom? That would square with what his teachers taught him in American history classes. Who were these heroes? Dead men? If the United States were attacked, would he sacrifice his life to defend his loved ones? Did men fight for honor, or was it out of mindless obedience? Bravery? Does Good, in the end, conquer Evil?

Something else nagged at Philip. He wanted to see the world. Should he enlist? Get trained to be a pilot on the job? If war came, as a pilot, he might avoid running into a wall of gunfire, following the orders of a general on some faraway hill. Would he fight with honor? He decided right then and there he would be a hero who lived! His parents, brothers, and the entire town would turn out to cheer his homecoming parade. Then, considering what Franklin, Newman, and Meacham might have experienced, he decided upon abandoning the entire idea of being a hero.

Delusions of grandeur again, he thought. *There is no war, and, therefore, I'm not going to be a war hero. I'm going to be a teacher.*

CHAPTER 5

Leaving Home

September 4, 1940

THE LATE SUMMER SUN SLITHERED THROUGH the Zumwalt boys' bedroom window. Philip rose from his bed and pulled a brown, double-breasted worsted wool suit from the closet. It was the only suit he owned. He tugged on the suit pants and buttoned up an open-collared white shirt. The pants were a bit short, accentuating his lanky stature. He carted his leather suitcase, satchel, and clarinet case to the backseat of his car. Homer and Wayne helped him stuff the two wooden Blue Goose fruit crates in the trunk. He folded his suit coat with care on the passenger's seat. After breakfast, the family gathered on the front porch.

Philip hugged his mother and kissed her on the cheek. Ruby Zumwalt's diminutive frame was no indication of her strength of spirit and intellect. As a schoolteacher herself, she set an example of hard work, discipline, and self-control for her students, the same lessons she instilled in her sons on a daily basis.

"I'll try to make it home for some Sunday dinners, Mother," Philip said.

"We'd like that. Maybe for church, too?"

"Sure."

"Be good to those youngsters over there, Son. Give us a call when you arrive. Call collect," Lonnie instructed.

Philip shook hands with each of his brothers. "Homer, Wayne. Good luck at Western and go easy on the girls."

The boys smiled and shook their heads at their brother's nonsense.

Turning back to his father, Philip stretched out his hand. "Take care of Mother, Dad."

Lonnie shook his eldest son's hand. "I will, Son. You take care of yourself."

Ruby, Lonnie, Homer, and Wayne stood on the porch and waved as Philip backed down the dirt driveway. Lonnie stood stoic with his jaw locked. His two other sons joined their mother in wiping away their tears.

Philip drove west on Bridge Street, and he, too, fought back his conflicting emotions. The anticipation and excitement of a new job wrestled with the sadness of leaving his family. He dismissed the lump in his throat. Steering his Chevy north, he negotiated Pittsfield Road's bumps and potholes. Lush green foliage stretched to the highway's edge. The road dipped through a valley and rose to a peak. Metaphoric. Climbing a mountain. A challenge. He remembered his mother's words, "Nothing worth having comes easy."

Even though Payson was only a little over an hour's drive from Nebo, he would never call this place home again. His route ran parallel to the Mississippi River just a short distance from Hannibal, Missouri, the birthplace of one of his favorite writers, Mark Twain. The morning breeze wafted through the open car windows and cooled him as he turned north on Route 96. The image of El waving at him as she departed through the blue-curtained doorway remained fresh in his mind.

He whistled and sang, a joy-filled minstrel. Soon he would be teaching the children of Payson the subject he loved. Superintendent Virgil Johnston had assigned Philip the additional classes of World Problems and Economics, but his main responsibility would be to direct the entire music curriculum, including band and mixed chorus, plus serving as freshman class sponsor.

He looked forward to his new job and giving it his best shot. His plan, however, would remain the same: save his money over the next two years and then head out for his adventure, whether that took him to Chicago, pilot school, or places he had only ever dreamed of seeing.

An hour later, the sign outside the small, rural town informed Philip he had reached his destination:

PAYSON, ILLINOIS
POPULATION 456

As he drove by Payson-Seymour High School, he felt a twinge of nervous energy and excitement well up within him. Was he actually up to being a teacher? The sprawling single-story limestone building sparkled in the morning September sun. A regal white, vertical spire adorned the roof above the entrance. Resembling a miniature castle, the structure was a testament to the high regard the community had for its fallen hero, Charles W. Seymour.

Philip drove down West State Street, turned left on North Park Street, and arrived at his new home. Parking his coupe in front of the two-story white boardinghouse across from Payson's Central Park, he read a small sign with peeling black-and-white paint, which sat lopsided in the overgrown lawn: STALEY'S BOARDINGHOUSE, NO VACANCIES. The place didn't seem quite as nice as he'd hoped.

He hauled his luggage and clarinet case up the sidewalk to a front porch badly in need of a fresh coat of paint and turned the doorbell. A woman opened the door. Her face was weathered and wrinkled, but her smile exuded kindness.

"Good morning, Mrs. Staley. My name is Philip—"

"Yes, yes, my dear boy, do come in. Welcome to Payson. So, they tell me you're a musician."

"Yes, ma'am," Philip said, holding up his clarinet case. "The next Benny Goodman."

They shared a laugh.

"Well, Benny, your room is upstairs, first one on the left. Happy to have you here."

Philip deposited his bags and crates in his room. The boarding-house was adequate, and Mrs. Staley seemed welcoming and more than accommodating. The single room included a bed, an upright dresser, and a small desk and chair. He settled in, putting his bags and clarinet in his closet and stacked the pile of books on the floor next to the bed. He pulled out a jelly jar full of coins and placed it on the dresser along with his books about aerial combat, *Winged Victory* and *Air, Men and Wings*. The local legend of the Vin Fiz had long ago planted a yearning in him to fly. He would continue to save up his pennies in the jar and hoped one day soon he might be able to afford flying lessons. If there was a war, he planned on enlisting to become a pilot. If there was no war, being a pilot would in no way hinder his pursuit of becoming a famous songwriter and performer.

This wasn't home yet, but it would do. He descended the stairs. Mrs. Staley stood in the doorway that led to the parlor, smiling. Philip was delighted to discover a familiar-looking upright Spinet piano in the corner. He walked over to it and struck middle C.

"Still in tune, Mrs. Staley."

"Still in tune, Philip. That piano came all the way from Albany, New York, with my husband's family. He loved to play. You do play, don't you?"

"Oh, yes, ma'am. My grandparents gave our family a piano much like this one. I've played it every day since I was five years old."

"Well, feel free to use it whenever you like. Would you mind play-ing something for me now?"

Mrs. Staley sat in a rocker adjacent to the piano. Philip took a seat at the upright and began to play some Chopin.

"Beautiful, Philip, just beautiful. Nocturne opus nine number two, I believe."

"Why, yes, ma'am. You sure do know your classical music, Mrs. Staley."

"I suppose I do. Mr. Staley loved all of it. He played every night. Chopin, Beethoven, Bach, he even loved the modern classics, especially Gershwin. He passed away a few years ago. I miss hearing the music. Please feel free to play that old piano anytime."

"I'll be happy to do that, Mrs. Staley. I do have a question for you though."

"Why, certainly. What is it?"

"Well, Payson sure seems like a friendly town, and I'm guessing that you know most of the families that live here."

"Most of 'em."

"A friend of mine from Western wanted me to look up a family he knows—the Robinsons. Are you familiar with them?" His body trembled just thinking about El and their night at the Casino.

"I certainly do. A fine family. They live on the corner of Bittersweet and Sycamore Streets, just a few blocks from here. Doc Robinson's the town's doctor. He and his wife, Sandra, have three daughters. I believe the oldest will be a senior at the high school this year. I think her name is Elinor."

Stunned, Philip nearly fell off the piano stool. A million questions raced through his mind. *How could El be a senior at the high school? Impossible. Didn't she realize I might be her teacher? I told her I was going to be a teacher. Surely, Mrs. Staley is mistaken.*

Mrs. Staley looked concerned. "Are you all right, Philip? You look like you've seen a ghost."

"No, ma'am. Really, I'm fine," Philip responded, dismissing the knot in his stomach.

"I'd be happy to ring up the Robinsons and arrange a visit."

"Oh, no thank you, Mrs. Staley. That won't be necessary."

He realized he now had a far more serious problem. Philip vividly remembered his initial interview with Superintendent Johnston.

"School board policy makes it clear, Mr. Zumwalt—relationships outside of school between teacher and pupil are strictly forbidden."

Johnston's voice had been authoritative and resolute. "Any teacher crossing that line will be automatically dismissed. Understood?"

"Yes, sir," Philip had responded.

"Such a thing is forbidden. It is *taboo*." Johnston's dark eyes had peered into Philip's, striking the fear of God into him. At the time, the idea of crossing that line was the furthest thing from his mind. Now, the memory of the interview and Johnston's edict, his final word, echoed in Philip's mind, over and over. What had he done?

CHAPTER 6

First Day of School

September 9, 1940

THE ALARM CLOCK WOKE PHILIP from a dream. He sprang from his bed early on this Monday morning, the first day of the school year. He soaped up what few whiskers he had and shaved them off with his straight razor. After brushing his teeth, he dressed in his brown suit and white shirt. He knotted his red silk tie and stood with perfect posture staring into the pockmarked mirror and his own deep blue eyes. "Good morning, class. My name is Mr. Zumwalt, and I will be your teacher this year."

Pleased with his reflection, he dabbed Brylcreem on his dark brown hair, combed it straight back, and made a slight part on the right side of his head. He laced up his brown oxford shoes and walked into the hallway, ready for his first day of teaching. His only major concern was how he might react if he saw a certain student by the name of Elinor Robinson.

"Good morning, Mrs. Staley."

The dining room table was covered with a modest, worn white cotton cloth. Philip was one of four boarders at Mrs. Staley's. She had told him the other three were traveling salesmen and rarely present for her delicious breakfasts.

"Good morning, Philip. Coffee?" Mrs. Staley smiled.

"Yes, ma'am. Thank you."

She passed a serving dish and a cup of coffee to him. He placed two fried eggs and three strips of bacon on his plate and took a sip of coffee.

"Nervous?" she asked.

"Not really, just excited."

Philip devoured his breakfast. After some polite conversation and a second cup of coffee, he excused himself and thanked his landlady. "That was wonderful, Mrs. Staley. Have a great day."

He took the stairs two at a time, brushed his teeth once more, and grabbed his worn brown leather briefcase. A gift from his uncle Ernest, it was one of Philip's most prized possessions. His uncle was a veterinarian and the pride of the family. When Philip received the gift upon his graduation from college, his uncle had told him, "Got a few miles left on it, my boy, but no worse for the wear."

The screen door clapped behind him as he strolled up North Park Street, turned left onto West State Street, and walked up the front steps of Payson-Seymour High School. The 1940–1941 school year was officially underway.

Elinor Lynne Robinson approached her senior year at Payson-Seymour High with an air of self-assurance. Dressed in a blue-and-white polka-dot blouse and a khaki pleated skirt, she strolled up the narrow brick sidewalk lined with giant oak and elm trees. The walkway wound right to the front steps of the picturesque building. Doric columns framed the front door, where a large arched window shaped like a half-moon sat upon a transom light.

"El!" Esther Scarboro screeched. "El!"

"Essie! Can you believe it? We're seniors."

Walking arm in arm into the school's main entrance and gliding down the terrazzo-tiled hallways, Esther had a news flash for El. "Have you seen the new music teacher? He's dreamy! I was working for Mrs. Peterson in the front office when he came for his interview with Mr. Johnston. We were sure hoping he got the job. Looks like he did." Essie laughed. "However, he does have one of those odd German-type names—Mr. Zumwalt," she whispered. "Not a good thing these days, ya know, Hitler and all."

El's knees nearly buckled. "What's his first name? Do you know?"

"Hmm. I'm not sure, but I think it is Philip—like my first cousin."

What was I thinking? Didn't he say he was a preacher?! Well, even that wasn't appropriate, El thought, now panicked. *Maybe he's not our real teacher, maybe a substitute. Oh, silly girl, what difference would that make?*

"You, okay, El?" Essie asked. "You look a little flushed."

"I'm fine. Too much sun yesterday, probably. Well, I can't wait to lay my eyes on this new teacher. Is he a sub? I mean, if he's that dreamy and all, I guess it doesn't matter, does it? What's he teach?" She was doing her best to hide her dread. She had no idea how she would ever face him.

"Band, World Problems, and Economics, I think. He's no sub. Mrs. Peterson said he was a graduate of Western Teachers College. A music major, I think she said. I'm sure he'll have the combined chorus, too."

"Must be pretty smart to know about all those subjects." El knew she couldn't tell even her best friend about what had occurred at the Casino. What had she gotten herself into? Walking the rest of the way to her first-hour class in silence, she smiled and half listened as Essie babbled away about her latest love, Cecil DeWeese, and what a wonderful year it was going to be. At that moment, El wasn't so sure.

Arriving at the main office, Philip picked up and scanned his class lists. World Problems—*Elinor Robinson!* Band—*Elinor Robinson!*

Mrs. Peterson noticed his exaggerated sigh. "Are you all right, young man?" she asked.

Regaining his composure, Philip replied, "Oh, yes, ma'am, I'm fine, just fine." Weak-kneed and flummoxed, he staggered into his first-hour classroom. *World Problems? I'm the one with the problem*, he thought. Any illusions he once had of romancing the girl he knew as El had vanished. He was a fool after all.

Entering the doorway of their classroom, El and Essie slid around the corner, straightened their skirts, fluffed their hair, and walked into World Problems class. Mr. Zumwalt was printed in bold white chalk letters on the blackboard.

The temperature stretched toward eighty degrees, and the room smelled of fresh floor wax. El's cheeks burned and her stomach turned over as she took a seat in the back of the room. Out of the corner of her eye, she watched Philip's every movement. He stepped from behind the podium, stood next to his desk, and shifted his weight from one foot to the other. His white shirt was already streaked with perspiration.

El had thought about that night at the Casino every day. She had not laid eyes on Philip in almost two weeks, not since they parted at the Blue Room. That night she could barely keep her eyes off him; now, she made every effort to avoid making any eye contact. Butterflies darted about in her stomach.

Ten seniors and juniors fidgeted in the heat, anticipating the novice teacher's first words. Teaching a class on World Problems had promised to be somewhat difficult on its own merits, but Philip could never have anticipated the distracting effect of the girl seated in the back row. He did his best to diminish what they had shared. *Okay, we danced a few dances, so what? And she did give me permission to kiss her.* He slogged forth.

"Good morning, class. My name is Mr. Zumwalt, and I'll be your World Problems teacher this year." He coughed from the chalk dust, which also left some unsightly residue on the front pocket of his pants.

"We sure got enough of those," someone blurted from the back of the room.

"Hey, can we call you Mr. Z?" asked Randall Yarborough.

"I suppose, sure." Moving back behind the podium, he called the roll.

When he came to El's name, he didn't look up.

El could barely breathe. "Present," she replied.

He moved to the blackboard and printed, "W __ R!" and turned back toward the class. Essie was passing a note to El. He smiled at Essie and shook his head. She looked down and then back at him, apologetically mouthing, "Sorry."

El slipped the note into her textbook.

Philip moved on and began his lesson with a simple question. "So, what's happening across the Atlantic Ocean, class?" The class sat silent. "Let's see. How about if I give you a clue?" He turned and pointed to the blackboard. A few members of the class laughed under their breath at the clue's simplicity.

"War!" Cecil DeWeese blurted out. "The Nazis are takin' over countries over there. But I for one hope we don't get caught up in it. Mr. Charles Lindbergh, a great American hero, says we oughta stay out of it."

From there, a spirited discussion and debate erupted until Philip interjected, "The Treaty of Versailles, signed by the countries involved in 'The War to End All Wars' took away much of Germany's ability to maintain a functioning economy. That led to the ascension of a Fascist government and its leader, Adolf Hitler."

Philip resisted the urge to steal a glimpse of the girl in the back row. Instead, he smoothly transitioned to a summation of the discussion, followed by a preview of the next class.

"In our next lesson, we'll explore the specific reasons that led to Germany invading other European countries. We'll be discussing the formation of the League of Nations following the Great War, and its influence upon the current state of affairs in modern-day Europe." The bell rang. Philip stopped. Unable to help himself, he looked right at El. If he had been daring, he would have winked. Instead, he dismissed the class with a smile and said, "Until we meet again."

"I'm guessing that'll be tomorrow," Essie said.

"That's correct, Esther. I'll see all of you tomorrow."

When El and Essie reached the hallway, El opened the note and read, *See, I told you he was dreamy.* El thought, *You have no idea, Essie, no idea at all.*

Ralph Guthrie saved Philip a seat at the faculty lunch table in the library. Guthrie was the math teacher at Payson, a friend of Philip's, and a graduate of Western. He had been at the high school since the fall of 1939. He had recommended to Johnston that Philip would be a welcome addition to the Payson-Seymour faculty.

Philip greeted the teachers gathered at the table and sat next to an attractive young woman. Her coal-black hair was cut in a modern bob framing her angular face to perfection. She put out her hand. "I'm Ina Harper. I teach English here."

Philip shook her hand. "Philip Zumwalt. Music, World Problems, and Economics. Pleased to meet you, Ina."

"My aunt Millie, Mrs. Staley, tells me you're a musician."

"I'd like to think I am." Philip laughed.

"Which instrument?"

"Piano and clarinet, but my passion is writing music."

"What kind?"

"You name it. I love it all."

Ralph interjected, "Philip was one of the top musicians at Western. You should hear him pound those keys!"

"I would love to some time," Ina said. "How were your classes, Philip? Any problems?"

"No. No problems at all. The students are great."

"Well, don't tell anyone you heard it from me, but watch yourself with Randall Yarborough," Ralph said. "He'll charm the socks off you, but if he doesn't get what he wants, he'll run to his daddy. Yarboroughs are used to getting their way. David Yarborough is the wealthiest man in Adams County, and last spring he got elected to the school board."

"What about Randall?"

"Spoiled rotten. Apple doesn't fall far from the tree, you know. Got a bit of mean streak in him, just like the old man. Beat up one of his classmates in the parking lot after a school dance just cause the other boy was talking with his girlfriend." Ralph looked at Ina for confirmation. "Robinson girl. Elinor, I believe. Am I right about that, Ina?"

Ina nodded.

Ralph's description of Randall startled Philip. Was he really El's boyfriend? Would his jealousy and temper ever cause him to harm El?

Ralph continued, "Word is alcohol gets the best of him sometimes, just like all the rest of his relatives—on both sides."

Coach Loy laughed. "Gets the best of most of us some of the time, Ralph."

"Can't argue with that, Art," Ralph replied.

The remainder of lunch, Philip and his new colleagues ate their sandwiches, drank their coffee, and discussed a variety of topics. One topic that didn't emerge was what a first-year teacher does if he is infatuated with one of his students, the same student who is dating a school board member's son with a bad temper and a drinking problem.

Ina was the first to leave the lunch table. Standing a few inches over five feet, dressed in heels, a crisply pressed white blouse, dark skirt, and pearl necklace, she projected a degree of sophistication and elegance not often seen in a small Midwestern farm community.

She turned to the table and, with a hint of drama and humor, quoted Shakespeare,

"Once more unto the breech, my dear friends."

The table joined her in a laugh.

As Philip entered the music room, he took a deep breath and descended the steps. Now he bore an even more serious burden, one requiring him to walk a delicate tightrope for the remainder of the school year. His vigilance in safeguarding El's well-being would have to be from a safe distance, undetected. His yearning for her must remain hidden from the good folks of Payson, and he would have to treat her as if she were just another one of his students. Striking such a balance was the only way he could survive.

CHAPTER 7

Ulterior Motives

October 12, 1940

NEARLY A YEAR HAD PASSED since Philip held Kate Uphouser's hand at Western's 1939 homecoming dance, an evening when it seemed as if they were walking on air. A first-place dance trophy—second year in a row. A match made in Heaven. They would talk endlessly about their favorite subjects: Broadway musicals, literature, movies, poetry, a future together. They would start out in Chicago, make a name for themselves in the music entertainment business, and then move on to New York's small off-Broadway theaters. In the end, their dreams landed them on the Great White Way, Broadway.

But there was no future together. In July 1940, Kate had called it all off. No fireworks, no harsh words. Instead, a quiet, civil conversation between two consenting adults. Kate was headed to Chicago, and Philip could not afford to do the same. Trout said it was because he wasn't rich enough for her and told Philip he thought she was just a stuck-up snob. Philip thought Trout was wrong, but a recent letter from Bob Everetts, one of his friends from college, confirmed that Kate was dating a wealthy guy from Lake Forest. No surprise.

But now, Kate was coming to Quincy. Why? Why had she asked Pat to ask Billy to ask Philip to accompany her to the Adams County Fall Festival Formal? Ecstatic that he and Pat had reconciled, Billy had no insight for Philip about what Kate might have up her sleeve.

On the afternoon of the dance, Billy Epperson parked his 1938 Chevy National Series AB Coupe in front of Mrs. Staley's boardinghouse. The maroon paint, shining black fenders, and black-and-silver wheels sparkled in the bright sunlight.

"Quite a ride, Kid," Philip remarked as he walked up to the car.

"Hop in, Nelly. Another Saturday night at the Casino for the Posse, at least for two of us. The ladies are comin' in on the train from Chicago around three. Pat said they'd catch a cab from the train station and meet us at the hotel around five."

Wearing his only suit and a blue tie, Philip was as ready as he would ever be. He never knew what to expect with Kate. During the drive to Quincy, Philip and Billy had some time to catch up. "Had any dates yet in Payson? Hey, doesn't that sweet thing you were kissin' on in the Blue Room live there?"

"You won't believe this, Billy . . . she's a student at the high school. In two of my classes *and* the mixed chorus."

"What? The hell you say!" Billy almost ran his coupe off the road. "You can't be serious, Nelly. You better steer clear of that. You need a job, not a scandal."

"I'm not about to get fired. I actually enjoy my job, so far. I'm staying as far away from her as I possibly can."

Conversation between the two lifelong friends continued as Philip updated Billy on his brothers' progress at Western. "They seemed to be adjusting well. Both of them are dating. Homer is on the basketball team, and Wayne's singing in the men's glee club. They are hitting the books hard. They'd better, or Mother will kill them." They both laughed.

"Speaking of dating, Nelly, do you suppose Kate's coming down here to try to reignite the flame between you two? Think she might have some regrets?"

"Ha! Fat chance. Nah. Knowing her, there's an ulterior motive."

"Yeh. Who knows with dames? Pat's all worked up over Perry Como, though. She asked me if we could go to the Fall Festival Formal. I asked her why, and she said, 'Simple—Perry Como.' Could be Kate feels the same way. Hell, they're even putting themselves up at the snazzy Lincoln-Douglas Hotel for Saturday night."

"So, me coming along, you sure that was Kate's idea, not Pat's or yours?"

"It was Kate's," Billy answered emphatically.

Philip shook his head. There was no sense in trying to figure out the mysterious Kate Uphouser. Now he changed the subject. "So, how *did* you and Pat get back together?"

"We patched things by writin' letters. I guess she missed me, and I sure missed her. There's an English teaching position opening up at Nebo next year, so maybe it'll all work out. Mr. Dennis is retiring, and the board already told Mr. Meacham he's gonna be the principal."

"Good for him. Is he still a little crazy?"

"Maybe. But he's always been good to me. I think bein' in a war makes any sane man a little crazy. He married a real nice gal from Pleasant Hill, though, and her folks own a farm."

"Gotta love farmers. My grandparents are farmers, you know."

"I remember a weekend we stayed out at their place. Your grandma asked us to go out to the chicken coop and bring her back a half dozen eggs. Man, did that henhouse ever stink!"

Philip laughed in agreement. "Yeh, but my grandma was a lot more than a chicken farmer. She was an accomplished pianist and musician. I think they had a piano in their home before anyone else in Pike County. They got a new one when I was five years old and handed the old one down to my mother. She started me playing the day it arrived."

"Well, you're the best damned piano player I ever heard, so it must be a pretty good one. Hey, they give you your clarinet, too? 'Cause, man, you play that thing like old Benny Goodman." Billy smiled. He considered Philip to be just about the most talented musician he'd ever known, even if he wasn't quite as good a clarinet player as Goodman.

"Naw, they just gave us the piano. I had to buy the clarinet. Say, who's the band tonight?"

"You born under a rock or something? It's Ted Weems and Perry Como. I hope there's room on the floor to dance. I got some new moves to show Pat."

"Like Trout?" Philip asked, smiling.

"Aw, c'mon, Nelly. Trout can't dance. He's a spastic. But I'll tell you one thing, that grin of his charms all the ladies. Now, as for me, I got the grin *and* the moves!"

"So, you think it'll be crowded?" Philip secretly hoped that a large crowd might prevent him from seeing a certain someone who might be at the dance.

"Oh, yeh. That place will be hoppin'!"

The Lincoln-Douglas Hotel soared above the Quincy landscape. Made of solid red brick and gray granite stone, the eight-story hotel stood proudly advertising two of Illinois's most famous sons. Philip and Billy, not quite as famous, entered through the hotel's double doors.

"Damn," said Billy, "looks just like a picture in a magazine of the lobby of some fancy New York hotel."

Sunlight filtered through high arched windows, drenching the lobby and adjacent lounge. The couches appeared to be upholstered with pure gold silk. Stately leather club chairs, each with a stand-alone ashtray, were scattered about the lounge. A sparkling chandelier hung in the entrance, and another floated overhead in the lounge. Both had crystal bulbs suspended in air, hanging like stalactites.

"Miss Carpenter and Miss Uphouser, please," Billy addressed the gentleman behind the reception desk.

Dressed in a tailored burgundy jacket with a black bow tie, the receptionist responded, "I'll be happy to ring their rooms, sir. One moment, please."

Rooms? It never dawned on Philip that Kate might have her own room. Wild fantasies raced through his brain. He came back to his senses when he saw Pat and Kate exit the elevator.

The blond and the brunette could have been sisters, and in some respects, they were. They had been members of Kappa Delta Pi, a sorority at Western. In their elegant dresses, they looked like Hollywood actresses. Pat's yellow floral print with puff sleeves and peplum panels flowed around her knees. Kate twirled in a circle and modeled her bias-cut tangerine chiffon, which exposed much of her back.

Wow, Philip thought.

"Zummie!" Kate squealed her pet name for Philip, a name he abhorred, a name only Kate could get away with calling him. She ran into his arms and kissed his cheek.

"Hello, handsome," Pat said, also pecking Billy's cheek.

"Was your train on time?" the Kid asked.

"Yep, right at three o'clock. Gave us time to freshen up," replied the always-flirtatious Kate.

"You sure did that," Philip said. "You two look like a million bucks."

"Hungry, ladies?" Billy asked. "I reserved a table for us at a private club on the Mississippi called the Triple Oaks. The steaks there are supposed to be delicious."

"I'm famished. Sounds great to me," Pat said.

"Let's go. I don't want to miss a minute of Perry Como." Kate twirled around again. "You do still dance, don't you, Zummie?"

Philip grinned at her. "I just hope you can keep up with me, Kate."

"Don't worry about that," she said with a wink.

They piled into Billy's Chevy. Pat sat next to Billy, and Kate perched on Philip's lap.

After a scrumptious dinner at the Triple Oaks, over which they chatted about the good "old" days at Western, current events, and future aspirations, Billy pulled his Chevy into the parking lot at the Casino. A long, leisurely line snaked toward the entrance to the pavilion.

Music by the Ted Weems Orchestra floated through open windows and doors. Upon entering through the familiar leather-covered doors, Philip was grateful his previous wish had been granted. The dance hall was packed. It was a temperate night for October in Illinois. Candles and small displays of cornucopia decorated the tables that lined the elevated level surrounding the dance floor. Philip felt uneasy.

Kate grabbed his hand. "C'mon, Zummie. They're playin' 'Jumpin' at the Woodside.'"

Philip took Kate's cue and spun her out onto the dance floor. They were swinging as if they'd been transported back to the dances at Western. The overflow crowd separated and then gathered around them, applauding the two dancers. Kate and Philip swayed and dipped alone in the middle of the floor. Kate matched every step, every one of Philip's moves. Oblivious to the attention, the smooth sounds of the swing music sent signals to his feet. He danced like he had never danced before. His eyes were focused on his partner, who, once again, had worked her sultry magic, complementing his every step as she glided around the dance floor.

Billy and Pat cheered along with the crowd. "Go, Nelly! Go, Kate!" Billy yelled.

The tempo mounted with a soaring trumpet solo. Kate was nearly flying as Philip spun and twirled her. They laughed—carefree, in perpetual motion. The song ended with everyone clapping and cheering, a moment of ecstatic spontaneity. Ted Weems joined the applause as he approached the microphone, "Let's hear it for that fine couple!" The crowd cheered. "We'll be right back after a brief break."

Kate's blond hair clung to the sides of her head and her pale-blue eyes shimmered, exuding the excitement she always had when she and her favorite dance partner took the floor. She was radiant, and she knew it. She slipped away from Philip and then glanced back with a come-hither look. He followed like a puppy. The crowd drifted outside and to the tables lining the observation deck above the dance floor.

Philip was back on his game. "Cocktail?" He'd been to this show before.

"Sure," replied Kate. "A sidecar, please."

"Yes. I remember."

He brought her the drink. Had she missed him? Was there a remote chance they'd get back together like Pat and Billy had? She thanked him, took the glass, and sipped. He offered his handkerchief. She accepted and mopped her brow.

Placing her glass on the table, Kate pulled a cigarette out of a silver case and a lighter from her purse. "Oh, that's right, Zummie, I'm sorry. I forgot you don't smoke. Any vices yet?" There was a suggestion in her voice. "Oh, stupid me, I forgot you had a glass of wine at dinner. Becoming quite the cosmopolitan guy. Are you actually drinking bourbon?"

Philip smiled, trying his best to act sophisticated. "An old-fashioned, to be exact." He lifted the glass, toasted her, and then placed his glass on the table. Taking the lighter from her hand, he lit her cigarette. It had been their shared love of music that led to their initial friendship, a friendship that had evolved into something more for Philip. Whenever they danced, it was as if they were attached by an invisible cord. When they were onstage together, Kate singing and Philip playing a torch ballad on the piano, the duo brought down the house. Looking across the table as she sipped her sidecar and smoked her Lucky Strike, it was obvious to Philip that her mind, even now, seemed to be elsewhere. Maybe Trout was right.

"Wow, Mr. Z, you sure can dance!" Randall Yarborough stood right behind Philip, who turned in his chair. His eyes locked in on the young woman standing next to Randall. El looked away, seeming totally bored.

"Well, thank you, Randall, and a good evening to you, Elinor." Philip stood as he greeted the two seniors. "Miss Kate Uphouser, I'd like you to meet two of my students from Payson, Miss Elinor Robinson and Mr. Randall Yarborough."

Kate extended her hand across the table. "My pleasure."

El minded her manners and exchanged a cordial nod with Kate, then added, "Pleased to make your acquaintance, Miss Uphouser."

Randall took Kate's hand in his and shook it. Starry-eyed, he gazed adoringly at this woman who looked like she had stepped right out of *Modern Screen* magazine.

"Well, enjoy the rest of your evening," Philip said as he pulled Kate toward the dance floor. "See you Monday morning."

As they slid away, Kate remarked, "Oh, Zummie, your students are so adorable. They look so young. That girl is quite cute. What was her name?"

"Elinor," Philip answered. "Elinor Robinson."

Cute? Oh, I'm cute, am I? A fire burned within El. *We'll see about that.* What was this feeling? She'd read about such stupidity in books but never actually experienced her stomach clenching like an angry fist. She grabbed Randall's hand and disappeared into the crowd of dancers.

Zummie? How many aliases can one guy have?

Ted Weems and his orchestra's next set started with "Begin the Beguine." Philip led Kate onto the dance floor as Perry Como entered the stage and began crooning.

"Isn't he just divine?" She sighed.

Philip wondered if the song was prophetic. Would the embers that had been sleeping begin to burn once again? It felt good to have her in his arms, even if she was paying more attention to the guy onstage. The song ended, and the orchestra segued into "Moonlight Serenade." No need for the dancers to even pause. Philip and Kate were entwined as they floated across the dance floor. He looked for El and Randall as the night wore on, but the overflow throng was an answer to his earlier wish.

Philip and Kate sashayed around the dance floor. He dismissed any thoughts of El and Randall. Kate wrapped her arm around his neck and cradled her head into his chest. She looked up at him. His eyes locked with hers. Three sidecars had taken their toll. She kissed him on the cheek and then moved to his lips. He let himself fall into her kiss.

CHAPTER 8

As Time Goes By

JUST BEFORE MIDNIGHT, TED WEEMS INTRODUCED the orchestra's final song. "We hope you all had a delightful evening and that you'll come back to see us when we return to this wonderful town. So, good night to Quincy, Illinois, the Gem City. And now, with tonight's finale, 'As Time Goes By,' the incomparable Perry Como."

Perry's tones were smooth.

> "You must remember this
> A kiss is just a kiss, a sigh is just a sigh . . ."

Philip wondered which it would be tonight—a kiss or a sigh.

> ". . . the world will always welcome lovers
> As time goes by."

He collected Kate's coat from the checkout girl, tipped her a dime, and joined his companions in the parking lot. As the couples piled into Billy's coupe, Philip heard El's giggle. He looked back over his shoulder and saw her walking with Randall toward his red Ford convertible. He exchanged a glance with El, and his stomach turned in knots. He turned away, climbed into the Billy's car, and closed the door.

Kate sat snuggled on Philip's lap as Billy drove back to the hotel. All four were sloshed. After Billy haphazardly parked his car on the

◆ 51 ◆

curb in front of the hotel, he stumbled around to the passenger side door and opened it. Kate staggered off Philip's lap. He tumbled out of the seat. Pat fell into Billy's arms.

Kate's incoherent come-hither look seemed to be another clear invitation. Then came the magic words. "Would you mind seeing me to my room, Philip?" she said, for the first time this evening not calling him by the nickname he despised.

"Of course," Philip replied. Of course, he would see her to her room. Basic politeness.

He wrapped his arms around her, nearly carrying her to the elevator. Billy and Pat disappeared. Acknowledging the operator's presence with a nod, Philip hoped Kate wouldn't deposit her Triple Oaks dinner on the parquet floor of the elevator.

"Good evening, sir. Ma'am. Which floor, please?"

"Sss . . . six," Kate slurred, putting her arm through Philip's. She looked up at him in a drunken haze and smiled.

Philip wondered what the elevator operator might be thinking. Undoubtedly, he had witnessed many such scenes, overserved men and women on an elevator liquored up and headed to a clandestine room. Philip imagined himself in just such a room. Kate enters in a silky nightgown. She stretches out across the soft sheets of a four-poster bed and beckons him to join her. He takes her in his arms. At last, the passion that had burned in them the past four years would be consummated.

The elevator operator's announcement jolted him back to reality. "Sixth floor, folks. Have a pleasant evening."

He stood Kate upright as they stepped into the hallway. "Do you have the key, Kate?"

She fumbled with her clutch, found the key, and gave it to him. The key was attached to a gold-colored medallion with the numbers 636 etched onto its surface.

"It was such a lovely evening! You're still my favorite dance partner," she said in a drunken stupor.

"You're not so bad yourself." He found the room, opened the door, and led her to the bed, hoping the rest of the evening would be just as he had imagined. The room did its part. A golden silk duvet covering the bed accentuated its elegance. Kate stumbled and fell onto the mattress, out cold.

Philip checked to make sure she was alive. Once confirmed, he took off her heels, removed her chiffon gown, pulled back the bedding, and tucked her in. He left her key on the dresser and closed the door behind him.

Billy's car was still parked outside, the door unlocked. He stretched out on the seat and pulled his suit jacket over him. He didn't regret the evening. Kate was the perfect dance partner. He'd fulfilled his role, been the perfect date and, in the end, a perfect gentleman. Everything was perfect except his sleeping arrangement. Dozing off, his thoughts were only of El as Perry Como's voice played in his head:

> "Woman needs man
> And man must have his mate
> That no one can deny."

Philip was sprawled out when Billy woke him the next morning with a sardonic, "How'd it go last night?"

Philip rubbed the sleep from his eyes and lied to save face. "I honestly don't remember what happened last night. Let's get some breakfast. I definitely need some food." He wondered out loud to his best friend, "Why *do* you think Kate came with Pat?"

Billy had no definitive answer to his buddy's question. In Sprout's Diner, inhaling his bacon and eggs and slurping coffee, he set forth one plausible conjecture. "Maybe she figured out she made a mistake. You two looked pretty familiar with each other last night. I had a hard time keeping my eyes on the road. You two were sure sneaking in a few kisses on the way home."

"She was drunk, Billy."

"Whatever you say. But it looked to me like she was absolutely enjoying your company!"

"Well, good for her, but I have other plans. I've been thinking about all of this and it makes sense to me to postpone my Chicago plan temporarily. Fame and fortune will just have to be put on hold for a while." He laughed. "I was planning on saving up for a couple of years to head to Chicago, but, hell, if I can join the Army Air Corps once the school year ends, I can pursue my other dream of being a pilot. Plus, the Army will pay me to do it."

"What? Are you crazy, Nelly? Why would you do that? Because Kate jilted you?"

"No, not because of her. I've got my reasons. I guess I just want to do something adventurous before I become an old man."

"I don't know, Nelly. If we do go to war, you're liable to get plenty of adventure. The wrong kind, the kind that gets you killed. You might never get to be an old man. The war over there in Europe's one helluva mess."

"That's a chance I'm willing to take. Nothing ventured, nothing gained."

"What about what's-her-name—Elinor? You think she would want to see you taking off?"

"Believe me, that's a mess, too. And a dead end, I'm afraid."

That night, Philip received a phone call from Kate at Mrs. Staley's.

"I'm so embarrassed by my behavior last night. Please, please accept my apology. One too many sidecars, I fear." Her voice was soft and sweet. "Thank you for taking care of me, though. You're always a gentleman, aren't you?"

He was surprised by her sincerity. "I try to be, Kate."

"I came along with Pat because I had something I wanted to tell you face-to-face. I'm in love, Zummie, and I think I'm getting proposed to next weekend."

"Oh," Philip said, disguising his surprise.

"Pat told me she was coming down to see Billy. I just figured that'd give me a chance to see you and tell you my great news. Plus, what red-blooded American girl wouldn't want to lay her eyes on Perry Como? You have to admit we had a blast last night!"

That we did, you in your lush four-poster bed and me on the seat of Billy's car. He came to his senses. "Yeh, it was great. So, who's the lucky guy?"

"He's wonderful. You're gonna think he's swell."

I bet I will.

"His name is Steven Woodley. He and his parents live in Lake Forest."

Appropriate. Philip's brain was trying to figure out what to say next, but Kate let him off the hook. She continued talking even faster than she normally did. "I met him at the theater during the summer. He came backstage and introduced himself. His parents helped finance a few of the Chicago Theater productions. They own some big manufacturing company. Well, all that's beside the point."

Is it?

"He asked me out and I accepted. We've been dating ever since then, and, well, I guess the rest is history. I do hope you can meet him before the wedding."

"That's great, just great. I'm happy for you—really." In a moment of clarity, he realized he was no longer in love with her. "I appreciate the call, Kate, and don't worry about last night. It was great. Best wishes to you and Woody."

"Why, Zummie, how in the world did you know his nickname?"

"Just a wild guess."

CHAPTER 9

The Road to War

OCTOBER'S BRIGHT YELLOW AND APPLE-RED LEAVES began to litter the high school's lawn as Philip prepared the band and mixed chorus for the upcoming Fall Festival parade and concert. His World Problems class followed the progress of the war in Europe and its impact around the rest of the world. El conducted herself as any normal high school senior might. She won the role of Lovey Riley in the school's fall drama production of *The Life of Riley*, played her tenor saxophone in the band, sang in the mixed chorus, and behaved as the model student she was. No words were spoken in private between El and Philip following the Fall Festival Formal.

Whenever he saw her, an unfamiliar feeling welled up inside him. Avoiding eye contact, he feared all the fine qualities that had captured his heart that night at the Casino might tempt him into making a foolish advance. She made him feel so alive! But he understood that pursuing her would result in his immediate dismissal. Such a scandal would tarnish his name and disgrace his family.

In late November, Philip introduced the topic of the latest presidential election to his World Problems students. Recapping the results from the election, which had taken place on November 5, Philip asked, "Why do you think that President Roosevelt was elected to an unprecedented third term?"

"To keep us outa the war," blurted Jimmy Blauser.

"He never shoulda been elected. The Democrats are gonna ruin this country." Cecil DeWeese's face twisted and turned bright crimson. "That's what my dad says, and I agree with him."

"I can see you're upset, Cecil," Philip answered, "but the fact is, he did win the election. The question is, why?"

Randall Yarborough responded, "The precedence of the two-term presidency was suspended because the American people must have had confidence in old FDR to keep them safe, even though he is a you-know-what Democrat." He grinned at Cecil.

"And what, pray tell, is wrong with being a Democrat, Randall?" El asked.

"Well, nothing, I guess. I did say the people had confidence in FDR, and, uh, he has kept us safe. I guess."

"*I guess*? You're danged right he has. We're not in a war, are we?" El shot back.

"Well, uh, no." With that, Randall surrendered.

Philip stepped in to save Randall. "An excellent point, Randall. We all want to be safe, don't we?"

"After all, this is the land of the free and the home of the brave, isn't it, Mr. Z?" Florence Marshall proclaimed.

"It sure is, Florence. Many men have died to keep this nation free. Let's just hope that many more don't meet the same fate. After listening to the veterans in my hometown, I can assure you none of them think war is a good thing. In my humble opinion, our president is doing his best to keep us both safe and out of the war. I think we can all agree so far he's been pretty successful on both counts." Philip sat on his desk, his long legs dangling. "I do hope once all of you are old enough to vote, you'll form your own opinions about the issues of the day and vote according to your conscience, whether you're a Democrat or a Republican. Above all, you should try to be well educated regarding current topics, whether of local, national, or international interest. If not, then I've done a horrible job as your World Problems teacher."

The students laughed.

"Ah, we don't think that's true, Mr. Z," Essie said.

"Well, thank you, Esther. Now, as for the present, there is no more pressing problem to explore than the war in Europe and the threat to the United Kingdom, or Great Britain, as some call it. We'll discuss that issue in greater detail tomorrow, plus the threat of Japanese aggression in the Pacific. During the past decade, they have occupied Manchuria and parts of China. Recently, they joined the Axis alliance with Italy and Germany. Please read the next chapter in your textbook. There just might be a quiz on that chapter."

Philip winked just as the bell rang.

Life in Payson was different. Philip had become accustomed to days and nights of stimulating conversations during his college years. Excited by the subjects he studied and his participation in a variety of the college's musical performances, college life had agreed with him. The late-night discussions revolving around politics and the mysteries of religion and life had provided hours of stimulating debates and intellectual sparring. Pure enjoyment.

Evenings were now spent developing lessons plans, reading up on current events in the public library, listening to music, or playing the piano either in the music room or at Mrs. Staley's. He had thought he might find teaching somewhat exciting, but overall it had turned out to be a bit tedious. He loved the discussions and the performances, but grading tests and essays was underwhelming to say the least.

Teaching World Problems required him to keep up to date on the daily reports of the events in Europe that filtered through the radio, newspapers, and magazines. Many of the war's details were too horrifying to share with his students. The terror wrought by Nazism struck fear into the citizenry of the free world, especially the United States.

Conversations over lunch with Ralph and Ina included frequent discussions about the Nazi occupation of various European countries.

The president had convinced Congress to appropriate money for assistance to Great Britain and France. But the reality was that the meager support would most likely not be enough to stop the onslaught of the German blitzkrieg. Philip wondered how much longer the United States would be able to stay out of the war. The idea of enlisting became more intriguing every day.

Darkness enveloped the back door of the high school as he turned the key, opened the door, and descended the stairs to the music room. He flipped the light switch. The band instruments remained securely stored in the cabinets along the walls, his music stand was positioned at attention in the front of the room, patiently waiting for him to tap his baton, and three rows of twelve metal chairs stood in rigid formation.

He sat down at the piano, still thinking of El. Did he create this situation, or had she? Who was to blame? It didn't matter. He realized he was obsessed with her. Even given the impossible circumstances, was it possible she, too, might actually have feelings for him? And even though the young lovers had had a few too many drinks that night in the Blue Room, their chemistry was undeniable. There was no way he could explain any of this to himself, let alone to anyone else. Whenever she walked into a room, his stomach churned. If his arm accidentally brushed against hers when she came to his desk to ask a question, the same bolt of electricity he'd felt in the Blue Room surged through his entire being. Was this really love or only fascination? He played the song and sang softly:

> "It was fascination,
> I know . . .
> And I might have gone
> On my way
> Empty-hearted . . ."

He would have to go on his way empty-hearted, not allowing his feelings to go any further. Thoughts of having an intimate relationship with El must end, at least for now. He had to quit torturing himself. His livelihood was at stake, as well as the reputation of his family and his own as a teacher and a gentleman. But the daydreams and internal debate persisted. Returning to read the stack of papers on his desk, he was haunted by the song continuing to play in his head.

He slammed the desktop with both hands. "Dammit!" he yelled. "What am I doing?" For a moment, just a moment, he fought to restrain the anger. In a rare fit of rage, he grabbed a stack of papers and flung them across the room. The song sat bitter and ironic in his mind. He threw his stapler. It rattled off the music stand. Next, his pencil cup flew through the air, striking a folding chair with a satisfying *crack*.

That first night at the Casino was still *real*. The touch of her skin against his, the smile that still drove him crazy, and her eyes, her captivating eyes. Had she actually driven him crazy? *For cryin' out loud, you're a teacher! You can't have a schoolboy crush on one of your students!* But he couldn't shake the images of her. He looked down across the room, the floor strewn with the items thrown in his furious outburst, his desk in total disarray. He was a fool!

CHAPTER 10

The Show Must Go On

November 25, 1940

THE BAND FILED INTO THE DANK BASEMENT music room carrying their instruments in orderly procession and settled into their chairs. Philip smiled and began class.

"I hope you all had a nice Thanksgiving, found a little time for practice, and are as excited as I am about our upcoming Christmas concert."

Students nodded or gave a thumbs-up.

"If you'd like to check out your instrument over the Christmas break, please remember to use the sign-up sheet."

The percussion section unclothed their drums and took their place at the rear of the room. Randall stood tall in the back row with his section mates. El in the front row. *A safe distance*, Philip thought.

El positioned the reed on the mouthpiece of her saxophone. Barely able to breathe, her palms grew sweaty and her heart raced. She connected the mouthpiece to the gooseneck, then the black neck strap to the hook on the saxophone. Stealing a glance at Philip, she pushed the neckpiece into the sax's body. She had missed seeing him. Although it was only a four-day break, it seemed like an eternity, just as every weekend did. And now here he was, big as life, in front of her and her classmates—strong, kind, but in charge. Sitting down, she caressed the sax, placing her fingers in the ready position. Having diligently practiced the songs that were to be performed at the Christmas concert, she was ready to impress her music teacher.

Philip tapped his baton on the worn wooden music stand. "Let's begin with 'Winter Wonderland.'"

The band members placed their sheet music on their metal stands.

"Good posture now, hands in position." Philip raised his baton as the students raised their instruments. The music filled the room as he let the band play the piece all the way through. "Good. I need just a little more air from you trumpets, less treble from the saxes. Let's get a little more separation on those last two chords. From the top now." He raised his baton. "One, two, three."

They played the song again.

"Excellent, good, keep that space. A little more balance and blend, saxophones." He dared to look right at El, then turned toward the clarinets. "Good, good tone, clarinets."

El hoped she hadn't blushed when his eyes met hers.

"Okay. Now let's hear the trumpet section one more time, but with a little more rhythm unity. From the top of the second page."

El smiled to herself. Here was a man who knew exactly what he wanted. As he raised his baton one more time, she thought, *And so do I.*

CHAPTER 11

Politics, Poetry, and a Holiday Kiss

December 16, 1940

A S THE BITTER MIDWESTERN WINTER COVERED Payson with a fresh blanket of snow, Philip thought often of his brothers. He mailed a letter to Homer at Western Illinois Teachers College that read:

Dear Homer,

I hope you and Wayne are well and studying hard. Have you seen Mother and Dad? I hope they're well. Last I heard from Mother, Grandmother Sidwell was nursing a bad cold. If you get home, give them all a hug from me.

Things are going well here. My students seem to be gaining a new appreciation of classical music. I have introduced them to the works of Bach, Beethoven, Strauss, and Wagner. Makes me wonder about the current aspiring musicians in Europe. Given the state of affairs, I wonder if any artists will survive. I've been reading in the newspapers that many of the Jewish artists have been relocated to ghettos and camps. The same is true for Jews of all occupations. Apparently, Hitler considers the Jews a threat to Germany. I imagine there is little attention being given to aspiring youth interested in the arts.

Seems to be quite a debate going about President Roosevelt's

Lend-Lease Plan. Many of my students feel strongly that the United States shouldn't be involved in the war at all. I think most of them are echoing the opinions of their parents who are sick of war. The other side of the argument is that to neglect the Allies of the United States would set a dangerous precedent and might allow for the Nazis to control the entire European continent without much resistance. War or no war is the issue we face. I don't see an immediate solution.

Yesterday afternoon, my band students performed admirably at the Christmas Concert. It was a wonderful program—they played "A Winter Wonderland," "White Christmas," "O Come All Ye Faithful," "Away in a Manger," "Deck the Halls," "O Holy Night," and we ended the program with "Silent Night." The audience gave the students a standing ovation. I'm very proud of their progress.

Later that evening, I accompanied the Mixed Glee Clubs as we strolled around Payson and sang Christmas carols. Quite a day!

Be well. Watch out for those ladies at Western, they'll break your heart. Ha! I don't think I ever told you about what happened to Kate Uphouser and me this fall. Quite a story. We'll catch up at Christmas. Take care.

Your brother,

Philip

The war in Europe and Japanese hostility in the Far East dominated the newspapers and radio. Philip did his best to stay abreast of the newsworthy events, both home and abroad. On occasion, however, he sought retreat in his room at Mrs. Staley's, where he found some extra moments to compose—not music, but poetry.

Last night I dreamed of a beautiful song,
Its melody haunting and wild,
But I also dreamed of a beautiful maid
Who looked at me and smiled.

And what is a song compared to a smile
From a maiden who's lovely and fair
And whose lips are inviting, and soft and warm
And offered for you to share?

But, alas, my dream was ended too soon.
I awoke and the maiden was gone,
And the song was forgotten, its melody lost,
And my soul was sad and forlorn.

He also took advantage of Mrs. Staley's offer to play her piano. He would work for hours on new compositions. Music lifted his spirits. Writing poetry provided a catharsis. He looked forward to the second semester and began to design lesson plans introducing his students to swing music. His lessons would include the music of one of his favorite composers, George Gershwin. He smiled to himself. *Maybe I should write a poem about being blue and rhapsodic.*

A predicted late-afternoon snowstorm on December 20 sent the students home early for the start of their Christmas vacation. The sunlight dwindled as Philip sat at his music room desk. World Problems essays sat in front of him, waiting to be read. He placed a Bing Crosby Christmas record on the music department's phonograph and began singing "Adeste, Fideles" along with Bing. His mind drifted to El, her soft, sophisticated voice stuck in his brain.

"That's such a lovely song."

He stopped singing. The record continued to play. It *was* El. *Say something.* "Elinor! You startled me." Trying his best to act normal, he smiled at her as she entered the room. "I'd have thought you'd be out enjoying your Christmas vacation. It's a fine afternoon for sledding or building a snowman. Looks like there's quite a snowstorm coming."

She responded with an innocent smile. "Well, I do love the snow, Mr. Z. That's why I bundled up and decided to go for a walk. It sure is a winter wonderland out there." She sang:

> "In the meadow we can build a snowman,
> then pretend that he is Parson Brown."

She could see on his face that, in spite of his stoic posture, her flirtation rattled him. "Pops might get the sleigh out tonight. It's already a lovely snowfall. Wanna ride out to the meadow?" She laughed. She sang out again, her voice sweet and mellow:

> "Sleigh bells ring, are you listening?
> In the lane, snow is glistening,
> a beautiful sight, we're happy tonight,
> walking in a winter wonderland."

Philip applauded. "Very nice. Perhaps I should consider you for a solo."

"Perhaps." She flashed her smile. "I was just out in the neighborhood. The light was on, and I heard the music so I decided I'd see if someone was down here. Pastor Ericson asked me last Sunday if I would play some Christmas carols at our church's Christmas Eve service. I said sure, but, like a knucklehead, I was in such a hurry to get out of school this afternoon, I forgot to sign out my sax after class ended."

Philip got up from his chair, opened the cabinet, and stepped aside as El retrieved her instrument. "Don't forget to sign the sheet and remember to bring it back after vacation."

"Geez. I'm sorry, Mr. Z. I hope I didn't do anything wrong, barging in here and all."

"No, no, you didn't do anything wrong. It's just that . . ." His throat and chest tightened. "It isn't a good idea for students to break into the school, that's all. But I think it's very nice that you want to play for your church service." He made a feeble attempt at a smile.

She interrupted him, "Not to be disrespectful, but I didn't exactly break in. The back door wasn't locked, and all I wanted to do was see if someone might be in the building so I could get my sax. I thought maybe a janitor was cleaning up, but I sure wasn't expecting to find you." She gave him another innocent look—her best imitation of Scarlett O'Hara.

"I know, but this sort of puts me in an awkward spot. You do understand, don't you?"

"Oh, my goodness. Who would ever think such a thing? I'm so sorry. How stupid of me. I wouldn't ever want to cause any trouble."

"Oh, I know. I know you wouldn't." Philip was trying his best to be the responsible teacher. *Does she have any idea how much I'm attracted to her? Do women instinctively know such things?* Philip cleared his throat. "I think you'd better take your sax and head on home, Elinor." Looking out the window at the top of the basement wall, he observed, "It looks like the snowfall's piling up out there, might be rough sleddin'." *God, I am so insipid.*

"I didn't come on a sled." El giggled.

Dressed in her black Wellington rubber boots, full-length wool coat, and wool cap, she stood before him a self-sufficient, independent young woman totally prepared for the elements. Then why did he feel such a strong urge to protect her?

"You walked then?"

"I did. Maybe you could walk me home. Keep me safe from the boogie man or old Jack Frost."

Philip felt himself caving in. "If you'd like, sure."

El loved his attention, the way he looked at her, but she didn't want to appear needy. "I'm fully capable of making it home on my own, you know." Tomorrow night would be the shortest night of the year, but she prayed tonight might last forever. The music room was dimly lit. Would he give in at long last, take her in his arms, and kiss her?

She came to her senses; she dared not think such a thing. He was a teacher, and she was a student. He was almost aloof as he stood at his desk and stuffed a stack of papers and two books into his brief-case. She had been so naive. She'd honestly thought he said he was a preacher. Maybe even that was wrong, kissing a preacher. He didn't look like he was much older than her. Maybe she should have told him she was a senior in high school and that her job at Harris's drugstore was only part-time, in the morning, every other Saturday. That would have ended it right there, ended what had turned into a magical evening. She had been caught up in the moment. He made her feel special, appreciated, desired, like some high-society, classy socialite. "So, are you going home for Christmas?" she asked.

He edged closer to her, turning his back toward the desk. "Headed out in the morning. The family's getting together in Nebo on Sunday."

"Our family's going to all be together, too. Christmas is my favorite time of the year."

As Bing Crosby concluded another classic carol, Philip smiled and said, "Mr. Crosby sure knows how to put someone in the mood for Christmas, doesn't he?" He removed the record from the player and placed it in its paper sleeve. "I love December. Christmas, and then my birthday's on December thirtieth."

"Really? How old will you be?" El prodded.

"Twenty-one. Skipped a couple of elementary grades. When I graduated from college, I was only twenty. How about we keep that little secret between the two of us?" He winked at her. Now he was doing some teasing. "Hey, we better get going. The snow really is piling up out there."

"So, you *are* going to walk me home?" El sensed victory. Chivalry over discretion. To top it off, her knight in shining armor was a lot younger than she had ever imagined. Was it possible her dreams might come true?

"I'd be happy to." Philip's confidence returned as he wrapped a wool scarf around his neck, pulled a dark stocking cap over his ears, buttoned up his herringbone wool coat, and pulled his tan leather gloves over his hands. "Here, let me carry that for you." He reached for El's saxophone case and opened the door for her. She buttoned up her coat.

There were two entrances into the music room, one from inside the building and one to the outside. Dread came over him. What if someone discovered him alone with a female student after school hours? He was in a dangerous situation, and the sooner he got El out of his room the better.

Just as he reached for the light switch, he heard footsteps coming down the inside stairwell. The door opened. It was the custodian, Mr. Jones. "Everything okay here, Mr. Zumwalt?"

Relieved, he replied, "Oh, yes, Mr. Jones. Just closing up. Miss Robinson forgot her saxophone, and I was just getting ready to help her get home in this awful storm."

"Well, sir, you better get movin'; that storm's bearin' down, that's for sure. Have a wonderful holiday, Mr. Zumwalt, Miss Robinson. Don't worry about the door, I'll lock everything up after you've gone."

"Thank you, Mr. Jones."

El stepped through the doorway ahead of Philip and started up the unlit stairs. Mr. Jones closed and locked the classroom door behind them. With the exception of a single shaft of dim light streaming unencumbered beneath the back outside door, the stairway was dark. Even in the filtered light, Philip could see her alluring figure beneath the winter bundling.

El paused, looked back, and then turned and proceeded up the stairs. He caught her momentary glance. A spark of desire shot through him. He dashed up the stairs two steps at a time until he was within an arm's length of her. He reached for her in the darkness. Just as he did, she opened the door, and the chill of the midwinter night froze his pursuit. She stepped outside. He followed, greeted by a fullblown blizzard.

The falling snow was thick, an ivory shower of icy spears slashed across the prairie. As they made their way down State Street, sparse gaslights flickered and cast a faint golden glow upon the evening's twilight. The five blocks to El's home seemed to Philip to be a mere few feet. Padding through the snow, they talked and laughed about the past semester.

"Hey, are Miss Van Dever and Coach Lloyd having an affair?" El blurted.

Philip stuttered, "I honestly don't know, Elinor. Just schoolyard gossip, I imagine."

She switched to a far more serious topic. "Do you think we're going to war?"

"I do, but FDR's being cautious for a reason. He's sly like a fox. I'm sure he has a plan in mind. He's just not showing his hand."

"Pops said when the Nazis invaded France and occupied Paris, they even stole priceless pieces of art and hid them away."

"Hard to imagine how desperate the German people must have been to follow a madman like Hitler. All of it's insane, El. War's insane."

"Well, here we are," El said as she turned right toward a brightly lit house. The Robinson home on the corner of Bittersweet and Sycamore Streets stood in front of them covered with freshly fallen snow. They made their way toward the front steps. El turned toward him. "Thank you for walking me home. I hope we didn't startle Mr. Jones."

"I think we might have," replied Philip. His dread returned. *What if he reports to Mr. Johnston that I was alone with El in the basement music room?* Philip thought.

"Enjoy your vacation. I hope you and your family have a very merry Christmas! See you next year!" El released a carefree, silly laugh, took the saxophone case from Philip's hand, and then turned serious. "You're really quite extraordinary, you know."

She bent down from the porch step to where he stood in the foot-deep snow and caught Philip by surprise. Softly she kissed him on the cheek, then darted across the frost-covered porch, and vanished through the front door. Once inside, she looked out at him through one of the leaded-glass sidelights and waved good night. He waved back.

Electricity flowed once again through his veins, just like their first night in the Blue Room. He wanted to hold on to the moment forever. The fresh snow partially covered the street signs. Squinting through the flurries, his brows and lashes wet with snowflakes, he could see a portion of the street sign on the corner where he stood. The only part visible was "sweet." Had he lost his mind? Should he run back to her, hold her, kiss her again and again, look into her eyes, and tell her how madly in love with her he was? Discretion prevailed.

Looking back at the porch through the falling snow, he could barely see if the backlit silhouette was still peering out the sidelight. He waved again, hoping she might be waving back, but she was gone.

As he plodded toward Mrs. Staley's, the snow crunching beneath his boots, he thought only of El. Touching the cheek where she had so sweetly pressed her lips, he remembered again the word Johnston had used to warn him: *taboo*.

Contemplating the word for a moment—a word that terrified him—it occurred to him there might be other options, ones that would include Elinor Robinson. She had to be a part of his life.

He felt as if he could float away like the snowflakes that disappeared into the night. He *was* in love! Should he shout it out to all who lived on State Street or Brainard? Should he yell it out at the top of his lungs to the inhabitants of the brown house sitting on the corner of Bittersweet and Sycamore? Would all the citizens of Payson, including the Robinsons, think he had gone mad?

Calming himself, he decided it wise to remain mute for the time being. As a new citizen of Payson, he realized it would be most sensible to respect the solitude being enjoyed by the quiet town's residents as they relaxed in their cozy homes. But he couldn't deny he longed for a future that included more of El's kisses. Their time would come and, until that moment, he would have to be content with reliving his night in the Blue Room and tonight only in his mind. He must be patient.

The last day of school, May 24, 1941, was a mere six months away. A red-letter day, a day already marked on his calendar. *Then* he could pursue Miss Elinor Lynne Robinson, a Payson-Seymour High School graduate, with every ounce of charm he possessed. *That* would be the day he would put his plan into action.

He walked up the icy front steps of Mrs. Staley's porch and opened the door to a wonderful scent—fresh-baked cookies! On the dining room table was a plate filled with sugar cookies decorated with red and green icing. Mrs. Staley shuffled down the stairs in her slippers and robe to greet him.

"Are these for the taking?" he asked.

"Of course, they are, my dear. They're just for you. When are you going home for Christmas, Philip?"

"If the roads aren't too snow-packed, I plan on taking off in the morning, ma'am. I'll be back in a week or so though."

"There's milk in the refrigerator. Whatever you don't eat, please take home to your family."

"Thank you, Mrs. Staley. That's very kind of you."

"Good night, Philip, and merry Christmas! I'm headed up to bed now. I'll see you in the morning before you leave. We'll have a little breakfast together."

"I'd like that. Thank you, again, Mrs. Staley—for everything. And a merry Christmas to you."

Philip gobbled up three cookies, washed them down with cold milk, and walked into the parlor to play the piano. He stopped short. Sitting on the table next to the piano was a package wrapped in white paper and decorated with red ribbon and a red bow. On the attached tag appeared his name, penned in bold letters. He opened the package. Inside a box, he found a note accompanied by a collection of sheet music. Shuffling through the music, he was overwhelmed: Gershwin, Berlin, Miller, Porter, Crosby, Cantor, and the classics—Chopin, Mozart. There were Christmas carols and "The Star-Spangled Banner." He unfolded the note and read:

Dear Philip,

This music belonged to my late husband. You make that old piano sound like it used to. I hope you will play these songs for some-one someday, just like he did for me. Your talent should never go unnoticed or unappreciated. Enjoy!
Sincerely,
Millie Staley

Philip wondered what he would ever be able to give Mrs. Staley in return. She had opened up her home to him and every day made him feel like it was his home, too. He placed one of the pieces of sheet music on the piano, sat down on the bench, and began playing, *pianissimo*. His favorite Christmas carol, "Silent Night," drifted up the stairway. Maybe Mrs. Staley had not yet fallen asleep. The night preceding the shortest night of the year remained silent except for the soft melody floating through the boardinghouse.

Once he finished playing the carol, he gathered up the music, wrapping paper, ribbon, and bow, and then tucked the note in his pocket and walked to his room. He touched his cheek one more time and smiled. It had been a wonderful night; the ungraded essays could wait until he returned from Christmas break. He went to his room, crawled under the warm blankets, and slept in heavenly peace.

CHAPTER 12

The Harlem Renaissance
and Another Deal

January 6, 1941

AS PROMISED, PHILIP BEGAN THE SECOND SEMESTER in his band class with a discussion of music appreciation, specifically modern music. "How many of you know about the Harlem Renaissance?"

El hesitated and then raised her hand.

"Okay," Philip said. "Let's try again. Anyone ever heard of Duke Ellington?"

This time Essie and Florence joined El, delighted they knew that Mr. Ellington was a famous band leader.

"How about Billy Holiday or Louis Armstrong?"

Still only three hands went up.

"It would be impossible to discuss modern music, or swing music, as it's called, without mentioning the Harlem Renaissance. Some of the greatest jazz, syncopated rhythms, and improvised solos came out of Harlem. Those great artists I just named gained much of their fame playing at the famous Cotton Club, which sadly closed its doors last year, but the music they left us is worth listening to. Here's a sample of one of Mr. Ellington's biggest hits."

Philip walked over to his Birch portable phonograph. "I used to listen to radio broadcasts of the Cotton Club performances, and that's when I fell in love with jazz and swing music. It was where I first heard this song." He placed the needle on the record.

"It don't mean a thing if ain't got that swing
(Doo wah, doo wah, doo wah, doo wah)
(Doo wah, doo wah, doo wah, doo wah)
It don't mean a thing, all you got to do is swing"

Most of the students were tapping their feet to rhythm of the song, and others were swaying their heads.

"It makes no difference if it's sweet or it's hot
Just give that rhythm ev'rything you got
Oh, it don't mean a thing . . ."

The record ended. The students applauded the rousing number, except for Randall, who sat rigid.

"You all right, Randall?" Philip asked.

"Me? Yeh, Mr. Z. I'm fine. I just don't care for nigg—uh, I mean that kind of music."

"I understand. We all have different tastes in music. I just wanted to introduce the class to something other than classical or John Philip Sousa this term. Stay with me here. I'd like to play another one I think you might like." Philip cranked his machine and placed another platter on the turntable. He set the needle. It was Louis Armstrong.

"Oh, when the Saints
Go marching in
Now when the saints go marching in
Yes, I want to be in that number
When the Saints go marching in . . ."

Philip ignored Randall's scowl this time and continued the lesson. "What I'm sure many of you know from taking Miss Van Meter's history class is that there was a migration of colored folks from the Southern states to the North. Escaping Jim Crow laws and the Ku Klux Klan was essential to their survival. Many colored musicians ended up in New York, in Harlem. There were writers, artists, poets, singers, and songwriters, and Harlem brought fame to some of those individuals who otherwise might never have been noticed. I was discussing this with Miss Harper, and she shared a poem I'd like to read to you. I think it captures the spirit of that artistic renaissance."

Philip opened the book of poetry and read a few stanzas of "Harlem Night Club" by Langston Hughes, purposefully leaving a couple of the more scandalous stanzas out.

Sleek black boys in a cabaret.
Jazz-band, jazz-band,–
Play, plAY, PLAY!
Tomorrow . . . who knows?
Dance today!

White ones, brown ones,
What do you know
About tomorrow
Where all paths go?

Jazz-boys, jazz-boys,–
Play, plAY, PLAY!
Tomorrow . . . is darkness.
Joy today!

"What I would like you to understand is that music, like poetry, holds a mirror up to each of us and to the society in which we live. What do you think Mr. Hughes's poetry was telling us?" Philip was surprised to see Cecil's hand. "Go ahead, Cecil. What did the poem say to you?"

"I think he was telling us to live for today because who knows what tomorrow might bring? I mean, that's pretty true, don't you think, Mr. Z? With the war in Europe and all."

"I don't know," Randall countered. "I think Hughes was just a lazy good-for-nothing who just wanted to play around and dance and write stupid poems. Not saying that poetry isn't a good thing sometimes, but this one just doesn't make any sense to me at all."

El's hand shot up. "I agree with Cecil. We need to find all the joy we can in every day. We have no idea where our paths are going, and I, for one, think we should dance whenever we get the chance."

"Hey, El, maybe you're the poet," Essie said, laughing.

"Well, I suppose it's safe to say we all interpret poetry and music in our own way," Philip said with a smile, "and I guess that's why there are so many different forms of expression. Tomorrow we'll listen to another of Mr. Armstrong's hits, 'Ain't Misbehavin'.' Until then make sure you don't—misbehave, that is."

The students laughed as the passing bell rang. Philip was gathering up his papers and stuffing them in his briefcase when Randall approached his desk.

"Sorry if I it seemed like I was misbehaving, Mr. Z," Randall said, smiling. "My family just doesn't much care for the colored. They've had some bad experiences. I understand what you're trying to do, introduce us to all types of music and I appreciate that, I do. But you need to know that my family isn't the only one in our town who feels that way. I like you, Mr. Z, but I'd be careful if I was you. That's all— be careful."

"I appreciate that, Randall. Thank you for stopping by," Philip said calmly, though he felt heat rising to his face with a certain sense of disgust.

Randall nodded and headed for the door.

"Say, Randall?"

"Yes, sir."

"How do you feel about Jewish people?"

"Uh, pretty much the same as the coloreds."

"Just wondered because, on Wednesday, we're going to begin a unit on George Gershwin, my favorite modern composer."

"Oh, he's not a Jew is he, Mr. Z?"

"You mean Jacob Gershowitz? I'm afraid he is, but I have a feeling you're going to like his music anyway."

"Maybe I will, Mr. Z, maybe I will."

Philip forced a smile as his anger drained. "See you in Economics this afternoon, Randall. Have a good lunch."

During his lunch, Philip shared what happened in his class with Ralph.

"Randall's correct about one thing, Philip. Be careful. There are some powerful people around here who might take exception to you introducing the music they played at the Cotton Club or reading Langston Hughes's poetry. Payson folks are good folks, Philip, but they're a bit set in their ways," Ralph said.

"Oh, I'm sure of that, Ralph, but I think our students need to understand the world is a bigger place than Payson. Randall's a smart kid; he could be a great leader. If we can open a young man's mind, that could make a real difference in his life. Don't you agree?"

Ina joined the conversation. "Ralph's right, Philip. Be careful. I heard they fired a music teacher in Pittsfield for just playing Billy Holiday's recording of 'Strange Fruit' in class. People around here don't like to be reminded of lynchings and the Klan. They're afraid of colored people. They're afraid of anything that's not familiar."

Philip smiled crookedly. "Like jazz?"

"From what I've heard, Randall comes from a long line of Klan members," Ralph cautioned. "Maybe just rumors, but his grandfather was supposedly a knight in the Klan over in Alton. I don't imagine they'd much appreciate some of the things you and I might be saying in our classes. Sometimes we've just got to meet these kids where they are and bring them along a little at a time. I'm afraid doing that when they're seniors is mighty tough."

"Maybe you're right, Ralph, but if not now, when?" Philip answered with a shake of his head.

Philip and Ralph's many teachers' lounge conversations and political chats were ongoing. They agreed on most of what the president was doing, even how FDR was adept at pulling the old political two-step. Keeping his campaign pledge to the American people not to go to war was of the utmost importance to FDR, even though reports poured into the White House daily detailing the looming threats the Nazi government posed to the free world. The American citizenry did not want to send their boys across the Atlantic to fight. And since the Nazis presented no immediate risk to the United States, most people were content to let the British take on the Germans. The president, however, was keenly aware that in order for Great Britain to carry on that fight, they needed more resources.

After much debate, that is what FDR asked, and he made it abundantly clear during a radio broadcast with his closing words: "We must be the great arsenal of democracy. For us this is an emergency as serious as war itself. We must apply ourselves to our task with the same resolution, the same urgency, the same spirit of patriotism and sacrifice, as we would show were we at war."

Near the end of January, Philip explained the Lend-Lease bill to his World Problems students.

"FDR's plan was to help save England and Western civilization. He compared his proposal to one neighbor lending another a garden hose to put out the fire in his home. The president told those at the press conference, 'What do I do in such a crisis? I don't say neighbor, my garden hose cost me fifteen dollars, you have to pay me fifteen dollars for it. I don't want fifteen dollars. I want my garden hose back after the fire is over.'"

Some of the students chuckled.

Philip continued, "Debate exploded in the halls of the Senate and House over giving the president the authority to sell, transfer title to, exchange, lease, lend, or otherwise dispose of any defense article to any government whose defense the president deemed vital to the defense of the United States."

Debate in Philip's class also grew fiery.

"We need to stay out of that war." Cecil DeWeese was back on his soapbox. "Why should we send money to the British? Didn't we fight a war to get rid of them? Like I said, FDR never shoulda been elected in the first place."

"I don't like war, that's for darned sure," argued Florence Marshall. "But those Germans are killing innocent people and takin' land that don't even belong to 'em."

"I agree with Florence," El said. "And the Japanese are no better. They massacred thousands of Chinese in Nanking, right, Mr. Z?"

"Correct, Elinor. The Japanese are members of the Axis alliance with the Germans and the Italians. If you'll recall, we talked about Japanese aggression earlier, and the Nanking Massacre that occurred in December of 1937 was certainly an example of that. The estimates of those killed varies, but it was in the thousands."

"There's no simple solution to this war." Randall rose and stood by his desk as if he were addressing a joint session of Congress. "I remember what Florence said about freedom. The president wants to preserve freedom in the world, and if by loaning our allies the 'garden hose' to put out the fire of Fascism, then I say give 'em the hose. If we can keep our boys from getting killed in another world war, then I'm all for it."

"Amen!" said Jimmy Blauser.

The debate and discussion prompted by the lesson left the young teacher feeling exhilarated, but, in the end, Randall was right. There was no easy solution to this world problem, but it was clear the president and the prime minister were concocting their own new deal.

As class neared its end, Philip said, "We'll continue tomorrow discussing what are the potential results of FDR and Churchill's agreement. We will explore the pros and cons of Lend-Lease and how it might affect all of us."

The bell rang. As El passed his desk, Philip asked her to stay. "Would you have a minute or two to meet with me after school today, Elinor?"

"Sure. Where?" El said.

"Just come back here. Okay?"

"Okay. See you then." El dashed from the room, trying her best to conceal her delight.

Philip watched her go. His memory of the front porch kiss lingered. It had confused everything, but he knew he must be resolute if he was to carry out his long-range plan. The deal he had in mind was not as important to the world order as Roosevelt and Churchill's; however, his immediate future did hinge upon its successful negotiation. He would be businesslike—never easy in her presence.

At the end of the day, as students filed through the hallways, he waited. El entered his room. Trying his best to compose himself, he feared his heart might pound itself right out of his chest. "Thank you for coming, Elinor. How are you?"

"Fine, I guess." El gave Philip the *look* that made him weak in the knees, the one that took away all his defenses. "So, what's the summons for?"

He longed to take her in his arms but instead looked straight into her eyes. He had to face this problem head-on, be honest and firm in his dictate. His voice betrayed him; it was soft and gentle. "This isn't exactly a summons, but I have given our meeting on your front porch a lot of thought."

"*Meeting?* That's a strange word for it."

"I'm not sure what to call it, but whatever it was, we need to get a couple of things straight. That night was very sweet, but we have to have only a student-teacher relationship until the end of the school year."

Tears welled in El's eyes. Quite a turnaround from their moment on the porch. "I understand. I've tried my best to keep my distance, to just ignore you, but I can't help but wonder . . . after graduation we'd be free to, you know, get together. There'd be nothing to fear, no trouble, no scandal. Right?"

Philip longed to be close to her but couldn't surrender. The newly negotiated agreement had to be ironclad. True love would win out in the end. The feeling surging through his body every time he was near her was no illusion.

"So, we really won't have a problem after I graduate, will we?"

El was already making a strong case for their future. *She'd make a fine attorney*, Philip thought. He sighed. "We'll just have to talk about all of this after you graduate."

Philip was no Roosevelt, but the deal was struck. Until graduation, he was the teacher, El his pupil.

CHAPTER 13

Valentine's Day Dance

February 15, 1941

AS PHILIP ROLLED OUT OF BED on a chilly Saturday morning, it crossed his mind to pass on chaperoning the annual Valentine's Day dance at the high school to avoid putting himself in too casual a position with El. However, it was an extracurricular assignment he'd volunteered for at the beginning of the year, and his mother's voice rang loud and clear in his head, "You signed up for it, Philip, so get your lazy rear end out of bed."

He dressed in blue jeans and a flannel shirt and pulled on his leather boots. Snatching up his winter coat, he headed down the stairs. A hot cup of coffee and a biscuit sat on the kitchen counter. "For me?" he asked Mrs. Staley.

"None other. Try some butter and jam on that biscuit. They're fresh out of the oven."

"Thank you, ma'am." Philip sat, slurped the piping hot coffee, and treated himself to the biscuit.

"Where you off to, Philip?" Mrs. Staley asked.

"Going over to school to check on the dance decorations. Some of the freshmen signed up to help out. Miss Van Dever, Coach Lloyd, and Mr. Goins are in charge. I thought I'd see what I could do to lend a helping hand."

Fishing for a bit of salacious gossip, Mrs. Staley smiled wryly as she filled Philip's cup. "Well, I heard Miss Van Dever and Coach Lloyd might be an item."

"Why, Mrs. Staley. I wouldn't have any idea about that."

"They'd sure make a mighty fine couple."

"I agree."

"You goin' to the dance tonight?"

"Yes, ma'am."

"Ina goin'?"

"I imagine."

"You know, she and that boyfriend of hers from U of I are takin' a break," she said, giving him an encouraging look.

"Yes, we've talked about it. Well, I gotta get going. Hope it doesn't snow tonight. Be a big mess in the gym. Have a good day, Mrs. Staley."

Philip spent the afternoon helping the others coordinate the decorating of the gym. *Maybe there are some sparks between Joan and Art*, he thought, but he wasn't about to spread any additional unfounded rumors.

He assisted Lloyd and Goins in constructing a crude stage where the Valentine's Day king and queen would sit and preside over the royal festivities. Ina unexpectedly stopped by and caught Philip completely off guard.

"Well, Professor. So, you're handy with hammer and nails, too?"

"Hey, Ina. Yeh, I help my father build houses in the summer."

"Coming to the dance tonight?"

"Yeh, I signed up to chaperone. You?"

"I signed up, too. Would it be too much trouble to catch a ride? Just in case it snows, you know."

"Sure, pick you up at six thirty. I have ticket duty."

"That'd be swell. I'll help you."

El and Randall were one of the last couples to enter the gym.

Randall handed the dance tickets to Ina and turned to Philip. "The old gym doesn't look half bad."

"The committee did a great job, didn't they?" Philip replied.

Red and white streamers created a faux ceiling, and paper hearts and cupids decorated the walls. The small stage was set under one of the basketball hoops with large gold and silver king and queen crowns painted on a backdrop. A crystal punch bowl filled with red punch sat on a table under the other hoop along with an assortment of Valentine's Day cookies. A four-piece quartet played modern swing music.

When the band took a break, Mr. Johnston stepped onto the stage and tapped the microphone. "May I have your attention, please?" A spotlight shined on the superintendent, who stood in front of the Valentine's Day royal court. "It is my distinct pleasure to announce the Valentine's Day dance king and queen for 1941. Drum roll, please . . ."

The quartet's drummer had stuck around and obliged.

"The Valentine's Day king is Randall Yarborough!"

The students applauded politely. Randall stepped forward onto the stage, and Mr. Johnston placed a gold cardboard crown on his head. The superintendent whispered into his ear and then addressed the crowd, "Randall will now crown the queen."

Randall played his role to the hilt. He wandered through the crowd toward Essie and then darted toward Florence Marshall. Finally, he turned and placed a faux silver tiara on his date's head. Mr. Johnston announced, "And the Valentine's Day queen is Elinor Robinson."

All the girls squealed. Philip and Ina clapped.

"Such a sweet girl," Ina remarked.

"Yes, she is," Philip replied. Though he was proud of El and her popularity, a sick feeling arose in his stomach when Randall kissed her on the cheek in front of the entire crowd.

The band began to play "Cheek to Cheek."

"Come on, Ina," Philip said suddenly. "Let's dance. We might as well have some fun tonight, too."

Ina smiled. "I thought you'd never ask."

Philip looked over Ina's shoulder. He wondered if El was succumbing to Randall's charming advances. Had cupid's arrow pierced her heart? He spun Ina away from the sight that made both his heart and stomach ache again: El wrapped in Randall's arms, taking the song literally.

El peeked over Randall's shoulder at Philip and Ina as they glided along the dance floor. She closed her eyes, hoping the jealously welling up inside her would subside while fearing she was no match for Miss Harper.

CHAPTER 14

Let Freedom Ring!

May 9, 1941

SPRING ARRIVED FOR GOOD. CROCUSES BLOOMED, and the trees of Payson sprouted forth their deep-green leaves. On a cloudless Friday morning, Philip began the discussion in his World Problems class. "One year ago tomorrow, Winston Churchill was appointed to the position of prime minister of the United Kingdom, replacing Neville Chamberlain, who had resigned. It was the same day the Nazis began to bomb England. What a predicament for Mr. Churchill! How do you think you might have reacted in such a situation?"

"I'da been as scared as an old long-tailed cat in a room full of rockin' chairs!" blurted Cecil.

The classroom erupted with laughter.

"Were folks killed when the Nazis bombed England, Mr. Z?" asked Essie.

"They were," replied Philip.

"Like, how many?"

"Hard to say, but there have been a number of casualties, in London in particular. The news reports tell us that many of the children have been sent out of the city, and the Royal Air Force has been gallant in fighting off the Nazi bombers."

"Why don't we go over and help them?" asked Florence Marshall. "That's the least we could do. Aren't we their allies? Those Nazis are monsters. Why, they even burned books! How can they do that, Mr. Z?"

Philip leaned back on his desk. "So, you can see what a difficult situation our president and the members of Congress find themselves in, can't you?"

"We need to get over there and kick some you-know-what!" Jimmy Blauser exclaimed. "The president's too soft. We need to make a stand before we're all talkin' in German."

"Sounds like you've changed your tune, Jimmy," Philip countered.

"I don't know, Mr. Z. I don't want to go to war, but I think what the Germans are doing is wrong. Don't you think so?" Jimmy was reticent now.

"I don't think it's very smart to get involved over there," said Cecil. "Look what happened in the Great War. A lot of men died, including my uncle. Why, even the great Charles Lindbergh thinks we need to stay out of it."

"He's just a damned Nazi," blurted Jimmy.

"He is not! He's a patriot, a hero! He ain't no Nazi!" Cecil yelled back.

"Okay, boys," Philip said. "Calm down."

He moved the discussion along, allowing both sides of the argument to be discussed. Discourse was the lifeblood of his class. It hadn't occurred to him how much he would enjoy teaching World Problems. Ironically, the subject kept him abreast of what was going on, allowed him to weigh the pros and cons of going to war, and made him seriously contemplate his idea of enlisting. He had always loved music, but his social studies classes had become equally stimulating. This was such a discussion.

"Returning to Florence's question," Philip said, "of 'how can they do that?' There was another important historical event that occurred on May tenth. Seven years prior to their attack on England, the Nazi government supported the Main Office for Press and Propaganda of the German Student Association. The students called for the censorship of hundreds of un-German books, then publicly burned over twenty-five thousand volumes for the entire world to see, just as Florence mentioned. The demonstrations took place in most university towns and declared that it was time for a pure German language and culture. They attacked the Jews of Germany, claiming that they were undermining traditional German values."

"That was just horrible," Essie said.

"I agree," Philip answered. "The Student Association—students like you—advocated for the purging of the literature and writings of the likes of German-speaking authors Bertolt Brecht, Albert Einstein, Sigmund Freud, and Karl Marx. The Nazi party had most likely put the ideas into the students' minds and encouraged the demonstrations. Joseph Goebbels, the Minister of Propaganda for the Nazi Party, had declared 'The era of extreme Jewish intellectualism is now at an end.' He told a gathering of over forty thousand students in Berlin that through burning the books, the decadence and moral corruption of the German family and state would soon be terminated."

"They even burned the books of one of Miss Harper's favorite American authors!" exclaimed Florence. "Ernest Hemingway! I just can't get that image outa my head. Think of those thousands of books up in flames. It just ain't right, I tell ya. It ain't right."

El raised her hand. "I think the Nazis want to control the minds of all the German people. I mean, what do they think they're doing by burning books?"

Philip beamed. His students all nodded in agreement with El that burning books, any books, was a grievous act, and that the freedoms guaranteed by the First Amendment of the U.S. Constitution were something they believed worth defending. He had struck a chord. His students inspired him. He had rambled through the lessons on the

Constitution, covering the compulsory content required of him. What he taught his students months ago had gained even more significance now. The very words and principles dutifully recited in his class had actually precipitated a war—a war that might end the lives of some of the young men sitting in front of him.

The lesson of the day reminded him and his students about freedom's fragility.

CHAPTER 15

Battle Hymn

May 14, 1941

THE HIGH SCHOOL BAND'S REPUTATION had spread throughout the county. Their jazzy rendition of "When the Saints Come Marching In" and Sousa's majestic "Stars and Stripes Forever" fired up fans and inspired players at the basketball games. The band soon became the talk of the town.

The Christmas and spring concerts were even given a rave review by the Quincy newspaper: *"Illinois has a discovered a jewel in its midst. The Payson-Seymour High School band has been a breath of fresh air. Performances at both Christmas and Spring concerts have delighted the Payson citizenry, drawing high praise from residents. Superintendent Johnston calls the band 'the pride of Payson-Seymour High.'"*

Likewise, the combined girls and boys glee clubs, thirty-one members strong, received praise from the community. Payson residents were thrilled when the students serenaded the town with "We Wish You a Merry Christmas," "Hark the Herald Angels Sing," and "Silent Night." Members of both clubs sang in the county chorus and their combined performance of "The Battle Hymn of the Republic" at the spring concert merited a standing ovation.

As leader of both organizations, Philip was fast becoming a local celebrity. He had preached time and time again to his students, quoting his mother, "Nothing worth having comes easy. If it did, everyone would have it. To be good at anything requires great sacrifice."

The success of the music program under Philip's tutelage was not lost on Superintendent Johnston, who had received a very positive phone call from Mr. A. E. Houseman, the board of education president. The superintendent found Philip in the music room.

"Some of the board members have been talking about the upcoming graduation ceremony and wondered if the chorus could sing 'The Battle Hymn of the Republic.' Mr. Houseman said the song moved him to tears at the spring concert. What do you say, Philip? Can the kids perform it at graduation?"

"We'd be honored, sir," Philip responded with pride.

At the regular Wednesday morning meeting of the mixed chorus, he greeted his students with the news. "This is a great honor," he said. "I'm so proud of all of you. We'll need to have a few extra rehearsals before our performance. Everybody in?"

The next morning at 7 a.m., thirty-one sleepy-eyed students arrived. There were a few grumbles, but most were eager to rehearse. Philip led them through a brief warm-up. "Now, let's take it from the top. And let's give a big round of applause to the percussion and trumpet sections of the band for agreeing to accompany us once again."

The mixed chorus clapped for their classmates. Philip raised his hands, pointing at the trumpets as the song began. Even with early morning voices, the mixed chorus sang beautifully. The drum, trumpet, and piano accompaniment added to the majesty of the hymn. As the Amen echoed up through the ceiling of the music room into the empty hallways, Philip was gratified to see the result of the year's effort.

"Altos, be sure you're getting on top of your notes, still a bit flat. And, tenors, keep singing out with those big voices. This is a powerful song; we need to hear everyone at their very best. Okay, here we go." His hands raised, he once again directed the piano accompanist, drummers, and trumpeters to begin. The voices rose in unison following the stirring opening measures.

"Mine eyes have seen the glory . . ."

As the song reached its moving conclusion, Philip's eyes grew moist. He gazed out and witnessed the same passion from his students. He would miss them and moments like this. He noticed tears in El's eyes as the song concluded. Her vivacious, loving spirit flowed from her very being as she sang or played the saxophone or argued politics. The passion and enthusiasm with which she approached each and every day—all of that added to his desire to be with her.

"Glory, glory, Hallelujah!
His Truth is marching on.
Amen."

Graduation would soon be here. Commencement of more than one kind.

Glory, glory hallelujah, indeed!

CHAPTER 16

Resignation

May 21, 1941

HAVING WATCHED HIS STUDENTS MATURE in both their thinking and their musical skills, Philip was pleased. Maybe he was a good teacher, after all. It was the end of the school day when Mrs. Peterson appeared at the door of his classroom. "Mr. Johnston would like to see you in his office, Mr. Zumwalt."

"Any idea what he wants, ma'am?"

"No, sir. I do not. He just asked that you come immediately."

Philip walked down the hall, whistling. He had come to Payson unsure of what he might find, but now he felt a sense of accomplishment. When he arrived at Mr. Johnston's office, he took a seat and waited. Mrs. Peterson was uncharacteristically stern as she approached and announced, "He will see you now."

Walking into the superintendent's office, Philip grew uneasy. Mr. Johnston had a somber look of concern on his face. "Thank you for coming in on such short notice, Philip."

"Yes, sir. Is there something I can do for you?"

"Philip, there's a delicate situation I need to discuss with you, and I hope you are able to be honest with me."

"Absolutely, sir."

"I suppose I might as well get straight to the point. Are you in a relationship with Elinor Robinson?"

The question startled Philip, but he regained his composure. "No, sir. Well, I mean, uh, obviously we have a student-teacher relationship, if that's what you mean."

"Not exactly, Philip. I'm afraid it's come to my attention from a reliable source that you did have some inappropriate contacts with her."

"I'm not certain what that means, sir."

"Apparently, she told the son of my reliable source that she was in love with you and planned to marry you."

Philip did his best to disguise the elation he felt upon hearing of El's proclamation. He remained serious. "I wasn't aware of such a thing. If that was the case, she never shared that with me."

"You are aware of the board policy forbidding faculty to have relationships with students outside of school."

"Yes, sir."

"What were you thinking, son? Did you, in fact, meet Miss Robinson at a dance hall in Quincy?"

"I did, but I was not aware at the time that she was a student. The school year had not even begun yet, sir."

"Well, that certainly is in your favor, but have you been alone with her in your classroom?"

"Yes, sir. But that was only to clarify our relationship. Oh, and there was one time before Christmas break when she came to pick up her instrument."

"So, you *are* in a relationship?"

"Well, not exactly. I took to heart your advice about such a thing being taboo."

"Philip, unfortunately, you have placed yourself in the middle of a rather complicated situation. I was asked by the board of education to investigate the allegation that you were involved with Miss Robinson. I'll report back to them exactly what you shared with me and call you at Mrs. Staley's tonight if I have further information. Thank you for coming in."

"Mr. Johnston, I can assure you that nothing inappropriate has occurred between me and Elinor Robinson."

"Thank you for your time, Mr. Zumwalt."

Philip left Johnston's office in disbelief. Trying to contain his rage at being unfairly accused of such an indiscretion, Philip burst into Ralph's empty classroom.

"What's the matter, pal? You all right?" his friend asked.

"Not exactly. I think I might be getting fired."

"What happened?"

"Mr. Johnston just called me in and asked me if I was having a relationship with a student."

"Oh, dear God, I certainly hope not." Ralph studied Philip's worried face and became concerned. "Are you?"

"It depends on how you define relationship."

"What does that mean?" Ralph asked.

"I met Elinor at a dance at the Casino before school started, and to be truthful, there was chemistry between us. We spent the last couple of hours of the evening talking, and I guess we did kiss a few times, but I sure as hell didn't know she was a high school student."

"But you did kiss her, right?"

"They were purely *innocent* kisses. I swear to you, Ralph. I had no idea that she would be one of my students."

"News flash, Philip. There's no such thing as an innocent kiss, a kiss is a kiss. Have you seen her since, you know, other than at school or school activities?"

"We've talked privately a few times since then, but nothing happened. Well, except she did kiss me on her front porch, but just on the cheek. No one saw it, and I told her after that we could not have any further private contact until graduation."

"Oh, my, my friend. You've dropped yourself into a viper pit. I wish you'd told me about this. Teacher gossip, of course, but word is young Yarborough's been pursuing Elinor ever since they started high school, maybe before that. And since old man Yarborough's on the school board, falling for Elinor was a big mistake. "

"I figured as much. It sure makes sense now. El must have told Randall how she felt about me."

"I don't see any way out of this, Philip. Yarborough's a big shot around here and can get you fired at the drop of a hat. Maybe you should resign—to save face, I mean."

"But nothing happened, Ralph. I'm telling you; our kisses were innocent. Nothing happened beyond that and the kiss on the porch, which was, I swear, just a peck on the cheek. That was it. Honest."

"Doesn't matter. Yarborough's going to make sure his boy gets whatever he wants."

"Maybe we should ask Elinor what she thinks about that," Philip said and then dropped his head. "Maybe it *is* best if I resign. I've seriously been considering enlisting any way. Then, I can court El without any scandal. The last thing I want is to ruin her reputation."

"Enlisting in the military for reputation's sake sounds pretty drastic, pal, especially if we go to war," Ralph cautioned.

Philip chuckled despite his discomfort. "Nah, Ralph, this just cinches it. I've thought about enlisting in the Army Air Corps this whole school year, and with all that's going on in the world, I'm feeling the call. This is the right decision for me."

Mr. Johnston called Mrs. Staley's later that evening and asked to speak with Philip. If it was his intention to dismiss Philip during the phone call, he was never given the opportunity.

"Mr. Johnston," Philip said, "I'm afraid there's been a terrible misunderstanding about Miss Robinson and me, and I'm truly sorry about that. I'm not sure if this is the right time or not, but maybe what I have to tell you will clear things up for you and me. I've decided to enlist in the Army Air Corps, sir. I'll submit my letter of resignation following the graduation ceremony, and I hope that will satisfy all concerned."

"This was not how I wanted all of this to end, Philip. I will accept your resignation, but with regret. I wish you all the best and want you to know you're one of the finest teachers I've ever known."

"Thank you, sir, it's been my pleasure. It was a privilege to teach these young people. Truth is, I believe I learned as much from them as they did from me."

After Philip hung up the phone, he hoped his future with El had not been compromised. Realizing his longing for her had grown even stronger, there was a sense of relief. He believed he had made the correct decision, one he hoped he would not regret.

CHAPTER 17

Graduation

May 24, 1941

"ELINOR LYNNE ROBINSON." Superintendent Johnston's voice boomed.

El walked briskly across the temporary stage constructed on the front lawn of the high school for the ceremony. The five school board members, a pastor, and twenty seniors sat at attention as the superintendent read the names and the diplomas were distributed.

Dressed in her white pinafore dress and spectator high heels, El accepted her diploma from Mr. Goins, the senior class sponsor. Following protocol and tradition, she placed her diploma in her left hand and shook Mr. Goin's right hand, officially becoming a graduate of Payson-Seymour High School's class of 1941. Families and friends applauded. She winked at hers as she returned to her seat. Philip smiled as she walked by. She returned it with her own.

Randall was the final student to receive his diploma. Philip walked to the center of the stage. Followed by the mixed choir of the girls and boys glee clubs, he placed the sheet music on his stand and waited as the chorus members lined up. He smiled at his students, easing their stage fright, and raised his hands with a confident air. He nodded to the accompanist, the trumpeter, and the drums to begin.

"Mine eyes have seen the glory . . ."

After the performance, the board of education president, Mr. Houseman, approached the podium and addressed the gathering. "That was just beautiful," he said. "Glory hallelujah for this day." He signaled a nod of approval to Philip, made a few brief remarks, and then relinquished the podium to Mr. Johnston. The superintendent congratulated the Payson-Seymour High School class of 1941 and certified they were officially high school graduates. The new alumni were cheered once again.

Pastor Kermit Ericson stepped forward and offered the benediction. Speaking in a gentle voice, he raised his right hand toward the light blue sky overhead. "Please join me in prayer." The audience and graduates bowed their heads. "Dear Lord, in these times of great uncertainty, we ask thy blessings upon these fine young men and women. Keep them safe and in thy care. Watch over them; remind them of your charge as they go out into the world and help them do good for all. We ask this in thy great and holy name. Amen."

The twenty graduates marched off the stage and into their futures. The service was an emotional roller coaster for Philip. He wondered if El's thoughts were as much of him as his were of her. He had been nervous prior to directing the "Battle Hymn," but once the first note sounded, his fears were dispelled. He'd directed the choir with unbridled joy and his students had performed flawlessly. Though he was firm in his decision to enlist, he had to admit to himself that he would miss his students.

The graduates joined their families in a great celebration. Philip and Ina were surrounded by many of their students. As they offered their congratulations to the graduates, Ina hugged both the boys and the girls; the girls hugged Philip; the boys chose a handshake.

As the students departed with their families, Ina turned to Philip. "That song was absolutely remarkable. You've done wonders with those youngsters."

"Thank you, Ina." Philip took a theatrical bow. "They've really developed this year, haven't they?"

"Yes, they have. So, headed back to Nebo tonight?"

"No, I'm gonna pack tonight and take off in the morning. I'll be staying with my folks this summer, helping Dad and my brothers build a house over in Pleasant Hill."

"I'll miss you, Philip Zumwalt. Are you coming back next year, or are the rumors true?"

"I won't be returning to Payson-Seymour in the fall, Ina. I've informed Superintendent Johnston and my mother of my decision."

"You're enlisting, aren't you?"

"Yes. It'll give me a better chance of choosing which branch of the service I want. I've always wanted to be a pilot, and this might just be my opportunity. It's beginning to look like war is inevitable."

"I fear you're right."

"I talked to a recruiter in Springfield last weekend. He was pretty sure I'd qualify for the Aviation Cadet program. He told me if I enlisted now, I could ship out in August. Like I said, I haven't uttered a word of any of this except to Mother. I'm afraid Dad would be too upset."

"Your brothers?"

"I'll tell them before I enlist, but I imagine they'll sign up, too, especially if we go to war."

"I'll say a prayer for you."

"Thanks. What about you? What are your plans?"

"Ron and I patched things up. He'll be finishing up his master's degree and starting to hunt for a job."

"Well, there's a music position open here and a vacancy at your aunt's boardinghouse."

Ina smiled. "I suppose that would be nice, wouldn't it?"

"Yeh, you never know what might develop."

"Which brings us to another topic. Your love life—" Ina stopped mid-sentence when she saw El's mother, Sandra Robinson, approaching.

Sandra nodded at Ina and extended her hand toward Philip who shook it. "Mr. Zumwalt, you had those kids singing like the Mormon Tabernacle Choir! Simply lovely."

"Thank you, ma'am, but I don't think we're in their league yet," Philip replied, smiling.

"Elinor so enjoyed music this year and just loved your World Problems class. She came home almost every night talking about you and your classes."

"Thank you, Mrs. Robinson. Elinor's a fine young woman," Philip replied. "You and Dr. Robinson must be quite proud of her." Philip shifted his weight from one foot to the other, perspiration dripped from his forehead. Had rumors of his *inappropriate* behavior reached the Robinsons yet? Would Superintendent Johnston or David Yarborough have reported such a juicy bit of gossip to them? He quieted his mind and focused instead on Mrs. Robinson's reply.

"We are. She's starting nurse's training in the fall at Blessing Hospital in Quincy."

"She'll be a good one," said Philip. *Though she ought to be a lawyer.*

"I told her she'd be a darned good English teacher," Ina added, winking at Sandra. "She displayed a fine understanding and appreciation of literature in my class. I declare, it's a mystery to me where her love of literature came from. I doubt if you knew, Philip, but Sandra has a degree in English lit from the University of Illinois."

Sandra smiled at Ina and turned to Philip, ignoring her friend's recognition. "Mr. Zumwalt, we've invited Ina over for dinner tonight. I hope you wouldn't consider it rude if at this late hour we extend the same invitation to you. After all, it only seems fitting that on Elinor's graduation night she has the opportunity to dine with her two favorite teachers."

Philip responded, "I'd love to join your family and Miss Harper for dinner. Thank you so much for the invitation, Mrs. Robinson." How could he decline such a kind offer? Still, he worried he might be complicating his potential relationship with El even more. Was this her idea or her mother's? The last thing he wanted to do was to jeopardize their future together by acting too impulsively.

"Elinor loved all of your classes, Mr. Zumwalt. She would go on and on about the discussions you had in World Problems."

"We had some rather spirited discussions in that class for sure. There was passionate disagreement about the war in Europe and what our role should be."

Sandra's jaw tightened a bit. "Well, I must confess, I have a strong opinion about war, Mr. Zumwalt." She paused. "My cousin, James Campbell, was killed in the trenches in France. Our family still hasn't gotten over the loss. The whole thing just makes me sick to my stomach. I'm so sorry, please forgive me," she said as she dabbed her eyes with her handkerchief. "The whole idea of young boys dying in a senseless war brings me to tears. I could go on forever about the futility of it."

"I understand, Mrs. Robinson. Seeing all of these eager young people embarking on their adult lives with a possible war on the horizon is disconcerting," said Philip with a distinct tone of regret.

"Well, let's be festive for their sakes. I promise not to inject notes of despair tonight. Dinner's at six. We'll all celebrate with a glass of Dr. Robinson's French wine before our meal. Sounds divine, doesn't it?" She gave neither teacher a chance to answer the question. "See you both around six o'clock, then?"

Ina and Philip nodded and watched as Sandra Robinson found her husband in the crowd of graduates and their families.

Ina turned to Philip. "Sounds like we have a dinner date, Professor! And I don't think any of us better bring up the topic of war, do you? Walk me home?"

With that, she wrapped her arm in Philip's.

Nope, he thought. *We better not talk about either war or love.* Both topics were *taboo,* a word that had become all too pervasive in Philip's inner vocabulary. He could hear his grandmother's admonition in his brain as clear as if she were standing next to him: *Philip, my boy, this is a fine kettle of fish you've gotten yourself into.*

CHAPTER 18

Dinner at the Robinsons

PHILIP ARRIVED AT THE FRONT DOOR of the Johnston boardinghouse at 5:30 sharp. The superintendent's aunt opened the door.

"Good evening, Mrs. Johnston," he said.

"Miss Harper will be ready in a moment, Mr. Zumwalt."

Mrs. Helen Johnston was every bit as feisty as her nephew. She stood an inch or two under five feet and was almost as wide.

"I heard those kids singin' today!" she exclaimed, as she led the way into the parlor. "Lordy, lordy, made my eyes tear up. Why it was just marvelous, marvelous I tell you. Of course, I don't have to tell you, do I?" She motioned toward the love seat. "Have a seat, won't you?"

Ina seemed to float down the stairs. She was stunning in her black shift dress and ivory pearls. *Ronald Hague's a lucky fellow*, Philip mused.

Slapping his arm and then wrapping her arm in his, Ina said, "Ready to go, Professor? Sandra did promise us a glass of wine."

"Ready as I'll ever be."

Sandra and Doc Robinson met Ina and Philip on their front porch, along with El and her two sisters, as well as the Robinson dogs, Labrador retrievers, one black and one yellow. The young people lounged in white rocking chairs and sipped lemonade. Philip had not set foot on the porch of the home on the corner of Bittersweet and Sycamore since the night El had kissed him on the cheek. Doc Robinson rose from his wicker chair and greeted the pair, the dogs joined him, tails wagging. "Greetings, folks. Please make yourselves at home. Don't mind Moose and Stella. Gentle as lambs. Brother and sister, don't you know."

El called the dogs to her and commanded them to lie down. She beamed as she stood and greeted Ina and Philip. "How did we do on the 'Battle Hymn,' Mr. Z?"

"You were all terrific, Elinor."

Ina joined Sandra on the porch's white wicker couch. El motioned her twin sisters to her side. "Mr. Z, I'm sure you remember Eunice and Emily."

"Oh, yes. Your mother introduced them to me at freshman orientation. It's a pleasure to see you girls again."

"They're so looking forward to being in the music program with you. They're far more musical than me."

"We sure loved hearing the 'Battle Hymn.' It was beautiful," Eunice said.

"We're going to try out for band *and* chorus next year," Emily added.

"That's great. The good news is you'll also have Miss Harper for English." He pointed toward Ina seated on the couch. She nodded her head in recognition of Philip's compliment.

"Mr. Zumwalt, our sister loved your class and we talked a lot about the war in Europe during dinner." Emily looked at her mother with a sense of apprehension. "I know my mother doesn't like talking about it, but all of us girls are concerned about what's going to happen. Do you think we're going to war?"

Emily's question caught Philip off guard. "I don't honestly know, Emily. Some of my friends have decided to enlist just in case we do. They'd prefer to choose their branch of service rather than be drafted."

"Really?" said Doc Robinson from his new perch on the porch railing. "They're taking a mighty big chance, aren't they? What if we do go to war?"

"Oh, I'm guessing they're taking their chances on the belief that the president isn't interested at all in taking us to war," replied Philip.

"Maybe those boys are just looking for some adventure to spice up their otherwise boring lives," Eunice said, half giggling.

"I wouldn't classify war as an adventure, Eunice. More a nightmare," said Sandra, turning serious and looking at her husband. "Wouldn't you agree, dear?"

Bushwhacked, Philip thought, *and by teenage girls, no less. I didn't open the can of worms, Emily and Eunice did.* The question now was how to get out of this discussion. Doc Robinson came to his rescue.

"I would, indeed, I would," Doc answered his wife's question in a solemn, regretful tone. "I think the men who never went to war are the ones who find it glamorous. The best part of the war for me was discovering French wine." He chuckled in an attempt to lighten the conversation. "Might you both be interested in sampling some of my finest Bordeaux?" Doc directed his question to the two teachers.

"Yes, please do come inside," Sandra said. "Hopefully, the fans will provide some relief from this dreadful heat."

Doc left the circle of conversation and rejoined the group as they gathered in the parlor. He carried a decanter filled to the brim with red wine. Ina and Philip accepted the offer. The good doctor poured wine into four crystal goblets.

"How about me, Pops?" El asked. "I am a high school graduate, after all."

"I don't suppose it can harm anything." He looked at his wife for approval. She returned a cautious smile and reluctantly handed a goblet to her eldest daughter.

"Here's to our dear, sweet Elinor, graduate of the Payson-Seymour class of 1941!" Doc lifted his glass.

The others raised their glasses and echoed Doc's toast of "Cheers!"

Philip looked around. The Robinson home was a blend of antique furniture, tasteful rich fabrics, vases, and paintings from foreign countries. Lamps of all shapes and colors illuminated each room. Persian rugs covered the floors. And judging by the taste of the Bordeaux, Philip decided Doc stocked his wine cellar with the best France had to offer.

An elderly woman dressed in a stylish purple dress and a matching scarf around her neck appeared at the parlor door.

"Momma." Sandra took her mother's arm. "I would like to introduce you to Elinor's two favorite teachers, Miss Ina Harper and Mr. Philip Zumwalt. Ina and Philip, this is my mother, Edna Campbell."

"I'm so happy to meet you both," Mrs. Campbell said in her high, soft voice. "It seems all I ever heard about over our dinner table from Elinor was Miss Harper this and Mr. Zumwalt that. It is indeed a pleasure to finally meet you both."

"The pleasure is mine," replied Ina.

"And mine," seconded Philip.

Miss Betsy, the Robinson family cook, came to the parlor door and motioned to Sandra. "Dinner is ready, Mrs. Robinson."

"Thank you, Miss Betsy. Well, shall we all retire to the dining room? I imagine Miss Betsy has made enough delicious food to feed an army."

The family and guests followed Sandra into the dining room and dutifully sat at the seat where name cards etched in calligraphy were displayed. The table was set with lovely china, glittering crystal, and silver. Platters of sumptuous roast beef, bowls of mashed potatoes, gravy, corn, tomatoes, and a cucumber and onion salad beckoned. The platters were passed around as forks and knives were eagerly put to use.

"Miss Betsy's a wonderful cook, isn't she?" said Sandra to Philip, who was seated next to her.

"Yes, ma'am. The meal is terrific. I can't thank you enough for the invitation," Philip replied as he sampled each dish with fervor.

The wine and conversation flowed. Talk of the war in Europe dominated the evening's dinner, Sandra's discomfort notwithstanding. Seated across from each other, El and Philip exchanged furtive glances and then looked away, fearful of exposing their attraction for each other to those gathered around the table.

I guess one of the forbidden topics isn't taboo after all, thought Philip. He smiled at El as he took a bite of mashed potatoes. She dropped her gaze, smiled down at her salad plate, and then made eye contact with him. His heart raced.

After enjoying Miss Betsy's famous sweet potato pie with fresh whipped cream, Doc and Philip retired to the library. Doc poured out two snifters of brandy, and offered Philip one of his cigars. Philip was happy to accept the liquor but politely declined the smoke. Doc lit his and discussion immediately commenced around the global dilemma facing President Roosevelt. As he gazed around the room, Philip was astonished with the display and wide variety of books filling the library's dark wooden shelves—novels, nonfiction, biographies, and a full set of *Encyclopedia Britannica.*

No wonder El was so well-read and erudite, Philip thought.

As the ladies gathered in the parlor, Sandra turned to Ina and exclaimed, "Ina, I think you've found yourself a good one!"

El sat quietly, but her mind raced. *Miss Harper, beautiful, intelligent . . . has she fallen for Philip, too? I'll bet Momma thinks they're perfect. Philip and Miss Harper. Really? Maybe Momma's just checking up on him. Maybe she picked up on my feelings for him, doesn't want me to be hurt. Of course, she wouldn't want Miss Harper to be hurt either. Nor would I.*

The fire that burned inside reminded El of how she'd felt the evening she'd met Kate Uphouser. No matter, she had heard Ina was headed to Champaign for the summer to begin her graduate studies and wouldn't return to teach at Payson until the fall. Philip would be a mere hour away in Nebo. And she was no longer his student.

Ina smiled politely at her friend's inquiry. "Oh, Sandra. Whatever gave you that impression? Philip and I are just dear friends."

"Oh, I just thought, you know, we've seen you together at dances and concerts . . ."

El's ears perked up and she was delighted to hear Ina's response. "Oh, my dear, no. We are colleagues—companions, I guess you might say. He has been kind enough to escort me to school events, but I've been seeing a young man who is a graduate student at the University of Illinois."

"I see. Well, I'd suppose I better set the Payson rumor mill straight then. Too bad, you two make a lovely couple."

Ina turned the attention to El. "It's this young lady's night. Why don't we concentrate on her? What are your plans this summer, Elinor?"

El laughed. "Oh, I'm not sure, Miss Harper. Just take it easy, I imagine." *And work out my future with Philip.* "I'm excited about nurse's training in the fall, though."

CHAPTER 19

An Understanding

THE AROMA OF CIGAR SMOKE permeated the study. "So, how did you enjoy your first year of teaching, Mr. Zumwalt?"

"Oh, it was great, sir, but given the world crisis, it might be my last. It looks like men my age may be drafted into the service, especially if we go to war in Europe," Philip answered.

"I hope not," Doc replied. "War is too costly, in every way. I know."

"How do you think we can avoid the war, Doc?"

Doc answered with a complicated soliloquy outlining a plan where the United States might be able to save England and France by sending assistance but still avoid sending men to fight.

The smoke in the study was beginning to bother Philip's eyes. "Excuse me, sir. Where might I find the bathroom, Dr. Robinson?"

"Oh, up the stairs, first door on your right, Mr. Zumwalt."

Philip found the bathroom, washed his eyes with water, and returned down the stairs. He stepped out on the front porch to get some fresh air. Taking in the sweet smell of the summer night, he heard the screen door open behind him. It was El.

She whispered, "When are we going to talk about all of this?"

He was in "a fine kettle of fish," to be sure. Glancing out at the street and aware the porch was not a private space, he resisted putting his arms around her. "I don't believe this is the time and place. Do you?"

"You don't believe it is, huh? Then why in the world did you come over here tonight?"

"I guess when your mother invited me to dinner, I just thought it was your idea."

"Really?"

"Yes, really. I'm actually surprised Randall wasn't here celebrating with you and your family. The king and queen of Payson."

"Why would you say such a ridiculous thing? I'm not the least bit interested in Randall Yarborough. I never have been." El was flushed with indignation.

"Oh, really? You sure looked cozy in his arms at the Valentine's Day dance. And why did everyone at the high school refer to him as your boyfriend?"

"My boyfriend? How ridiculous. Teachers' gossip, I imagine. I finally broke things off with him two weeks ago, as if they'd ever begun. He just kept asking me out, and we have a rule in our family. If a young man asks you out, you are obliged to accept. Common courtesy according to my parents. Finally, I'd had enough, and I told him I was in love with someone else. He guessed it was you and I denied it, but I'm afraid I'm not a good liar."

"What did you just say? You're in love with me?"

"Yes, Philip Zumwalt. I'm in love with you. There, I said it out loud. Would you like me to shout it out from my front porch so all the neighbors can hear?"

Philip smiled. "All I want is to be with you. I swear that's the truth. I love you, too. I've waited for this day all year!"

El smiled, her eyes moist. "Me, too."

"Look, we have to tell your parents the truth."

"I know. I'll talk to them."

"And I promise I'm going to tell my family about us as soon as I get back home."

"Elinor!" Sandra's voice filtered through the screen door. "Where are you?"

"Out here, Momma. Just getting a breath of fresh air. Be right in." El stretched up on her toes and gave Philip a gentle kiss on the cheek. "Coming, Momma, coming!"

The evening concluded with the Robinsons escorting their guests to the front door. Pleasantries were exchanged. Ina hugged each member of the family with a thank-you. Philip offered his sincere appreciation to the Robinson family for their hospitality.

When Philip extended his hand to thank Elinor, she threw her arms around him, whispering in his ear so all could hear, "Thank you for being such a great teacher. It was a wonderful year." No kiss on the cheek this time, but she held him for a long moment in her embrace—he worried it might be a bit too long. Looking over her shoulder at Doc Robinson, Philip was relieved to find the good doctor seemed oblivious to his daughter's public display of affection.

Elinor released Philip, but he held on for a moment. "Thank you, Elinor. It was a pleasure having you in class. Keep practicing that saxophone. You never know, Glenn Miller might need a new sax player."

Everyone laughed, and with that, Ina and Philip departed. The moon was almost full and sat in the night sky overlooking the quiet village of Payson. As they walked down State Street toward Mrs. Johnston's boardinghouse, Ina said wistfully, "Aren't they the most wonderful family?"

"Yes, they are; they certainly are," Philip replied. He had come to this small town not knowing what he would find. One thing he had not counted on was falling in love.

As they strolled down the quiet streets, his head began to spin. Was it the wine, the brandy? The initial stage of his plan was completed. He had mailed his letter of resignation to Superintendent Johnston and Mr. Houseman. By choosing his branch of service, the Army Air Corps, he would fulfill his obligation to the military and realize his dream to become a pilot.

His feelings for El were stronger than ever. The gnawing in the pit of his stomach, the lightness in his total being, made everything as crystal clear to him as the Robinsons' goblets.

Ina did most of the talking on the way to the boardinghouse. Philip's responses were mostly *uh-huh*. When they reached their destination, they stopped at the bottom of the porch steps and sat down.

"Ina," he said. "Can we talk?"

"I'm all ears, Professor. Although I fear we both might have had a little too much wine."

"I have a confession, and I hope you won't think any less of me."

"I doubt that can ever happen, Philip. What's on your mind?"

"I met El at a dance at the Casino before I ever came to Payson. I had no idea she was in high school or that she would be a student of mine. On that night and ever since, I have yearned to be with her. I believe I can say, with a certain bit of certainty, she feels the same. We have not, I promise, acted inappropriately throughout the school year. We've had a few private conversations trying to sort all of this out, but that's all. Tonight, we confessed our love to each other. I fear her parents may not understand, given this strange set of circumstances."

"Oh, Philip. I'm not surprised. I'm a pretty keen observer of people, my friend, and I've watched you two all year long. A glance here, a cautious smile there. And tonight, you would have to be blind not to notice. You could have cut the tension in the air at the dinner table with a knife. Of course, possibly going off to war is going to complicate things, but I bet you two will figure it out. If I were you, though, I believe I'd have a conversation with Sandra and Doc sooner than later. Just my little bit of parting advice. It might be a little uncomfortable at first, but I'm certain if you and El really love each other, it will all turn out." She smiled at him as she rose. "It was a lovely evening. Good night and Godspeed, Philip."

He stood, relieved and grateful for her friendship. "Take care of your Music Man."

Ina turned toward the screen door. "I will."

"Ina, I think the world of you. You've been a dear friend."

"I feel the same way, Philip. I will always think fondly of you."

He returned her smile. "Good night, then."

"Take care of yourself, especially when you go flying off into the wild, blue yonder."

She hugged him, opened the screen door, and went inside. He walked slowly toward the boardinghouse he had called home for nine months and prayed Ina was right about El's parents accepting him. At the moment, the furthest thing from his mind was his upcoming appointment with the Army recruiter. Right now, he only knew one thing for certain. Ina was right: He needed to have an honest conversation with Doc and Sandra Robinson.

CHAPTER 20

Sweet Days at Siloam Park

I T WAS THE MORNING OF THE LONGEST DAY of the year when Philip began the hour-long drive from Nebo to Siloam State Park. His dark-blue Chevy turned onto the park's winding dirt lane. The morning sun glimmered through the lush pines as he zigzagged along the forest road. The Siloam Forest Home Hotel finally appeared, tucked away in the evergreens. Billy had been given a job as the summer maintenance man at the hotel. As part of his compensation, he was provided a room to live in for the entire summer and use of the park's facilities during the weekends.

The two lifelong friends hatched a plan. Billy invited Pat and Philip to spend the weekend and suggested to Philip he might want to ask El to come along. Philip's conversation with El's parents had gone better than expected, and permission had been granted for Philip to court El during the summer. However, spending the night at a hotel together was most certainly not a part of the agreement. Fearing her parents' disapproval, El and Philip devised a bit of a deceitful scheme, which included some of El's friends providing cover.

Philip carried his canvas bag up the back stairs to Billy's room, a sleeping porch on the top floor of the old hotel with windows on three sides. A single bed and dresser sat against the innermost wall attached to the main building. "We gotta use the shower in the maintenance shed and the outhouse next to it," Billy instructed. "So take care of your business before you come to bed."

"Not much privacy," Philip remarked, reminding himself of his recent enlistment and the unlikelihood he'd be enjoying much privacy in the months ahead as a member of the U.S. Army Air Force.

"Hell, nobody can see you up here except the birds and bees." Billy winked at him and laughed. "Besides, at night there's a great breeze. But I sure wouldn't want to be sleeping out here in the winter."

"So, where do I sleep?"

"In the bed, stupid."

"But where are you going to sleep?"

The Kid got a sheepish grin on his face. "Oh, don't worry about me, pal. I'll find a place to bunk somewhere."

"Okay, but I don't want to put you out," Philip said.

"Oh, don't worry. You're not putting me out." Billy winked again.

This time Philip got the message. He dropped his bag, walked down to the front porch, and plopped into a rocker. Wiping beads of perspiration from his forehead, he marveled that the thermometer already read eighty-five degrees at ten o'clock in the morning. He sighed and gazed out over the breathtaking vista of towering trees surrounding the mineral springs bubbling up within walking distance from the hotel—nature at its finest. A long semicircular driveway led to the hotel's front entry and a verdant green lawn extended from the hotel down to the springs. Shrubs and a colorful assortment of flowers lined the driveway. Philip rocked, nerves on edge, and waited. He'd been dreaming of this day for months, dreaming of being alone with El.

He sat up with a start as Billy and Pat burst through the screen door. "Come on, Nelly. We're headed down to the lake for a swim."

"I'll be down later," Philip answered.

Around noon, ensconced in his rocker, Philip spotted a coal-black Buick motoring up the gravel drive. Voices from the front seat drifted up to the front porch, "Isn't it divine, Essie! Billy told Philip it was heavenly. He was right!"

The girls bolted out of the car almost simultaneously. Philip's heart jumped as El stepped onto the driveway. In a lemon-colored linen dress with sandals and a white broad-brimmed hat, she glided up the sidewalk holding hands with Essie.

Philip rose from his rocker and stood on the porch. El blushed but contained her excitement. Stopping at the bottom of the stairs, she curtsied, batted her eyes, and smiled. Reaching down from the porch, he held out his hand. She took it. He pulled her up into his full embrace as their lips met.

She sighed. "My, my, Mr. Z. That's quite a fine way for a young woman to be greeted. Is that standard procedure around here?"

Her laughter still intoxicated him. "No, Miss Robinson. That treatment is reserved only for special guests."

"Thank heavens, I'm considered a special guest." El smiled.

Essie cleared her throat. "I suppose we'd better get checked in," she said to no one specifically.

Philip greeted El's best friend. "Essie, so good to see you. What a place, huh? I think this is going to be a great weekend."

"Oh, yes, Mr. Z. I mean, uh, Philip. I'm sure of that. We all had to tell our folks a heap a lies, but, yes, indeed, this is going to be one exciting weekend, for sure!" With that, she squealed.

Carrying the girls' bags and picnic basket, Philip led El and Essie into the hotel lobby.

Arriving at their room, El unlocked the door. Essie tossed her bag on the floor and threw herself onto her bed, laughing, "Wow! That was quite the entrance you made, girl."

El giggled as she unpacked her suitcase and arranged her toiletries on a shelf. "I sure hope Momma and Pops don't find out Jimmy and Cecil are headed up here, too."

"Only if Florence rats us out. We're sure naughty girls."

The rooms of the four-story hotel were modest; El's and Essie's had two twin beds and a dresser, a hardwood floor, and braided rag rugs. A large wooden fan hung from the high ceiling, keeping the temperature in the room bearable. The two graduates pulled on their bathing suits, threw on their straw hats, grabbed their picnic basket, and headed to the lake. Philip met them at the front door. He took the basket and, holding El's hand, escorted them down the worn path to the water's edge.

Billy and Pat had claimed some prime real estate on the lawn next to the lake and were stretched out on wooden chaise lounges under a large green umbrella when El, Essie, and Philip arrived. An additional umbrella and three more chaise lounges awaited the trio. Other hotel guests had begun to make their way to the lawn by the lake's beach.

The Payson girls' packed lunch was sufficient to share with all. The three girls talked, sunbathed, read, and cooled off with a dip in the crystal-clear lake while Billy and Philip tossed around a football. It was midafternoon when Philip and Billy swam out to a whitewashed timber raft with its attached diving boards, the highest of which intimidated Philip.

"Billy's such a show-off," Pat said. "That high dive scares me to death. I wouldn't go up there if you gave me a million dollars."

"Me neither," agreed Essie.

"Oh, I don't know. I think it looks like fun." El threw off her hat, sprinted toward the water, dived in, and quickly reached the raft. "Is it scary up there?!" she yelled up at Billy.

Philip hadn't yet braved the high dive but was delighted that El had joined him on the raft.

"Naw," said Billy. "I love jumpin' from high places. It gives a fella a thrill, right down here."

El giggled, but Philip couldn't believe his friend's crude reference.

"Well, I wonder if a gal will get the same thrill?" With that, she climbed up the high dive's ladder and bounced out to the edge of the board. "Bet you can't top this!" she called out as she dived in headfirst, barely making a splash. Popping up, she squealed, "C'mon, Philip. Try it. It's fun!"

Billy knew his pal was stuck. Philip wasn't going to admit he was afraid of heights. When he was seven years old, on a dare from Billy, Philip had fallen from one of the highest branches in the oak tree on the front lawn of Billy's home. Fortunately, nothing was broken, and, in the process, Philip learned a couple of valuable lessons: Don't take dares from Billy and stay away from heights.

El was back up on the raft. Her reddish-brown hair glistened in the sunlight reflecting flecks of gold. Her pink suit with its thin spaghetti straps clung to her body.

"C'mon, scaredy-cat," she said. "It won't kill you. Might sting a little if you don't hit the water just right, but it's not that bad. And it's so much fun—a thrill, even." She winked at him. "It makes me feel, you know . . . euphoric!"

Billy, halfway up the steps to the high dive, looked toward shore to make sure Pat was watching. Philip took a deep breath and started up the ladder. The railing steadied his wobbly ascent as he watched Billy once again dive headfirst from the dizzying height. Philip's pulse pounded. He looked straight ahead at a small island in the distance and walked out onto the diving board. *What a man won't do to win the heart of the woman he loves.* He took three possibly ill-fated steps and jumped. Surfacing, he heard El's applause. Well worth stinging arms, water up his nose, and risking his life, and it did make him feel somewhat . . . euphoric.

CHAPTER 21

A Dangerous Dance

"THE ROOM'S ALL YOURS, NELLY." Billy grinned. "Not like the days of shacking up at the Rooming House back on West Carroll. Remember, I'd sneak Pat in the back door and tell you to go sleep on the couch in Inness's room? Well, this little love nest is all yours, Romeo."

His directions were clear. Philip nodded, realizing where Billy was going to spend the night.

"Make sweet night music while you can," Billy added. "We might be off to war in Europe tomorrow if FDR has his way."

"Thanks, old buddy. You supply the liquor, too? A full-service love nest?" Philip quipped.

"As a matter of fact, my fine friend, I do have a little gift for you, compliments of my uncle, Jack Kinnamon. He passed away last month and left his only nephew a silver-plated flask. It comes with a full complement of Wild Turkey." Billy pulled a shiny flask from his bag and handed it to Philip.

Philip inspected the flask with admiration. "Nice."

"That ought to set you up for tonight. Bring that sweet young thing up here and make it a night to remember, buddy!" Billy noticed the look on Philip's face. "Hey, you're not still a virgin, are you?"

Philip whispered almost apologetically, "Yeh."

"Wow! You mean to tell me that you and Kate never—"

"Nope, never," Philip said.

Billy had a peculiar admiration for the unique combination of Philip's innocence and integrity but had to wonder if he was human. "Don't you ever get the urge?"

"Hell yes, I get the urge. I've had the urge plenty of times, but I resist it somehow. What did Trout call it? Protestant guilt?"

"Just have a couple of drinks and see what develops. Who knows, maybe you won't feel so guilty after all. She's sure cute, I'll give you that!"

"You take care of Pat. I'll be fine, don't worry about me."

The two friends laughed all the way down the back steps to the shower in the maintenance shed.

Essie's boyfriend, Cecil DeWeese, drove up to Siloam in the early evening, accompanied by Florence Marshall and Jimmy Blauser. Jimmy and Cecil had reserved a room together, and Florence would sleep in Essie and El's room. At least that was the plot the young graduates of 1941 concocted and related to their parents. Now it appeared that everything was working out so that each young couple might have their own room.

Awkward conversation rose and fell as the group of eight gathered in the hotel's pine-paneled dining room. Billy had made a dinner reservation, and the party was escorted to a round table with a red-and-white checkered tablecloth. Overhead, massive logs crisscrossed; high-arching crossbeams stretched across the expanse imitating a cathedral ceiling. Circular black cast-iron chandeliers hung down aglow with Edison lights inside frosted globes.

A massive stone fireplace dominated the center of the room, a monument to a time before a coal-powered boiler bestowed heat upon the hotel. No such heat was needed in the middle of June. A gentle evening breeze blew through the screen doors as the Payson graduates, accompanied by two Posse denizens and Miss Pat Carpenter, took their seats. The recent Payson-Seymour alums soon realized their former teacher was an integral part of the ruse. Mr. Z was now just Philip, a member of the gang.

Following dinner, they moved to the porch. Guests stretched along the vestibule, comfortably rocking and chatting. Everyone but Philip smoked a cigarette while watching the sunset. Billy and Philip shared their flasks, and soon each couple was off on a walk seeking privacy under the waning, romantic sliver of a crescent moon.

Philip and El strolled down to the mineral springs and found an empty bench. He put his arm around her. She snuggled into him. The summer evening was cool as they sat, talked softly, and held each other as they had the night they first met. Their intermittent kisses were gentle.

"It's gorgeous, Philip. A perfect evening."

"Better than I could have ever imagined." Philip looked into her alluring eyes. "Should we explore the mineral springs? Get all healed up from what ails us." He laughed, staring out at the springs covered with a hazy mist. The hot steam was inviting. "They do, of course, require the patrons to wear swimsuits."

"Well, of course, Mr. Zumwalt. A proper girl would always wear a swimsuit to the mineral springs." Her giggle, as always, made him smile. "Meet you here in ten minutes."

El raced through the front porch screen door and dashed up the stairs to change into her swimsuit, and soon the couple strolled down the gravel path to the springs. Alone, they slid into the water. The night air and pleasant scent of pine trees wafted over them. The tangy aroma of the mineral springs stung their nostrils as the hot water engulfed their bodies. They laughed at each other as they recalled their first night together. "I can't believe you actually thought I was a preacher," Philip said.

"There was a lot of noise! The Dorsey Band was loud. I can't understand why you didn't wonder why I was asking you all those questions about church," El replied. "But now that you've brought me to Heaven—maybe you *are* a preacher." She giggled. "This place *is* heavenly, Philip. Just look at the moon."

The reflection of the slight moon still glimmered on the mineral-infused water, and Philip momentarily peeled his eyes away from El to look. "Just being here with you makes it heaven."

She sighed. "Oh, my, aren't you the corny, romantic soul?"

He leaned in toward her. Their lips met. He ran his hands through the back of her water-kissed hair and down her shoulders. She did the same. He wanted to be one with her. He loved the feel of her hands caressing the back of his head. His hands moved down her back and then lower as music drifted out through the hotel's windows into the night air. The soft melody lingered over the mineral springs. Philip recognized the tune—a recording of *The Pavane in F-sharp Minor*.

The music and bourbon emboldened Philip. He wrapped his arms around her. They kissed, this time with passion. They stroked each other, hands searching each other's bodies, discovering places untouched and unexplored. Philip slid the straps of El's swimsuit down off her shoulders. The moonlight's reflection made her face even more irresistibly beautiful. She gazed at him with adoration. Fearing he had gone too far, too fast, he pulled his hand back. She took his hand in hers, guiding it back to where it had been, kissed him, and then whispered in his ear, "Let's go to your room."

Gathering his wits, he stood and pulled her up into an embrace. Her hands slid down his back; he caressed the back of her neck. Sweetness mixed with unbridled desire. Bliss. They walked hand in hand up the sloped lawn to the back stairs of the hotel and up to Billy's room.

Slipping through the door, they embraced and kissed again—clandestine lovers lost in the evening's moonglow. Philip twirled El just as he had done on the dance floor and guided her to the wall opposite the windows. Sheer curtains danced with the night breeze. Their eyes met. She placed her hand upon his cheek and raised onto her toes. Fumbling with the straps of her suit, he helped her strip it from her body. Glistening mineral water and sweat trickled down her soft, suntanned skin. He trembled with anticipation as he tasted her silky lips. If passion meant suffering, it was not so tonight. With raw desire they rolled from side to side on the narrow bed, kissing, caressing, and exploring each other's innocence. He pulled himself upon her.

She pushed him away. "I can't," she whispered, her voice tender. "Not here, not now."

She pulled the threadbare sheet over her. He turned away, embarrassed. Staring at the wall, he tried to regain his composure, ashamed of his longing.

She wrapped her arms around his waist, pulling herself against him. This dance had become too dangerous. "Please understand. I love you, but we must wait."

He surrendered and suppressed for now the desire that surged through his body when they touched. He would honor her request but would always yearn to be one with her, body and soul.

"I do, I understand," he said.

The faint sound of a bird awakened El, as the shortest night of the year had come to an end. She wrapped up in her sheet and looked out the windows of the sleeping porch.

Philip rolled over. "Good morning," he said. "Was that the lark, the herald of the morn?" he quoted.

"No, it's the nightingale, silly. There are no larks here, Romeo."

"Ah, I beg to differ with you, my love. The horned lark is indigenous to our little corner of the world."

El smiled. "Appropriate. I always feared you had a bit of the devil in you." Laying her head upon his shoulder, she adjusted the white cotton sheet draping her body and kissed him on the nape of the neck. "Go back to sleep, you horned lark devil. It is not yet day, and I shall be content to lie here and listen to the nightingale's evensong."

"Impressive. A Shakespearean scholar?"

"No, just had a good senior English teacher," El said with a flirta-tious wink.

Philip smiled to himself, rolled over, and got out of the bed. Today was the dawn of a new day, the first of many he hoped to awaken with his love by his side.

CHAPTER 22

Billy's Tall Tales

BILLY AND PAT JOINED EL AND PHILIP at a corner table in the dining hall and ordered breakfast.

El gave Philip a mischievous grin and turned to his best friend. "Okay, Billy, what's the explanation for Philip's ridiculous nickname?" she asked, pointing at Philip. "I've been dying to know since the first night we met." She let out her distinctive giggle. "Nelly? Really?"

Billy laughed. "He has to give his permission. Posse secrets."

El sported her pout and batted her eyes at Billy. "Please, oh please, Billy. You said you'd tell me someday. C'mon. Pleassse."

Philip laughed at El's Southern belle imitation. "It's a pretty silly story, but for all our sakes, just give her the short version, Billy. The girls have to get home before dark."

"Okay, the short version it is." Billy's speech was clipped, like he was reporting the news over the radio. "Halloween of thirty-four. The Posse was out looking for a good time. After collecting bags full of goodies, we decided to call it a night. But Trout was always up for a prank, and he convinced us to be his accomplices. One of his favorite shenanigans was to run through backyards and tip over the outhouses of unsuspecting neighbors. The target that night was Nelly and Trout's grouchy old minister, Pastor Harrison. Nelly wanted no part of it, but the rest of us were game. Being the good guys we are, we made sure the old geezer wasn't inside."

El's eyes widened and she looked over at Pat, who gave her a silly see-what-you've-gotten-yourself-into? kind of look. Philip just shrugged.

Billy's grin grew wider. "So, after we upended Harrison's outhouse, we laughed our you-know-whats off all the way home. Best part is, we never got caught by the sheriff." Billy's face lit up. "But here's where the story gets really good. Later that night, after Nelly returned home, he lit a lantern and headed to the family privy. After taking a seat, he started whistling a tune and then broke into song." It was difficult for Billy to giggle and sing at the same time.

> "Oh! My poor Nelly Gray,
> They have taken you away,
> And I'll never see my darling any more . . ."

"He was singing away, 'I'm sitting by the river' when the outhouse began to shake. Wasn't an earthquake though—some other pranksters were tippin' him over. Before he could react, he ended up facedown on the door."

"Yikes," El screeched, holding her hands over her cheeks.

Laughing, tears of pure joy ran down Billy's face. "The fellas who had so rudely interrupted Philip's business were howling so loud, Homer and Wayne heard the commotion all the way up in their bedroom. The singing troubadour became the butt of the joke that night, if you get my drift. Philip scrambled to pull up his pajama bottoms and yelled for help. I'm guessin' the stench would probably have eventually done him in." Billy snickered again.

By now both girls were giggling. Philip put on a good façade and laughed along with the others.

Billy continued, "Mr. Zumwalt, Homer, and Wayne ran outside to the rescue, tipped the outhouse back up, and saved our boy. Philip had recognized some of the voices—a few of the seniors from Nebo High. The tipping of the outhouse only left your sweet boy's pride slightly damaged. The next day came the coup de grâce. A few senior boys passed him in the hallway and addressed him in unison with a chorus of 'How's it goin', Nelly?'"

Philip smiled at El and again shrugged. El was laughing so hard, she could barely catch her breath. "I'll never look at an outhouse the same," she howled. "What about 'The Posse'? You guys have stuck together through thick and thin, haven't you?"

"Yeh. We were just a bunch of kids out to have a good time. I think it was in third grade that Inness labeled us the 'Pike County Posse.' He'd seen almost every cowboy movie ever shown at the Cozy, the movie theater in Nebo. We all loved movies, but Inness loved those cowboy movies most of all. We'd cheer out loud when the good guys in white hats, the 'Posse,' brought the bad guys in black hats to justice. Inness decided we were the good guys, and the nickname stuck. We all had other nicknames through the years, but in the end, we were known as 'Big Fish' Trout, 'Hawkeye' Harkness, 'The Giant' Inness, 'Nelly' Zumwalt, and me, 'The Kid' Epperson." The Kid took a sip of coffee. "I guarantee you one thing though, we'll have one another's backs for the rest of our lives. And this guy here, my boy Nelly, why, he's the best."

Philip smiled and shook his head. *What a bullshitter!* He had, however, been totally accurate about one thing: The Posse would always have one another's backs. No matter what.

The afternoon was hot and steamy as El and Philip strolled hand in hand down the gravel drive to the parking lot alongside Billy and Pat. El thanked Billy for sharing his stories and for arranging the stay at the park. Essie and the rest of the Payson contingent trailed behind.

Philip knew he would hold on to the memory of this weekend forever. Their night together had changed everything. He pulled El aside for a moment and turned somber. "El, I need to tell you something."

"I'm listening," she said.

"I enlisted in the Army Air Corps two weeks ago. I'm going to be a pilot. If we do go to war in Europe soon, I'd just as soon be flying airplanes. Plus, I think that might be the best way to win a war these days."

El cocked her head, not fully absorbing Philip's words at first. At his nod that she'd heard correctly, she hung her head. "Maybe we won't go to war," she said, fighting back competing emotions. When she looked up, her eyes narrowed. "Did you ever think of that?"

"Truthfully, when I signed up, it just felt like the right decision." Philip took her chin in his hands and looked into her tear-stained eyes. He continued, "I thought I needed to get away from all of this—figured I was no longer welcome in Payson and signing up would give me a chance to have a real adventure and pursue my dream of being a pilot. Oh, El, I've wanted to be a pilot ever since I was a kid. Problem is, after this incredible weekend, all I want to do now is be with you."

"Not sure why you would think that's a problem," El replied.

"That's not what I meant. I've made my decision, and that's that. I'm sorry."

The word *enlisted* turned El's stomach into the same knot every time she heard it. The thought of Philip leaving to join the Army terrified her. She listened intently, hoping Philip might help her make sense out of all this. Maybe she could change his mind, maybe if she begged him not to go. His next sentence short-circuited that notion.

"I just can't back out now. I'm scheduled to ship out in August, and I'd be a coward if I went back on my word."

Not wanting him to see her tears, she turned her head away, wiped her eyes, and faced him again. "Philip, you are an honorable man, the furthest thing from a coward. I may not like your decision, but I'll do my best to understand."

Philip placed her luggage in the backseat and opened the driver's door. They kissed and clung together before she slid into her seat.

"None of us knows what's going to happen in Europe," he said, bending down to the open window.

"I know," she said. "I learned that this year from my handsome World Problems teacher."

"I suspect even he doesn't know how all of this is going to end. But if we go to war, I'll make you a promise. I will come back. I love you."

"Billy warned me that you're a guy with big dreams, so go do what you have to do, but I'm going to hold you to your promise. Funny, I suppose you'd find my dream rather foolish."

"No. I wouldn't. Tell me your dream, please."

"What I've always wanted was to marry a wonderful man and have a family. That's my dream. Silly, isn't it?"

Philip smiled. "Not at all. Once the war is over, if there even is a war, I'll have saved up enough money to go back to school, and then it's my intention to make both of our dreams come true." Philip hoped El was encouraged by his use of *our*. He reached in over the open window and grasped her hand.

"Okay, soldier. Sounds like a plan," she said tenderly, taking his hand. "Our time will come, Philip. It will. The good news is, you're not leaving until August. There's a whole summer ahead of us."

Essie pecked Cecil on the cheek and settled into the passenger's seat. El started the engine, put the car in gear, and drove away. Philip waved as the Buick rumbled down the gravel road and headed back to Payson. Surely, she was right. Their time would come.

Summer of '41

IT WAS A RITUAL, A REGULAR ROUTINE; on Friday nights, after Philip finished work on the house in Pleasant Hill, he drove up and had dinner with the Robinson family. El and Philip enjoyed going to a movie or dance. Other evenings they'd stay at the Robinsons enjoying family time—ordinary moments. After the meal, Philip and Doc would occasionally retire to the porch and sip brandy, a taste for which Philip had now acquired. Doc would smoke a cigar as the pair discussed current world events and, of course, the possibility of war.

Doc may have been a medical doctor, but his passion was politics. A dyed-in-the-wool Democrat, he agreed with President Roosevelt's handling of the crisis in Europe. This Friday night, Doc stopped rocking and said, "So, young man. Let's talk a bit more about your intentions. It appears to me that you and my daughter have developed a rather serious relationship. Is that true?"

"Yes, sir. It is. We've discussed our future together, and I believe we agree. I will honor my enlistment, and El plans on completing nurse's training. Neither of us knows exactly what's going to happen, especially if we go to war." He leaned forward, elbows on knees, and looked the doctor straight in the eyes. "I can tell you this, sir. I do love your daughter. She's a wonderful person, and, if the world doesn't turn completely upside down, I hope to be back on this porch in the near future asking you for her hand."

"Well, sir. It sounds to me like you two know what you want. I hope we don't go to war, and I hope to see you back here making that request of me—and Mrs. Robinson, of course."

"Of course, sir."

Doc rose. "Well, time to turn in. See you next weekend?"

"Wouldn't miss it, sir."

Back in the parlor, Philip bid Sandra and El good night. El escorted him to the porch. "What were you and Pops talking about?" she asked.

"Us? Oh, nothing. Just baseball."

"Humph! Baseball, my eye. Philip Zumwalt, you're a terrible liar. Time for you to go home. Good night!"

"El?"

"Yes, Philip."

"You do know I love you, right?"

"I do. And I love you, too. Now good night."

He gently took her in his arms and kissed her. She faked swooning as he hopped off the porch and skipped down the sidewalk.

"Baseball! Well, I never," she said as she turned toward the front door. "Pops! Pops!" she called. "We need to talk."

Philip arrived at his old boardinghouse, where Mrs. Staley allowed him to stay in the spare bedroom on weekends. She was seated on the porch.

"How was Miss Elinor tonight?" she inquired.

"Perfect," Philip replied.

"A good evening then?"

"Yes, ma'am. It was a great evening, as always."

"Don't let that girl get away, Philip."

"Don't worry, Mrs. Staley. I don't plan on that ever happening."

El and Philip's Saturday dates also took on a regular pattern; in the early afternoon, after El's morning shift at Harris's drugstore, she would rush home, prepare a picnic lunch and the young lovers would walk to Payson's Central Park, across from Mrs. Staley's boardinghouse. Sitting on a blanket on the lawn under the shade of an old oak tree, they lunched on sandwiches and fruit and sipped on the famous Robinson lemonade.

This particular day, El was stretched out on a blanket staring up at the sky. "Aren't the clouds magnificent?"

"They sure are," Philip answered.

The cirrus clouds resembled wispy white birds darting across the blue sky, floating unencumbered by time and space.

"Soon you'll be flying right up there with them."

"And you'll be cleaning bedpans," he joked.

"I'm trying to be sweet and make you out like a hero, and you go and say something like that." She punched him in the arm. He rolled off the blanket, laughing. "Oh, why don't you go fly a kite?" She jumped on top of him and started tickling him.

He rolled her over, defeating her feeble attempt to pin him to the ground. Instead, he pinned her hands above her head and kissed her.

"Wow! I'll say one thing. You flyboys sure can kiss!"

"That's not all we can do."

El blushed. "Not here, silly. We're in the middle of town."

"So?"

"So?!" She jumped on him again, tickling with all her might, until they ended up in a laughing heap. The day passed as they finished eating their lunch, soaking up the sun, laughing, and pretending they didn't have a care in the world. As the clouds drifted by, reality drew closer with the realization that their summer of bliss would come to an end all too soon.

CHAPTER 24

Goodbyes, Training, and Exams

August 23, 1941

AUGUST TURNED UNSEASONABLY BRISK as Philip, dressed in his wool overcoat, stood silent with his parents and El on the platform of the train station. The St. Louis Iron Mountain & Southern train would soon transfer him to his duty station at Jefferson Barracks. As the train pulled in, he shook his father's hand and kissed his mother on the cheek, and then wrapped his arms around El. Their kiss was both passionate and regretful.

"You be careful, soldier," she said.

Philip wiped the tears from her cheeks, turned, and grabbed his suitcase. "I will, don't worry. See you in a few weeks!" he shouted over the train's screeching whistle.

The conductor called out, "All aboard!"

Philip raced toward the steps leading to the bowels of the passenger car and jumped onto the platform. He slid into an open window seat and waved to his loved ones as the train headed south. He was glad to see his parents standing close by El, all three waving together. He had traveled a mere few hundred yards when reality set in. Not wanting the other passengers, especially the soldiers, to see his tears, he kept his forehead pressed to the window and wept quietly. It was too late to turn back. His adventure had begun.

September 14, 1941

Dear El,

I am still celebrating passing the Aviation Cadet perception test. Now all I have to do is pass the rest of the exam next Friday, and I'll officially be an Aviation Cadet.

It's been too long since I left your embrace. Although I only spent eighteen days at Jefferson Barracks, all of it was miserable. The drill instructors barked out orders and put the fear of God into us from the moment we stepped off the bus. After being issued our clothing, we were assigned to a barracks and a bunk. Later in the day, we were lined up in formation and given a pep talk by the company commanding officer. Most of our training at Jefferson consisted of close-order drill when it wasn't raining and lectures on military protocol when it was.

We've learned about military discipline and courtesy, how to wear our uniform, the articles of war, war bonds, and National Life Insurance—even the discussion of a topic too embarrassing to mention, even to a nurse.

Please keep your letters coming, it seems that is all I have to look forward to these days.

Was transferred to the Thirty-Fourth School Squadron at Scott Field on the tenth of September, and since then have been taking even more tests. Once those are all completed, I will be given a classification, a classification which will determine what job I'll have for the rest of my military career. I hope that when all is said and done, my test results will qualify me to be an Army Air Forces aviator. I miss you so.

Love,

Philip

September 28, 1941

Dear Philip,

My schedule of classes has been, to say the least, rigorous. I am gaining such valuable experience in my practicums tending to the patients at Blessing Hospital. I must be honest with you, many of my duties leave me nauseated, the latest being the application of leeches to a patient who had cancer on his face. I have hardly had one moment to myself, thus the lack of letters. It's certainly not because I don't love you, my darling, you know I do. I promise to do my best to write more often, but it seems that all I do is go to class, nurse, and sleep. I love being a nurse, but I do so hate that we are separated.

I yearn for your letters, and do tell me everything that you are doing and learning. I think you are so brave for pursuing your dreams. I know it will all work out in the end. I do think about you night and day (Cole Porter—ha!). See? I did learn something from my adorable music teacher. Can't wait to see you.

Love,

El

CHAPTER 25

First Diary

October 29, 1941

LATE IN THE AFTERNOON, PHILIP WALKED into the Belleville Military Store at Scott Field and picked up a small black book. "I'll take one of these, a pen, a cap, and a belt," he said to the clerk, parting with some of the hard-earned cash he'd saved from his year of teaching and summer construction job.

On the front of the book, his first diary, was an etching of an eagle with spread wings surrounded by a laurel wreath. Five words were engraved in red: "My Life in the Service." When he returned to his barracks, he opened the diary and read the introduction:

> *Your experiences in the armed forces of your country are your part of living history. By all means KEEP A DIARY! Times without number, historians and writers have found more information of real human interest in diaries of enlisted men than in the studied accounts of generals and admirals. This book, conscientiously kept, may prove to be the living record of your destiny five hundred years from now!*

Reclining on a scratchy woolen blanket, he thought, *Five hundred years from now, who would even know that I ever existed? Why keep an account of what I did? What am I doing? Escaping?*

As he contemplated writing, he wondered if he was ready for an adventure that might turn dangerous. Up to this point, he was overcome with boredom and wondered if he hadn't made the biggest mistake of his life. He was ready to learn how to fly an airplane. His whole body felt the excitement of the coming months of training. Perhaps his tedious life was about to end. He wondered if his musings would be of interest to his children someday. Ready or not, a great adventure was in his future. Only time would tell. He opened to the first page, wrote his name, and then filled in the blanks on the next page.

**THE FOLLOWING PAGES CONTAIN
THE DIARY OF MY LIFE IN THE SERVICE**

This simple record of my daily experiences and
thoughts has given me pleasure in the writing
of it. If for any reason it leaves my possession,
I would like to have it forwarded to:

Name <u>Mr. Alonzo Zumwalt</u>

Address ______________________________

City <u>Nebo</u>   State <u>Illinois</u>

After writing his father's name and his hometown in the proper spaces, Philip A. Zumwalt made his first entry:

October 29. Purchased this diary at Belleville Military Store. Also a garrison cap and belt. In school today, I passed 18 WFM in code.

Most pages of the diary contained a quote from the Bible or a famous author or politician at the bottom of the page. He read the quote at the bottom of the first page:

All actual heroes are essential men,
And all men possible heroes.

—E. B. Browning

CHAPTER 26

Bad News

PHILIP RETURNED FROM THE EVENING MOVIE and sat down to write El. He missed her terribly and hesitated to share his latest setback. He decided to be honest with her—to always be honest with her. In the difficult days of separation that lay before them, their relationship would only survive if they were able to share both good and bad news with each other. Risking his vulnerable ego, he wrote:

November 9, 1941
Dear El,

So sorry you had to work last weekend. After I found out I was going to receive a weekend pass, I called you. The nurse in charge said she would give you my message, but I fear that did not happen. Bad news—I failed the Aviation Cadet eye test, unstable left eye. I have to admit, I'm devastated! I was reassigned to radio operator school after I passed the code test. Been playing the piano in the dayroom to soothe my bruised ego. Denny, the squadron morale officer, wants me to be on some programs, and Boyle, an excellent singer, wants me to accompany him. Went to the U.S.O. in St. Louis yesterday and then to the St. Louis Symphony last night. It was incredible. It didn't cost me a cent. All I had to do was wear my uniform. Joseph Szigeti was the violinist. I was moved to tears. I only wish you would have been there with me.

Tonight, I went to the movie Week-End in Havana *with Alice Faye, Caesar Romero, Carmen Miranda, and John Payne. They actually have some pretty good films that they show to us here. The food isn't half bad. I am learning all about the military way of life—very strict discipline. I do hope that the radio operator school will be somewhat interesting. I listen to the radio in the barracks every night. There are often some pretty good programs, even classical music some of the time and your favorite, swing tunes. I'm trying my best to keep up with my letter writing. Army life can get quite tedious. Some weekends I've read 3 or 4 books. That's how I pass the time when I am not in school or training. Fighting boredom is the real war we wage here.*

From your letters, it sounds like just the opposite. I am so happy that you are enjoying some of your training and that being a nurse is agreeing with you, except maybe for the leeches. I miss you greatly and can't wait for our next time together. Perhaps we will both be home over the holidays. Maybe we could reenact last year's scene on your front porch—remember? I think of you every day and I remain faithfully yours.

Love,

Philip

Putting aside his daily boredom with Army life, Philip was excited to finally send some good news home to El. Just the thought of possibly seeing her in the near future made military life a bit more bearable.

Scott Field

November 19, 1941

Dear El,

I hope that you received my letter last week letting you know that I've secured a weekend furlough for November 22; I am also hoping that perhaps you have been able to arrange for some time off. Not much different here—school, practicing the piano whenever I get a chance, K.P., and rain. I have received letters from Dad, Harkness, and Inness. Things seem to be going well at home. Dad has been doing some carpentry work for Mr. Trout. He says that Fish hasn't changed a bit, although he thinks he might be getting a little more serious. He is still dating the gal from Quincy, the redhead. Do you remember her from the dance?

Hawkeye writes that law school is difficult, but that he is enjoying the big city, its history and especially the seafood. Even though he's still a Cubs fan, he loves attending Red Sox games at Fenway Park.

Inness reported that Pittsfield had a great football season, but he is thinking about joining the Army or the Marines, especially if we get involved in the war in Europe. He says the more he hears about what Hitler and the Nazis are doing the madder he gets. I don't think I would want The Giant on any team against me.

Billy wrote and told me his classes are going well and that he's preparing the basketball team for the upcoming season. I'll bet he's a taskmaster. Pat got the English job vacated by Mr. Meacham, who became principal. I wonder if Billy will be popping the question soon.

Went to see the movie Dive Bomber *tonight. Sometimes I wonder if I really want to get up there in a plane. Those guys that are fighting in England are real heroes. I recall the speech Churchill gave devoted to the pilots defending Great Britain. He said, "Never was so much owed by so many to so few." Pretty true, I would say.*

I am taking an A.C.I. radio course and have resigned myself for now to be content to be a radio operator. I am considering applying for a communications officer appointment but will have to complete this training first. Enough for now. I do hope that we will be together soon.

Love,

Philip

Philip wondered if being a communications officer wouldn't be a safer appointment. There was a lot to consider, and the specter of war still loomed on the horizon. He wondered what momentous decisions were being weighed at the White House. How far would the United States go to assist its allies?

He looked forward to celebrating the holidays at home. He ached to see El and also hoped he would have some quality time to spend with family and friends. His initial wish would go wanting, but the latter was about to be granted.

CHAPTER 27

The McCravens' Party

November 22, 1941

ROSIE MCCRAVEN WAS A FORMER STUDENT of Philip's and also the object of Philip's brother Homer's affection. When she discovered that Philip would be coming home on leave, she told Homer that her parents would like to throw a party in Philip's honor. Homer thought it was a fine idea, and so plans were made for the homecoming of Payson's adopted son.

Philip hitchhiked home on Saturday morning and that evening rode shotgun as Homer drove the family car to Payson. Billy, Pat, and Wayne rode in the backseat of the old Chevy.

"I'm curious, Homer, how did you meet Rosie?" Philip asked.

"At Harris's drugstore last fall. I was just killing time waiting for you to finish up at the high school. It was a Friday night. We just started talking. I'd guess you could say there was some chemistry between us. We began writing letters and, well, you know the rest. She's one fascinating gal."

Philip understood the feeling. "*Fascination* is a dangerous word, Homer. It can get you in a lot of trouble. Be careful."

"She told me you were her favorite teacher."

"I don't know if I was her favorite teacher or not, but that's sure nice of her to tell you that," replied Philip. "She was a junior in the band and mixed chorus. A delight to have in class."

"I'll bet she was!" Homer exclaimed. Not to mention, she was as pretty as any girl Homer had ever known.

The Zumwalts' old Chevy pulled up to the McCravens' house. The bungalow's windows glowed a warm welcome back to Payson for Philip and Homer. Rosie greeted them on the front stoop. She pecked Homer on the cheek. He blushed and grinned.

Walking in, Philip whispered to Homer, "Looks like maybe you learned more at college than English, math, and drafting."

Philip entered the parlor to Louie Armstrong's "Ain't Misbehavin'" playing on the McCraven phonograph. Nearly twenty folks had gathered there to welcome him home. They all put down their drinks and greeted him with a round of applause.

"Our hero!" Cecil shouted.

"Hail to the returning warrior," Essie added.

Ina Harper rushed toward Philip and hugged him. "It's so good to see you, Professor. We have a lot to catch up on. I miss you."

"It's great to see you, too, Ina. How's Ronald doing?"

A handsome, dark-haired man dressed in a Navy lieutenant's uniform approached with a cup of punch. "Here you are, Ina. Fresh from the bar."

"Philip, this is Ronald, Ronald Hague, my fiancé." Smiling, Ina flashed her engagement ring with a wave of her hand.

"Wow! Congratulations! A pleasure to finally meet you, Ronald," said Philip. "Ina never stopped talking about you. I'm guessing you completed your master's degree. So, congratulations on everything!"

"Thank you. And thank you for enlisting. I sure enjoyed teaching at Payson until I got called up," Ronald reported.

"He was in the NROTC at U of I. He just started the school year when he received his orders. Apparently, they need officers." Ina sounded both proud and regretful.

"Where are you headed?" Philip asked.

"Oh, I got a great duty station. Taking off next week for Hawaii. Pearl Harbor."

"You can't beat that."

"Where are you going, Philip?" Ina asked.

"Don't know yet."

Sandra Robinson rushed over to the group. "Philip, my dear. How are you?" She gave him a brief hug. "Oh, do please excuse me, Ina."

"He's all yours, Sandra. We'll catch up later, Philip."

Ina and Ronald turned toward each other, sipped their punch, and resumed an intimate conversation.

"It's so good to see you, Mrs. Robinson," Philip said. "I was hoping to stop by tomorrow."

"That would be wonderful, but Grandmama Campbell is nursing a bad cold, so I think we better take a rain check."

"Please send her my regards. I hope she feels better soon."

"I certainly will; that's very kind of you." Sandra turned back toward Ina. "And who is this handsome young officer?"

"Oh, I'm so sorry, Sandra, meet my fiancé, Ronald Hague. Ronald, this is Mrs. Sandra Robinson, one of my dearest friends in Payson."

"Pleased to meet you, Mrs. Robinson."

After a few minutes of pleasantries, Sandra took Philip's arm. "Well, I've monopolized enough of you two lovebirds' time, and Philip and I have a bit of catching up to do. Please excuse us." She pulled Philip to one side of the room. "Elinor was so disappointed that she wasn't able to come tonight. They're working our poor dear to death. And you—oh my, you've lost so much weight. Don't they feed you in the Army?"

Philip only smiled in response.

Taking him by the arm again, Sandra led him to the open door of Dr. Joseph McCraven's study. McCraven was the only veterinarian in Adams County. He and Doc Robinson had been friends for years. They shared similar political views, loved FDR, and both were avid St. Louis Cardinal fans. Sandra and Philip found the two friends discussing the future of their favorite team and the odds of ever beating the reigning World Champions of baseball, the New York Yankees.

"I hope Rickey didn't make a mistake trading Mize." McCraven was smoking his pipe and blew a puff of smoke from his mouth.

"We didn't get much for him—a pitcher, catcher, and some cash— but Rickey's a smart fella, and I think the Musial kid and 'Country' Slaughter will get us some runs with their hitting and base running. Why, Joe, I'll bet you here and now we're in the World Series come the end of next September. Mark my words." Doc stuck out his hand to his friend. "Ten bucks?"

"No thanks, Don," replied McCraven. "I just hope we aren't fighting a war over in Europe by that time." McCraven rose to stoke the fire.

"I hope not, too," Sandra interrupted. "Dr. McCraven, you remember Philip, don't you?"

She and Philip crossed into the cozy, lamp-lit study, a red Persian carpet muffling their steps. Doc sat in a houndstooth cloth armchair by the study's fireplace. McCraven placed the iron poker in its rack and turned to greet his visitors.

"*Remember* him?" he said as he shook Philip's hand heartily. "How in the world could I forget him? Seemed to me he was a fixture at your home nearly all summer. Good to see you, my boy. How's the Army treating you?"

"Just fine, sir. It's been quite an experience."

"So, how's the flying going?" asked Doc, rising to shake Philip's hand. "I guess that beats digging ditches and fighting in trenches, that's for sure."

"Yes, sir, well, the pilot thing is sort of on hold for now, but if we do go to war, I hope I'll get a chance to fly."

"Good for you, young fella," said McCraven. "I think we're going to need all the best young men we can find. I'm afraid we're going to have to take after that devil, Hitler. Not a good man, no sir, not good at all. Enough of that. Tonight's a night for celebration. Let's fatten you up, son. Mrs. McCraven and Rosie have been cooking all day long. Please join your brothers and friends, and have yourself a sandwich and a drink or two."

Philip looked out into the parlor where Homer was sipping a cocktail and talking with Rosie. Wayne had sidled in next to Mary Lou Wagle, one of Rosie's classmates who had also been in Philip's band. *Both of my little brothers have grown up*, he thought, smiling to himself.

"Yes, yes. Do eat something, Philip," Sandra said, leading him back toward the study door. "Donald, don't you think he's too thin?" she called over her shoulder, her forehead wrinkled with concern.

"Nonsense, my dear. You look fit as a fiddle, my boy," Doc said, nodding at him.

"Thank you, sir. It just feels great to be home."

"I am so glad you consider Payson home," Mrs. Staley said as she emerged out of the crowd and hugged her favorite boarder. She pulled him through the study door and fully into the party. "Did you see that Ina got engaged? Isn't that exciting?"

"Sure is," Philip replied. "Ronald seems to be a great guy."

"Have you been able to see Elinor?"

"No, ma'am. I haven't seen Elinor since I reported for duty. Between her schedule and mine, it just hasn't been possible. I'm hoping she might get some time off this weekend, but it doesn't look like it." Philip's dejection registered on his face and his eyes dropped momentarily to the floor.

"Well, that can't last forever, Philip. I am certain you two will be able to see each other soon. Pick up your chin, my boy." She tenderly put two fingers under his chin and lifted it up. "Tonight we need to celebrate. After all, we aren't at war, are we?"

"Not yet. Let's hope that remains the case, Mrs. Staley. Now, how are you?"

The two continued to chat away like the long-lost friends they were. Conversation and beverages flowed abundantly throughout the evening, and the hors d'oeuvres prepared so meticulously by Mrs. Etta McCraven and her daughter were consumed with delight. But, for Philip, the homecoming was incomplete. Absent was the one person he had his heart set on seeing. Now, it was her turn to be on duty.

CHAPTER 28

Ordinary Days

EL WAS DEVASTATED THAT SHE HAD MISSED the McCraven party. She had hoped that perhaps at the last minute she might receive a pass, but an emergency on her floor terminated that fantasy before it was barely able to begin. When she sat down to write Philip, she did her best to disguise her disappointment, but she wanted him to know how much she was looking forward to some time together over the Christmas holiday.

Blessing Hospital, Quincy, Illinois
November 23, 1941
Dear Philip,

I only have a minute to write in between classes. I am so sorry to have missed the get-together at Rosie's. I talked with Momma on the phone last night and she is worried about you. She thinks you look more like a beanpole than usual—ha! See, I haven't lost my sense of humor. She said you were still handsome though, thank Heavens! I do hope we will both get a break at Christmas, and I will do much better on the front porch than I did last year. Do you think, my darling, that we will be going to war? I pray every night that we will not get involved in that awful conflict. I hope they are treating you well. I can't wait to hold you in my arms again. Do take care.

Love,
El

Philip was excited to receive El's letter and looked forward to another front porch rendezvous. He couldn't wait to hold her in his arms, too. He longed for simple, ordinary days and wrote telling her so.

Scott Field

December 2, 1941

Dear El,

The party at Rosie's was swell, but it would have been so much better with you there. I think Homer is head over heels for Rosie. She is a sweet girl, and I am pleased to see my brother so happy. Wayne talked all night with Mary Lou. It was great to see the Payson folks again. Your parents and Mrs. Staley all looked well. I had a nice conversation with all of them. I met the fella who replaced me, Ronald Hague, a nice young man originally from Iowa. He got his degree from the U of I where he was in the Naval ROTC program and just got called up. Quite dashing in his uniform. Ina and he are engaged. A fine couple. He played the piano at the party and is quite a talent. He and I talked about what he had been teaching in the World Problems class. He thinks that FDR is being persuaded by Churchill to enter the war.

Ralph Guthrie was at the party, too. He thinks FDR is merely using his rhetoric to posture against Hitler, but that it would not be to his benefit politically to enter into the war. Send the weapons to the Brits and Ruskies and let them do our fighting for us. Plus making all of these weapons will help our economy and we might gain some territory from the Brits through the Lend-Lease deal. I think your father is right; FDR is a cagey politician who has no interest in sending us to war. I agree with Ralph.

I stood in line last week for Christmas furlough, and it looks like I'll be coming home. I hope you can do the same. I took exams for telephone procedure and circuit analysis last Friday and then headed over to the enlisted men's club and played the piano. A group of fellas gathered round and sang songs from **The Mikado,** *quite a rousing evening. On Saturday, I went back to the St. Louis Symphony and heard the great Arthur Rubinstein. He certainly gives a pianist something to aspire to. On Sunday evening I saw a fine and moving picture,* **One Foot in Heaven,** *with Fredric March and Martha Scott. I wish you could have been there.*

Jim Burke, one of the men in my squadron, and I were having a pretty deep conversation the other day about home and what we miss most. I told him that I miss ordinary days, the days like we had this summer, days where we would go to the park and just talk. Days when we would walk downtown, grab a soda pop at Harris's, and dream about where we would be in a year, five years or more. I wonder where we will be. I hope we'll be sitting on our porch sipping lemonade, or relaxing by a warm fire reading books—comfortable in our silence. Ordinary days, El, that's what I yearn for, and Burke agreed with me.

Time to go. I hope you will be able to send me a letter so I know how your ordinary days are going, but I am guessing you haven't had too many of those. I received your picture today. You look so beautiful and your nursing uniform is quite stunning. I miss you, your laughter, and everything about you.

Love,

Philip

Philip carefully placed the picture of El on top of his belongings in his footlocker so that every time he opened the footlocker there she would be. Rumors were floating around the camp that the troops would be receiving a furlough sometime before Christmas day. He opened El's next letter with eager anticipation, hoping for news of a break in her duty schedule, maybe a day or two over the holidays when they could be together.

Blessing Hospital
December 4, 1941
Dear Philip,

Not much to report here. I've been notified that we'll have a week off at Christmas, so I do hope we'll be able to spend every spare minute together. Training is still rigorous, and I even had to apply more leeches the other day. Ugh! I have started smoking more and more to stay awake. I guess the cigarettes still make me feel euphoric—ha! So happy you got to see everyone at the McCravens. I hated to miss it. And how exciting about Miss Harper!

By the way, did you hear about the First Lady snubbing the Duke and Duchess of Windsor? What a scandal!

I cannot wait to see you over the holidays. Take care.
Love always,
El

Philip wondered why the First Lady would do such a thing. Upon further investigation, he discovered that it was rumored the Windsors were Nazi sympathizers. *Well, good for the "other Eleanor,"* he thought. *How wonderful that our First Lady has such spunk! She doesn't take any nonsense from anyone, not even the royals!*

Philip tucked El's latest letter in his footlocker and reclined on his cot. His friend Matt Zachal was playing his Spanish flamenco guitar a few bunks away. Philip was looking forward to the upcoming weekend when he and Zac planned on attending the St. Louis symphony.

CHAPTER 29

A Date That Will Live in Infamy

December 6, 1941

PHILIP AND ZACHAL CLAIMED THEIR PAY and headed to St. Louis. Zac was part Latino, passionate, and flamboyant—a pugilist, especially when women with whom he had shared his poetry and intimacy were whisked away by another man. Philip's nickname for his new friend was "The Latin Lover." Zac called Philip "Z."

A poet, Zac enjoyed penning tomes laced with eroticism, chronicling his torrid love affairs. He would share his compositions with Philip in English, but Philip couldn't help but wonder if some of the language might have been even more evocative in Spanish. However, even in English, the subject matter left Philip slightly uncomfortable.

Zac loved music, too. He played his guitar with astonishing flair. Philip was pleased that Zac had finally decided to tag along and take in the St. Louis symphony. Despite their diverse backgrounds, their shared love of music had led to an amiable friendship.

After flunking the eye test portion of the physical for flight school, Philip had resigned himself to becoming a combat radio operator. If things went well with his training, he would still get to fly, just not as a pilot. For now, he needed a distraction and could think of none better than the symphony. El had positively answered Philip's letter bearing the bad news, encouraging him to keep trying. Philip missed everything about her, especially her positive attitude. Even after pulling an extra weekend shift, she never complained.

Philip and Zac attended the Saturday evening performance of the St. Louis Symphony, ending their night at the USO. Entering the hall, they were greeted by a haze of smoke and the stench of stale beer mixed with cheap perfume. Combined with the sound of an out-of-tune, tinny piano, Zac proposed finding someplace else to end their Saturday evening. "C'mon, Z. Let's get outta here. This place stinks!"

Philip had a better idea. Seeing the drunken GIs who populated the room, leaning on nurses and local girls rather than dancing, he approached the current piano player. The doleful young soldier was doing his best at the worn-out piano, but when Philip offered to play a few tunes to give the fellow a break, he gladly accepted.

As soon as Philip started playing, the drowsy spirits of the current clientele were inexplicably awakened. A mixture of swing music and popular songs inspired soldiers, sailors, nurses, and civilians to flood the dance floor with newborn enthusiasm. After a few tunes, they gathered around the piano wrapped in one another's arms and sang a few of the songs familiar to all. Such moments made Philip feel alive. Even as war loomed, he was able to lose himself in the music, in the thrill of entertaining.

Inebriated couples finally dispersed, stumbling out into darkness. Their alcohol consumption had enhanced their ability to dance and sing, and Philip was pleased to think his piano playing possibly made them feel better. Taking their minds and his away from the uncertainty of their future was most rewarding.

December 7, 1941

Philip and Zac each procured a cot at the Forest Park tent city. Sleeping until noon, they dressed in their uniforms, returned to the USO for a sandwich and a Coke, and strolled back up Market Street to the Municipal Auditorium Opera House.

The St. Louis Symphony's afternoon performance featured guest conductor Charles O'Connell. "I'm actually enjoying your classical music," Zac admitted. The splendor of the massive Municipal Auditorium in the daylight was impressive. "And this building, Z, my friend? *Magnifico!*" Zac said, wide-eyed.

O'Connell was just as magnificent. Directing the symphony with aplomb, he brought the music of Bach alive. Philip and Zac joined the rest of the packed house in showing their appreciation with a thunderous standing ovation. The curtain closed signaling intermission.

As Philip and Zac made their way to the grand foyer, the hallways were abuzz. The impassioned conversations were not, however, about the splendid performance rendered by O'Connell and the symphony. Instead, an intermittent whispered word or two drifted toward them: "Pearl Harbor." "Japs." "Sneak attack."

Philip politely interrupted an exchange between two Army officers. "Excuse me, sir. What's going on?"

A young, dark-haired Army captain turned toward Philip. His moist eyes indicated that whatever was happening was serious. The captain cleared his throat and answered Philip's question. "War, soldier, we're going to war. The Japs bombed Pearl Harbor this morning."

"Pearl Harbor? In the Pacific?" Zac asked incredulously.

"Hawaii. The Japs hit us without any warning. The majority of our ships in the Pacific are docked there. Most of them are destroyed. Major casualties. The president doesn't have much choice in this one. We were attacked. Our guys didn't have a chance." The officer shook his head and turned back to commiserate with his fellow officers.

Philip was not certain what shock felt like, but a strange feeling welled up deep inside. He wondered if Ina's fiancé had survived. News of the sneak attack spread rapidly through the opera house. Japan had declared war on the United States and its allies. All soldiers were being ordered to return to their fields and posts immediately.

When Philip and Zac returned to their barracks, there was a sense of foreboding. Some soldiers sat or laid on their bunks in silence; others were making wisecracks, saying it was about time. Philip propped himself against his pillow, pulled out his pen and diary, and began writing about the events of the day, an unforgettable day. He concluded his entry:

> I keep saying to myself, "We're at war—at war," but I can't make it seem real—most of the fellows are joking about it all. Most are relieved that everything is clear. We have a job to do.

December 8, 1941

At approximately 12:30 p.m., President Roosevelt delivered a radio speech to the nation. Philip mixed in with a group of men who gathered around a radio in the dayroom. The joint session of Congress had convened in the congressional chamber. The soldiers joined the nation as they listened attentively to President Roosevelt:

"Mr. Vice President, Mr. Speaker, Members of the Senate and House of Representatives: Yesterday, December 7, 1941—a date that will live in infamy—the United States of America was suddenly and deliberately attacked by naval and air forces of the Empire of Japan. . . ."

The president continued with information that was news to Philip and his fellow soldiers, who had gathered around the radio in the dayroom:

"Yesterday the Japanese Government also launched an attack against Malaya. Last night Japanese forces attacked Hong Kong. Last night Japanese forces attacked Guam. Last night Japanese forces attacked the Philippine Islands. Last night the Japanese attacked Wake Island. And this morning the Japanese attacked Midway Island . . . As Commander in Chief of the Army and Navy, I have directed that all measures be taken for our defense. But always will our whole nation remember the character of the onslaught against us. . . ."

The president was lighting into the Japanese, and Congress lapped it up. They responded to his condemnation of Japan with resounding and sustained applause. FDR continued and assured the nation that not only would the country be defended but also, "This form of treachery shall never again endanger us. Hostilities exist. There is no blinking at the fact that our people, our territory, and our interests are in grave danger. With confidence in our armed forces—with the unbounding determination of our people—we will gain inevitable triumph—so help us God."

Philip's eyes teared up as he listened to still more applause from Congress. Now he understood Colonel Franklin's devotion to General Grant. On the surface, war made no sense at all, but this seemed different. President Roosevelt's words inspired him. He was prepared to run through a wall of gunfire to defend his country. He would not blink in the face of danger! The news that would reverberate around the world came next. The president was even more solemn and resolute as he concluded his speech:

"I ask that the Congress declare that, since the unprovoked and dastardly attack by Japan on Sunday, December 7, 1941, a state of war has existed between the United States and the Japanese Empire."

"That seals the deal, boys, we're goin' to war." Burke sounded almost elated. "I enlisted looking for a good fight, and it looks like we found one."

"Yeh, forget any Christmas furloughs, fellas," Zac grunted. "And I'm guessing that goes for the symphony, too, Z."

Christmas at home with El and his family was no longer a possibility. Everything had changed. He sat quietly on his bunk with the realization that, from this moment on, his life would never be the same.

Zac was right. Bad news traveled fast. All Christmas furloughs were canceled. A good news flash came across the wires that cheered up the soldiers in the Thirty-Fourth Squadron at Scott Field: The boys in the Pacific had sunk a Japanese battleship. Philip turned in an application to become a radio communications officer. "Remember Pearl Harbor" was America's new slogan. Philip and his buddies were ready for action.

On December 11, Germany and Italy declared war on the United States of America. The Axis alliance was complete. As the men in Philip's tent sat on their cots reading magazines, he pulled his diary from his footlocker and wrote:

> That defeat at Pearl Harbor will only be avenged in the blood of many Japanese! Today's news is optimistic. The Japanese battle fleet is avoiding conflict, the British and Dutch are holding their own in Malaya, the Russians' new giant offensive is rolling forward, and the British are driving steadily forward in North Africa. Rumania declared war on the U.S. today. That's a joke. Received letters from Dad and Mother. Mother's contained a five-dollar check.

It turned out Zac's prediction was not entirely accurate regarding new Army policy. Philip did attend the St. Louis Symphony on Sunday, December 14, and relished the performance of noted pianist Ida Krehm. And, on December 20, Philip once again claimed a seat at the opera house and came away enthralled by the performance of the guest artist, Igor Stravinsky.

Philip learned that the minor stigmatism that had caused him to fail his Aviation Cadet exam was going to be overlooked, and he was now permitted to submit an application to flight school. In the meantime, he spent his days in radio communications school classes, and his nights passed tediously while writing; reading letters, books, and magazines; listening to the radio; and going to the movies. The weeks between Pearl Harbor and Christmas seemed like years. The idea of spending the holidays away from home lowered everyone's morale.

Perhaps a bit of divine providence prevailed, or maybe the commanding officers at Scott Field simply determined that morale was sinking too low. For whatever reason, the soldiers were granted Christmas Day leaves. Philip phoned home to ask his parents to pick him up on Christmas Eve.

CHAPTER 30

Christmas Eve

December 24, 1941

E L INVITED PHILIP TO COME TO PAYSON for dinner, under the singular condition that his parents wouldn't mind. They didn't. Ruby gave Philip her blessing with a caveat: "Please drive carefully. There's an awful storm coming. And, if at all possible, please try and make it back for the eleven o'clock service at church. But, if the storm gets too bad, I'm certain Mrs. Staley would let you spend the night."

Philip agreed. Borrowing the family car for the evening, he drove to the Robinsons with a knot in his stomach. Sliding up the Robinsons' circle driveway, he parked the car, wrapped the Army-issue wool scarf tightly around his neck, and buttoned up his double-breasted brown coat. Upon opening the car door, he was greeted by December's flurries. Concealing a small package in his coat pocket, he walked toward the front door. His combat boots crunched upon the partially shoveled snow-covered sidewalk. Head down, he plowed ahead into the fierce north headwind.

"Philip!" El bolted through the front door and ran down the steps, falling into his arms. He grabbed her, kissed her, and then gently pushed her away, holding her at arm's length, and smiled. Snowflakes fell upon her long, auburn hair and melted. She returned his smile, as they embraced near the same spot where she had kissed him on the cheek over a year earlier.

Whispering in her ear, he held her tightly, wrapped her in his coat, and guided her onto the porch and through the front door.

After El helped him remove his coat, hat, and scarf, and hung them all on the coat tree, the evening's plan came at him in rapid-fire. "My family can't wait to see you. After dinner, let's take a walk, just the two of us. Mrs. Staley told Momma that she would love to see you, and Momma told her we would try to visit her this evening. She told Momma she hoped we would have a chance to stop by. Of course, she told Momma that she knew your time was precious and would understand if we weren't able to stop."

"I can't think of anyone I would love to see more." Philip hesitated. "Except, of course, you and your family." He winked.

Grandmama Campbell appeared in the foyer hallway with a tray of mugs filled with hot chocolate topped with whipping cream. "Goodness gracious, don't you look handsome in your uniform. How about a nice hot drink? Dinner will be ready soon."

"Grandmama, you're the best," El gushed. She relieved her grandmother of the tray and offered a mug to Philip.

"Thank you, Mrs. Campbell. I'm so happy you're feeling better. Last time I was home, Sandra told me you had a bad cold."

"Oh, it was a doozy, I tell ya, but you can't keep a good gal down." With that, she turned and headed back into the kitchen. "Miss Betsy, what can I do to help?"

"Momma and the girls are still getting ready upstairs," El reported, as they entered Doc's study, each with a mug in hand.

"Who goes there? Some suitor calling upon my eldest daughter?!" Doc bellowed. "Bring that soldier in here, Elinor."

El led Philip through the door. Doc rose from his desk chair and shook Philip's hand. "Welcome home, young man. Haven't seen you since that soirée at the McCravens' house. Quite a celebration, wasn't it?"

"Oh, yes, sir. It was great to get a break from the Army, that's for sure," Philip replied.

Doc returned to his leather chair behind the large mahogany desk. Philip claimed the club chair that faced the man who he one day hoped would be his father-in-law. El sat next to Philip on the arm of the chair.

As they sipped hot chocolate, Doc puffed on his cigar. "Looks like we're going to be in the thick of this war, my boy. Hirohito made a big mistake listening to his generals. In my humble opinion, the Congress and the president made the correct decision. FDR's a fine leader. He guided us out of the Great Depression and now he'll lead us to victory over the Axis powers. Mark my words, son, it's not going to end well for those Fascist bullies."

"I think you're right about that, sir. The men I've served with are dedicated to winning this war as soon as possible. I just hope England can hold on," Philip said.

"Old Winston Churchill, now there's a warrior for you! He was a soldier, you know. I don't think England could be in better hands. He's at the White House right now making his case to Roosevelt." Doc blew a smoke ring.

"I don't know, Father," El said. "It just seems to me that war is all about men fighting over land and money."

"I beg to differ with you on that, Elinor," her father replied. "This war is about more than land and money. There's a basic difference in the philosophies of our governments. The Nazis are Fascists through and through, and their dictator wants to control what people think—even how they act. There are even reports that they're harassing the Jews for no good reason. Why, they're nothing but a gang of bullies. And, my God, look at what those Japanese have done. Not only have they committed terrible atrocities against the Chinese people, why, they had the audacity to attack *us*! I suppose the biggest question FDR is facing is, who do we go after first?"

"I'm in full agreement with Prime Minister Churchill on that," Philip said. "We need to take care of the Nazis first. But the Japanese may end up being just as big a threat. If they get control of the Pacific, that would be a major problem for the Allies."

"Hard to say," Doc replied. "After they hit us at Pearl Harbor and the Philippines, it seems they were not content to merely hold on to what they had. I expect they'll go after Australia next."

"There's a lot of territory out there in the Pacific to hold on to," Philip responded.

"See, that's exactly what I mean," El argued. "*Territory*. Just like a bunch of silly boys arguing in a sandbox over who gets the biggest pail and shovel."

"I'm sorry, El, but I have to agree with your father on this one," Philip said almost apologetically. "We're hardly talking about a sandbox. We may be talking about the entire world, and I do feel that the Axis powers are intent on doing us harm. Pearl Harbor was no accident. I think we have every right to go to war."

El turned away. The last thing she wanted to do on this evening was argue with the man she loved. She bit her lip and simply nodded. Words and phrases came from her father's mouth, but she paid only partial attention, lost in a haze of sadness. Doc had pulled a copy of St. Augustine's *Confessions* from his bookshelf. Augustine's words floated up to the ceiling along with his stale cigar smoke. They seemed as distant and irrelevant to El as the war itself.

"'Principles of a Just War' . . . a just cause . . . we were attacked . . . a right intention . . . what is more right than the restoration of freedom?"

El couldn't maintain her silence. She got up from the arm of the chair. "Father, no one wants war. All most folks want is to live in peace, have food, shelter, and good health."

"That may be true, Elinor, but I also believe people want their freedom, and that is something worth fighting for. Here's what Augustine wrote. . . ."

El looked away and scanned the books in the library, diverting her attention from her father's discourse.

"Here it is . . . 'Any man who has examined history and human nature will agree that no human heart does not crave joy and peace. One has only to think of men who are bent on war. What they want is to win; their battles are bridges to glory and to peace. . .'And the only way to peace and freedom now is to win this damn war. And I hate to say it, but that will require great sacrifice."

El looked down. She wasn't going to divulge her most passionate rebuttal. What she really wanted to say was that she didn't want the man she loved to go to war and be killed. That was a sacrifice too great. Instead, she turned and headed through the study doorway. "I'm certain dinner is almost ready. Please excuse me. I need to go and help in the kitchen."

Both men stood as she left the study and then returned to the comfort of their chairs.

"I don't know, Doc, but I have to tell you that I fear, even though Augustine has a point, those bridges to glory and peace are a long way off." Philip returned the conversation to its origin, how to win the war. "In your opinion, sir, who's a bigger threat, Germany or Japan?"

"I agree with your earlier premise, Philip. Take down those damn Nazis first. If they get control of the oil fields in the Mideast, we're in for a long, protracted struggle. Hitler made a big mistake invading Russia. He created a two-front war, and it's going to get mighty cold in Russia this winter. Those Russians are tough people. According to the news reports, the Nazi strategy was to defeat old Ivan before winter set in. But the Russians counterattacked, and the newspapers say that the German Army is suffering greatly in the cold."

"I hope so," Sandra said, entering through the library pocket doors. "Anyone who burns books must be evil to the core. I am certain that you two have not quite solved the world's problems yet, but it is time for dinner, and we promised Philip we would have him home for the Christmas Eve service. Please come to the table."

"Oh, that's quite all right, Mrs. Robinson," Philip said, trailing her and Doc to the dining room. "If I don't make it back, my folks will understand."

"I am certain having you there worshipping tonight is very important, Philip. Let's sit down and eat," Mrs. Robinson replied as she offered Philip the chair next to El.

CHAPTER 31

The Lighting of the
White House Christmas Tree

FOLLOWING DINNER, THE ROBINSON FAMILY GATHERED in the living room. A giant blue spruce nearly touched the top of the ten-foot ceiling. Decorated with bright ornamental globes and wooden figures depicting toy soldiers, cars, fire engines, and Santa Claus, it was the largest Christmas tree Philip had ever seen up close. A single medallion depicted the Savior's birth in the manger with the words "Happy Birthday, Jesus" inscribed upon it. Candy canes were scattered among the branches, along with small candles on tin trays waiting to be lit. Sandra sat on the divan with Eunice and Emily on each side of her. The two Labs stretched out on the floor at their feet. Grandmama Campbell rested in the wooden rocking chair, an afghan draped over her lap.

Philip sank into a chair covered with red embroidery next to the big Philco radio in its cabinet of faux zebrawood. Brown dials and pushbuttons could be tuned to any broadcast band station. Two bands of shortwave were available for foreign broadcasts. The reception was clear as a bell, according to Doc.

Doc turned the radio on, adjusted the dial, and tuned in to the local station. It relayed the broadcast of the lighting of the White House Christmas tree, originating from station WOL of the Mutual Broadcasting System out of Washington, D.C. El again reclined on the arm of

Philip's chair and held his hand. Her father continued tinkering with the dial, eliminating the static coming from the radio's speakers.

"For goodness' sake, Donald. It's fine," said Sandra. "Please sit down."

Finally content with the resulting crystal-clear reception, Doc took his seat in the leather chair opposite Philip and El, on the other side of the radio.

The announcer's voice resonated through the tan grill cloth covering the speakers: "Good evening, ladies and gentlemen. We are speaking to you from the south portico of the executive mansion, the White House in Washington, D.C. . . ."

Local committee members in charge of the lighting of the White House Christmas tree began the ceremony with their greetings, followed by a lengthy prayer from Cardinal Joseph Cardijn. Members from both the Girl and Boy Scouts brought salutations to the First Lady and President Roosevelt.

The moment arrived that the Robinson family, Philip, and most of the country's citizens had been waiting for. The president spoke to the nation: "And now for the ninth time I light the living community Christmas tree of the nation's capital."

Hundreds of miles away from Payson, the National Community Christmas Tree stood ablaze in dazzling white lights on the White House lawn.

The sound of church bells echoed through the speakers. Doc struck a match and lit the wick on a long brass candle lighter. After igniting one of the candles on the tree, he passed the lighter to Sandra, who lit another candle. Grandmama followed suit, as did each of the Robinson daughters. Emily handed the candle lighter to Philip, who lit the final candle on the tree. He sat down just as the president came on.

"Fellow workers for freedom," Roosevelt began in his commanding voice, "there are many men and women in America—sincere and faithful men and women—who are asking themselves this Christmas: How can we light our trees? How can we give our gifts?" For the next five minutes, the president spoke eloquently of the challenges that faced the American people in the upcoming days of war and the sacrifices that would have to be made. Just before the president introduced the prime minister, he concluded with "Our strongest weapon in this war is that conviction of the dignity and brotherhood of man which Christmas Day signifies—more than any other day or any other symbol. Against enemies who preach the principles of hate and practice them, we set our faith in human love and in God's care for us and all men everywhere. It is in that spirit, and with particular thoughtfulness of those, our sons and brothers, who serve in our armed forces on land and sea, near and far—those who serve for us and endure for us—that we light our Christmas candles now across the continent from one coast to the other on this Christmas Eve."

"Hear, hear!" cheered Doc. "Did you hear that, Philip? By Jove, he was talking about you."

"Why, in the good Lord's name, are you talking like an Englishman?!" exclaimed Sandra. "Who do you think you are, old Winston Churchill himself?" She pointed to the radio, reminding him that the prime minister was due to speak in just a moment.

"What in the world could be wrong with talking like old Winston? He is quite an orator, don't you agree, old chap?" He winked at Philip.

Following Doc's lead, Philip replied in his own finest English accent. "I quite agree with you, my good man."

El turned away from the laughter, choking back tears. The president's message had been powerful and inspirational, but the soldier sitting next to her was one of those that the leader of the United States was talking about. The last thing she wanted in this world was to sacrifice the love of her life, no matter how noble the cause.

As they bantered, President Roosevelt lauded the Allied nations and gave particular praise to the British people and their leader. He turned the microphone over to that very man, his friend, Winston Churchill. The newspapers had reported that Churchill was staying for the month at the White House, visiting the president and First

Lady. He would be celebrating Christmas with them and addressing the U.S. Congress on December 30, 1941—Philip's twenty-second birthday.

The Robinson living room fell silent. They listened intently as the prime minister began, "Fellow workers in the cause of freedom . . . I spend this anniversary and festival far from my country . . ."

Philip had long admired Churchill, an intelligent and brave man. On this Christmas Eve, those gathered around the radio learned the prime minister had a single mission on his mind: He wanted the United States to commit its arsenal of democracy to the cause of defeating the enemy that threatened his homeland.

The prime minister continued, "Let the children have their night of fun and laughter. Let the gifts of Father Christmas delight their play. Let us grown-ups share to the full in their unstinted pleasures before we turn again to the stern task and the formidable years that lie before us, resolved that, by our sacrifice and daring, these same children shall not be robbed of their inheritance or denied their right to live in a free and decent world. And so, in God's mercy, a happy Christmas to you all."

Churchill had thrown down the gauntlet. Philip looked over at Eunice and Emily and was reminded of his own brothers and his former students. What about the children that he hoped El and he would bring into the world? Would they live in a world free from tyranny? The radio played three Christmas carols to conclude the ceremony. Philip and El held hands as the final carol played. They joined the other family members and all those standing on the White House lawn so far away singing "Silent Night."

Philip looked around the room, soaking up the moment. A year earlier, he had received a kiss on the front porch of the Robinson home. He walked through a snowstorm, ate sugar cookies, and played this same carol on Mrs. Staley's piano. On that night, he had begun to formulate his plan. He eventually arrived at a decision that took him on an unforeseen path. He did not regret his choice. He looked at El and her family, a family he'd been barely acquainted with a year earlier. Now he hoped this would soon be his family, too.

The words of the president and the prime minister had inspired him. He feared that war would, indeed, be horrible, but this war *was* necessary. He would fight against the principles of hate. He would fight so the children that El and he would bring into the world would be free. He would fight to the death to defend his country and the people he loved. This was a night he would return to in his memory for the rest of his days.

El slid down the arm of the chair onto his lap, and he gently held her hand. He didn't want to let go. He didn't want to ever let her go.

Doc had also been moved by the speeches. "God bless Mr. Roosevelt and Mr. Churchill," he said.

"God bless us all," whispered his wife.

The candles burned down while the family listened to some commentary offered by reporters at the White House. Doc turned off the radio. Philip joined El at the hall closet, put on his coat, thanked the Robinsons for a lovely evening, and said his goodbyes to the family. A chorus of "Merry Christmas" followed him as he made his way to the door. He gazed at them, wondering how long it might be until he saw them again.

"Merry Christmas to all of you, and a Happy New Year," he said.

"I'll be back in a while," El said as Philip helped her put on her coat. "We're going over to see Mrs. Staley and wish her a merry Christmas."

Sandra escorted them to the door. "Mrs. Staley is such a dear lady. Please tell her merry Christmas from our family, and the same to your family, Philip. I hope you have a lovely Christmas."

CHAPTER 32

Of Gifts and Holy Nights

EL AND PHILIP HELD HANDS AS THEY WALKED toward the park. Snowflakes fell gently. They reached the old oak tree where they had picnicked nearly every Saturday in July and August, and Philip drew El in for a kiss. She clung to him tightly. He opened his coat and wrapped it around her, feeling the warmth of her body next to his. If only time could stand still, if only they could be lost in ecstasy, in a warm place of retreat, nestled by a cozy fire, their bodies linked by a love assured to last a lifetime. But that wasn't possible now, not in this moment.

As they separated, Philip reached in his coat pocket and offered El a small red package wrapped with a diminutive white bow. "Merry Christmas, El," he said.

She removed her leather gloves and opened the gift. "Oh, Philip, darling. It's beautiful." She pulled a gold lavaliere from the box. Three narrow threads extended from a golden chain. Hanging from the gilded strands was a pearl surrounded by three more gold threads, and dangling from the encircled pearl was a second pearl.

"It was my mother's. I confessed to her that I was in love with you. She insisted I give this to you. It was hers, and her mother's before that," Philip spoke, choking back tears. "It's a token of my love for you and confirms my promise. I love you, Elinor Robinson. I have loved you from the moment we first met. But I must be honest with you, my dear, I don't think we should get married now. The world's too crazy, and I don't want you to be stuck as a widow."

"You promised that wouldn't happen, remember?" she said, her face wrinkled with concern.

"I know I did, but that was before the reality of war set in. The only thing that's important now is that you know I love you. You know that, right?"

"I do, and I'll wait for you. I promise I'll wait. The day you come home I'll meet you right here under this oak tree and you can propose to me properly, just like a gentleman should. But this wonderful lavaliere is really all I'll ever need." She cradled the necklace in her palm, holding it out, inspecting every inch. "It's so beautiful. I can't believe your mother would ever part with such a lovely necklace. I'll cherish it always."

"Here, let me help you put it on." Philip pulled off his gloves, took the lavaliere, and placed it around her neck.

She turned and he fastened it. Rotating back, she cradled his face in her hands. "Thank you." She kissed him and then reached into her purse and offered him a package wrapped with bright gold holiday paper. "Merry Christmas, my love."

Philip tore open the package. "*The Great Gatsby* by F. Scott Fitzgerald!" he proclaimed. "I've heard of this."

"A few of the girls at the hospital said it's quite a juicy story, and so I read it. Nick, the narrator of the book, kinda reminded me of you. He's so idealistic and such a dreamer," she explained. "I thought you'd like your own personal copy."

"I love it. I'll keep it with me at all times. It'll be my good luck charm. Thank you, my darling." He sweetly kissed her upon her nearly frozen forehead. "It's too darned cold to be out here. Let's get over to Mrs. Staley's. I have a gift for her, too, and I need to make it home in time for the Christmas Eve service. I wish you could come with me."

"Someday I will. We'll be together for every Christmas Eve and

Christmas Day and all the ordinary days of the year, just like you and your friend Burke talked about. I know we will."

They walked across the park to Mrs. Staley's. Philip delivered a small charm he had purchased in a pawnshop in St. Louis to Mrs. Staley, who still wore the charm bracelet her husband had given her. The afternoon Philip had seen the diminutive piano charm in the shop, he had to buy it for his favorite landlady.

Mrs. Staley was overjoyed to see them and cried once she opened the gift. "Oh, my goodness! Gracious sakes, Philip. You shouldn't have. It's perfect. I'll put it on my bracelet tonight. Can you two stay for some hot chocolate?"

"Just one cup, Mrs. Staley. I have to get back to Nebo for the eleven o'clock service," explained Philip.

"Oh, I understand, dear. Please tell your folks hello."

After a short conversation, the couple hugged the kind landlady and wished her a merry Christmas. "Momma and Pops asked that I convey happy holiday wishes to you, too, Mrs. Staley," El said.

"And a merry Christmas to the two of you and your families. Thank you for making a little time for me. Take care and God bless." Mrs. Staley dabbed the tears from her cheeks with her handkerchief as she waved goodbye from her doorway.

El and Philip took their time walking back to her home despite the frigid temperature.

Standing at the door of the Zumwalt family car, El looked into Philip's downcast eyes. "When will you be home next?"

"I honestly don't know. I've got to return to the field tomorrow and should get my orders sometime soon. The first sergeant made it clear there won't be any furloughs for quite a while. The great news is that the brass is going to waive my failed eye exam since it was only a minor stigmatism. So, I'm hopeful my appointment to Aviation Cadet training will come through before they ship me overseas. If so, I'll get to come home before I deploy. Of course, you never know with the Army."

"Be safe, my love."

"Now that I have my good luck charm, how can I not be? I have you and all of this to come home to." He took El in his arms and kissed her. They held their kiss, wanting it to last forever.

"Have a wonderful Christmas with your family. It's going to be a great new year. Think of the adventures we're going to have!" El choked back her tears. "I promise you that I will be praying that every Christmas from here on out we'll be together. We'll celebrate this holiday for a hundred years to come and look back on these days with nothing but fond memories. I love you with every inch of my being, Philip Zumwalt."

"I love you, too, my dear, dear, sweet Elinor. Until we meet again," he said with his best Shakespearean English accent and grinned.

"O think'st thou we shall ever meet again?" El replied playfully, caught somewhere between laughing at her silly lover and crying.

"I doubt it not," Philip said, leaving out the part about woe and the sweet discourses yet to come.

They kissed again. El stood waving on the circular driveway, clinging to her lavaliere as Philip's car disappeared.

Philip stopped the car in front of the Nebo Christian Church. He sat and opened the book El had given to him. Her handwriting appeared on the title page:

To Philip,

"Tomorrow we will run faster, stretch out our arms farther . . . And one fine morning—"

One fine morning we will be together as one and then we will share the rest of our tomorrows together.

Love,

El

Christmas 1941

They would share their tomorrows together. Philip was certain of that. He sprinted up the church steps and slid into the foyer, clomping the snow from his boots. Steam rolled off his coat. He hung it on a hook and snuck into the sanctuary. The congregation sat in prayerful silence, heads bowed. Pastor Harrison finished his prayer as Philip took a seat beside his mother. She sensed his presence and looked over at him. He was afraid she would be angry that he was late, but instead she smiled. Ruby loved her son more than he might ever be able to imagine. She took his hand and held it tightly. He nodded to his father and brothers, who all acknowledged him in return. He looked down the pew and mouthed, "Thank you" to the Zumwalts' neighbor, Forman Fields, who had picked up the family and transported them to the service.

Pastor Harrison's sermon had none of its usual fire and brimstone on this snowy Christmas Eve. Instead, he preached gently about the need for love and peace in a world distraught with hate. The war had changed everyone, even Pastor Harrison. He spoke with a reverent tone of the sacrifices the members of the armed services were about to make so that those gathered might still be free to worship on such a holy night without persecution or fear of imprisonment.

Philip joined in the singing of the last verse of one of his favorite hymns, "O Holy Night." The Zumwalt's neighbor, and long-time member of the congregation, Grace Fields, sang the first two verses as a solo, and all assembled concluded the hymn.

Following Pastor Harrison's benediction, Philip's brother Wayne rose and sang "Silent Night." In the dim light of the candlelit sanctuary, the entire congregation joined in singing the last verse.

As the families filed out into the snowfall, a few congregants lingered in the foyer to express their gratitude to the Zumwalt boys.

"Lovely, solo, Wayne. Just lovely."

"You sure know how to play that trumpet, Homer. Never heard 'Hark the Herald Angels Sing' sound so good."

"You will be in our prayers, Philip. God bless you and all the soldiers."

"Thank you for your service, Philip. Be safe."

The boys acknowledged the compliments and good wishes. They shook the men's hands, hugged the women they knew, and nodded respectfully to those with whom they were less familiar.

Midnight. The church bells signaled the hour as Philip walked with his mother and brothers to their car. The snowfall intensified as Nebo was transformed into a winter wonderland. With a delighted laugh, Philip ran through the snow to the old Chevy, opened the door for his mother, and joined his brothers in the backseat. By the time they arrived home, it was Christmas.

Philip hopped out of the car, once again opened the door for his mother, and made a request. "Would it be all right if I have a moment to myself, Mother?"

"Of course, dear," she said, disguising her own anxiety.

He stood alone on the porch steps and looked to the sky. The reflection of the half-moon lit the soft falling snow ever so dimly. It had been a good night. El loved her lavaliere, Mrs. Staley was thrilled with her piano charm, and now he had a good luck charm. He figured he would need one.

What he didn't know was that Franklin Delano Roosevelt and Winston Churchill had made a momentous decision. Philip wasn't thinking about them, the war, the Army, or whether or not he would be a pilot. The inevitable fight for the freedom of humankind was not, on this night, of the least consequence to him. No, tonight he was only thinking about this holy night, this night divine. Even as the snow turned to freezing sleet, there was a warmth deep inside him he had never experienced. He looked at the half-moon. In its diminished state, even the moon seemed lonely tonight set against the cloudy, gray winter night. Philip imagined its pain matched his because he already missed El.

CHAPTER 33

A Birthday Decision

PHILIP RETURNED TO THE BASE FEELING HOMESICK, but radio school and military communications systems kept him so occupied that he had little time during the day to pine for his loved ones. Evenings were another story. At night, he wrote in his diary, immersed himself in El's Christmas gift, read letters from those he loved, and penned his own. To El, he wrote:

> . . . late-night fire drills caused much swearing and griping. Newspapers and the radio provide us with the latest updates on the war, but I spend most of my free time reading and listening to symphonies on the radio or writing letters to you, the folks, or my brothers. I loved The Great Gatsby. I think it is my all-time favorite book. Perhaps that's because you gave it to me.

It was Philip's first birthday away from home. No birthday cake, no family, and worst of all, no El. He was twenty-two years old as he once again placed his pen onto the diary page.

> Tues. Dec 30. Had a chance to become an instructor today but turned it down. I was tempted for a moment considering that the folks and El want me to stay so badly. However, I

couldn't stand to spend my next three years in this place. I'm putting all hope into my chance of getting that Aviation Cadet appointment.

On New Year's Eve, Philip was granted a twenty-four-hour pass. He called El to give her the good news, to thank her for her card and the box of candy she had sent, and to plan to get together for New Year's Eve.

After a brusque hello, El launched into a tirade that left Philip shell-shocked. "You're a stupid, idiotic fool, Philip Zumwalt! Why in the world did you turn down the instructor's position? You could stay close by and we could see each other, at least on weekends."

"Only on the days and nights you're not working," he said sarcastically.

"That's not fair! I have to complete my training, you know that!"

"Okay. I do understand, but there's also a war to fight, and I need to be a part of it. I don't want to be a coward. Plenty of men are gonna die, El, but hear me loud and clear, I don't plan on being one of them. I couldn't live with myself if I run away from combat. The good news is, since we are at war, I was told my stigmatism would be overlooked and I could retest for the Aviation Cadet program. I want to fly. You know how important it is to me."

"You're impossible. If I could, I'd throw this necklace at you through the phone. I don't want to say any more. I'm afraid what I have to say, I might regret later."

"Just go ahead. Say it."

"Oh, you're intolerable—all of you! Randall just enlisted in the Marines with your buddies, Trout and Inness. You're all crazy, just like this damnable war." El was beside herself, angry, shouting, and holding back the tears.

"You women just don't understand. We men—"

Click!

Well, all right then, thought Philip. *A man's gotta do what a man's gotta do.*

El's duty shift stretched from New Year's Eve to New Year's Day. She was so upset with Philip that it was almost a relief not to be celebrating with him. She loved him, but something inside her feared the worst. The year 1942 loomed ahead, now resembling what their relationship had somehow become—unpredictable and enigmatic.

The Cadet Exam

P HILIP REGRETTED HOW HARSHLY HE HAD SPOKEN to El. With great remorse and contrition, his next letter struck quite a different tone.

January 4, 1942
Dear El,

Please forgive me. I know that it's hard for you to understand why I feel the need to go to war and not be with you, but as much as I believe in our love, I also believe in duty and honor. If I don't help protect our country and our freedom, then I would never be able to live with a clear conscience. I hope we might be able to talk on the phone. I love you and miss you.

It's colder than blue blazes (although that seems a bit contradictory, anyway it's danged cold here). I got up and went to breakfast this morning. It was the first time I'd gotten up for a Sunday breakfast, but please don't tell Mother. I know she'd want me to be attending church. I'm having a rather hard time with my faith right now. Things seem so confusing, just something I need to figure out on my own.

Later, I came back to the barracks, got into bed, and listened to the radio all afternoon. After dinner I listened to the symphony, then went to see **Tarzan's Secret Treasure** *with Johnny Weissmuller* *and Maureen O'Sullivan. Maybe when we see each other I'll beat my chest and say, "Me Tarzan, You Jane!" Ha!*

I retake my Aviation Cadet exam tomorrow. I'm certain I'll pass. I do sincerely hope that you are not too upset with me. I told you that I'll return and I'm a man of my word. I'm hopelessly in love with you, but I need to do this for my country and for myself. Please understand!

All my love,
Philip

Philip did pass his Aviation Cadet exam with a flourish. When he met with the board, he was told that once he graduated from communications school at Scott Field, he would go directly into the Aviation Cadet program. He had not been completely honest with El regarding his acceptance into the program. Although he believed himself to be a man of honor and would never tell El a bold-faced lie, sometimes a man had to stretch the truth a bit. It was true that he did not want to leave her a widow—or worse yet, a widow with a child. But he neglected to tell her that one of the criteria for admission into the AvCad program was that the candidate be single. He would make good on his Christmas Eve promise, but attaining officer status and being a pilot were too important to him to give up. And achieving both would give him greater career opportunities after the war ended.

Philip fought off boredom and resigned himself to the seemingly nonsensical regimens of the Army. The remainder of January he concentrated on his classes and went to the movies at the theater on Scott Field nearly every night. The movie that had inaugurated the new post theater was the Abbott and Costello comedy *Keep 'Em Flying*. Philip hoped he soon would be.

After completing the required transportation forms, he would travel by train to his new post in Florida. A typhoid-tetanus shot and a smallpox vaccination were indicators foreign service was inevitable, but he anticipated his orders for the Aviation Cadet program should arrive soon. That assignment would keep him stateside until he completed the training.

He had done everything possible to become a pilot but was also well aware that his future was now in the hands of the U.S. Army bureaucracy and perhaps other unknown forces yet to be determined. If his AvCad orders did not arrive in time, he would be shipped overseas as a combat radio operator. Either way, he was well aware that he would soon be thrust into combat. He was more curious than fearful. What would his future hold? He wondered if the gypsy fortune-teller had told him the truth. . . .

CHAPTER 35

Zeralda's Prophecy

FIVE MONTHS EARLIER, PHILIP HAD ATTENDED the Illinois State Fair. Skeptical but willing, he took a friend's advice and visited a fortune-teller. Her tent was staked out a few yards behind the fair's midway.

Ancient, scraggly faced, and wrinkled, Zeralda sat somber in her dark tent. The ceiling and walls were covered with silk fabrics of deep maroon, dark blood red, blue, and green, all of it eerily draped and flecked with spiderwebs and dust blown in from the adjoining midway. Her gray-white hair fell upon her shoulders under a bright-red scarf wrapped as a turban. Her blouse, draped below her shoulders with a string tied in a bow, made a feeble effort to cover her ample, sagging breasts. Her nails were painted bright red to match her lipstick, and her dark, puffy eyes focused intently on Philip across a table covered with gold-and-red striped cloth.

It seemed to Philip as if her eyes were peering into his soul. He was confounded by the fact that those same eyes conveyed a certain degree of empathy. Did this woman possess some real mystical knowledge of the future? A crystal ball waited under a white cloth. Philip sat.

"You have come to discover your fortune and your future, young man?"

"Yes, ma'am."

She removed the cloth from the crystal ball. With long, lingering strokes she caressed the air above it. "You are in love," she intoned.

"Yes, I am."

"There were abundant storms that early on disrupted your love life; for now the waters are smooth, but the storms will reemerge. You are restless. Thirsty for a new chapter in your life."

"True."

"You are planning to enlist in the Army Air Corps."

"I am."

"I see a great adventure in your future. You will be rewarded with medals of silver and gold. I see the military and you are in an airplane. You will serve for three terms."

"I hope not."

"Oh, yes, and you will meet with unexpected dire circumstances at an uncommon hour, but do not fear. Your treasure will not be left in gold or silver coins, but in another form, one money cannot buy."

"What will that be?" Philip asked, trying not to sound anxious.

Zeralda shook her head. "That is all I can foretell at this time, but I can assure you that you will find love."

"I suppose that's reassuring. Thank you, Madame Zeralda."

Philip was twelve years old the day he and his brothers became the beneficiaries of a hefty fortune left behind by a band of gypsies who had temporarily taken up residence in Nebo. The gypsies disappeared as mysteriously as they had arrived, stealing off into the night from their campsite down by the Lower Bay Creek. Led by Homer, the boys later recovered the bevy of coins hidden in an underwater cave and kept them as their own.

Philip now wondered if he and his brothers should have left the gypsies' coins alone.

The fortune-teller had thrown in a specific reference to medals of gold and silver—a coincidence? Was there a gypsy curse on the brothers? What sort of "dire circumstances" awaited him? War certainly would have its share of those. Even with all his concerns, though, he was comforted by the old woman's promise that he would receive some kind of mysterious treasure—even if he did have to serve three terms of enlistment. *I guess it's going to be a long war,* he thought.

He likened his fantasy to a bad plot of some pirate adventure. Curses and karma and all legends that surrounded such folklore were, most likely, just nonsense. *Most likely*, he assured himself.

CHAPTER 36

Meet Me in St. Louis

PHILIP CLOMPED OVER THE SNOWY PATH leading to the mailroom. He claimed three letters, one from his mother, one from Wayne, and one from El. He tore open the latter with pure exhilaration.

January 11, 1942
Quincy, Illinois

Surprise!

Dear Philip,

Received your letter. I can honestly say that I do not understand, but I will try because I am hopelessly in love with you, too.

Lots of things have happened since I wrote you last. Charles Ruby and Don Callahan were kicked out of school for getting drunk at a basketball game and coming home on the bus. Ruby is back in school. Payson is quite low on teachers. Johnston is doing guard duty at the bridge. Guthrie is gone, and Sims is going to the Army. Goins is acting as superintendent, and I don't know what they are going to do about Ag. The rumors about Miss Van Dever and Coach Lloyd were true. Now, they are actually dating. Quite the scandal for Payson. Essie dumped Cecil—broke his heart!

How are you doing and do you expect to move? That is a crazy question because I'm positive you can't answer it. Have you heard from your brothers at Western? I do hope they stay in school. It seems like all the men are being swept up by the war. I do suppose it is necessary, but it all seems so frightening.

Congratulate me. I'm not flunking yet, but I wish I had your head to knock on. We get capped the first week in February. No kidding, I can hardly wait. Really, can you picture me as a nurse? As usual, we are working pretty hard and have semester tests coming up. The only thing that makes me feel good about such things is the fact that they will end my college courses—chemistry and microbiology. Do you blame me?

So, speaking of chemistry, I have some good news. One of the girls hails from the St. Louis area. We finish finals and then we get a weekend off. I could get a ride to St. Louis on January 31st and maybe we could see each other. I would love to go to the symphony with you. You make it sound so romantic. Let me know. I wear my necklace every day and think of you every day, too. I do hope we will be able to see each other and that this awful war will not get in the way. Tell all of your friends "Hello" for me. I would love to meet them, but I am hoping we will have some time just the two of us. I think I had better say so long for now or I may forget to wake up when that clock r-r-rings in the morning at 5:30. No kidding! Until St. Louis, maybe? I will be there even if I have to sneak onto Scott Field and kidnap you. Now maybe I'm being romantic. Please take care of yourself.

Love,

El

On a bright, clear afternoon the last day of January, Sally Storzbach, El's best friend from Cadet Nurse training, dropped El at the Majestic, one of the finest hotels in St. Louis. "Have fun!" Sally said, giggling.

"Honestly, Sal, I'm so danged nervous about all of this," El confided. "You won't tell anyone, will you?"

"My lips are sealed," Sally assured her. "For cryin' out loud, El. We're at war. Your fella might be shipped overseas. Lord knows how long it will be until you see each other again. Like I said, have fun! I'll pick you up at ten tomorrow. My folks would like us to attend church with them. After brunch we can head back to the hospital. See you tomorrow." Sally put her black Ford sedan in gear and drove off to her home in Webster Groves.

Dressed in her mother's mink coat and carrying her suitcase and dress bag, El walked nervously into the enormous lobby and waited. At three o'clock Philip strolled through the hotel's revolving door. Not a word was spoken. Their eyes and lips met simultaneously. It had been over a month since their exchange of gifts under the oak tree in Payson's Central Park. El had long since forgiven Philip for his decision to go to war.

"My, my, quite the statement!" Philip said, holding her back for inspection. He had never seen her in a mink.

"Oh, this old rag?" She joked. "Momma didn't want me to freeze to death, so she insisted that I borrow her coat for the weekend."

"Well, it's almost as stunning as you. You look wonderful, old rag and all." Philip laughed. "Come on, let's get you checked in. I reserved a room for you."

El playfully batted her eyelashes. "Well, I guess I'm not sure what you have in mind."

"I just want us to have some time alone. We have reservations at Antonio's Italian Restaurant on Market Street, then we'll taxi over to the Municipal Auditorium Opera House. Yehudi Menuhin is the guest soloist. He's wonderful."

Philip accompanied El to the registration desk. "The reservation is in your name, but don't worry. Your reputation is safe; I'll not be spending the night. I have to report back to the Field by midnight."

El hid her disappointment.

"I'm so proud of you. You're actually going to be a nurse! Will you take care of me when I'm an old man?"

She laughed.

The desk clerk appeared. "Good afternoon, ma'am. May I help you?"

"Yes, Elinor Robinson." She looked at Philip. "I believe I have a reservation."

"Yes, ma'am." The clerk secured a key from one of the minute cubicles stretched like a beehive behind him. "Room 711. I hope you will find your accommodations satisfactory. Please let us know if you need anything."

"Thank you, I most certainly will." El took the key from him and turned to Philip. "What time, soldier?"

"Dinner reservations are for six. I'll pick you up at five-thirty. See you then, nurse." Philip smiled, offered his silly, nonmilitary salute, executed a perfect about-face, and walked through the revolving door onto Pine Street.

The room was lovely. El hung up her dress, removed her golden lavaliere, and ran a bath using a little sachet of scented bath powder. She sank into hot, soapy water in the deep porcelain tub, dreaming of how the night might end and how her future with Philip was really just beginning.

The evening she'd met him at the Casino, she'd had no idea what a kind, thoughtful, and loving man he was. It turned out it wasn't one of her ordinary infatuations. Even with his rain-drenched hair and suit and his gangly arms and legs, she'd found him dashing, and his smile totally disarmed all her defenses. He was a divine dancer. So genuine. He even listened to what she was saying. Disguising herself with the mature elegance of Ginger Rogers in her classiest roles, she'd had no idea she would run in to her own Fred Astaire. Without any warning, there he was, sitting by himself at a table with a virgin ashtray. She smiled. El and Nell, quite a pair. Deep in the luxury of the bath, she allowed herself to dream of what her idyllic life with this extraordinary man might be someday.

After her painted nails dried, she slipped into her black silk undergarments. Arranging the dark seams on the backs of her prized silk stockings so they'd run straight down her shapely calves, she snapped them into her corset. She slipped on a black rayon cocktail dress with red accents and rhinestone buttons, zipped up the back, and then clasped her lavaliere around her neck. She slid on high heels and looked in the full-length mirror with approval. Her auburn hair was longer than it had ever been, silky and shiny. She laughed at herself preening in the mirror and then complimented her reflection. "You look just like Ingrid Bergman, Miss Elinor." Grabbing her evening clutch and mink coat, she entered the elevator and exited into the elegant lobby without betraying her heightened sense of apprehension.

Philip was waiting on a circular couch, dressed in his uniform. He stood to meet her. "Wow!" Starstruck, he held out his arm. She wrapped hers into his. "Shall we?" he said.

"Let's go, soldier. Show me this city!" They exited the hotel arm in arm, oblivious to the bitter January chill. Their eyes locked; all anxiety melted away. This would be an evening they would hold on to for the rest of their lives.

A romantic dinner by candlelight at Antonio's found El and Philip laughing, trying their best to avoid splattering their clothing with the delicious marinara sauce covering their spaghetti. Giggling, they playfully tucked their napkins into their necklines and spread them down to their laps.

Philip hailed a taxicab and requested that the driver take them to the opera house. He put his arm around El and kissed her on the cheek, enjoying the softness of her skin. As they emerged from the cab, El looked up at the colossal gray limestone building in front of her. "Oh, Philip!" She stood in awe beneath the massive Corinthian columns lining the entrance to the auditorium and the opera house.

He smiled, watching her stare up in wonder. "Wait till you see inside," he said.

The lobby stretched two stories tall. White marble pillars lit by brilliant sconces gilded with gold metal supported the ceiling where golden chandeliers cast iridescent beams of light upon the ionic columns. Long rectangular windows sat recessed within the columns bordered by golden hieroglyphics. Gold was everywhere. El stood motionless, astonished by the splendor.

Philip could hardly contain himself. "You haven't seen the half of it." He led her through the enormous mahogany doors that opened into the opera house. The entire space was also bathed in gold. Opulent crimson curtains hung along the side aisles and stretched across the expansive dark marble stage. The theater was filling up fast as they shuffled along the row to their seats.

El stopped and looked up at the balcony and the ornate ceiling. "This place is magnificent, Philip."

"Someone told me it holds thirty-five hundred. Amazing, isn't it?"

"I'll say."

Minutes later, the curtains opened and the overflow audience applauded the conductor, who appeared onstage followed by Yehudi Menuhin. El heard a woman behind her say, "He's a Jew, isn't he?"

"Yes," a man's voice replied. "I'll bet he's glad he's here and not in Europe."

El shot Philip a stunned look of disbelief at the man's insensitivity to Menuhin's plight.

The moment the St. Louis symphony and Menuhin began, the entire theater was entranced. Menuhin was masterful; performing in flawless synchronicity with the orchestra, he moved through the program, which included Vivaldi's "Four Seasons Concertos" and selected pieces from Bach, Beethoven, and Mozart.

The concert ended with Menuhin's rendition of Gershwin's "Summertime." Touched now by El's sensitivity, Philip offered her his handkerchief to wipe away her tears. The music had pierced her soul.

They were such a long way from the music room in the basement of Payson-Seymour High School, but the music that Philip had exposed her to was, at last, being completely understood. The finale drew a thunderous standing ovation and chorus after chorus of "Bravo! Bravo!"

Walking toward the exit, El teased Philip. "So, did you request Gershwin just to woo me?"

Philip winked affirmation. "Wasn't Menuhin wonderful?"

"Beyond words. Why would Hitler want to destroy someone who is able to create something as beautiful as that?" El asked sadly.

Philip shook his head. "I don't know. I honestly don't know."

They walked from the opera house up to Washington Square Park and found an empty bench. Philip brushed the snow away. They nestled together.

"Are you cold?" Philip asked.

"Not tonight. I have my love to keep me warm—and the mink coat." She laughed, gave him the look that always melted him in his tracks, and whispered, "Do you have to get back tonight?"

"I do. The first sergeant ordered us to be prepared to leave at a moment's notice; packed up and ready to go. Knowing the Army, we'll probably be waiting around all day tomorrow, at least. Some of my buddies claim that the military motto is 'Hurry up and wait!' What about you? Are you going back tomorrow?"

El nodded. "Sally's picking me up at ten. We're having brunch with her parents after church, then driving back to the hospital in the afternoon. But here's my real battle plan, soldier," she said, turning serious. "Once I graduate and you get assigned to wherever on God's green earth they send you, I'm going to join you there. I'm enlisting in the Army Nurse Corps and putting in my request to go wherever you are."

"Not a good idea, El. The Army doesn't always give you what you ask for. Plus, I'll probably be going overseas into a combat zone, and combat zones, just in case you haven't heard, are dangerous, even for nurses."

El was her usual stubborn self. "I don't really care. I'm going to do whatever I can to be near you. Maybe Pops can pull some strings for me. He knows some people in FDR's administration, you know."

"Hey, how about pulling some strings for your soldier boy? Make sure I get my orders to report to AvCad before they send me overseas."

"Well, I'll see what I can do. Of course, we won't be able to get married until this stupid war is over. Nurses have to stay single, too, you know." She flashed her ever mischievous smile. "Apparently, pilots can't be married either, but I suppose you already knew that, didn't you? So why don't you go and win this stupid war as fast as you can? Go fly your airplanes. I'll come and be a nurse wherever you're flying. And don't try and talk me out of it. My mind's made up. Don't get me wrong, my darling. I know what you and all of the other men have to do, and it is noble. I realize what we believe in is threatened. So, why don't you go win this damnable war and get back to me as soon as you can? And, if I can help, then you must support me, too. Okay?"

Philip nodded in surrender.

She cradled his face and kissed him. "C'mon, let's walk. You and this coat aren't really keeping me very warm."

They strolled back to the Majestic Hotel, each hoping the night would last forever. Philip had promised himself he would simply kiss El good night and return to base. She handed him her key. As he opened the door, he made another inalterable decision. Sweeping her off her feet, he carried her into the luxurious room. He set her down and spun her around just as he had done so many times on the dance floor. She stepped away—no longer afraid.

The mink slid off her arms to the floor. She turned her back to Philip. Emboldened, he wrapped his arms around her. She slipped away, stopped, looked over her shoulder, teasing him, beckoning him to try again. He advanced slowly, his hands moved over her shoulders, and he slid the zipper down the back of her dress. She stepped out of it. The dress and mink comingled on the plush, intricate multicolored carpet. He twirled her around.

Languidly, she removed the lingerie that remained. Her piercing green eyes bore into his. The moonlight filtered through the windows, outlining her flawless, willing body. Nubile and intentional, she moved toward him, unbuttoned his jacket, unbuckled his belt, and loosened his tie. Pulling him by his tie over to her bed, she released him momentarily. He removed his shirt, pants, and boxers. They tumbled in their clumsy nakedness onto the sprawling bed.

The nurse and the soldier awash in their passion—a majestic evening. They consummated their love, entwined in the rapture of the single moment in time they had been given. El and Nell, or Ginger and Fred? It mattered not. They were two lovers dancing the night away, surrendering to their own private ecstasy.

There was no "But soft! what light through yonder window breaks?" in the morning's early hours. Instead, the unusual sound of a horned lark's high-pitched song drifting through the closed curtains awakened the sleeping couple. Hurried kisses interspersed with Philip's scrambling to get dressed. The room was cold. El draped the mink over her naked body and stood on tiptoes at the door as her solider made his exit.

Having overslept, Philip prayed his unit had not shipped out. Throwing on his overcoat, he hurried out the door and dashed to the elevator. Turning for one final look at El, he raced back to the doorway and held her in his arms. He took her face into his hands and cradled it like fine china. "Turns out I wasn't a fool the night we met at the Casino. That was, by far, the luckiest night of my life."

"Mine, too," she whispered.

He held her as long as he possibly could, kissed her, turned, and sprinted into the open elevator. She stood in the doorway and waved goodbye just like the first December night when she'd kissed him on her front porch. She had watched him through the door's sidelight then, smiling, knowing in her heart he was the man she would love for the rest of her life.

Philip smiled bravely as the elevator doors closed. She grinned back, tossing him a kiss. He pushed the button for the lobby as the elevator doors closed. Wiping his tears on the sleeve of his coat, he exited the elevator and crossed the lobby. His chest ached as he departed the hotel, pushing through the revolving doors.

El ran to the window facing the street and tugged at the frozen frame with all her might. Coaxing it open, she yelled at Philip just as he opened the door to a yellow cab. "Until we meet again, my sweet Philip! I will always love you!"

He turned around, saw her leaning through the open window, wrapped in her mother's fur coat, and thought, *How can I leave her?* A bitter gust of arctic air pierced his wool overcoat. His entire body began to shake—he didn't know if the chill running through his body was caused by his emotions or the frigid wind. He looked up. She could not see the tears streaming down his face. Neither could he see hers.

He stood erect, at attention, and threw his silly two-fingered salute toward her. "Until we meet again, my beautiful Elinor. I will always love you, too!"

She shut the window, threw herself on the bed, and sobbed. How would their story end? He would keep his promise, wouldn't he? Of course he would. Philip was a man of his word. She could count on that.

Philip slid into the backseat of the cab, slammed the door, and, once again, wiped his eyes. The cab driver's voice was uncharacteristically soft and sympathetic. "Where to, soldier?"

Soldier. That was now who he was. Duty called. He had a job to do. It was his decision, his decision alone, one he would accept without regret. He knew she would wait for him. Fighting back his tears, he replied, "Scott Field, please, sir."

PART TWO

CHAPTER 37

Connections in San Francisco

June 5, 1942

ESPITE HIS REPEATED INQUIRIES ABOUT HIS ORDERS for the Aviation Cadet program, Philip had not received his orders directing him to report to one of the flight centers. Instead, in late May, his orders reassigned him to Hamilton Field in San Francisco, California. From there he would depart to somewhere in the South Pacific. He exchanged letters weekly with El. In his correspondence, he mentioned his new Army pals, Patrick Charles "Chuck" Winter and James Burnett "Burnsy" Burnside, who would accompany him on his flight to San Francisco. They had all completed radio operator school and were headed to "God knows where." Philip responded that knowing they would be going together on the first leg of the journey brought the three soldiers some sense of comfort.

After months of preparation, frustration, and waiting, they were finally off to war. Their journey to San Francisco had been circuitous; Morrison Field in West Palm Beach, Florida, MacDill Field in Tampa, Florida, across the south by train through New Orleans, and then west to Duncan Field in San Antonio, Texas. Their orders instructed them to catch a flight to San Francisco, their last scheduled stop before the South Pacific.

"After we land in California," Winter told Burnsy and Philip, "I'm gonna contact one of my old high school buddies. We played basket-ball together. He was a senior when I was a junior."

The trio sat on olive drab, metal benches in the twin-engine Doug-las C-47 along with twenty-five fellow soldiers being transported to Hamilton Field. They settled in and fastened their seat belts.

Winter continued, "We started out in the same grade school together in my hometown of Winston-Salem, North Carolina. Now he's Captain Thomas Beauregard Wilson, a B-17 pilot. Took some Jap shrapnel in his arm in the Philippines and got shipped back stateside to recover. I guess the nickname we gave him back in grade school must have stuck when he joined the service. We called him 'Bo.' He told me his Flying Fortress crews always called him Captain Wilson to his face, but behind his back they used another nickname, called him 'Old Man Bo.'"

"Old man? Hell, how old is he? I thought you said you went to school together?" Burnsy questioned.

"He just turned twenty-six. Guess that's old in our world. Must make me Old Man Winter." Winter laughed. "Compared to you young whippersnappers, I guess I am. He was a real hero, though. Got a Pur-ple Heart and a Silver Star for gallantry. He was lucky to survive the attack by the Japs."

On Saturday night, June 6, 1942, Philip and Burnsy met Captain "Bo" Wilson. On that particular evening, Wilson was no war hero, sim-ply a friend of Chuck Winter, a friend with connections. He distributed twenty-four-hour passes to Winter and his buddies—good for one last night of raisin' hell.

Burnsy agreed. "We're gonna party all night long. Live it up before we go over and get our asses blown to smithereens by the Nips."

Philip laughed and shook his head. His pal sure had a unique way of expressing himself.

They landed at Hamilton, and Wilson picked them up in his 1941

Ford sedan. Burnsy and Philip held on in the backseat as the pilot drove recklessly down US-101. *Captain Wilson must think if he pushes down on the accelerator hard enough, his car just might take flight,* Philip thought.

All in one piece, the soldiers arrived at their destination, 363 Sutter Street in San Francisco. A parking attendant relieved Wilson of his car keys, and the entourage marched confidently up to the nightclub entrance. Billboard posters enclosed in glass framed the entry advertising show times, meal prices, and pictures of featured entertainers.

A single flyer caught Philip's eye. An attractive young Chinese woman dressed in a skimpy swimming suit adorned one side of the poster. The opposite side beckoned in bold letters a tantalizing message, "Come along please! I'll show you how to have fun—in Chinese." The men sprinted up a flight of stairs to the club called Forbidden City.

The ballroom was visible through the anteroom, which opened into a wide passageway. Expansive and grand, the space was filled with tables covered in white linen. All were ornamented with small rice-paper lanterns and graced with a full service of white china and silver. The tables formed an elongated U and surrounded a wooden parquet dance floor that jutted out in front of a large stage. An extravagant red-velvet curtain stretched behind the entire width of the stage. Pagoda roofs, gold-gilded ceilings, and festive, colorful rice-paper screens depicting Chinese characters, dragons, and ancient Chinese architecture all added to the ambience. The décor gave Philip the distinct feeling that he had been dropped into a nightclub in the real Forbidden City of Peking, China.

A petite Chinese woman greeted the party of four at the reservation desk, asking, "May I help you, gentlemen?"

Dressed in their uniforms, they were simply ordinary customers to the hostess, until Wilson spoke. "Captain Thomas Wilson, ma'am. I believe I have a reservation for four."

"Yes sir, Captain Wilson. Right this way." With a gesture, the hostess signaled a man dressed in a black tuxedo waiting in the entrance to the ballroom and dining area.

The man approached. "Captain Wilson?"

"Yes, sir," Wilson responded in his distinctive Southern accent.

"It is my honor to meet you. I'm Frank Huie, manager of the Forbidden City. Please follow me. Right this way, sir. Mr. Low will be joining you later."

Mr. Huie escorted the Wilson party to a table near the stage. Philip looked at Winter and shrugged his shoulders as if to say, *Why the royal treatment?* "What's the deal? Do they treat all of us GIs like this?" he whispered. "And who's Mr. Low?"

"I don't know," Winter said. Once the party was seated, he asked, "Hey, Bo! Do you know all these guys personally or what?"

"You might say that. Charlie Low, the owner here, has a cousin who used to live in the Philippines. One night I was just sittin' by myself in a bar in Manila, minding my own business. I look over and some smart-ass Army lieutenant is giving this Chinese woman a tough time. I mean he's really being a total jerk, calling her all sorts of terrible names, had his grimy paws all over her. She kept asking him to leave her alone, but he was too drunk to know any better. I stepped in and asked him nicely to leave the lady alone. That's all."

"Bullshit!" cried Winter. "I heard the story from some guys who were there. The lieutenant got mouthy with Bo, so Bo grabbed his gonads and lifted him right off his damn stool."

Everyone laughed.

"Coulda' been a scuffle, I guess. I'm guessing I had too damn much to drink, too, that's for sure." Wilson's soft drawl heightened his attempt at modesty. "I guess the doll was grateful that I helped her out, and we sort a hit it off after that. Anyway, we became friends, if you know what I mean, so when things got hot over there, I told her I had some buddies who were transporting Americans back to the States. I just got her a ride here to California, that's all."

A cocktail waitress appeared. The GIs ordered a round of drinks.

Winter and Burnside requested scotch and sodas, and Philip an old-fashioned.

Wilson was the last to order. "I'll have a Cuba libre, darlin'. And please put that on my tab, ma'am."

"I sorry, sir, but Mr. Low tell me all drinks at this table on the house."

"Well, please tell him that's mighty kind of him." Once she left, Wilson continued his story. "So, I show up here after I get out of the hospital, a little R & R, you know, and I'll be danged, but this young beauty is a dancer right here at the Forbidden City. One night, I decided to wait for her after the show. She remembered me right away. Southern-boy charm, I suppose." Wilson smiled with less modesty now. "We went out for breakfast and then just kinda picked up where we left off, if you know what I mean."

Winter laughed. "Yeh, Bo, we know what you mean. We knew the first time."

Wilson continued, "That's when I found out she was Charlie's cousin. Charlie had heard about how I defended her and asked her if he could meet me. Ever since then we've been pretty good pals. So now whenever I come here, he takes care of me." Wilson paused to wink, then continued, "And my friends."

Philip may not have been at all familiar with the Asian culture, but he understood the meaning of loyalty to one's family.

Winter raised his scotch and soda. "A toast to our hosts, to Captain Bo and Mr. Low!"

"Damn," said Burnsy. "So, Chuck, now you're a poet, too? Hell, yeh, cheers!"

The soldiers around the table hoisted their glasses and repeated, "Cheers! To Bo and Low!"

CHAPTER 38

Living for Entertainment

HOURS PASSED AND DRINKS FLOWED. Philip could see that Bo Wilson was a good man. No wonder Charlie Low held him in such high regard. A complimentary three-course Chinese dinner followed the men's third round of cocktails, delighting their senses with scintillating aromas and flavors.

As they were cleaning the last remnants of the sumptuous meal from their plates, a full orchestra appeared onstage and began playing an assortment of big band music. The dance floor filled quickly. From behind the curtain a young man appeared and took the microphone as the dancers stopped to applaud.

"Larry Ching," reported Wilson. "The Chinese Frank Sinatra."

Ching began to croon, and Philip was almost immediately transported back in his mind to the Casino. Even the lyrics were fitting.

> "I'll be seeing you in all the old, familiar places
> That this heart of mine embraces all day through . . ."

Larry Ching held the last note with a smooth tone that Sinatra himself might have admired. A Chinese man dressed in a tuxedo with a white jacket and shirt and black trousers and bow tie emerged from behind the orchestra and stood at the microphone. "Let's hear it for Larry Ching." The crowd applauded once again. "Ladies and gentlemen. A special welcome this evening to all of our brave soldiers and sailors." A cheer erupted.

"That's Charlie Low," Wilson informed his tablemates.

"We have some special surprises for you this evening. Very special. But before we get started, everyone repeat after me: We live for entertainment."

The crowd responded in enthusiastic unison. "We live for entertainment!"

Philip looked around the room. Hundreds of people were jammed into the ballroom. GIs mingled with nurses, all in uniform. Some GIs danced with civilian women. Young dandies in tuxedos shared cocktails with California actresses and models. Movie stars or not, the civilian women wore luxurious, shimmering evening gowns, so tight they looked as if they'd been poured into them. Standing four-deep at the fifty-foot bar or seated at a table for four or more, the audience was ready and willing to be entertained. The smell of sweat and smoke mingled with the sweet bouquet of jasmine and burning candles.

"So, here we go," Charlie Low continued. "Please welcome the Tai Sings Dancers."

Philip was spellbound. The Tai Sings Dancers performed a traditional Chinese dance and then removed their fabulous cheongsams to reveal scanty burlesque outfits.

"Damn, Z," Burnsy sighed to Philip, "these gals are *exotic*."

Philip nodded without taking his eyes off them.

The movement of the chorus line combined synchronized elegance and titillating dance steps. The dancers formed a kick line in a V. Once the line separated, Mai and Wilbur Tai Sing glided onto the dance floor. Waltzing, they appeared to be almost floating on air. The Tai Sings and their dancers received a rousing applause.

As the orchestra struck up "Taking the A Train," Charlie Low approached the Wilson table carrying a magnum of champagne. Following close behind Mr. Low was an attractive Chinese woman.

Wilson rose from his chair, kissed the woman on the cheek, and offered her his chair. She accepted. Two tuxedoed men immediately produced chairs for both Wilson and Low.

"Boys," Wilson announced, "I would like y'all to meet the owner of this fine establishment, Mr. Charlie Low, and his cousin, Dai Low."

By now, all the men were standing. Wilson made the introductions. They paid their respects to Mr. and Miss Low and took their seats.

Low moved his chair next to Philip and set the large bottle of champagne on the table. "This ought to hold you boys for a while," Low said as he uncorked the bottle. With a loud *POP!* the cork sailed toward the ceiling.

Wilson nodded his gratitude toward the owner. "That's mighty kind of you, Charlie."

"This him?" Low inquired of Wilson.

"Yes, sir, sure is."

"Captain Wilson tell me you play a pretty good piano!" exclaimed Low.

Philip wasn't sure how he should respond to Low's inquiry. He didn't have to. Burnside took over.

"Yes, sir, you oughta hear Philip play, Mr. Low. He's a real Eddy Duchin. Real smooth. When he plays Gershwin's 'Rhapsody in Blue,' why, it's like old George himself is playin' it. He plays the whole danged thing from memory, no sheet music or nothin'. Philip's the real deal, sir." Burnside might as well have signed up right then and there to become Philip's talent agent.

"Would you please play that for us here, my friend? 'Rhapsody in Blue' is one of my favorites. It would be an honor to have a serviceman perform for us. The orchestra's piano is already onstage. The rest of you boys, enjoy this bottle of Dom Pérignon. 1926. Very good year! You Captain Wilson's friends, you friends of Charlie Low."

The piano beckoned Philip to the stage. "I'd be honored to play for you, Mr. Low."

Philip followed Charlie Low to the stage and stood before the overflow crowd. Low gave him a grand introduction. "You want to be entertained?"

The audience responded with an enthusiastic "Yes!"

"This soldier a warrior, and a piano player, too. I give you Mr. Philip Zumwalt. Please."

The patrons joined Charlie in polite applause. Philip sat at the ebony Steinway grand piano as the audience quieted. Striking the opening notes with confidence, he felt instantly at home. His fingers danced across the smooth keys with precision. His face lit up with a smile of delight, his head bobbing and his body swaying. Rhythm and melody exploded with grandeur from the belly of the exquisite instrument. His fingers skipped, bounced, and leaped—left to right on the keyboard, striking low notes, then high notes. It was as if his fingers were an extension of his soul frolicking across the ivory and ebony keys. As he struck the final note, the patrons rose as one, exploding with applause and cheers of "Bravo!" Philip took several bows and, flushed with excitement, headed back to his table.

Charlie and Dai Low were still standing as Philip approached the table. "You got job here after this war over," said Low, still applauding.

"Damn, boy, you're good!" Wilson slapped Philip on the back.

"Thank you, sir."

"No 'sirs' here tonight. In the Forbidden City, we're just GIs havin' a good time. I'll be back fightin' in the Pacific with you boys soon, maybe a month or less, so let's just have some fun tonight. And till I get over there with you, don't let those mosquitos swallow you up." Wilson's laugh boomed and echoed across the room.

CHAPTER 39

A Formidable Foe

WILSON'S ELATION TRAILED OFF as the evening wore on. Looking at these young soldiers soon destined for combat, he turned serious. "Here's one thing you boys need to know, might put your minds to ease a bit. B-17s are great airplanes. Over fifty thousand pounds with a wingspan of a hundred feet or more. Powerful as hell. Four twelve-hundred-horsepower Wright engines. *Flying Fortresses.* Sturdy. Reliable. That's what they are, no doubt about it. And on top of all that, a range of almost four thousand miles."

Philip, Burnside, and Winter could fill in the rest. Learning about B-17s had been part of their training. The Flying Fortress flew at a ceiling of thirty-seven thousand feet with a maximum speed of 323 mph. The typical Fortress was armed with at least six fifty-caliber machine guns, one thirty-caliber machine gun, and a bombload of forty-eight hundred pounds. Its minimum crew usually consisted of nine men, including a pilot, copilot, navigator, bombardier, engineer, radio operator, ball turret gunner, waist gunner, and tail gunner. Most of the enlisted men's positions might soon be assigned to any one of them.

"Never underestimate your enemy, fellas," Wilson warned. "The Japs are tough SOBs, just like us. They got a pretty good hold on the Pacific right now." He smiled at Dai. "But we're gonna win this goddamned war and then this beautiful woman and I can start a family of our own."

Dai smiled back with a vigorous nod. She leaned in closer to Wilson, and he squeezed her petite hand in his large, calloused one. Philip felt happy for the lovers, although it made him miss El even more.

Mr. Low excused himself. Winding his way through the crowd, he sat down at a table with movie stars Jane Wyman and Ronald Reagan. Dai stayed moored to Wilson, gracefully sipping on her flute of Dom Pérignon.

Philip was enjoying his last stateside "soirée," as Doc Robinson might have called this extraordinary evening. Part of his plan had been fulfilled. Traveling far from Illinois, he had seen the magnificence of the Atlantic Ocean, the Gulf of Mexico, and now the Pacific. He had ridden the rails through states he'd only previously read about in histories of the Civil War or geography books.

He figured Wilson was right. Out in that wide expanse of ocean beyond the bay, he would face men from another culture, and he wondered if he would be able to kill another human being. Some of the men he might kill were no more responsible for the attack on Pearl Harbor than he was. In all probability, they believed they were defending what they loved, just like him.

No regrets tonight though. Playing Gershwin on a Steinway in the Forbidden City nightclub in front of an adoring audience of hundreds of people made this a night to remember.

After downing his fourth old-fashioned, Philip reminded Winter and Burnside they had a plane to catch. Thomas Beauregard Wilson had made a lasting impression. An officer and a gentleman, albeit a drunken officer and gentleman on this evening, Bo Wilson had taught the former teacher a lesson he would never forget: Do not, under any circumstances, underestimate your enemy.

"There's one good thing about serving in the South West Pacific, boys," Wilson said. "If you live long enough to get a furlough, those Aussie women are incredible." Wilson winked and flashed his charming smile at Dai. "Of course, they're not as fine as the women right here in good old San Francisco."

I wonder if the Australian women are exotic, Philip thought, smiling, although he had no intention of partaking.

Mr. Low returned to the table. "I wish you all good luck." He looked straight at Philip, "Young man, I mean what I said earlier. You very talented. Stay alive over there, and after you get back to the States, give me a call. The world need to hear the kind of music you play. It make us all better people."

"I couldn't agree with you more, sir," Philip responded. "Music sure does lift the soul."

Low extended his hand to Philip. "You call me Charlie. Okay?"

"Uh, sure . . . Charlie." Philip shook Low's hand and then watched as he disappeared into the crowd.

Wilson slurred as he seconded Philip's assertion. "You're right about one thing, son. Music sure does lift the soul. Why, there's even a rhythm to the smooth runnin' of a plane's engine or a bomb whistlin' a tune of doom as it drops outa' the bomb bay or the poppin' of the fifty cals. Yes sir, my boy, the music of war. That's what that is. And that'll stir your soul. I goddamn guarantee it."

Philip swirled the ice in his glass, took one last swig, and rounded up his pals. He wondered if his soul would really be stirred. They thanked Wilson and left him with the gorgeous Dai Low and another Cuba libre.

The inebriated soldiers caught a cab and headed for Hamilton Field. The war was waiting for them. The evening had been enlightening for many reasons. As for Philip, he left with an appreciation for his new Chinese friends. They were good, decent human beings. He regretted that some Americans continued to cling to the antiquated idea of "The Yellow Peril," although Asian, Chinese, and Japanese were not the same. Still, many Americans feared both. Philip felt such fears were unwarranted. The Japanese had attacked Pearl Harbor. They were now the enemy, not China. He knew for certain he would someday return to the Forbidden City and play the piano once again for Charlie and Dai. But after spending an evening with Captain Bo, he also knew another thing for certain: What he was about to face was going to be no soirée.

CHAPTER 40

A Vast Expanse

NEWS OF THE VICTORY AT MIDWAY flew through the ranks and lifted morale. Philip jotted a quick note to El. He couldn't wait to fill her in on his thrilling experience at the Forbidden City.

June 7, 1942
Dear E!,

Packed and ready to go. We're scheduled to begin our flight tonight at midnight. One of Winter's high school buddies took us to a fancy nightclub, The Forbidden City in San Francisco. It was quite a shock to me when the owner of the place, Mr. Low, asked me to play the piano. Evidently, Winter had told Captain Wilson, our host, that I could play. So, I did! On a grand Steinway. It was amazing. There were hundreds of folks all dressed up in tuxedos and fancy dresses and quite a few GIs also, even a few nurses. Anyway, it was truly grand, just like the piano. Ha!

I talked with Captain Wilson late into the night. He was wounded in the Philippines, even got some medals for combat. Quite a guy. He let me know that we were headed into some tough times, but I don't want you to worry. I told you that I'm coming back from this crazy war, and I will. I miss you, my darling, but I will write as soon as we land in Australia. In spite of everything, I have to admit

that this is an exhilarating experience. I hope things are going well
for you. I think it's only appropriate that you should be at Blessing
Hospital, for you surely are that for me. Have to finish packing.
   All my love,
   Philip

Philip, Winter, and Burnside abided by the enlisted men's favorite dictum, *hurrying* back to Hamilton Field just in time to *wait* almost twenty-four hours to take off. Midnight on June 8 found them airborne, heading for Hickam Field on the island of Oahu, Hawaii.

During the nearly fifteen-hour flight, the side gunner turned to Philip. "Hey, pal. You ever fired one a those?" He pointed at a fifty-caliber machine gun.

"No, sir," Philip answered the staff sergeant.

The sergeant looked over his shoulder toward the cockpit. Making certain no officer heard his reply over the roar of the B-17 engines, he approached Philip and whispered in his ear, "Don't call me sir, son. I work for a livin'."

"Yes, si—I mean sergeant," Philip replied sheepishly. The gunner gestured for Philip to move into position to fire. Philip settled in behind the machine gun. "Isn't this against regulations, sergeant?"

"Naw, what the hell, you'll need a little practice before one a them Zeroes comes at ya wantin' to blow your balls off."

Philip cautiously pulled the trigger. Startled by the force, the recoil, and the noise generated by the weapon, he was surprised by how powerful he felt. He pitied the enemy that had the misfortune of being struck by one of the lead-coated rounds that went whizzing out into the dark.

Wilson had told Philip the Pacific Ocean was two and a half times larger than the Atlantic and that all the world's land mass would fit nicely into the Pacific with plenty of room left over. "Water as far as the eye can see, son! The sky and the ocean meet, and if you didn't have instrumentation, you wouldn't have any idea where in the hell you were." Wilson had not painted a pretty picture of aerial combat in the South Pacific. The ocean that once seemed so far away stretched out beneath Philip's plane.

The sergeant confirmed Wilson's observation. "Lotta fuckin' water down there, boy. Ya better hope this old junk heap don't go down." He belted out a hearty belly laugh.

Wilson had also given Philip a stern warning. "Being lost in the Pacific means almost certain death. Being shot down by the enemy, being the victim of mechanical failure, or even running out of fuel all carry the same sentence. One mistake by a pilot, a copilot, a navigator, or an engineer could result in your ship ending up in the drink—a place that's already a graveyard for hundreds of flyboys."

After Philip's initial exposure to a fifty-caliber machine gun, he nodded off to sleep with the staccato beats of the weapon's discharge dancing in his head.

June 9, 1942

After a decent night's sleep, Philip and his crew landed at Hickam Field, Oahu, Hawaii, at 4 p.m. Hawaii time. Three days had passed since he'd sipped cocktails and taken the stage at the Forbidden City. All that was now a world away. The plane flew over Pearl Harbor. Looking out the window, Philip couldn't believe what he was seeing—ships, planes, buildings so blown apart he could barely distinguish one from the other. Witnessing such devastation roiled his gut. He recognized his anger as an alien feeling, one he had rarely experienced. His fists unclenched. Having surveyed the damage, he understood something new. One of the sergeant's comments stuck in his brain: "Some say we're too damned soft. We were lucky the Japs retreated after Pearl Harbor. They totally kicked our ass." Philip hoped he wouldn't be soft. He wondered if what he felt was hatred or revenge or both. It didn't matter.

Reports of superior Japanese air, naval, and land forces spread through the ranks. Despite the odds, Philip was confident he and his brothers in arms would prevail. Upon their arrival at Hickam, he and his crewmates found bunks and slept for nearly seventeen hours. He would remain in Hawaii until June 22.

Hickam Field, Hawaii (Oahu)

I landed there six months after the raid that started our war with Japan, but battle scars were still everywhere. Wrecked planes, bullet marks on hangars, bomb scars, all could be seen. The barracks showed only too well what had happened there. No windows, bullet holes in lockers, stains on the sidewalks, machine gun marks on the walls. Pearl Harbor just across the fence suffered as much. The whole story was not told at home. Our Navy suffered more than realized. I have talked with many who lived through that day of hell, and I hope to never go through the same . . .

It was later in the evening before his departure when he wrote to Billy Epperson.

June 21, 1942
Dear Kid,

Hope the Army is treating you well. I find it hard to believe that you signed up to jump out of a perfectly good airplane. As for me, I hope I never have to use my parachute. Word in the Stars and Stripes *is that General Bradley is getting you fellows into fighting shape. Do take care, old friend, and punch Adolf in the nose for me if you get a chance. I honestly think if it weren't for him, we wouldn't be in this mess. We're scheduled to leave Hawaii tomorrow and, after some island hopping, we ought to get to Australia by the end of the month. Went through Hickam Field and Pearl Harbor. Reminded all of us why we are fighting.*

Hawaii is a paradise, no doubt about that, and the Pacific Ocean is beautiful. It's blue for as far as the eye can see. The water that comes down from the mountains is crystal clear and cold as an Illinois January morning. I've mostly been reading and playing the piano at the PX. The good news is that I'm drawing per diem pay. I've received 170 bucks in actual cash up to yesterday. It's my intention to save up enough money to be able to buy El a ring, but please don't spill the beans to Pat. Any word on the rest of the Posse?

Made some great friends and spent a memorable night in San Francisco. Got to play the piano at The Forbidden City nightclub—quite a gig.

Saw a mongoose the other day. They have some rather odd animals in these parts. We heard some gunshots last night. Rumors floating around that it was a Jap submarine. Been reading, doing crossword puzzles, and got my third tetanus shot. It rains here pretty constantly; this place is a sea of mud. Lt. Emery says we should be sergeants within 3 to 4 months. I hope so, but it sounds too good to be true. I could sure use the extra dough.

Actually got to drink some real milk for breakfast the other day, first glass since leaving the States. I sure do miss good old American food. Mother wasn't the greatest cook, but even her meals were gourmet compared to Army chow. I yearn for some good fried chicken or pot roast. Makes my mouth water just to think of it.

We flew over several volcanoes, one of which, Mauna Loa, is still active. Smoke was rising out of the crater. One mountain was so high that there was snow on top of it. A couple of my buddies were involved in the Midway battle. They said it was terrifying and the noise was deafening. Met a guy from Galesburg, Illinois, named Driscoll and discovered that we know quite a few of the same people—small world, especially I suppose when we are at war.

I'd better sign off. Take care of yourself, Billy, and give my love to Pat if you talk to her. I haven't heard from El lately, but I think the mail has a tough time catching up with us. I hope General Bradley's not working you guys too hard in that Louisiana heat.

Congratulations on getting your butter bar. Thank Heavens I don't have to take any orders from you. I imagine I'll be getting commissioned in the near future either as a communications officer or if I finally get my orders to return to the States for flight school. Keep me posted on Inness and Trout. I fear that they might be over here already with the Marines. Word is that it's going to be some tough slogging. We have to secure a foothold in the Solomon Islands. If we don't, the Japs will be able to control the South West Pacific, and if Australia falls, we're in big trouble. I have no idea where we're headed, and if I did, I couldn't write it here (censors). Just got word we fly to an atoll tomorrow. Hard to believe that a year ago we were having the time of our lives in Siloam State Park. Funny how life has a way of keeping us humble. Stay in touch.

   Posse forever,
   Nelly

The following morning, Philip rolled out of his bunk at 4:00 a.m., showered, shaved, and ate breakfast before boarding the plane that would take him and his crew closer to Australia. They flew to Palmyra Island, an uneventful trip, other than he was able to get some practice operating the radio onboard. He later jotted in his diary, *Palmyra is a ring of sand with some palm trees on it and a lagoon in the middle. Covered with guns and planes . . .*

The next day they were off to Canton Island, another ring of land with a lagoon in the center. Crossing the equator and international date line drew an explanation from Bobby Freeman, an airman they picked up in Palmyra. "In the States, it's Wednesday, but here on the other side of the international date line it's Thursday. Today in the States is tomorrow here. We just jumped from Wednesday to Thursday. Lost a day, vanished into thin air. Yesterday is today."

"Suits me just fine," responded Winter. "A six-day week. Just as long as they pay us our humongous salary for the entire month—and we get our per diem."

"Thirty bucks a month. Yahoo!" Burnside added sarcastically. "Maybe enough for some pretty native girl to do my laundry for me. But what the hell? We get free room and board—a real bargain."

"Where we're goin'," moaned Freeman, "I doubt if they have laundry service of any kind. From what I hear, all there is over there are flies, snakes, mosquitos, and Japs."

A five-and-a-half-hour flight on June 26 landed them in New Caledonia, where the airport runway was pure iron ore. The air was heavy with red brick dust, blanketing anything not covered with tarps or sheets. The dust reminded Philip of home. He was a long way from the brown, dusty streets of Nebo, a place he thought he would never again call home. Now, getting back there, and back to El, was all he thought about.

Landing at Amberly Field in Ipswich, Queensland, on June 27, the trip of seventy-eight hundred miles from California to Australia was complete. Philip and his friends were grateful to set foot on solid soil but anxious and uncertain about their next duty station.

Freeman's announcement upon their arrival wasn't exactly what they wanted to hear. "Yessiree, boys, if we aren't careful, this place might end up being our permanent home. The United States Air Force made a cemetery right here. Buried their first soldier here last month. I suppose there'll be quite a few to follow." A disconcerted look passed among the men. "I sure as shit don't wanna spend eternity in this hellhole, and I'm pretty certain none of you do either, so let's not be one of them."

"You got that right!" Winter exclaimed.

"Okay then," Freeman continued, "let's find ourselves a bar and drink to that."

The boys came across a broken-down bar—no Forbidden City,

but it would have to do. They spent the rest of the night toasting one another's health and well-being while sloshing down Australian beer. None of them had any intention of ending up six feet under in the Ipswich, Queensland's Cemetery. That was a toast they could all drink to.

On Saturday, June 27, 1942, Philip made the final entry in his first diary:

Ate supper and given a bed in a converted hangar. Took a shower, had a coke at the PX . . . then called it a day.

Back in the States, it was still Friday, June 26, 1942. Philip wondered what El was doing in Gem City on a hot summer Friday night. *Most likely tending to the needs of her patients,* he concluded. Nurse El. An angel of mercy, radiant in her freshly ironed Cadet Nurse uniform, full of life, exuberant, spreading her euphoria from room to room.

Philip looked forward to tomorrow. Wasting no time on the perplexity of the international date line, he purchased his second diary and began to record what life was like in the South West Pacific with the Fifth Air Force. What tomorrow held was unknown. He supposed that was always the way it was. Tonight, he would content himself with a good night's sleep and maybe be lucky enough to muster up a dream of his beautiful nurse back home.

CHAPTER 41

The Joads, Steinbeck, Rabaul, and Dostoevsky

Charleville, Australia
July 15, 1942

PHILIP AND BURNSY LEANED OVER their steaming cups of morning coffee at the Paris Café. Worn wooden tables and chairs were scattered throughout the narrow patio under a bright-red canvas awning. A blackboard scrawled with white chalk advertised available food items, daily specials, and prices. Rain dripped off the awning, adding to the dreariness of the day. Burnsy wore his olive drab field jacket over his fatigues to combat the inclement weather. Philip opted for his overcoat. Burnsy lit a Camel cigarette and opened his book, *The Grapes of Wrath*, to a bookmarked page.

"Any good?" asked Philip.

"Not bad, kinda depressing, all about this poor family called Joad."

"You bring it from home?"

"Naw, got it from the chaplain's library. Steinbeck's a good writer. I got a letter the other day from a buddy of mine in Aviation Cadet school. He said word is that Steinbeck was hanging out with some B-17 guys and the Army commissioned him to write a book about guys like us."

"If he wants real excitement he ought to fly over here and follow us around. He could title his book, *Waiting for War* or *The Soldiers Who Died from Boredom*." Philip was sick and tired of waiting around. Where in the hell were his orders for AvCad? The acronym SNAFU didn't even begin to describe the inefficiency of the U.S. Army Air Force.

Burnsy took a drag of his cigarette and snickered his distinctive chuckle. He returned to his book, but not for long. "Word on the street is that Dugout Doug is moving his HQ to Brisbane," he reported.

"Oh." Philip was reading his own book, *The Last of the Mohicans*.

"Yeh, the son of a bitch is the fuckin' Supreme Commander of the entire South West Pacific Theater now, even though he ran like a chickenshit out of the Philippines and left General Wainwright on Corregidor to surrender."

"Yeh. Pretty gutless." Philip didn't look up.

"He picked Kenney as the boss of the entire Fifth Army Air Corps."

"I heard Kenney's a good man."

"Let's just hope he keeps the Japs outa' our hair."

"I think that's our job, Burnsy."

"I guess, but I hear tell that we're gonna be flying outa' New Guinea."

"Really?"

"I looked it up, Z. Second goddamned biggest island on the entire planet. Said so right there in the encyclopedia in the chaplain's library. On the Pacific Ring of Fire. Jungles, rivers, swamps, rain forests, mountains, and a boatload of wild, nasty animals and natives."

"Sounds like paradise," Philip quipped, squinting over the top of his book. "Why in the world are we going there?" Burnsy had grabbed his interest.

"Glad you're finally paying attention, turd."

Philip laughed. "No need to get personal."

"Japs took the port of Rabaul, New Britain, in February of this year. There was an Australian Army garrison stationed there called the Lark Force. They put up a good fight, but the Japs won. Now Rabaul is the major Jap base for navy and land forces in the South West Pacific. And they're pretty damned close to Australia, if you get my drift."

"I get it." Philip nodded. "We've got to keep the Japs pinned down on Rabaul. I suppose it helped that we won at Midway."

"It did, but there's a helluva lot of little islands out there that the marines have got to take before we can gain any control for sure."

"I hope we aren't headed to New Guinea soon. I kind of like it here. Hey, did you say the chaplain has a library?" Philip asked, putting his book down.

"Yeh, he's got some pretty decent books. You might check it out." Burnside sipped on his coffee, took a drag off his cigarette, and turned a page.

Philip thought Burnsy would be considered by some a pseudo-intellectual, but his broad chest, floppy hair, and brusque, profanity-ridden manner could physically intimidate even the toughest soldier. Philip found the place where he had left off and continued reading. Both men read in silence, except for the clinking of glasses and coffee cups being gathered by the waiter. Up to this point, his duty station in Charleville had been tedious and monotonous.

When Philip returned to camp for dinner, all hell broke loose. Later, he recorded the event.

> Thurs. July 16
> . . . Just as we were sitting down to dinner, the air raid siren went off and we had to drop everything and run to tents. Grabbing our guns, gas masks and helmets . . . Freeman and I took out for the woods, ending up about a quarter mile from the field. After waiting an hour, nothing happened, so we came back. The all-clear signal sounded just as we got back to the mess hall, so we finished eating.

Following the false alarm, Philip headed to the mail tent and picked up a letter mailed from the States nearly a month earlier. As always, he recognized the familiar handwriting and anxiously tore open the envelope.

June 21, 1942

Dearest Philip,

Finally got a break from rounds and allowed to go home for a day. Pops and Momma picked me up and we arrived in Payson just in time to partake of one of Miss Betsy's scrumptious meals. I won't detail it because I daresay I don't want your mouth to water—rather unseemly.

The last time I was home, I spent a little time in our library. One of the doctors at the hospital, Ernest Thoroughgood, and I have become good friends. His name describes him well. He's a really good man. Don't worry, I filled him in on the competition. He knows <u>all</u> about you. Anyway, he told me I should read a book by this Russian author, Dostoevsky. It's about these brothers. I do like it very much. I am certain you would love it. Right up your alley. I think I would rather read about women, but that's another story, I guess. We had the book in our library at the house, so I read it. Parts I hated. Mean, mean people, deceitful, lying, terrible. But there were a couple of parts I knew immediately that I wanted to share with you. One portion reminded me so of you. Dostoevsky wrote, "Things flow and are indirectly linked together, and if you push here, something will move at the other end of the world. If you strike here, something somewhere will wince; if you sin here, something somewhere will suffer."

I hate to think of you being a sinner, I know you're not. I hate to think of you suffering, but I know you are. What you're going through with all of your friends is unimaginable to me or any of the rest of us on this other end of the world who are safely going to bed every night because you're defending us and this country and freedom. But we're all linked together—my thoughts, my spirit is linked to yours. It is linked with this unbelievable love I feel for you deep inside of me, which brings me to another quote from the same book I want to share with you:

"Love all God's creation, the whole and every grain of sand in it. Love every leaf, every ray of God's light. Love the animals, love the plants, <u>love everything</u>. If you love everything, you will perceive the divine mystery in things. Once you perceive it, you will begin to understand it better every day. And you will come at last to love the whole world with an all-embracing love."

Isn't that beautiful? Just think if everyone would abide by that idea, if we could just love everything? I am sure you think me childishly innocent, but sometimes we must have a dream of how things can be, not how things are, how horribly terrible they are for you and for me because of where you are and what you have to do. I do know this, Philip. Life is a mystery, especially during this terrible, terrible time, but if it is a divine mystery and if I want to better understand it, I need to try and love everything. I hope you know that I realize how dreadful this war is, as far as I can imagine it, but you must try, try to find some love somewhere, my dear. It is all that might get you through this awful ordeal. That is what I wish for you, a Great Love, one like ours, but maybe even one that exceeds ours. That is my wish. Please write whenever you have an opportunity. Your letters make my day.

All my love,

El

CHAPTER 42

The Chaplain's Library

July 18, 1942

EL'S LETTER AND BURNSIDE'S TIP ABOUT a library led Philip to visit the local chaplain. It was a cloudless Saturday morning when he walked into the chaplain's office. A handsome, middle-aged black man with snow-white hair greeted him.

"Reverend Donald Kelley at your service, young man. How are things in the Army Air Force?" On each of the lapels of the chaplain's jacket was a gold pin displaying the letters U.S., and below each pin rested a silver cross. A pair of silver bars were embroidered on the middle of the epaulets resting upon the chaplain's shoulders.

Philip was not interested in discussing the Army Air Force or even his faith. All he wanted was access to some books. "Fine, sir. Should I call you Father or Captain?"

"Oh, neither, my boy." The chaplain laughed. "I'm Protestant. Methodist, to be exact. Not Catholic. That would be either Father Norman Mirabelli, or Father Thomas Shea." The pastor had a good sense of humor, and Philip immediately liked him. "Father Mirabelli's over in Brisbane, Shea's at Port Moresby. If you're Catholic, that is. And if you would, please just call me Reverend. You're new around here, aren't you?"

"Yes, sir. Came over end of June."

"Well, I'm here to help. No high-pressure tactics around this place to bring you to the Lord. Entirely up to you. But if you do need someone to talk to, I want you to feel free to stop by. I'm not here to judge you or anyone else, so don't be afraid to tell me what you're really thinking. Please, have a seat, son."

Philip sat at a small, round wooden table across from the chaplain. Softening a bit, he replied, "I think I've gotten myself into a real mess, Reverend. That's what I think. And right now, I'm just trying to figure it all out."

"Combat yet?" the chaplain asked.

"No, sir, not yet. What I'm really here for is to find a book. My buddy told me you had a pretty good library here."

"Well, I think we do, if I do say so myself. Browse as long as you'd like." The reverend gestured toward an open doorway and led Philip into his humble library.

Philip followed Kelley into the small room, full of dusty shelves and books. "Any classics? I'm looking for a book by Dostoevsky."

"Up on that top shelf to your right. I believe you'll find his books there. All the books are arranged alphabetically by author."

Philip gazed up. Allen, *Anthony Adverse*. Balzac, *Droll Stories*. Barringer, *Gerfalcon*. Bellamann, *Kings Row*. There it was: Dostoevsky, *The Brothers Karamazov*, *Crime and Punishment*, *Notes from Underground*, and one titled *The Idiot*.

He climbed a few rungs up the ladder and grabbed *The Brothers Karamazov*. He continued to consider the books remaining on the shelves. Roberts, *Northwest Passage*. Sandburg, *Lincoln: The Prairie Years II*. "Any Hemingway or Fitzgerald?"

"Nope. Can't keep those fellas on the shelf. Soldiers run off with 'em and never return them."

"Too bad. They're fine writers. A friend of mine first recommended them to me. Is the book about the brothers any good? I have two myself—brothers, that is." Philip laughed. "Another friend of mine from back home told me I should read this one."

"Sounds like you have quite a few friends back home, son."

"I'd like to think so, sir."

"In my opinion, *The Brothers Karamazov* by Dostoevsky is one of the finest pieces of literature up there. Of course, being from Illinois, I'm a bit partial to the Sandburg biography of Lincoln, but we only have the second volume of *The Prairie Years.* My goodness, I sound like a librarian, don't I?"

"Not at all, sir. Where are you from in Illinois?"

"Galesburg. Birthplace of the poet and Lincoln's biographer, Carl Sandburg. I suppose that's why I'm partial to Mr. Lincoln. Illinois boy and all."

"I'm from Illinois, too."

"Oh, whereabouts?"

"A small village called Nebo."

"Nothing wrong with small towns! Always good, God-fearing folks in small towns."

"I agree with that. You certainly seem to know quite a bit about literature, Reverend," Philip said.

"Well, I've had the opportunity to read quite a bit at night." Reverend Kelley smiled. "You boys normally come in the next day to confess your sins."

"I thought you weren't Catholic."

"Doesn't deter your buddies. They just want to talk, and so often it has to do with some sort of justification for what they think is sin. I just tell them that's their choice—sort of the message in the book about the brothers you asked about."

"Really? I think I did read one of his other books in World Literature class at Western. One of those up there." Philip pointed. "Yes, there it is. *Crime and Punishment.* He was a Russian, right?"

"Yes, oh yes, he was a Russian, indeed. So, you're a college grad? Not an officer, though?"

"No, sir. Most likely will be soon. Just waiting for my orders."

"I see," replied Kelley. "Well, take the book. Let me know what you think."

"Thank you, sir. I really appreciate this."

"You're most welcome. Enjoy, but I need to warn you, the book is—how can I say it?—a bit dark."

"Well, it couldn't be any darker than this war, could it?"

The good reverend paused and then responded in a sober tone, "I suppose not."

Philip tucked the book under his arm and headed back to his tent. He spent the weekend listening to the radio and devouring the novel. He wanted to immediately write El and tell her how much he loved the book, especially when he came to the portions she had outlined in her letter, but the one part of the book that impacted him the most was a chapter titled "The Grand Inquisitor," a chapter that had confused Philip enough that he wanted to talk it over with Reverend Kelley. Perhaps the good pastor could answer some questions.

Monday evening, after dinner, Philip knocked at Reverend Kelley's door, book in hand.

"My, my, Philip, finished reading the book already?"

"I couldn't put it down."

"Still, my boy, that's an eight-hundred-page novel," replied the reverend. "You must be a very fast reader."

"I guess." Philip focused on Kelley. He hoped this man of God might have some answers. The pastor, in Philip's mind, was both honest and wise. "I found the novel, as you said, a bit disturbing, but also thought-provoking. The chapter entitled 'The Grand Inquisitor' puzzled me, though."

"Not uncommon. That's a reaction of many readers. Come sit, please."

Philip obliged and took a seat once again at the library table. "Why the kiss?"

"An interesting question. You want my opinion?"

"Yes, sir."

The reverend smiled. His gentle, unassuming nature reassured Philip he had come to the right place.

Philip continued, "I was hoping you might be able shed some light on this. Why do you think Jesus kissed the Grand Inquisitor?"

"It's what God does, my son. In the face of the worst evil, he forgives. He understands our humanness. We're all sinners, Philip. The kiss is a symbol of that forgiveness. After all, He knows us because He created us. We can accept Him or not. That is our choice, but He accepts us no matter what."

"No matter what? Even if I drop a bomb out of a plane and kill another human being?"

"That's a tough question to answer, my son, to be sure. One I, too, find confounding. I believe that life is sacred. We've all of us humans been created by God. I suppose I rationalize this war as an answer to good over evil, over tyranny, injustice, the murder of innocents—that perhaps we have an obligation to defend the powerless."

"Perhaps?"

"Listen. I'm not omniscient, only God is, so I just try to figure things out the best I can from this altitude."

"Believe me, Reverend, I haven't found any answers flying around up there, either."

"Not surprising." Kelley's face expressed his compassion.

"We were attacked. I get that. And Hitler's a monster, but I have to tell you, Reverend, this is all quite confusing." Philip's strong and argumentative voice trailed off, lost in a sense of despair and resignation.

Kelley returned to the book discussion. "Let's get back to the Grand Inquisitor, shall we? The Inquisitor is telling Christ that mankind cannot handle free will and that freedom is what causes suffering. If the church just takes over and tells you what to think and how to act, then the church can take over your sin. He accuses Christ of rejecting the powers that could have made it easier for us here on Earth. Christ rejected authority, miracles, and mystery, and now the church has capitalized on all three. The Inquisitor argues that all the people really want is security, not freedom. I suppose that is what's happening right now in Germany, in Italy, in Japan, isn't it?"

"I'm afraid you're right there, Reverend."

"But it doesn't matter. The essence of the kiss is what matters. Forgiveness and love. That, my friend, is the message. Even now. And you must know that you are forgiven and loved by a power greater than you. The toughest part for you boys is that you need to learn to forgive and love yourselves."

"The newspaper reporters write a lot about the ultimate sacrifice our servicemen make. I wonder if that means the ultimate sacrifice is that *we* are going to hell?"

The pain in Philip's eyes was evident to Kelley. "My dear boy, I told you that I do not have all the answers, but I do not believe there is such a place."

"I beg to differ with you, sir. I have talked with men who say they've stormed its gates due north of us in Rabaul."

"On Earth, maybe. But I believe that God is the center of all things, seen and unseen. He loves us and he forgives us. Man created hell, not God. But here is what I do believe, Philip. If there is a hell below or one on earth, I believe God loves you so much, He will even be *there,* in either place, for you."

Philip bowed his head. "When I read the passages my girl from back home sent me, I realized that I should try and love everything, but it seems so impossible. I guess it might be the only way to try to survive, though. That Russian was a pretty wise fella, wasn't he?"

Kelley smiled. "Yes, I think he most certainly was."

Philip handed him the book and extended his hand. "Thank you, sir. Thank you for everything."

The reverend took Philip's hand and placed his other on the young man's shoulder. "Godspeed, Philip, my boy."

As Philip left Reverend Kelley, deep inside he fervently hoped that the man of God and the Russian author were both right. Here at the other end of the world, his actions would have consequences. He wanted to love everything. He truly wanted to perceive the divine mystery in this madness, but he knew sin was inevitable. He was going to need all the love and forgiveness he could possibly receive, and he hoped that God, in His infinite mercy, would indeed be accompanying him to hell.

Philip wanted to follow El's advice, but in war, love seemed so out of reach. Wilson had left him with another piece of advice that sent chills throughout his body. "It's kill or be killed, my good man," he told Philip that night at the Forbidden City. "Kill or be killed. Damn shame, but that's just the way it is." The look on Wilson's face had told Philip all he needed to know about the horror of war he would soon encounter. A chill ran through Philip's entire body. The complete incongruity of war, the fear of the unknown, and the possibility of death prompted him to pen the following, which he sent along with a letter to his brother Homer:

My Will

Since the U.S. is a nation at war and I am a member of her armed forces and faced with the perils that such service carries, I, Philip A. Zumwalt, being of sound mind and body, do make this will. My books are to be given to my brother Wayne, all of my personal possessions to Homer. He has been told what to do with them. All money resulting from my death is to be administered by my mother in the following manner: Wayne is to be given at least one, preferably two years in the university of his choice, to emerge with all possible advanced study in his field. I do this because I feel that Homer is more capable of achieving success on his own. However, if after Wayne is settled on a life work, Homer has not achieved his hopes, I admonish Wayne to provide all financial assistance in his power to see that this is done. They must remember to always help each other

in every way. Any remaining money or income is to be used to make my parents' subsistence more certain. I am not afraid to die, and I beg them not to take my death too hard if it should come.
*   Philip A. Zumwalt*

Having contemplated death a great deal during the past year and having written his last will and testament, the possibility of his death became a reality for Philip. It now permeated his consciousness, his existence. Living on the faint promise of rumors, he and his buddies hoped against all hope that MacArthur was devising a grand plan that would defeat the Japanese in short order. One of his earlier wishes had been granted: His life and the lives of the men in the Sixty-Fourth Squadron was in no way dull.

Nov. 6, 1942

The Nineteenth Bomb Group is definitely going home. The Ninety-Third Squadron is being replaced by the Sixty-Third, the Thirteenth by the Sixty-Fourth, and the Twenty-Eighth by the Sixty-Fifth. The 403rd Squadron, the other member of the Forty-Third Group, is going to Milne Bay. It now seems that the Forty-Third Group is being transferred to Mareeba and an outfit of B-24s is taking their place at Iron Range. The Sixty-Fourth has nine airplanes to work with, and a large number of men, experienced combat crews included, who have not been in Australia long enough to be sent back home will be transferred into the outfit within the next few days. Probably we will see action within the next two weeks. It now seems that my crew will have a major for a pilot—that is, if we remain a crew. My worst fear is that we will be split up completely. If we do fly with the major, I believe that it would be safe to say that six months from now I will either have several medals—or be dead. Certainly I will be an experienced combat man. Even now I am one of the few men in the squadron with any experience at all, and even that experience will not help me in a bombardment outfit. There are only twenty men who have seen as much action as I. All this will be changed when the crews from the Thirtieth come in. Beginning soon, we shall see more combat than most of us want. At least life will not be dull no matter what else it may be, and I'm glad I'm here to see it.

Philip's "combat" missions to this point had been mostly a collection of reconnaissance flights devoid of exchanging fire with the enemy or dropping bombs on designated Japanese targets. The word *combat* would soon take on an entirely new meaning.

CHAPTER 43

First Combat Mission

November 15, 1942

A HALF-TON TRUCK DEPOSITED PHILIP AND HIS CREW to *Taxpayer's Pride,* Plane Number 44448, the designated lead ship assigned to bomb the harbor of Rabaul, New Britain. Take off was scheduled for 1215. Major Jack Bleasdale was the pilot.

Philip was to assume the positions of assistant radio operator and side gunner. He climbed up into the bowels of the Flying Fortress and checked the strap on his fifty-caliber machine gun, making certain the weapon could be swung into action. In order, he double-checked his supply of ammunition, the interphone controls, suit heater outlet, oxygen regulator, and portable oxygen unit. Moving next to the radio operator, Quentin Blakely, he went through the same procedure with the radio equipment, double-checking the command set, the liaison set, radio compass set, interphone equipment, marker beacon equipment, radio altimeter, and IFF radio set.

Each member of the crew conducted his own check of equipment. Philip could hear Bleasdale completing the cockpit list with copilot Lieutenant Adelberger. The major read an item on the checklist, and if it was complete, Adelberger responded with "Check!"

As Philip went through his own procedures, he overheard Bleasdale's litany. It was the same for all B-17 pilots each and every time they put a plane in the air. "Lock tail wheels . . . brakes set . . . interphone on

. . . trim tabs set . . . check generators . . . check manifold pressure . . . run up engines . . . gyro set . . . generators on."

The power of the engines surged, rattling the fuselage and its inhabitants. The checklist was complete, and the major was ready to take his plane into combat. He addressed the crew over the interphone: "Prepare for takeoff."

The Flying Fortress lifted off the ground. The takeoff was smooth, without incident. All nine crewmembers collectively heaved a sigh of relief and settled in to do their jobs. Up front sat the pilots Bleasdale and Adelberger. The navigator, Lieutenant Hansen; the bombardier, Lieutenant Hand; and the engineer, Sergeant Craig, joined them in the forward section of the plane. Blakely and Philip operated the radio and the side guns. Corporal Stewart manned the ball turret gun, and Private Honald was assigned to the tail gun.

Philip dreamed of one day becoming the officer who recited the checklist to his copilot. He smiled, thinking of Billy. *Probably another delusion of grandeur.* He sat back in his seat, content to be a part of this combat crew. The plane flew effortlessly over the Solomon Sea at approximately twenty-five thousand feet. The night was clear, the flight smooth.

Bleasdale pulled back on the B-17's yoke. The plane ascended and headed north. Soon they would fly over the volcanoes on Rabaul, bounce through the ack-ack, and drop their bombs on their designated targets in Simpson Harbour.

The airmen's leather aviator caps and the earphones contained within the earflaps muffled the roar of the engines. With his interphone off, Philip was left with visions of the possible brutality that surrounded his current existence. He preferred thinking about conversations at the club, not much peace and quiet there, but it beat the hell out of what he was about to experience. The silence was deafening. These were infinite spaces, like the ones philosopher Blaise Pascal wrote about in one of the philosophy books Philip had read from the chaplain's library.

Philip was as terrified by these infinite spaces as Pascal had been in the comfort of his cozy study in mid-seventeenth-century France. Had Pascal, or any of the other philosophers, ever endured anything even remotely like what he was about to face? It was easy preaching to his students. He had talked repeatedly of the political ramifications of war, trying his best to explain the intricacies of American foreign policy, discussing the brutality of the Nazis, and vilifying the Japanese for their slaughter of the Chinese in Nanking. He had done his best to not romanticize war while standing in the shelter of his classroom or lounging with El under the shade of the gigantic oak in Payson Park. Even then, he knew war was the furthest thing from being romantic.

Now, here he was, a man of peace, a victim of his own boredom. He had sought out this adventure and would soon come face-to-face with his own naivete. This was no delusion, and it certainly wasn't grandeur. He would never have enlisted had he been aware of what man was capable of doing in a time of war. The damage modern weapons inflicted upon human flesh was beyond a person's imagination.

He had visited friends in the field hospital, talking to them as they lay helpless, missing limbs or eyes or portions of their skulls. Regular guys. They'd shared cocktails and beers, sung around the piano at the Allied Fighting Forces Club, and talked about the things they all had in common—their families, their wives, their children, their girlfriends back home. Without warning, their manhood and their future had been ripped away, replaced with unceasing pain and regret.

Philip had no idea what was coming. He prayed his training was sufficient. His fellow airmen's personal experiences filled in some of the blanks, but they claimed that Wilson had sugarcoated combat. Sitting in his tent or at the club or the USO, Philip had listened intently to the horrors survivors of previous missions had experienced. They spoke in whispers, as if they were afraid that their boasting about survival might somehow curse their next flight.

So, this was glory? Fear engulfed every inch of his body. In a few minutes, fragments of metal and steel-headed bullets might tear him and his fellow crewmembers apart. The aluminum fuselage that encased him and his crew would not impede the projectiles of death. He had heard countless tales of unfathomable damage the indiscriminate rounds might inflict. It was impossible to envision such bloodshed. There was nowhere to run, nowhere to hide inside the bowels of a B-17. Each side was fighting for survival, to protect their friends, their brethren in arms—to defend their own country. None fully understood the mutilation their weapons might cause unless the participant had experienced or witnessed the carnage firsthand. The stench of burning tissue and coagulated blood would be unforgettable. Philip was well aware that the terror wrought by this war would imprint images into men's minds that would haunt the surviving veterans for the rest of their days.

One of his conversations with Ralph Guthrie came to mind. "We'll probably have to go to war, Philip," Guthrie had prognosticated. "But remember what Thomas Jefferson once wrote: 'The most successful war seldom pays for its losses.'"

One had to wonder what spoils the victors would receive after this war finally ended. Philip believed there would be enough losses to go around. He rose from his seat and braced his body over his locked and loaded weapon. He was fully committed to protecting himself and his crewmates. He was prepared to kill. The knot in his stomach tightened as the nose of the plane descended into a steep dive. Out the starboard waist-gunner window, white clouds gave way to black puffs. The infinite spaces had abruptly filled with impending death or worse. Lieutenant Hand broke the silence, his order echoing throughout the plane, "Bombs away!"

Philip couldn't sleep following his first mission. Nightmares. Bright flashes of light, the smell of gasoline and smoke remained locked in his senses. His dreams filled with the shrieking high pitch of orders screamed out with urgency. Fear was ever present; prayers could be heard, filtered through the deafening noise of engines and machine guns. These men, these brave warriors, all wished the din of violence and the fear of death would disappear, simply dissipate into blessed silence, into a peaceful quiet. But Philip's night was far from peaceful—never a sound sleep, only a half sleep—fearing his dreams were all too real.

First Bombing Raid

Pilot—Major Jack Bleasdale

Radio Operator—Sgt. Quentin Blakely

Co-Pilot—2nd Lt. Adelberger

Assistant Radio—Sgt. Philip A. Zumwalt

Navigator—1st Lt. J. W. Hansen

Ball Turret Gunner—Corp. Leslie Stewart

Bombardier—2nd Lt. Hand

Tail Gunner—Pvt. Honald

Engineer—Sgt. Dennis Craig

Plane Number—44448 (Taxpayer's Pride)

On Nov. 14, 1942, we flew to Port Moresby, New Guinea, and loaded ten 500 lb. demolition bombs aboard our plane. As extras, we tied incendiaries in clusters of threes and loaded about forty of them by the side gun positions. About 12:45 on Sunday, Nov. 15, we took off for Rabaul, New Britain. Aim was to strike shipping in the harbor. Our plane was the lead ship. On our first run over the target, we passed completely by without realizing it. Then we saw the searchlights after another plane and turned back. It took me several minutes to realize that the flashes in the clouds just above us were from antiaircraft. Some smaller stuff fired at us fell short, but, all in all, the ack-ack was light. One searchlight beam passed within several feet of our wing. Bombs dropped as we watched other planes come in, which was the best part of the raid. The antiaircraft, the search beams, the flares lighting up the harbor, and the bombs bursting on the ground and on the water made an exciting picture. One plane got caught in two light beams and streams of tracers came both at it and from it. Two huge fires were started below that could be seen fifty to seventy- five miles away.

As we passed over the city of Rabaul, Craig and Blakely had tossed out some of the incendiaries, but a huge number were still left. At first it was decided to drop these on Gasmata, but fearful of our gas supply, the major changed his mind, so we dropped them at some lights we saw just before leaving New Britain. Working as swiftly as we could, I untied the clusters and Stewart tossed the bombs, one at a time, out the side window. We left a long string of about twenty little fires burning behind us, none of them apparently very serious. Just before reaching New Guinea, the plane struck a very bad air pocket and dropped about a thousand feet straight down. It was a shock I do not care to experience again. The rear interior of the plane looked as if it had been through a tornado. We landed again at Port Moresby about 7:30 a.m. and went straight to bed.

CHAPTER 44

A Sorrowful Morning

November 21, 1942

ON A NORMAL SATURDAY MORNING, sleeping in and grabbing extra shut-eye was a luxury the GIs coveted. On this particular morning, it wasn't the thunderstorm outside or the incessant rain dropping on the roof of the enlisted men's tent that awakened Winter from a dead sleep. Philip awoke, too, and watched as Winter slipped through the tent flap door. He had responded to the sound of soldiers screaming at one another in the early dawn. Throwing on his fatigue pants, Philip followed Winter through the door, out into the downpour.

Through the monsoon, First Sergeant Nyman had stopped yelling. Changing his strategy, now he was calmly approaching Master Sergeant Joseph O'Scannell. "Put it down, Joe. C'mon, Sarge. You don't want to do this."

Philip observed Winter walking equally cautiously toward the surreal scene. The master sergeant stood in the middle of the muddy road, a .45 pistol in his right hand, a bottle of whiskey in his left. "Can't take it anymore, Pete." A brick of a man, all five feet ten, two hundred twenty pounds, O'Scannell knelt down, slumped over in the mud, crying in front of Nyman and Winter. He cocked the .45 with his thumb.

Lieutenant Emery emerged from the officers' tent and approached

O'Scannell. "Let's just take it easy, Joe. Everything's gonna be all right. Just put down your weapon."

"I'd rather not, sir. I'm goin' out on my own terms," O'Scannell slurred as he choked out his response.

Philip observed the macabre scene from just beyond his tent's doorway. He understood what the master sergeant was saying. The ungodly living conditions, the relentless bombing raids, the uncertainty of returning from a bombing run over ack-ack-ridden Rabaul, all contributed to a loosening of one's grip on reality. But Philip didn't want to see the NCO end up a suicide victim. O'Scannell was a good man, an honorable soldier.

Winter had the same idea. An expert poker player, schooled in deceit and misdirection, he moved cautiously behind O'Scannell, plotting to grab his weapon from behind. Philip realized this might be Winter's greatest gamble. The master sergeant quivered in the downpour. *A decorated NCO reduced to this,* Philip thought. *War. What price must we all pay to survive this insanity?*

Philip's stomach cinched as he witnessed Winter inch through the mud. Winter grabbed O'Scannell around the neck and grabbed for the pistol just as O'Scannell discharged a round into his skull. Blood and brain matter flew. Both O'Scannell and Winter collapsed onto the mucky road, covered in splattered blood.

The sound of the discharged weapon jolted Burnside out of his cot. He raced outside, bumping into Philip's back, and stopped, frozen in place, the rain cascading over them. For a moment, Philip, Burnsy, Nyman, and Emery stood wide-eyed and silent.

Winter was limp but breathing, collapsed over the master sergeant, the bloody remains of brain spattered over him. He pushed up off the ground, rose slowly, and joined the others gathered around the body. The men regained their voices.

"Jesus Christ!" yelled Emery.

"Dear Lord," Nyman said.

"Shit!" Winter shouted.

"Oh dear God," Philip whispered, looking over at Burnsy, who was shaking his head and murmuring, "Fuck, fuck, fuck."

O'Scannell lay lifeless, the .45 barely in his hand, the right side of his head indented with a circular hole rimmed with abraded skin, singed by the powder of the weapon. The brown liquid from the Jack Daniel's bottle spilled onto the mud-soaked ground. The master sergeant's hair was matted with dark blood and mud. His head rested in a watery mixture, a murky puddle of blood and whiskey.

Medics arrived and surveyed the body. A young corporal reported the obvious to Lieutenant Emery. As if they were pallbearers, the stunned soldiers surrounded O'Scannell's limp body and, assisting the medics, lifted him onto the stretcher. The medics draped a canvas tarp over the dead NCO and slogged away.

CHAPTER 45

A Lethal December

A S THE ONE-YEAR ANNIVERSARY of the bombing of Pearl Harbor approached, combat missions increased. Philip had traveled thousands of miles since hearing news of the infamous attack in the lobby of the St. Louis opera house. Nineteen forty-two had been an unforgettable year. He had witnessed death firsthand and been consumed by this perilous adventure he had pursued. His wish had been granted in spades—at least that was how his friend Chuck Winter, the consummate gambler, would have put it.

December 2, 1942

Pilot—Capt. Daniel

Radio Operator—S/Sgt. Blakely

Co-Pilot—Lt. Christopher

Radio Gunner—S/Sgt. Zumwalt

Navigator—Lt. Wexler

Ball Turret Gunner—Sgt. Stewart

Bombardier—Lt. Hand

Tail Gunner—PFC Fraser

Engineer—T/Sgt. Craig

Plane No.—19244

Crew awakened about 3 a.m. and took off about 4:30 to hunt for a Jap convoy off the coast of Buna. On the beach there, we saw landing barges and reported them to Moresby. Hunted several hours and finally located the convoy, consisting of four destroyers, near the coast of New Britain. As we made our bombing run, someone yelled "Zeroes," and I spotted one off our left wing, immediately opening fire. There were nine altogether, and we made one run, dropping four bombs, in spite of them. Ack-ack was heavy but inaccurate. We were circling for another run when Stewart came out of the ball turret and took one of the side guns. Later we learned that the door had fallen open and he barely managed to pull himself back into the plane. Naturally he had a severe shock.

For twenty-five minutes they attacked us, making individual passes from all directions. Only one of the top turret guns would fire and then only in short bursts, jamming often; the tail guns went out; the right side gun charging handle broke and for several minutes we were practically defenseless. At that moment, one Zero came straight in from the right side, all six guns blazing. Stewart was trying to load the gun, but at the sight of what seemed sure death, he stepped back and fell into a sitting position on the left catwalk. Tracers were everywhere and so certain was I that my end had come that I tensed myself in expectation of the bullets to come. Somehow, by a miracle, not a shot hit us or the plane. In desperation I seized a screwdriver and, in a few minutes, put that gun into action again. The next Zero that started in that way met a warm reception.

It was over as quickly as it had started. Working furiously to load the ammunition boxes, we became aware that the sky was empty. At first we refused to believe they were gone, and we finished filling the cans with spare ammunition, but gradually realized that we were safe and began to check damage. Our No. 2 motor was shot out, but otherwise we had no bullet holes, nor was anyone hurt. A tribute to the bad shooting of the Japanese! We made it back to Jackson Field without incident and, after eating, went to bed, for physically and mentally all were exhausted. Next day we learned that for the mission the entire crew was to be recommended for the Silver Star for Gallantry in Action.

December 27, 1942

Pilot—Capt. Daniel

Radio Operator—S/Sgt. Blakely

Co-Pilot—Lt. Marcroft

Radio Gunner—S/Sgt. Zumwalt

Navigator—Lt. McCord

Ball Turret Gunner—Sgt. Stewart

Bombardier—Lt. Hand

Tail Gunner—PFC Fraser

Engineer—T/Sgt. Craig

Plane No.—1-2649

Observer—T/Sgt. MacConnell

Took off about 11:00 p.m. for a bombing raid on shipping in Rabaul harbor as there were about 90 ships there. As we came in for our bombing run, several searchlights began hunting for us, and one of them flashed squarely on us. Suddenly the whole sky seemed to light up as 16–30 other lights immediately went on. I first started shooting with the right side gun, changed to the left, then, aiming one with each hand, fired both of them together. After a few minutes of this, Blakely came to my aid and we fired until both our guns went out.

All the time we were under the concentrated fire of every antiaircraft gun in the harbor. It so exceeded anything else I had ever seen that I was dazed. The plane was bouncing and trembling from the concussions, when suddenly we were hit and went into a steep dive. I found myself lying on the roof, and as we pulled out came down on the floor on my head. Blakely made a rush for his parachute but was unable to get it on as we went into a second dive. The searchlights still held us. I could hear the tinkle of broken glass and knew that we were hit, and I gave myself up for a dead man. The navigator later told me that he cursed bitterly at being shot down on his first mission.

As we came out of that dive, we were doing 400 miles an hour, but for the first time we had broken free of the lights. In a few minutes more we were away from the harbor and out of range. A quick survey showed that no one had been wounded, though bruises and cuts were numerous. I had a huge "goose egg" on my head, Fraser had a wrenched knee, MacConnell had been struck across the leg by a 30-calibre machine gun—hardly anyone was untouched. Our No. 2 engine was shot out, and the interior of the plane was a wreck. We feared that we might not be able to make it back to Moresby, so everyone wore parachutes all the way. However, we came in on three engines with several minutes of gas left. All had taken a physical beating, so went straight to bed. The entire crew agreed that never in all their flying had they come so close to death before. It could come little closer without reality. We had seven holes in the plane.

Philip sat quietly on his cot. It was the evening of his twenty-third birthday—no fanfare, no celebration. He wondered if his family would think of him tomorrow, lifting their glasses in a toast to their hero. *Hero?* He felt as if he was the furthest thing from such a moniker. What would 1943 have in store for him? Maybe Madame Zeralda was a fake, her prophecy a lie. He would survive, make it home, and keep his promise to El. He decided to write—first to El.

December 30, 1942
Dear El,

On my birthday, I can only think of you and how much I miss you. My memory of you took me back to one of our special places and I decided I would try and write a poem about it. I hope you like it.

The Old Oak Tree

Where will we be,
How old, how grown,
Together or alone,
Until we once again see

The Old Oak Tree?

Will youth have passed us by
Without thought or care?
The blink of an eye.
Were we naïve or unaware?

Love bloomed once
On summer's day
A picnic lunch,
As we found our way.

Winter's eve
With gifts so true
We did believe

In a love so new.

Making a promise then and there
To find each other, no matter where,
A forever love we would bequeath
Together, as always, beneath

The Old Oak Tree.

Philip A. Zumwalt
12/30/42

My prayer tonight is that this war will soon end and I will be home in your embrace. I love you as much as life itself.
Yours forever,
Philip

He sealed and stamped the letter, pulled his diary from his foot-locker, and wrote late into the night.

Someday, when this war is only a grim memory, its sharp edges softened by sentimental musings, I imagine that many films will be made in an attempt to tell the story of aerial combat in the South West Pacific. The truth will never be told . . . One man expressed himself this way, "If I see a fellow with combat wings, a new dress uniform, and much rank, I know he just got in from the States, but if he's wearing an old uniform, is wearing no sign of rank, and looks like a tramp as well as being usually drunk, I know that he's a fighting fool." The old combat crews have proven their worth, not through their appearance on the ground, but through their activities in the air. Actions speak louder than words.

Completing his final sentence, he closed up the diary. *I once was a fool for love and now I'm a fighting fool,* he thought. Though he did not love everything, an impossibility that El had proposed, he loved many things: music, great literature, philosophy, and even, to some degree, religion. It went without saying that he loved his family and El. What confounded him was that now he had to add one more item to his list: combat. Strange. There was a certain exhilaration in cheating death. There was a certain pride he felt when taking down an enemy Zero, in defeating an adversary intent on dominating others. He believed in freedom, and now, he had to admit to himself, he actually loved something else—being a man of action.

PART THREE

CHAPTER 46

Letters and a Hospital Stay

January 21, 1943

PHILIP AND EL EXCHANGED LETTERS throughout the latter months of 1942 as often as possible. They wrote out of habit, an antidote to loneliness. Letters were similar, details of daily activities and the promise of undying love. Philip sat down outside his tent to read the latest. It had taken nearly three weeks to reach him, but he welcomed news from the home front.

January 2, 1943

Dear Philip,

Happy New Year! I am sorry that I have been so neglectful in writing. I have some sad news to report from the home front. My sweet grandmama Campbell passed away last week. She thought the world of you. What a wonderful woman she was, and what a life well lived! We will miss her terribly. Also, Mrs. Staley fell and broke her hip. She is here at the hospital, and I have been taking care of her. She talks so fondly of you. I do hope she can recover from her fall.

Now for the good news, I guess. Essie and Randall are getting married. Randall was wounded on Guadalcanal. The sad part of this news is Randall lost his right leg, just below the knee. A great deal of infection set in before the medics could tend to him. He was awarded a Purple Heart and sent back to the States.

As for little old me, it seems like I am always on duty or studying. Mrs. Staley is one tough lady. She is recovering nicely from her accident. Another of my patients died last night. He was a wonderful, elderly man—a retired professor of philosophy. Such a kind man. When he passed his entire family was around his bed. I cried. It was such a sweet moment. It is odd, isn't it, that both of us have witnessed death at such a young age? Who could ever have imagined such a thing? Of course, what you've seen is much more awful than what happens here. There are nights when I can hardly sleep imagining what you are going through or what I have just witnessed during my shift.

When I was in Chicago a few years ago, I met a young Japanese woman on the L train. She was reading a book. The title intrigued me, so I asked her about it. We had a lovely conversation. The book was **The Interpretation of Dreams** *by Dr. Sigmund Freud. This young woman told me about the unconscious mind and that our dreams are really "wish-fulfillment." All I can say about that is that as far as I am concerned, I only wish that my dreams would be fulfilled. If I say more, I fear the nasty censors will cut it out anyway.*

What I wanted to say in the first place was what a nice person the Japanese woman was, and she sure as heck didn't drop bombs on Pearl Harbor. Geez, Philip, she is studying to be a doctor of psychology. She wouldn't harm a flea! I think I might just go check out one of Dr. Freud's books from the library. Then I'll go home and dream of you. I heard he writes about all sorts of interesting things. Went to see **Casablanca** *with a group of doctors and nurses. What a great movie! I just love Bogart and Ingrid Bergman. Have you seen it yet? I hope you received my birthday card. Please take care. Here's looking at you, kid.*

Love,

El

He had not yet received El's birthday card. Philip wrote it off to typical military inefficiency, folded the letter he had received, and placed it in his footlocker with the others. Feeling a bit feverish, he delayed writing back to El at the moment. After his throat became so swollen he could hardly swallow, he checked into the sickbay.

The moment Dr. Goldman looked down Philip's throat, he informed his patient it was a case of tonsillitis. The infection was extensive, and Goldman wasted no time. He ordered Lieutenant Loretta Keno to prepare the operating room. When Philip awoke from the anesthesia, he barely noticed the burning pain in his throat. Rather, he thought he had died and gone to Heaven. A beautiful angel stood over him, wiping his forehead with a cold towel.

"Glad to see you awake, soldier. You gave us quite a scare," Nurse Keno said. She placed a cup of ice water next to him, lifted his head, and guided the straw into his mouth. He sipped. His throat was still on fire, but the cold water brought some relief, as did the soft touch of the nurse's hands.

It was days before Philip felt like talking. Nurse Keno made up for it. She constantly checked on him, gave him sponge baths, massaged his aching body, and talked incessantly about her family who lived in San Francisco. She had joined the Cadet Nurse Corps and volunteered for duty in a combat zone. It was as if Philip had his own personal nurse. Although he might have preferred that El fulfill that role, he was grateful she had followed her parents' advice and hadn't volunteered for duty overseas.

Loretta was, however, a breath of fresh air for him, witty with a good sense of humor. When he was finally able to talk, they discussed everything from movies and music to poetry. She was not only lovely but smart and a wonderfully competent nurse. He looked forward to seeing her every morning as she started her shift. Her auburn hair and

soulful eyes reminded him of El. He imagined El had the same captivating effect on her patients.

"Looks like you're going to get discharged today, Philip," Nurse
Keno said as she lifted his chart from the foot of his bed and made the
appropriate check marks.

"Believe it or not, I've really enjoyed our time together, Nurse
Keno."

"Please, call me Loretta. One of the other nurses said you're the
guy who plays the piano at the club, right?"

"Whenever I get a chance, I head over to the AFFC or the USO
Club. Seems like soldiers and the nurses like getting swacked and hitting the dance floor. My favorite time is when they sing along with the
songs I play. It's great fun. You should join us."

"Oh, I have. I hadn't realized you were the piano player. I was
quite impressed."

"Thank you."

"I need to tell you, I've enjoyed our conversations, Philip Zumwalt. You're an interesting man."

"Maybe our paths will cross at one of the clubs?"

"Oh, you can count on it. Now that I know the piano player, I plan
on being a regular." She smiled a smile he had seen before. His memory was still a bit foggy. Where had he seen such a smile? No matter.
She was a friend worth having, and in this war, that was a valuable
commodity.

February 9, 1943

The weather in Port Moresby was warm and balmy with intermittent
rain showers. Philip claimed the letter with its familiar writing at mail
call. He and Winter sat down outside their tent, separately reading
their letters from home. As Philip read, the smile on his face turned to

a frown and his brow furrowed. He continued to read, then wadded up the letter, and threw it on the ground.

"What's the matter, Z?" Winter asked.

"Nothing," Philip answered, but the look on his face and the clump of paper in front of him gave Winter the evidence necessary to conduct a further investigation.

"Bullshit, man. What's wrong?"

Philip ignored the inquiry. "You gotta cigarette, Chuck?"

"What?!"

"Just give me one."

Winter pulled an Old Gold cigarette from the pack in his pocket and handed it to Philip. "You need a light?"

"Naw. I think I'll just chew on it. Of course I need a light, you stupid dipshit."

Winter had never seen Philip like this. "Well, damn, if you're gonna call me names, light it yourself." He threw his Zippo lighter at Philip.

Philip fumbled the toss, struggled repeatedly to strike a flame, but finally lit the cigarette. He took a drag and coughed, took another, and pointed to the letter. "I always feared this day might come, Chuck. Just go to the second paragraph. Not exactly a Dear John, but that's probably coming next. Can't say I blame her."

Winter picked up the letter and read:

January 15, 1943
Dear Philip,

I hope this letter finds you well and dry. It sounds like the rain must never stop over there. My training continues with long hours, and so many monotonous chores, although such duties, as they call them, are necessary.

Writing this letter, Philip, is one of the hardest things I have ever had to do in my life. Our time together was wonderful—you are wonderful, but I am afraid I have betrayed you. I have a confession to make, and Lord knows I don't want you to hear this secondhand.

Many of the girls have taken to hitting the bars after their shift has ended. I've gone with them a number of times, and I must admit that it's a time for all of us to unwind. Some of the doctors join us, and I've become friends with one of them. In fact, I guess we are more than friends. I have feelings for him. He is such a kind man; even his name reflects his personality. He came to Quincy from Germany. His entire family and his fiancé were sent to what the Nazis called konzentrationslager. I asked Ernest what that meant and he told me that we would say concentration camp. Evidently, these are camps where they send Jewish people and other minorities in order to separate them from the rest of the Germans. I suppose it is much like they are doing with the Japanese that live here in America. Can you even imagine, Philip? What is wrong with the Nazis? What is wrong with us?

I have danced with him and some of the doctors and other fellas at the Casino. When we all go to the Casino on the occasional weekends we are off duty, we try to put the war and the hospital out of our minds. I must confess every time I dance with another man, whether a doctor or a GI on leave, I think of you. I'm so confused right now. I'm sure you can tell that, can't you?

But back to Dr. Thoroughgood. I know you would like him, Philip. He's a fine, gentle man. We've had numerous wonderful conversations about medicine, the war, and, of course, politics. It's quite an amazing story of how he escaped from Germany and made it to Quincy. He was a doctor in Germany but had to get certified here in the U.S. The folks at Blessing took him in and helped him. Now he is a certified physician and delivering babies. Anyway, he asked me out to dinner on New Year's Eve and I accepted. No harm, right? It just so happens that we went to the Triple Oaks and, lo and behold, who was there but your brother Homer and Rosie McCraven. The truth is that I'm so lonely, and I imagine you are, too. So, I think we need to trust each other and have the freedom to see other people.

I suppose this gives you every right to go out dancing with those pretty nurses over there or the Australian beauties (yeh, I've heard about them). I want you to enjoy what little free time you get, dear Philip, and I think this is best for both of us. I guess what I'm saying is we need to put things on hold. I realize this is painful for both of us, and I just wish this war would never have happened. I suppose matters of the heart are difficult to understand. I hope you will.

Sincerely,

El

"For Christ's sake, Z. You big baby! She said she thinks of you when she's dancing with those other guys."

"You mean doctors. I can't compete with them, Chuck. They're there and I'm here, stuck in this shithole. Plus, I can tell she's falling for that guy. And she signed the letter *sincerely*, not *Love, El*."

"Oh, bullshit. Hell, this just gives you permission to live it up when you go on leave. How could she pick some guy over a handsome devil like you? Hell, you're such a catch I might take you for myself." Winter jumped on top of Philip and began to tickle him.

They rolled around in the dirt, punching and laughing. Philip's giggling was a much-needed cure for his blues. He knew now he had to get home. After all, just how long could El resist the charm of such a good, kind man?

Philip mulled over his response to El and the next day wrote his reply to her proposal:

February 10, 1943

Dear El,

I understand. In life, we must all make decisions, choices that affect our lives. We are, most likely, not fully aware of what the future has in store for us, but we go on the hope that whatever fate befalls us, it will be for the best. That is what I hope for you—the very best. If the feelings you have for your new friend are real, then

I will surrender most graciously and do my best to move on. Even if it was for the briefest moment in time, my time with you was a treasure.

I do not choose to belabor you with my current circumstances, nor bore you with tales of woe. I am not fond of pity and certainly not coming from a person who I hold in the highest regard. You changed me and gave me a new sense of purpose, one that continues to exist even in the direst of circumstances. Tomorrow is a day, but as the poet says, Today is called the present for a reason, it is a gift and I plan on making the most of each and every moment. I encourage you to do the same. You must not feel guilty about your change of heart, nor should you expect me to ever stop loving you. That would be impossible. I will always love you, you will always be with me. I wish you the very best.

Sincerely,
Philip

CHAPTER 47

R & R in Sydney

Sydney, Australia
February 25, 1943

PHILIP, LEWIS GODLOVE, AND JIMMY SLEPKO arrived in Sydney for some much-needed R & R. The GIs thought R & R should be changed to R, R, R & R. They needed rest and recuperation, but also relaxation. Most of all, they were looking for some *adult* recreation, recreation that came in all forms: lying on the sands of Manly or Bondi Beaches, eating decent food, staying in fancy hotels, and experiencing the Australian nightlife with all its trappings, including the beautiful women.

Lewis Godlove epitomized his name, a Bible-toting Baptist from Arkansas. Once the war ended, he told Philip he would resign his teaching position back home and become a minister. His evangelical skills aside, he had yet to convince Philip that every word in the Holy Bible should be taken literally. Philip appreciated Lew's dedication to his faith, though, and respected his persistence in spreading the "Good News."

Lew and Philip sparred incessantly over the merits of organized religion, but both valued the arts. Listening to music and going to see motion pictures assuaged their otherwise mostly miserable existence, although they conceded survival remained their top priority.

Each, in his own way, had led an innocent and sheltered life. Lew had reluctantly relented within the past few months to partake of alternative liquid spirits. Alcohol took away the gnawing sting of battle experienced by weary airmen. The booze momentarily allowed them to escape the horrors of aerial combat. That they might have killed another human being haunted their own existence. Both men had lost entire crews with whom they'd served. The specter of death cursed them with recurring nightmares. As they unpacked in their room at the Rose Bay Hotel, Philip sought an answer to a question that had bothered him for nearly two months. "Lew, do you think that Meyer Levin is in Heaven?"

Lew laughed. "What kind of a question is that, Lucky? Or is that just the start to another of your poems?"

Being the sole survivor of two crews that never returned to base had earned Philip his latest nickname.

"No, come on, man, get serious for a minute. I mean, you know, Meyer was Jewish. Do you think Jesus has a monopoly on all the real estate up there?"

"According to the Holy Bible, Philip, I'm afraid unless Levin took Jesus as his Lord and Savior at the last minute—I'd have to say no, he's not in Heaven."

"You're kidding, right?" Philip's voice betrayed his incredulity. "You mean to tell me a good man, a hero, like Levin's not in Heaven? You're full of shit, Lew. How can you be so certain about that?"

Lew tossed his underwear in a top drawer. "Look it up, my good man." Pulling a Bible out of his duffel bag, he began thumbing through the pages. "Right here, Philip. John 14:6, *'Jesus saith unto him'*—and that would be Thomas, doubting Thomas—*'I am the way, the truth, and the life: no man cometh unto the Father, but by me.'*"

"That just seems arrogant to me. What about a poor African tribesman who led a good life but never got out of the jungle, maybe a missionary never found him? Is *he* going to hell?"

"That's what the Bible says," Lew responded.

"The Bible also tells us not to kill anyone or commit adultery, right? So, does anyone who doesn't follow the Ten Commandments go to hell, too?" Philip continued his quarrel. "Besides, Lew, the Bible was written centuries ago. And much of what was written, in my humble opinion, was metaphoric."

"Wow! Metaphoric. I didn't even know that was a word. You can second-guess the word of God all you want, pal. I guess we'll just have to agree to disagree. For me, the Bible *is* the holy word of God passed down from generation to generation. It is the Truth with a capital T."

"Well, you can believe what you want. I just have a hard time believing in a God who'd send Meyer Levin to hell. I just can't believe that's true. Isn't it possible everyone gets one final chance to, I don't know . . . you know, to believe or confess their belief in God or what-ever the omnipotent power might be called?" Philip's voice conveyed his anguish. "I just have to believe that God would show more mercy than that."

"Anything's possible." Lew shrugged his shoulders. "Sergeant Levin was certainly a good man and God is merciful. If we repent our sins there might be a chance, even for a Jew. Maybe Levin did see the light."

"The light? What light would that be, Lew?" Philip's rage inten-sified, his voice rising. "And a 'chance for even a Jew,' what does that mean? I think the only lights those guys saw in the end were the damned spotlights or the flash of ack-ack in their side windows."

"I hear you, Lucky. I hear you. Calm down." Lew was composed, measured—rarely emotional about anything. "I understand your rea-soning, at least to some extent. One thing this war has taught me is that sometimes there aren't any good answers to all these questions we want answers to. Like this war—one huge paradox, that's what this is. Life's mysterious enough without the war, wouldn't you agree?"

"Yeh, especially after we've been dropped right here in the middle of hell. Paradox? No! It's just a big pile of shit."

"Well, buddy, we're not in hell right now. We're in paradise—wine, women, and song."

Philip smiled, tired of arguing. "Yeh, you're right, Lew. Time to live it up. But, hey, wouldn't you rather go to a revival?"

"Not tonight, pal. Just need to revive my sanity. I might be a stick-in-the-mud sometimes, Lucky, but I'm human, too. And as long as Jesus forgives me—remember that merciful God I told you about?—then I plan on doing just a little bit of sinnin'. Keep things interesting down here on Earth."

"Sinnin' it is, Lew. We deserve to enjoy the few days we might have left. How about we start at Kings Cross? We're not gonna solve any of life's mysteries tonight. But just for the record, as far as I'm concerned, Meyer Levin is in Heaven. At least, that's the way I see it. If I've got my history and Sunday school lessons right, Jesus, the Son of God, was a Jew. Am I right about that? And, honestly, I'm not even sure Jews believe in an afterlife. But if there is one, I suspect it's something beyond our wildest imagination. And, whatever it is, whatever we call it, I'm betting we'll all end up there—together."

Philip had made his point. He imagined Lew would think he was a blasphemer or needed more formal religious training. It did cross Philip's mind that he might need to talk with Father Shea when he returned to Moresby. El's letter had turned his world upside down, and sometimes he wondered if he hadn't lost hope in everything: love, God, the Bible, the inherent goodness of humankind. He rolled over in his bed and decided to take a nap, hoping some sleep might temporarily ease his pain.

In the early evening, Philip pressed his dress uniform and strolled with Lew down King Street. The bustling thoroughfare was teeming with rowdy soldiers, sailors, and prostitutes. Philip flagged down a taxi. "Theatre Royal, please," he instructed.

White Horse Inn was being performed at the theater. "Nothing like a good opera to get our juices flowing!" Lew exclaimed. "Then, let's say we get smashed!"

El's memory haunted Philip. Even on a balmy summer evening in Sydney, on a well-deserved R & R, where a man just needed to be a man, he couldn't get her out of his mind. If he went to a cabaret or a dance hall, she was there. If he attended an opera, she was there. Even the exquisite Australian women reminded him of her. Did any of it really matter though? Wasn't he now eternally damned to hell, like his pal Levin? His faith had been shattered into a million pieces. He knew he'd killed other human beings, maybe innocent civilians, even women or children. Would a merciful God really forgive that? How was he any better than the enemy who committed their own atrocities and lived by their own set of rules? What did their God say about all this? What about Buddha? How were the Japs judged on Judgment Day? How could a loving God allow all this to happen? What could a man honestly believe in anymore?

He'd read in one of the philosophy books he borrowed from Reverend Kelley about Blaise Pascal and the Grand Wager. Pascal wrote that the wise decision regarding the existence of God was to decide in God's favor. By doing so, one gained all. By not doing so, one lost all. One could gain eternal life if God existed; if not, one would be no worse off. If you bet against God, win or lose, you either gained nothing or lost everything. Philip thought such a theory was dishonest. After all, if God was just and omniscient, wouldn't he know that the bettor was only hedging his bet, that he wasn't a true believer? Wasn't that the only way to get to Heaven?

Philip's head hurt. Questions without answers. Lew had earlier given Philip his answer. "Either you believe in God or not, Philip," he said. "It all boils down to faith. Some have it; others don't."

For the moment, Philip was just happy to be alive. *Alive*—the operative word. He looked forward to the operetta. *After that,* he thought, *if my head's going to hurt, it might as well be the result of a little sinnin'.*

The grandeur of the Theatre Royal was no delusion and the

operetta relieved Philip's despondence for a few hours. Philip and Lew met Slepko at the Australia Hotel on Castlereagh Street. They ate steaks, drank beer, and people-watched. Wilson was right on two counts: The Japs were tough SOBs, and the Australian women were beautiful. Philip wondered if just looking at Australian women constituted sinnin'. Not all was smooth and friendly, however.

Tension had been brewing between some GIs and the Aussies. The war had worn thin the nerves of the soldiers from both countries. The Battle of Brisbane had only intensified the uneasiness. Rumors circulated earlier had been substantiated.

Slepko had the details. "Last December, a riot took place in Brisbane. There was a brawl between U.S. MPs and Australian enlisted men in late November. A buddy of mine stationed there told me about it. Fifteen Australian servicemen were shot by U.S. military machine guns and piled up on the post office steps."

Bitterness over the incident was still fresh in the Australian camps and was exacerbated by the U.S. forces being paid better and receiving higher-quality rations. U.S. troops were even given preferential treatment by Australian merchants and hotel owners. To add salt to the wound, the American Post Exchanges, or PX, as the stores were called, offered items to U.S. servicemen that were forbidden, rationed, or excessively expensive for Australians. The Aussies were upset that Americans were dating their women and were convinced that the GIs' access to affordable cigarettes, alcohol, ice cream, and silk stockings gave the Americans an unfair advantage. It was no surprise that thousands of women from Down Under were either engaged or married to American soldiers and sailors.

"We need to tread lightly around the Aussies, fellas. They're all pretty pissed at us," Slepko warned. "I'd hate for any of us to wind up in jail and ruin our R & R."

After dinner, Philip took off on his own and left his buddies at the hotel. He wandered the streets of Sydney and discovered a music store. After purchasing some sheet music, records, and needles for his phonograph, he drifted into the PX and bought stripes, shoulder patches, and wings insignia. He would have them sewn onto his uniform later. After a late night at the movies, he switched hotels. He awoke Saturday morning in a comfortable bed in one of Sydney's finest hotels, the luxurious Great Southern. Ready to greet the day after a sound night of sleep, he was armed with a fresh, positive attitude. Adventure awaited.

Exiting through the massive mahogany doors of the Great Southern, he stepped out into the brisk, sun-laden morning and took a deep breath. It was the beginning of a day that would end up holding great promise, a day he would meet someone who, like all of his experiences lately, was unforgettable.

CHAPTER 48

Betty

PHILIP AND LEW HAD ARRANGED A LUNCH DATE with two Australian women they'd met the previous night at the opera. Lew would escort Betty Hittman and Philip would accompany Beryl Penfold. Philip was content to be Lew's wingman and had no intention of having any kind of relationship with a woman other than a platonic one. At lunch, the two soldiers confirmed evening dates with the ladies and reserved a table at Rose's Nightclub.

After purchasing corsages, the soldiers proceeded to Betty's apartment at the Kingsclere Flats on Macleay Street, met the women, and taxied to Kings Cross. At Rose's, the quartet lived it up. The jazz ensemble, consisting of a piano player, drummer, and two horn players, kept the place lively with popular songs from the U.S. The two couples waltzed, fox-trotted, and two-stepped the night away. Their dancing was punctuated with their prodigious consumption of alcohol. Philip was by far the most skilled dancer, even though slightly smashed. He started the evening dancing with Beryl, but for some unknown reason, during the evening, he switched partners with Lew.

Before he turned in for the night, Philip pulled his diary from his duffel and sat at the hotel desk to write about his evening.

Ended up with Betty—really some "gal"! Godlove took Beryl home, and I took Betty home. Ate at a small restaurant. Arranged for a date tomorrow night. Came to hotel by taxi. For some reason, Betty and I get along well together. She's very frank and very smooth. Smart, poised, well-groomed, and very attractive. Comes of a rather wealthy family. She likes Americans and never dates Australians. Also, usually goes out with officers.

I am, I have learned, the second enlisted man she has ever been out with—Godlove was the first. Beryl's family is also wealthy. I have an invitation to their home for lunch tomorrow. What a day!

After sleeping in late, Philip dressed and waited for a phone call from Lew to confirm the lunch date at the Penfold residence that had been arranged the night before. He felt no guilt. He had a wonderful time with Betty, the lovely Australian socialite. *And what the hell*, he thought, *El's letter, after all, did give me permission to see other people. And just what did that phrase mean to her anyway?*

Lew's call never came. Philip called Betty to inform her of the confusion and ate lunch alone at the hotel. Lew arrived back at the room around 4 p.m. without mention of his oversight. Maybe Beryl hadn't even remembered inviting Philip and Betty to lunch. Perhaps they had all overindulged. One thing was certain, Lew didn't spend the night in the room he and Philip shared. *None of my business*, Philip thought. Besides, the upgrade in accommodations was even better minus Lew's snoring.

On Sunday evening, February 28, Lew and Philip called on Betty. It was news to Philip that Lew had already arranged a date with Nellie, Slepko's ex-girlfriend. *I guess Beryl Penfold's disappearance will remain just another one of life's mysteries*, Philip mused.

Betty, Nellie, Lew, and Philip had dinner at the most exclusive restaurant in Kings Cross, the Claremont. Each meal set the soldiers back a little more than six dollars and fifty cents in American dollars. Philip was now the one who overindulged. The group decided to explore the shops and pubs on the Corso at Manly Beach on the other side of Sydney Harbor. It sounded like a great idea, but once the ferry launched, Philip became seasick and spent the remainder of the voyage on the lower deck of the craft, losing his expensive meal over the ferryboat's side. Given his exposure to turbulence in the B-17s, Philip was surprised at his inability to navigate the crossing without being nauseated. Once back on dry land, he recovered completely.

Later in the evening, he escorted Betty back to her apartment. The Kingsclere was the tallest residential building in Sydney. Modeled after apartment buildings in New York City, it was constructed of brick and sandstone, stood eight stories tall, and towered over all the Victorian mansions and row houses in the neighborhood. It was Sydney's first high-rise block of flats. Philip was impressed by the stateliness of the building's exterior, but upon ascending the spiraling mahogany staircase, he was awestruck even more at the luxuriousness of Betty's residence.

The evening had turned unseasonably cool by the time the couple arrived at apartment 8 on the third floor. Adorned with a stained-glass panel, the front door exuded elegance, only to be matched by the intricate parquet floors. The focal point of the living room was a stone fireplace surrounded by camel-colored leather furniture arranged around an intricately woven wool rug that lay in front of the fireplace. Betty entered the living room and turned on the Tiffany lamp that sat upon a polished dark oak table. Oil paintings from every corner of the globe hung on her walls—Rome, Jerusalem, New York City, London, Paris.

"This is quite a place you have here, Betty."

"Thanks to Mother and Father. They wanted me to have my own space. Thought I needed to have my independence."

"Have you traveled to all of these cities?" Philip asked, referring to the paintings with a wave of his arm.

"I have. Again, thanks to my generous parents. They wanted me to see the world. I love to travel, but given the situation now, I would just like to find a job of some sort and help with the war effort. I volunteer at the Red Cross a couple of days a week, but I want to do more."

"We could use all the help we can get. Can you fly an airplane?" he joked.

"I think I'll leave that up to you," she replied with a chuckle. "How about a sandwich and some tea? I fear you lost most of your dinner on the ferryboat ride."

"That'd be swell." Philip was embarrassed that he hadn't fared well on the boat ride but put his embarrassment aside when he spied Betty's phonograph. Next to it, a collection of records was stored in a small, intricately carved cabinet. He pulled one out and walked down the hall toward the kitchen. "Copland. I love him. Do you mind if I play this one?"

Betty was finishing up making the sandwiches and heating up the teakettle. "Oh, please do. I love Copland, too. A great American composer. I can see why you admire him."

Philip returned to the living room, placed the record on the turntable, turned the crank, and lowered the needle. He smiled as the Introduction to "Billy the Kid" filled the apartment, reminding him of his best friend.

"Billy the Kid!" exclaimed Betty. "Good choice. One of the musicians who has been staying here in apartment six on the second floor told me at a party last week that Copland has composed a new musical work. I think he said it's called "Fanfare for the Common Man." Word has it that Copland wrote it for the Cincinnati Symphony."

"Sounds marvelous. The common man and woman in America need some fanfare for all they do. It's the common man who is fighting this war, that's for sure."

"Why don't you start a fire in the fireplace, Philip? There's a bit of a chill in here tonight."

Philip followed her instruction. As he stoked the fire, he heard the teapot squeal. Moments later, Betty emerged from the kitchen with a tray of sandwiches and two steaming cups of tea. The couple sat basking in the warmth of the blazing hearth listening to Copland's music. Philip stared into the fire—hypnotic.

"A penny for your thoughts," Betty whispered.

He got up, put on another record, Copland's "Appalachian Spring," and returned to the couch. "Oh, nothing really. I dreamed this would be one great adventure, but instead it's been a nightmare—no escaping the horror. I don't sleep well anymore."

"I know what you mean. Just volunteering at the hospital two or three days a week, I've seen things I never imagined. I just try to block it all out when I come home, but that's not easy to do."

Philip had his own images, the ones that haunted him. He didn't want to expose Betty to the terror he replayed in his mind. "I wonder, what is the sense of all of this? I just want it to end, that's all."

"It will. It will someday."

The fire burned down as they quietly sipped their tea. Betty excused herself, left the room, and returned with a small book. "One of the wounded soldiers gave me this book of poems the other day, written by a man named Eliot, T. S. Eliot. Silly name to me, why didn't he just use his first and middle names? T. S. seems a bit pretentious, don't you think? No matter. This soldier said I should read one of his poems. He told me he thought Eliot might be onto something."

"I know of Eliot," Philip said. "Which poem?"

"'The Hollow Men.' A strange title, don't you think? Anyway, I was reading along and not understanding much of it, but when I got nearly to the end, it's like it slapped me in the face."

"What'd it say?" asked Philip.

She opened it. "This is the part, right here." Betty read from a dog-eared page:

> "Between the essence
> And the descent

Falls the Shadow."

"I guess that says it all, Philip, doesn't it?"

"I don't know. You've caught me a bit off guard here, Betty. I feel like I'm back in Poetry 101 in college."

"Okay. I'll give you that one, but here's the big question. What is the essence of all of this? What is any of this going to prove? It seems like we're all descending into a sort of personal, dismal hell on earth— an all-encompassing insanity. An insanity affecting all of us."

"It is insane. I agree. But I have to constantly remind myself we didn't start this war. What madness, in God's name, drove Hitler and the Japanese to do what they did? Was it greed or was war necessary for them to survive? All I know is that I have to believe we're on the right side of this struggle; otherwise, I couldn't do what I've been doing. Saint Augustine would call our war a 'just war.'"

Betty nodded, and Philip noted the compassion etched across her comely features.

He continued, "*Essence?* Hmm. An interesting word. I believe at the core of our essence there is a degree of good, maybe even good with a capital G, like the *good* the ancient Greek philosophers talked about. If we can find that common good in mankind, if we can help each other find that, then maybe someday the world might be at peace." He took a sip of his tea and wondered if what he had said made any sense at all.

Betty reaffirmed his reasoning. "Yes, but I think Eliot has a point. There's a shadow that falls over most things; life isn't black and white. We can't always classify events simply as good or bad. But even in our descent, even when we're caught in the gray ambiguity of this war, even in our worst moments, we have the chance to ascend and ultimately discover the essence of our being."

"And what, pray tell, is that?"

"Love, Philip. It's love. Even in the most terrible conditions at the hospital, I see it. It isn't Hollywood love, kissing and spooning. It's bigger than that. I've witnessed it with my own eyes. I'm not grateful for much of what I've seen in the hospital, but I am grateful for that. Amidst all the suffering and pain, I have seen unconditional love and caring that each one of those doctors and nurses administers to their patients. It's amazing."

Philip rose from the couch and paced toward the fireplace. He turned and looked sympathetically toward Betty. "No, I get it. I've seen it, too. In the middle of a battle, men enduring their worst, most horrific moments are at their best. Even willing to sacrifice their own life for their buddy. I can't explain it either, but I've seen it firsthand. I guess it's exactly what a Russian author wrote years ago. If we love everything, we'll be able to perceive the divine mystery in our lives."

"That's awfully profound, Philip, but don't you think that's almost impossible to do? Where did you learn that?"

"From Elinor, Elinor Robinson. The girl I told you about. The girl I was in love with, the girl who decided she just couldn't wait any longer." Mentioning her name aroused the painful feelings he still harbored deep inside.

"Oh, I'm so sorry. That must have been terrible for you. A Dear John?"

"I guess you could say that."

"I do remember you mentioned her. El, right?

Philip regained his composure. "Yes. El. It was El who sent those words to me. They were from a wonderful book, *The Brothers Karamazov* by Fyodor Dostoevsky. Loving everything is so difficult, especially when you lose those things you love, like the love of your life, or your best buddies, men who were like brothers to me. So, Betty, even though I realize this is insanity, I have to believe that we are sacrificing for good over evil. Even in the midst of my own personal descent, I have to believe that in the end when we remember this war, the essence of it will be something positive that ended with a world at peace. So maybe love will triumph in the end. I pray it does. I have to hope, with all due respect to Mr. Eliot, that we will emerge from the shadow into the light of a brighter future. I truly hope we can." He turned his head and wiped his eyes.

"I think maybe you're the poet. Here, I'd like you to have this." She handed him the book, *Collected Poems: 1909–1935* by T. S. Eliot.

Touched by her generosity, goodness, and friendship, he smiled and thanked her. They finished their tea in mutual silence. There was no further analysis of T. S. Eliot's "Hollow Men" or talk of war or nightmares or friends lost in combat.

"Copland is amazing, isn't he?" Philip said.

"Indeed, he is." Betty looked at him with admiring eyes.

Philip had seen the look before, but he was determined to fight the temptation to take this friendship any further. He rose from the couch. It was nearly an hour past midnight. "Thank you so much for the tea, sandwiches, and book. I better get going. Good night, Betty."

Philip returned to his room at the Great Southern, sat on his bed, opened the book, turned to the table of contents, and leafed through the pages. He found the poem Betty had shown him and read it in its entirety. Tears flowed as he finished the final stanza. The faces of his friends, all killed in action, flashed through his mind—all who had made the ultimate sacrifice. He laid back on his pillow. *Who knows for certain how it all ends?* he thought.

He read the final stanza once again to himself in silence:

> *This is the way the world ends*
> *This is the way the world ends*
> *This is the way the world ends*
> *Not with a bang but a whimper.*

CHAPTER 49

A Surprise at Romano's

THE LIFE OF AN AMERICAN SERVICEMAN on furlough agreed with Philip. For each day remaining, he pressed his dress uniform, sent flowers to Betty, and ate at the finest restaurants. Betty and he took in the stage play *My Sister Eileen* at the Minerva Theatre. On Wednesday, March 3, they dined at the Claremont again. After dinner, Philip in his dress uniform and Betty in her resplendent, off-the-shoulder, gold brocade evening gown landed at Romano's, one of the most popular nightclubs in Sydney. They checked in at the reservation desk and were unexpectedly escorted by the maître d' to a table reserved in the front row.

The smell of Betty's orchid corsage was intoxicating—as intoxicating as the woman Lew brought to the table to join them. "Miss Joy Nichols," he announced, "meet Miss Betty Hittman and Mr. Philip Zumwalt."

Niceties were exchanged. Betty waited until the opportune time to whisper into Philip's ear, "Joy's one of our most famous singers, Philip."

Joy's long chestnut-colored hair cascaded around her shoulders, her bright blue eyes sparkled, and her smile was radiant. She immediately put the table at ease. Charming, with a wry sense of humor, she seemed genuinely interested in her new friends, especially when Lew told her of Philip's talent as a piano player. "Maybe you could accompany me one of these days, Philip," Joy said.

"I'd love to, Joy," Philip replied. "But you need to come up with a gig pretty quick. We head back on Tuesday."

Joy and Philip shared a laugh.

"I'm sorry to say, I don't have a performance booked until the weekend after that. It would have been so nice to have a soldier accompany me," she said.

"Yeh, that would've been great!"

The four of them toasted the night with a rare bottle of imported 1928 Moët champagne. The club's owner, Renzo Romano, appeared at the table to offer his salutations and a complimentary tray of sweets to the star and her friends. The sweets were divine, but Philip cringed at the cost of three guineas (nearly sixteen American dollars) for the bottle of champagne. He cursed Charlie Low under his breath for introducing his taste buds to the fine, bubbly drink. He took another sip without even the most remote warning of the evening's next surprise.

Mr. Romano pulled up a chair to the table. Lew offered a flute of champagne and Romano accepted. He sipped and then turned to Joy. "Miss Nichols, would you do my modest establishment the honor of performing tonight's closing number with our orchestra?"

Joy smiled and looked over at Philip. "I would love to sing for these brave men," she said. "But I have one condition."

"Anything you want," Romano replied.

"I would like my friend to accompany me." She pointed over the table at Philip. "Are you up to it, Philip?"

Philip hesitated but only for a moment. "Are you kidding me? Of course, I'd love to!"

"How about 'They Can't Take That Away from Me'? It's one of my favorites. If it's okay with you, Mr. Romano?"

"If that's what you want, that's what it'll be. I'll inform the orchestra. Do either of you need sheet music?"

Philip and Joy both smiled.

Joy responded, "I don't think that'll be necessary, will it, Philip?"

"No, ma'am."

The evening wore down. It was well past midnight when Mr. Romano appeared on stage. "Ladies and gentlemen, it is my distinct pleasure to introduce you to an Australian treasure, Miss Joy Nichols, who has graciously agreed to sing our closing number for us. She will be accompanied by one of the U.S. Army's finest young soldiers, Mr. Philip Zumwalt."

Philip escorted Joy onto the stage and took his seat at the piano. "It is such a *joy* to be here tonight at Romano's," Joy said. The crowd laughed. "Mr. Romano was kind enough to ask me to sing a song for you, and we'll get right to that, but first, I want to thank all of you soldiers, sailors, and airmen. Whether from the U.S. or Australia, know how much we appreciate your sacrifice while keeping the rest of us safe. As a tribute to you courageous servicemen, I have requested that one of your fellow soldiers accompany me on the piano tonight." She pointed to Philip. "Sergeant Zumwalt, let's do this!"

The saxophone wailed as Philip began to play. Joy sang:

> "There are many, many things
> That will keep me loving you
> And with your permission
> May I list a few?
> The way you wear your hat . . ."

The clientele, including Betty and Lew, were mesmerized as Joy finished the song with flair.

> "The memory of all that—
> No, no—they can't take that away from me."

The audience erupted with a standing ovation. Philip joined Joy as they held hands and took their bows. Betty and Lew continued their applause as Joy and Philip approached the table. "You two were wonderful," Betty said beaming.

Mr. Romano came back onstage, thanked Joy and Philip, and then led the crowd in a rousing rendition of "Waltzing Matilda" as the crowd sang and filed out.

Betty whispered into Philip's ear as they exited Romano's and hailed a cab. "How about a nightcap at my place?"

"Sounds great."

"Isn't Joy just the best?"

"She sure is. I still can't believe she asked me to accompany her."

"Well, good sir, you were wonderful, too!"

"Why thank you, kind madam. It did cap off a wonderful evening."

Philip took Betty's hand and helped her out of the cab. After a short walk, they entered Kingsclere's foyer and rode the elevator up to her apartment. She unlocked the door, excused herself, and headed into the kitchen. This time Philip took the initiative to start the fire. Sinking into the leather couch, he closed his eyes.

Nightmares had tortured his soul. Most nights he got only a few hours of sleep. He'd tried to exorcise the demons. Writing about them helped him cope somewhat. He thought maybe spilling his guts onto paper would be cathartic, but in the end, his fears remained. He wanted to love everything like the Russian author had advised. But how could he? War truly was hell, in every way. The only certainty in his life now was his love for El. Despite her misgivings, her love was as real to him as the violence he had experienced in the confined chamber of the death machine that now dominated his existence.

Betty returned to the living room and stood at her buffet. Various bottles of liquor sat in display on a silver tray. "How about some cognac?"

Philip nodded. Betty poured the reddish-brown liquor into a crystal snifter, delivered it to Philip, and sat down next to him on the couch. "Thank you for starting the fire. You're getting pretty good at that," she said. "I just love a cozy fire."

"I like it best when it's contained," he said. "Thanks for the drink." He lifted the snifter in a toast to his hostess. They sat quietly, sipping on their cognac.

"Are you okay?"

"Me? Yeh, I'm fine. Being with you has been amazing, Betty, but I have to be honest. All of this time here has only made me miss my girl back home even more. When I got the dreaded Dear John letter, I was heartbroken. I suppose I still am."

Betty listened. Gazing into the fire, she responded after a long silence. Her eyes were moist. "I understand, Philip. I really do. It's hard to lose someone you love. Mine was an Australian officer. Robert died on Rabaul, a member of the Lark Force. I miss him. He was so much like you, Philip, one of the really good guys. My time with you has made me feel so alive again." Betty paused. "You and I have something special, something I haven't experienced in a long time. It's strange, isn't it? Even in the midst of all this tragedy, there is still hope. Even in the midst of this awful war, there is still love."

Philip tenderly took her hand. "Sounds like you're the poet now, Betty. I'm so sorry for your loss. Sorry for all of this. But you're right. We must hold on to hope, and we've both witnessed love in ways we might never have imagined before. I'm afraid that you and I might love each other for a night or a week or who knows how long, but we both know all of that would only be temporary."

Betty bowed her head, hiding her tears. "Yes, as perfect as this has all been, I appreciate your honesty. If you love Elinor as much as I think you do, it will work out. I doubt very much that she's going to let a good one like you get away. But being separated is so difficult, isn't it?"

"It is."

She interrupted him. "I really think it best if we say goodbye tonight. I don't trust myself, and I'm guessing you might feel the same."

"I'm afraid you're right about that."

Philip could hardly look into the moist, blue-gray eyes of Betty Hittman, but he did. The smell of the orchid and her perfume, as well as her complete sincerity, would bring most men to their knees, begging for just one night of bliss. He rose from the couch. "Goodnight, Betty. Thank you for everything. Do take care of yourself." He leaned over and kissed her on the forehead.

"You, too, Philip. Goodbye."

At the door he paused but resisted looking back. He knew he had made the right decision. What he wrote earlier in his diary was still true. Betty was quite a gal. He would never forget his nights and days in Sydney. No one could ever take that away from either of them.

March 9, 1943

On Tuesday morning, Philip awakened at 8 a.m. and ate breakfast with Lew. "Some jerk stole my extra pants out of my room last night. I need to head over to the MP station and report it. Can you pick up my train ticket and meet me back at the Red Cross?"

"Sure. I'll see you a little later," Lew answered.

After filing his report with the military police, Philip tried unsuccessfully to cable some money home to Wayne. At 9:30 a.m. he met Lew at the Red Cross.

"Here's your ticket. We leave for Townsville tonight. Have to be at the station at seven," Lew said. "This is for you, too. Betty asked me to give it to you." Lew handed him a letter. A single word appeared on the envelope, written in blue ink: *Philip*.

He opened it.

Dearest Philip,

Even though things did not end up with us being together, like I thought they might, I just wanted you to know that my prayers are with you and that I will never forget our time together. As I told you, you are the perfect gentleman. Your dear El has herself one fine man. I pray this war will end soon and everyone will be able to go home to those they love.

I hesitate to write this, Philip, but I have always been honest with you, so here it goes. I sincerely hope that your life with El goes as planned, but if things go amiss, perhaps you might consider a trip to Sydney. Here's to both hope and love. I promise the next bottle of Moët will be on me. Take care, soldier.

Love,
Betty

CHAPTER 50

News of the Posse

PHILIP MISSED HIS FAMILY, ESPECIALLY HOMER. Good news arrived back at the home front in few and far-between parcels. With great delight, he sat down and recounted to his brother the latest such news.

March 12, 1943

Dear Homer,

We arrived back in Townsville last night, a rather uneventful trip. Had an overnight stay in Brisbane where I called upon Muriel Ross, remember her? Mother reminded me to look her up if I got a chance. She's a Red Cross volunteer. We ate lunch together and had a chance to catch up and talk about home. It made me even more homesick. I had a great time in Sydney. A group of us hung out together, ate some great food, went to a few clubs, and saw a wonderful operetta. I met a fine woman there named Betty Hittman. I think we will always be great friends. We shared some wonderful moments together.

On the train to Townsville, Lew Godlove and I joined a drinking party. There were a couple of Red Cross nurses in the compartment and one of them was from Illinois. Her name was Lt. Annie Baum. Her father graduated from the U of I and we got to talking about growing up in small towns. When I told her I was from Nebo, she acted like she had seen a ghost. I asked what was the matter, and she launched into a story about a couple of Marines she'd met when she was stationed in Brisbane.

She'd just received her first Saturday night pass and joined her nurse friends who were invited to a party at the Breakfast Creek Hotel. Quite a hot spot in Brisbane, she told me. The soldiers flocked there—beer, music, and right behind the hotel there were a couple of brothels. A parrot evidently sat out on the hotel's veranda and when the women of the night walked by on their way to work, the parrot would blurt out, "Here come the whores. Here come the whores!"

Anyway, that particular night, the First Marine Division stormed into Brisbane like they were retaking Guadalcanal. Quite a few of them ended up at the hotel. Annie was sitting at the bar having a drink when a Marine came up to her. She told me, "He flashed this big grin at me and said his name was Trout—Big Fish, they called him." She went on, "We had a few beers and danced. He went on and on chattering about his hometown, his friends called The Posse, and his new bride, DeAnne. Then this large man came over and joined our table for a minute. Trout introduced him to me as the Giant. His real name, Trout said, was Jerry Inness. Later, he introduced us to an Australian girl he'd been flirting with all night. Her name was Trudy."

Needless to say, I was elated to be getting news of these guys! They were alive and partying just like it was Saturday night back at the Casino.

She said Steve told her I was going to be a pilot, and then, when the war was over, a famous composer. After way too many beers, he started talking about his unit, The Old Breed. He and the Giant were on Edson's Ridge. Annie told me he laughed and said, "If we hadn't held 'em off, the Japs would have taken back the island. If that would have happened, we'd all be having to learn Japanese by now."

I asked her if they were okay and she told me they looked awfully thin to her, even the Giant. He told her the other members of the

Posse were safe. Me in Australia, Harkness in England, and Epperson, most likely, on his way to North Africa. One thing she found hilarious was how unique Steve and Jerry's laughs were. She said they laughed all night long and so did everyone who was with them. Their R & R was short-lived though; the next day, they shipped out to Melbourne headed toward another campaign. She said, "I really hope I'll see them again."

I told her, "So do I."

Quite a story, huh? Please share it with the Ross, Trout, and Inness families, if you get a chance. Be safe and well.

Your brother,

Philip

Philip received a letter from Homer written over a month earlier. He was pleased that, at that particular time, at least, the entire Posse was safe.

February 7, 1943

Dear Philip,

Just got off the phone with Pat. She got a call from Billy and rumor has it that his airborne division is headed overseas. She's worried to death, but he told her that being a football hero and all, no Krauts are going to kill him. I guess that, just like you, most of these men would rather be home with their families, but it looks like we are in it for the long haul. Bottom line is they attacked us. I am in the NROTC now and will receive orders once I graduate. Pat also told me she had talked with Harkness's parents. He landed safely in England and will be flying B-17's on bombing raids over Germany. I don't even want to try to imagine what you and all of your friends are going through.

Rosie and I broke up. I'm guessing the same is true with you and El as I saw her out to dinner with some other guy in Quincy. It was the same night Rosie and I decided to split. Don't be too brokenhearted, Philip. I'm pretty sure there are plenty of fine women who would love to be on your arm. I had a date with Ida Dell Kinnamon last weekend. She's swell. We really hit it off. Be safe, brother, and remember you don't have to be a hero. You already are in my eyes.

Best always,
Homer

Homer's letter was no surprise; it only affirmed what he already knew, but he was not about to give up his love for El. Her being with another man didn't mean anything. After all, he'd spent time with Betty. El had been honest with him about seeing other people. There was nothing more to it than that. Deep in his soul, Philip believed they would be together. It was a belief he chose to hold on to.

CHAPTER 51

Valentine's Day
and a Cablegram

ANOTHER WEEK PASSED. MORE RAIN, another mission. Middle of March, early in the morning, Philip returned to his tent following another successful raid over Rabaul. He discovered a letter with unfamiliar handwriting on his desk.

"Sergeant Nyman said I could bring it to you," Burnsy reported. "Looks like it's from your little gal back home. Hey Z, does she know you were gallivantin' around Sydney with that rich dame?"

"Nothing for her to know about, pal. Nothing happened. Miss Hittman and I were and still are just friends." Philip didn't care for Burnsy's allegation, but it was a common assumption about the men who returned from R & R. As Kipling wrote in his poem "Tommy":

Single men in barracks don't
Grow into plaster saints.

"Man, I'd like to have a friend like that." Burnsy laughed.

Philip opened the letter knowing it wasn't from El. Instead, it was a letter from Pat Carpenter. He prayed it wasn't more bad news from home.

February 14, 1943

Dear Philip,

Happy Valentine's Day! I'm sorry I've been so neglectful in writing. Seems like I'm always grading English papers. Now, Mr. Meacham has placed me in charge of the library and the Speech Team. Ugh! Too much work. I'm pretty certain Billy hasn't had a spare moment to write to you, but I wanted to send you our news. Billy gave me an engagement ring the night before he shipped out. Lord only knows where he's headed. Hush, hush.

Stopped by to see your folks last week. They seem to be doing fine. Your mother talked a lot about her students, and your father is pretty busy building houses in Alton. They reported that both of your brothers are well, and they're thrilled every time one of your V-mails arrives.

I feel terrible about you and El. Your mother told me El returned the lavaliere you'd given to her; sent it in the mail with a nice note to your mother. She wrote to your mother that she was just not ready to make a permanent commitment and that she was seeing another man. It just didn't seem right to El to keep the necklace. I'm so sorry, Philip. I imagine this isn't the best news you could receive on Valentine's Day, but I am certain once you return to the States, you two will figure it out. I always felt that you were made for each other.

I pray every night that all of you boys will come home safely, and I send you all good wishes and luck.

Your friend,

Pat

Philip folded the letter and placed it in his footlocker with the others. That pretty much sealed the deal. Strange that El wouldn't let him know that she had returned the lavaliere to his mother. Unlike her. He was more disappointed than angry, but he remained convinced their love would survive this awful war. Pat's reporting how much the

V-mails meant to his folks made him feel guilty that he hadn't written home in a while. He jotted a letter, walked to the post office, and sent the following cablegram home to his mother:

Dear Mother,

Just to let you know that I am safe and got to enjoy a respite from my duties. I've had a memorable few days in Sydney. Met some fascinating people. Even got to accompany Joy Nichols, a famous Australian singer, for one of her numbers. I also had lunch with Muriel Ross in Brisbane. I am so happy you told me she was over here. Tell her folks she seems to be doing fine.

Hope Homer's training is going well. Sent a letter to him today. Give Wayne and Dad my greetings. Keep those "Banners" coming; I love reading the hometown news. Miss all of you and hope to be home soon.

Love,

Philip

CHAPTER 52

Of Wounds and Tears

March 28, 1943

LATE ON A SUNDAY AFTERNOON, Philip reclined on his cot. He had planned on reading, listening to the radio, and taking a nap. There were days he didn't mind hanging out in his tent. It was somewhat entertaining to listen to his tentmates kibitzing or arguing about various topics from sports to women. He had been with Burnside and Winter since their training days at Fort Morrison. Ed Stevens had joined them, a fine young man. Philip felt as if he had almost become a mentor to the ball turret gunner from Mountain Lakes, New Jersey.

Burnsy sat outside the tent and was conversing with one of the Papuan women. Big and strong with his bushy brown hair hanging over his right eye, Burnsy ignored the Army Air Force's guidelines regarding haircuts. Philip was intrigued with the scene unfolding through his tent's open flap. Was it possible Burnsy was attracted to the woman? It reminded Philip of a scene in a Tarzan movie. Although he felt like a voyeur, Philip couldn't resist watching.

Burnsy stood half naked in his jungle fatigue shorts. Hanging around his waist in desperate need of washing, they needed to be added to the pile of clothes being scrubbed by the woman. Philip thought Burnsy's body could also use a good scrubbing.

The dark-skinned woman was also half naked, a common sight at the base. She was wrapped in a multicolored linen skirt. Philip had come across a new word in his reading the other day—*beatific*, meaning blissfully happy. It appeared to Philip that Burnsy was definitely beatific when this particular native woman was in his presence. Ruth was her name. Burnsy had taken on the task to teach her English, a task he seemed to relish.

Philip watched as Burnsy faced her and put his hands on her shoulders. "Let's stop for a moment, Ruth. I'd like to teach you some new words."

She nodded, as if she understood, but continued to rub his shirt with all her might against the washboard. He grabbed her hands. She looked into his deep hazel eyes.

"Stop, please," he whispered.

She nodded again.

"Ruth, today I am going to teach you four new words. Each pair of words looks the same when I write them down on paper, but they have completely different meanings. They are called homographs," he said.

She gave him a puzzled look. "Hom . . . o . . . gr . . . again, please. I not understand word."

Philip wanted to intercede and tell him that he was trying to teach her a far too complicated portion of the language. Instead, he lay quietly on his cot pretending to read while he continued to eavesdrop and watch through the unzipped door of the tent.

"Okay, never mind the word. I know this might be a bit confusing, but it's important to know that words can look the same but have different meanings. Do you understand?" Burnsy said.

Ruth replied, "Maybe. I listen to you. You explain. You good at explaining things."

Philip thought, *I can't wait to hear this. Homographs. Ha!*

"So, when I cry, a tear comes from my eye," he told her, and then he scratched out a word on a blank piece of paper. "There. T-E-A-R."

"Like when you sad?"

"Yes, exactly."

"Are you sad, Sergeant Burnside?"

Philip imagined Burnsy was sad and probably wishing he could escape with Ruth to some peaceful part of the island and leave this horrid war behind. It was obvious sweet Ruth had pierced Burnsy's tough exterior and somehow found her way into his soul.

He answered her, "Yeh, sometimes I am, Ruth, but that's beside the point now. Stay with me." He ripped the sheet of paper in two. On the other piece of paper, he told her he was going to write the word again.

"Why you do that, Sarge?" Ruth asked.

"No, what you would say is 'why did you tear that paper in half, Sarge?' See, it looks like the same word, but it means something entirely different. Get it?"

"I think so. First word mean tear in eye, second word mean tear up paper, but they look the same when you write down on paper."

"Exactly. Very good, Ruth."

"I need to get back to laundry, Sarge."

"One more, Ruth." Burnsy turned over the pieces of paper and wrote something on both. "First word is wound." He pointed to the scar on his arm where a piece of shrapnel had grazed him. "This is a wound, Ruth."

She smiled. "I happy it not go in your heart. I would have tear then."

Burnsy smiled in return. "Yeh, me, too. But another meaning for the same word means wrapping something around something else."

Again, Philip observed a look of confusion on Ruth's face.

Burnsy pointed toward the bottom of the tent. "See the rope is wound around the stake."

"Oh," Ruth answered, "but none of those words sound the same."

Now she's got him, Philip thought. *His intellectual equal. Could it be? Is Burnsy in love with Ruth?* He wondered about the possibility of their future, of all their futures. How many tears, how many wounds, how many lives will be torn apart by this insidious war? He also wondered if Burnsy was thinking at this very moment how sublime it would be to lay with Ruth, wound in her warmth and love.

He couldn't help himself. He closed his eyes and thought of El, and he yearned for the same—to lay with her in the bed of their room at the Majestic, to linger, wound in each other's arms, to have stayed there—forever.

He wiped away an uninvited tear from his cheek, closed his book, and shut his eyes. Beatific he was not.

CHAPTER 53

There the Dance Is

BURNSY'S TENDERNESS TOWARD RUTH OFTEN SURPRISED Philip. Seeing two people so much in love started him thinking of El once again. He slid off his cot and settled into the chair at his jerry-rigged writing desk—a plank of wood nailed onto a pair of ammo crates. Throwing caution to the wind, he wrote:

Dear El,

There are times I can't help but think of you, times when I have to share what I'm thinking about because I know you will understand. While on leave in Sydney, I met a woman named Betty Hittman, a wonderful person. She reminded me of the poetry of T. S. Eliot, who I had read in college and liked very much. Born in St. Louis, he later moved to England. Betty gave me a book of his poetry, and I was initially quite taken by a poem entitled "The Hollow Men." As I read more of his poetry, I became more and more captivated by his language. Apparently, he is currently in the process of writing a longer poem entitled "The Four Quartets." I imagine he might have finished all four parts by now, but in the book Betty gave me the First Quartet was actually the last poem in the book. It was entitled Burnt Norton. When I read that poem, I thought of you, especially the following verse:

"At the still point of the turning world.
Neither flesh nor fleshless;
Neither from nor towards;
at the still point,
there the dance is. . ."

When I think back to the moments we spent together, most of them could be defined like that, not just when we were dancing, but nearly every, single instance. The world stood still, El. It reminded me of acciaccatura, the musical term I taught you in band. Remember? A grace note, ornamental, a timeless note, a momentary pause, maybe even a moment of grace. It's there, and then it's gone. Time frozen in place.

Those moments of ours remain still in my mind. When I think of them, there is lightness in my soul. It exists somewhere deep inside of me, completely defying explanation. Perhaps that is the mystery that so many religions have tried to solve.

It reminded me of what you wrote to me, quoting Dostoevsky, ". . . if we love everything then we'll perceive the divine mystery in things." In war that has been so difficult. I want to love everything, but these have been days of darkness for me. It's like a mystery. I am confused and confounded. Moments of anger and madness, beyond my wildest imagination, dominate my thinking.

Losing four of my closest friends sent me spiraling into a state of mind too dark to even describe. Here, at the other end of the world, I yearn for you, for real love. I yearn for peace. When I roam out into the woods that surround my tent, I find a certain degree of peace in the silence there, but it only makes me long to be back in your arms, to go with you, once again, to the still points we shared, where the light of goodness, your goodness, lessened my darkest fears. I not only felt loved, I felt safe.

I miss you more than you can ever know, but I also understand what you are feeling. I still plan on keeping my promise. I will come

*home. By the way, just in case you might still have feelings for me,
let me assure you that Betty and I are just good friends, kind of like
you and Dr. Thoroughgood.*
    Yours Truly,
    Philip

He placed his pen on the makeshift desk, crawled back into his cot,
and slept.

CHAPTER 54

Tent Talks

March 31, 1943

WEDNESDAY EVENING CLOSED with another bull session in the tent. Topics ranged from the mystique of Australian women to available books to read to surviving the next mission. Word around camp was that the evening movie had been canceled, worsening Stevens's foul mood. He swatted a gigantic mosquito on his neck, splattering his own blood all over his cot. Classical music played on the phonograph.

"I like this music. Kinda *exotic*." Burnsy loved the word.

"Fauré, a French composer," Philip stated.

"Maybe you need to play this record for some dame, Winter. You might get laid," Burnsy teased.

"Savin' myself for my wedding night. Not sleeping around with those Aussies or the natives like some of you guys," Winter was quick to respond.

"What exactly do you mean by that, pal?" Stevens sat straight up in his cot. "I hope you're not calling Australian women prostitutes!"

"Call it whatever you want, Ed," said Winter. "I'm just telling you that I'm not interested in these foreign gals. I'm saving myself for a purebred American woman."

"Well, you got your opinion and I got mine. I think the Aussies are swell, don't you, Lucky?" Stevens looked to Philip for some affirmation. He had heard Philip had been acquainted with an Australian woman during his last leave.

"Yeh, well, don't knock the natives until you've tasted the local delicacies," Burnsy said.

Winter offered his defense. "I'm not saying all the Aussies are ladies of the night, but you have to admit there's a lot of 'em out there making a damned good livin' off of GIs."

"Not the ones I've met," Stevens countered. "They've all been real classy, and most of 'em coulda had an officer if they wanted. I'm just happy Chic chose me."

"How about we just listen to some music and read our books, or whatever you fellas are reading. Let's just agree to disagree on the lovely Australian ladies and the Papuan women," Philip negotiated, hoping for some peace and quiet.

"Hey, why'd they cancel the movie tonight, anyway?" Stevens growled.

"The projector broke down, numbnuts," Burnsy answered.

Philip suspected that Winter's cloaked accusation still lurked in the dank humidity of the enlisted men's tent, gnawing at Stevens. The soldier rolled over on his cot and pouted like a three-year-old. The recording ended. Philip turned off the phonograph and tuned the radio to the Armed Forces Network station. Big Band music. Sinatra was singing.

"Ol' Blue Eyes!" Stevens had recovered. "I'll bet he gets all the ladies."

"If Frankie ever makes it over here, you better hold on tight to Chic. I saw him back in the States right before the war broke out. He was one smooth customer," Philip said with a playful, dramatic swoon.

"He won't get Chic, no matter how handsome he is or how good a singer he is. She's in love with me."

"Really?" Winter retorted, tossing out more disparaging remarks about the Australian women. "Loves you? You mean she loves the booze you buy her and the flowers and the presents. That's what she loves, rookie, not you. Don't kid yourself. These dames don't love any-one more than any other. They're gettin' what they can get. Livin' for the moment, just like us. It ain't love, pal."

"No, she does! She *really* does love me, Chuck," Stevens said, turn-ing serious. "We're gonna get married when this whole thing is over and settle back in Mountain Lakes."

"Assuming this war ever ends," Burnsy said.

"So, Lucky, what happened with that Australian beauty of yours? Godlove told me she was a knockout." Stevens was still trying to build his case.

"Yeh, and Slepko said she's got a load of lettuce," Burnsy added.

"Could be," Philip replied. "She's swell, but we're just friends."

"Why? I thought your little sweetheart back home dumped you. At least that's what you whined about after you let me read her letter," Winter said.

"Let's just say the jury's still out. I plan on getting back to the States soon, and I'm not giving her up without a fight. As for Miss Hittman, she lost her fiancé, an Aussie officer in the Lark Force. Tough deal. That's it, end of story."

"Did ya get lucky, Lucky?" Burnsy smirked.

"Fuck you, Burnsy," Philip responded, swearing uncharacteristi-cally and thrusting his middle finger at his buddy.

"Still friends with her?" asked Stevens.

"Yeh, friends," Philip replied. "Damned war confuses everything!"

"Yeh, it does. Sorry, Lucky. Afraid I struck a chord," Burnsy actu-ally apologized. "I didn't mean anything by it. I'll bet she was a real good gal."

Philip's reply was nearly inaudible. "Yeh, she was."

Burnsy blew a smoke ring. "I guess I'm just a no-good son of a bitch. My motto is, 'Get what you can get.' It's not like we're gonna see tomorrow anyway, right? I'm not picky like old Chuck. And you guys can make all the fun you want to of Ruth, but she's one fine woman."

"I hope you treat her with some respect," Philip said.

"You're damned right I do, Lucky. She's a good person, in a lot of ways."

"I have to tell you, fellas. Betty was great—attractive, smart. Just about anything a guy would want in a woman, but I didn't want to use her just because she's a skirt. If I'm going to fall in love with a woman, I have to be willing to make a commitment to her. I guess I'm just old-fashioned that way. Besides, the whole thing with El is up in the air. I mean we both have the freedom to see other people. I really don't want her just sitting around pining for me. I want her to have a life."

Burnsy was back. "You're still living in the dark ages, Lucky. We might all be dead tomorrow. I say love the one you're with, old buddy. Love the one you're with."

Philip contemplated Burnsy's contention and replied, "I know I should just be living for the moment right now, too—happy to be alive and, like you say, Burnsy, get whatever I can. Live life to its fullest. But there's something inside me that just, I don't know, won't let me do that. Maybe it's because I really do love El with all my heart. Is there anything wrong with that?"

"Good for you, pal. Y'all need to stick to those good old American dames!" Winter proclaimed.

"Hell, you don't have to really love 'em, Lucky. You just have to, you know, *love* 'em, if you get my drift." Burnsy was back on a roll. "And if you're really lucky, Lucky, it'll be more than two at a time."

Winter threw his magazine at Burnside, who was doubled over in laughter.

# CHAPTER 55

Of Prerequisites
and *The Last of the Mohicans*

"**Y**OU GUYS EVER WONDER IF ANYONE** back home has a clue about what's going on over here? I mean, what's really going on?" Philip's question curtailed the laughter. "I hope the time will come when we get the chance to tell folks back home the truth."

"Is that what you're writing about in your diary? Us and the war? You could get in a lot of trouble for that, couldn't you?" Stevens asked.

"It might be a little dangerous, but it helps with my sanity. Cleanses the soul," Philip replied.

"Our souls could sure use some of that," Burnsy remarked.

"If the folks back home knew what we've been going through, I think they'd raise holy hell. When this insanity is finally over, I'm gonna write a book and tell people what it was really like out here, flying with the *Forgotten Fifth*. Of course, that requires a pretty extreme prerequisite."

"What's that?" asked Stevens. "A prerequisite?"

"In this case, Ed, that would be staying alive," Philip told him.

"You've done a pretty good job at that."

"Yeh, but I'm afraid flying with McCullar is definitely lowering my odds."

Burnsy agreed. "McCullar's a helluva pilot but too much of a daredevil for me. Flying with him is almost a sure ticket to buying the farm. It's crazy to fly a sixty-five-thousand-pound airplane two hundred feet above a target to drop a load. We're just asking for it. Of course, I guess it does give a flyboy braggin' rights. I mean, all the men think McCullar's a hero, but that skip bombing shit's for the birds."

Everyone laughed, and then an hour of silence ensued.

Stevens interrupted the peace and quiet. "So, you really gonna write a book, Lucky? That why you're always writin' in those diaries of yours?"

"Yeh, helps me remember what happened here, day to day," Philip said. "When I get home, I hope I can make some sense of all this. Folks need to know what war is really like. Maybe then we won't have any more war."

Burnsy reentered the conversation. "I doubt that, Lucky. As long as man is on this planet, there's gonna be wars. It's inevitable—too much greed."

"Hey, if you do write a book, make me look good, okay?" Stevens requested.

"As good as I can, kid." Philip laughed.

"Speakin' of books, you got any good ones I can read, Lucky?" Stevens had worked his way through most of the magazines but remained bored.

"There's a few in my footlocker. Look at Cooper's *The Last of the Mohicans*. It's a good one."

Stevens opened Philip's olive drab footlocker and took out the book.

"Hawkeye's the name of the main character," Philip said wistfully. "I gave that name to one of my buddies back home. Now he's Lieutenant Harkness, stationed over in England. Dropped out of Harvard Law School so he could drop bombs on Europe. When the war broke out, he signed up to be a pilot. He's flying seventeens over Germany in broad daylight." Philip shook his head. "You gotta wonder who's issuing those orders! Flying in broad daylight. It's gotta be a turkey shoot for the Krauts. Hawkeye was one of the smartest guys I ever knew, a damned good man. I just hope he's still alive."

"It's nuts how they're sending those men into that shit during daylight, but that's the stinkin' military!" Stevens fumed. "They're crazy as hell, but maybe all of us have to be a little crazy, too, so we can win this goddamned war." As he spoke, he rummaged through Philip's footlocker. "Hey, Lucky, what's this other stuff? Damn, how many diaries do you have?" Shuffling through Philip's books and letters, Stevens held up two other diaries.

"Three. I imagine if the brass finds out I'm keeping 'em, I'm screwed. They're probably right. If we ever get overrun here, those diaries would be quite a cache for the Japs. Most of our missions and targets are contained in those journals. I tried to keep as accurate an account as possible to remind me what we've been through over here. When Captain Leonard was killed, some of the fellas told me a couple of officers came in and cleaned all his stuff out—took everything. They told his tentmates they'd send all of his personal effects home, but one of the first sergeants told me they burned his letters and a diary he'd been keeping."

"All of his personal stuff? Can they do that?" Stevens shook his head.

"Security, I guess. They can do pretty much whatever they want. Anyhow, they destroyed all of it." Philip was matter-of-fact. "Guess they don't want the Japs reading our love letters."

The soldiers chuckled, but right then and there they made a pledge to one another, agreeing that if any of them died, the survivors would do everything in their power to make sure their buddies' personal effects didn't fall into the hands of the brass.

Philip's mind drifted back to simpler times, nights when he and his brothers would retreat to their bedroom and share their most private thoughts. They trusted one another—whatever they discussed remained confidential and never left the room. On this night, Philip's struggle was overwhelming. He needed to share his grief, his disillusionment, his fear, and his hope with someone. He chose Homer.

March 31, 1943

Dear Homer,

I have some sad news to report. Last Thursday I received word that another of my friends is gone. Bobby Freeman's plane was shot down, and he perished in the crash. I'll need to notify May Gray, a girl he had been seeing over here. It's so difficult making friends and then losing them, Homer.

My newest friend is Ed Stevens. We met at Fenton Field in 1942 but became good friends after he arrived at the Sixty-Fourth Bomb Squadron and was assigned to my tent. He's small in stature, but tough as nails. A ball turret gunner on a B-17 has to be resilient. Manning the machine guns on the underbelly of a Flying Fortress is one of the most precarious assignments. Ed replaced Les Stewart. Les was a real character and one helluva ball turret gunner. I don't know how those guys climb down into that death trap, but they do. Thank God, they do!

A story recently circulated around here about another gunner whose turret stuck. The hydraulic system was so shot up that the wheels of the plane couldn't be lowered and the gunner couldn't get out. When the bomber crash-landed, the gunner was crushed to death. The other nine crew members survived.

"Just another rumor," Ed told me after hearing the story. I do think he's impervious to fear. All he seems to live for is shooting down Zeroes and marrying his Aussie sweetheart. Ed is the third gunner we've had in the last few months.

They call me Lucky now since two crews I served on have been lost at sea. I continue to play the piano and sing at the USO Club or the Allied Fighting Forces Club on the nights they're open. Takes my mind off all of this and breaks the monotony when we're not on a mission, but I wonder how much longer I can take this. I wonder when my number will be up.

Rumors have been floating around I've been accepted into the AvCad program. Once I receive my orders, I'll be sent back to the

States for training. Most likely my orders are, right now, at the bottom of a pile on some clerk's desk, lost in a maze of military red tape, but my hope is they'll come within the next few days, and I'll be home soon . . .

Philip took a break from his letter writing. The rain began to fall outside once again. Stevens turned to him. It was almost as if he had read Philip's mind. "Hey, Lucky. Any word on your AvCad orders?"

"A couple of desk jockeys told me they heard they were in the pipeline. But don't forget, we're in the Army. I'll believe it when I hold the papers in my hand."

The evening passed as the men listened to music and read. The tent was warm and felt like home now. Burnsy placed his girlie magazine on the floor and stared at the ceiling. "Hey, Lucky. You think we're all gonna die?"

"We're all gonna die, Burnsy, just not right now. Rumor has it, no one gets out of this world alive. But until then, we're gonna be big heroes. A New York ticker tape parade. I'll get my officer's commission and pilot wings, go to Europe, take out old Hitler, and then come back here and get Hirohito. FDR'll pin a medal on me, Old Dugout Doug will shake my hand, and we'll all live happily ever after."

Stevens entered back into the conversation. "Then what're you gonna do? I mean, you gonna get hitched to that gal back home?"

Philip turned thoughtful. "I don't honestly know, Ed, but here's a question for you gentlemen. Is it possible to love two women at the same time?" Betty's letter from weeks earlier made him wonder what would happen if El decided she no longer was willing to wait.

"Naw, I agree with Burnsy. Love the one you're with, buddy, love the one you're with. Or maybe even more than one, maybe two or three." Stevens was, at last, becoming one of the guys. He rolled over in his cot. "Right, Burnsy?"

"Fuckin' A!" Burnside grinned.

Philip laughed along with the rest of his buddies at Burnsy's irreverent sense of humor. He appreciated the carefree attitude of his tentmates but was tired of conversation. He would finish his letter to his brother later. "It's been real nice talking to you guys," he said, "but I'd like to listen to some music for a while. No offense?"

"Naw, none taken. We could all use a little peace and quiet," Stevens responded. He opened *The Last of the Mohicans* and continued to read.

CHAPTER 56

A Pyrrhic Victory

April 3, 1943

THE DEAFENING REVERBERATION OF THE ENGINES and the force of the propellers were a strain on the senses of any crew who ascended the metal stairway leading into the belly of a B-17. That was especially true at 0050. Being a flyboy in World War II in the Pacific Theater was not exactly like what the media portrayed. While Philip settled into his preflight checklist, he thought about a diary entry he'd made earlier:

The American public has, over a long period of time, built up a picture of clean-cut, alert young men coming into their aircraft in full flying equipment, prepared for a combat mission. Clean shaven, every hair in place, sleek and well fed, every man is an expert in his job and is a born airman, flying because he loves to fly. Alas, how different is reality!

A typical mission goes something like this. The crew is awakened about midnight, eats several half-cooked pancakes, drinks a cup of vile Australian coffee, and rides on a truck to the plane only about half-awake. As they lie around waiting for the pilot to warm up the engines, they are a motley group. Dressed in a variety of clothing, half American, half Australian, some are wearing shorts, some coveralls, some trousers; some have no shirts; no two have the same kind of headgear; several need a shave. What conversation there may be revolves around every conceivable subject from football to leave in Sydney, with emphasis on the coming mission. Usually, however, everyone is much too sleepy to talk. There are also extended sessions of muttered cursing at having to get up so early in the morning. The casual observer back in the United States would, from such an observation, feel certain that such men could not be an efficient fighting team, but results obtained prove differently.

As Philip looked around, he was reassured that he was sur-rounded by as worthy a group of young airmen as the Forty-Third had to offer, all were Fightin' Fools, and he even had to include him-self in that category. The crew was led by Major Ken McCullar, the premier heavy bomber pilot of the Forty-Third. McCullar's reputation was widespread across the South West Pacific; a living legend, the top skip-bombing pilot was also noted for bringing all his men and plane home in one piece.

Philip settled into his familiar radio operator's seat. If he was fortunate, he had to complete only two more missions—this one, one more, then home. He could even be going back to the States as soon as the day after he received his orders for AvCad. Either was a more than acceptable option.

When McCullar walked into a room, the women took notice and the men stood a little taller. Philip would be proud to be even half the pilot McCullar was. The pilot went through the checklist with copilot Second Lieutenant Byron Andrews. Once completed, he came over the interphone system. "We're headed to Kavieng, boys. Got a few eggs to unload."

Lifting off without incident was a normal takeoff with McCullar. Burnsy sat across from Philip, replacing Corporal Howard at the last minute as a side gunner and assistant radio operator. As they approached their target, Burnsy removed his headgear and turned toward Philip. "Like I said before, Lucky. This skip-bombing shit's for the birds!"

Philip removed his headgear. "No argument from me on that, Burnsy," he said, smiling.

"What the hell. It's as good a day as any to die. You're a good man, Lucky. We're gonna get through this war. We have to, that's what good men do. We fight to survive, just like Tom Joad. And, just like old Joad, I'm a man of action. I've learned a lot from you, pal, and I just want you to know I appreciate it. Bottom line is this, if a man's number is up, it's up—so be it."

"You're not going to die, Burnsy. We're gonna get out of this and win the war. Remember my plan?"

"That's your plan, pal, not God's." It was unusual for Burnsy to mention God since he normally purported to be an atheist.

Through the headgear McCullar issued an order. "Cease all radio contact, men. We're approaching the target."

The major was all business. Having practically rewritten the playbook on low-altitude bombing, he was admired by enlisted men and the brass. A handsome, cavalier, authentic American hero, he had only one problem: McCullar was so obsessed with killing the enemy, he often took risks that, in the minds of most, were too daring. Philip understood his urgency. Like all the other men, McCullar wanted to end the war as soon as possible and get back home to Mississippi.

The Flying Fortress went into a dive. The crew tightened their seat belts and held on as the plane descended. Four thousand feet, three thousand feet. The target came into view. Lieutenant David Schultz, the bombardier, readied himself. McCullar picked a light cruiser out of the convoy docked in Kavieng Harbor. Doing 200 knots, he leveled off his massive ship at 200 feet. Schultz released the load of four 500-pound demolition bombs, all with a four- to five-second delay fuse.

Philip and Burnsy manned their .50 caliber machine guns, moving separately, Philip to the left window and Burnsy to the right. They watched from their respective vantage points as the Japanese cruiser was blown out of the water and into a million pieces. The ship caught fire as the ammunition magazines it carried exploded. The Japanese sailors looked like ants swimming in a sea of oil and fire. McCullar circled the aircraft as the crew watched their target slowly keel into the water.

Philip's heart was heavy. How could he justify all this? He was an accomplice to murder, sending other human beings to a death too awful to even comprehend. The lucky ones were those of the enemy who were already dead when they fell into the fiery water. This was madness; all of it was madness.

"Well done, men. Well done," McCullar's praise echoed through the interphone system as he turned the plane south and headed back to Port Moresby. Antiaircraft artillery fire had commenced from the shoreline, but there were no Zeroes attacking. Philip scanned the horizon and the sky above, relieved there were no bogies. He heard a blast from behind that caused the plane to lunge. A cannon shell had hit the right wing, but McCullar was able to adjust—no damage to either of the props.

Philip yelled at Burnsy, "Whew, that was a close call, pal!"

As the plane continued its ascension, Philip clicked the safety on his weapon and turned to his friend. Although standing, Burnsy was slumped over his machine gun.

Philip was surprised Burnsy could actually take a nap in such an awkward position. "You takin' the rest of the morning off, Burn . . ." The name died on his lips when he saw deep red droplets dripping from the left side of Burnsy's skull, part of which was gone. His brain protruded from what remained of his head, a frothy mass of gray matter crowned with red bubbles, his hair dark with clotted blood. Philip froze in shock.

Corporal George Mowad slid away from his position as tail

gunner. "C'mon, Sarge. Let's lay him down. Pretty sure he's gone." Mowad helped Philip lower Burnsy to the floor of the aircraft.

"God dammit! God dammit!" Philip began to sob. "He wasn't even supposed to be here! He wasn't supposed . . ." He cradled Burnsy's mutilated head in his lap. His mind raced back as he wept uncontrollably—a motion picture sped up in reverse. Burnsy at the Forbidden City, Burnsy in the tent waxing eloquent, Burnsy sipping tea and smoking his cigarettes at the Paris Café, Burnsy being unmerciful to Winter and Stevens, Burnsy with Ruth.

The world came crashing down on Philip. The war had dealt its cruelest blow. How could Burnsy be gone? Death had long ago ceased to be impersonal, but this death was more intimate than he could have ever imagined, and he wanted nothing to do with it. *Wounds and tears.* Burnsy couldn't have chosen better words to teach Ruth.

Mission completed, McCullar landed the plane at Moresby at approximately 0800. Philip went directly to his tent and broke the news of Burnsy's death to Winter and Stevens.

The Greeks would have called the mission a pyrrhic victory. A light cruiser was sunk; hundreds of Japanese sailors had been eradicated. The skip bombing was successful. But at what cost? Philip sat on his cot, still shell-shocked. Doubt filled his mind as he wondered, *How much longer is Lucky going to be lucky?*

CHAPTER 57

A Time for Every Purpose

April 4, 1943

NEARLY A MONTH OF MONOTONY in Port Moresby had occupied Philip and his crew until the previous day's mission. He had no answers for Burnsy's death. Like O'Scannell, he found all this senseless. Still sleep-deprived and exhausted, he entered the service tent, the same place he went on Sunday mornings twice a month. He questioned the legitimacy of attending the service, but the local chaplain, Thomas Shea, was counting on him, and he had given Shea his word. He wished Shea had some answers to some of the questions raised in his discussions with Godlove. He shuffled in behind the simple wooden altar and took his seat on the bench at the upright piano—still not in tune.

The smell of jungle rot was wretched, but rare early morning sunshine brightened the venue. Foggy steam enfolded a half-dozen rows of wooden chairs populating the crude temple of worship. A few hungover soldiers and nurses straggled in, metal coffee cups in hand. Philip wondered if they, too, had come looking for some of the same answers he sought. They bowed their heads in silence.

Are their prayers the same as mine? Philip wondered. *Survival, an end to war—all war—a lasting peace?*

The seats gradually filled. Shea entered from the rear of the tent, dressed in his fatigues. The oak leaves on his uniform subtly displayed his officer status, but he was more concerned with the welfare of his flock, these sleepy-eyed GIs and nurses, than his rank. He incessantly prayed to his God to keep them out of harm's way. Shea was especially fond of Philip.

Philip noted Shea's gaze rest on him for a moment, and he thought back to their first encounter. It was late on a Saturday night three months earlier when Shea had heard Philip playing jazzy piano at the Allied Fighting Forces Club. Philip was surprised when the major approached him. Seeing the cross on the officer's lapel made him even more apprehensive. What was a pastor doing at the club this late on a Saturday night? The pastor's question was even more unsettling: "Would you be interested in playing some hymns at our Sunday morning church service?"

"Let me think about it, sir," Philip answered. "I did play at my church back home, and know most of the old hymns." Sleeping in had become a luxury Philip relished every Sunday morning. Relinquishing such an indulgence would be a sacrifice he wasn't certain he wanted to make.

"It would only be twice a month. Sergeant Nelson will play the other two."

"I guess I could do that, sir."

"Thank you, my son. I'll look forward to seeing you."

The pastor and the radio operator shook hands. An agreement was made. Philip would play for the chaplain, and the chaplain would pray for Philip. Having earlier decided to take Pascal up on his wager, Philip realized that he had not, perhaps, reached the mountaintop of religiosity. However, his deal with the pastor and God suited him for the time being. It was somewhat logical, and given his current situation, what did he have to lose? Living in this world of murderous missions, orders, operating procedures, bombs, and death, there wasn't much that made sense anymore.

This Sunday morning, on a nod from the chaplain, Philip began to play "Blessed Assurance." Memories of Nebo, his family, and the white shiplap-sided church they attended every Sunday morning came flooding back. He held on to his emotions and played the hymn. It crossed his mind that maybe their prayers might be sent forth to him tomorrow. He was a long way from home, light-years from those days of innocence and assurances, a time when the future seemed like it was his—a family who loved him, a woman who adored him. He was a teacher, doing a worthwhile job with a steady paycheck. His plan was foolproof: Save up some money, marry the woman he loved, and pursue his bigger dreams. *If you want to make God laugh, make a plan—just like Burnsy said,* he thought.

Chaplain Shea's short sermon ended with a prayer. "Dear Lord . . ." Shea paused, searching for just the right words. "We know that none of us is perfect, no one person, no one government, not even one religion. We remain the sum of our parts, good and bad. War magnifies both, bringing out the best and the worst in all of us. We ask that in the not-so-distant future, your forgiving grace will transcend all of our doubts and fears, and that your divine love will, at last, bring our world peace."

Philip sat in a front-row chair adjacent to the piano. He was completely still, his hands folded in prayer. He wondered if such a thing would ever be possible. World peace? He dropped his head even farther onto his chest, deeper into prayer, praying for the miracle that would answer Father Shea's plea.

The chaplain continued, "You have taught us through scripture and the book of Ecclesiastes that to everything there is a season and a time to every purpose under Heaven. A time to be born and a time to die, a time to plant and a time to pluck up that which is planted, a time to kill and a time to heal, a time to break down and a time to build up, a time to weep and a time to laugh, a time to mourn and a time to dance."

Philip's mind drifted back and he smiled to himself. *A time to dance—oh, for just one more dance with El.*

Shea concluded, "A time to love and a time to hate, a time of war and a time of peace. I pray, dearest Lord, that you bring the peace that passeth all understanding to this troubled and war-torn world, and I pray most fervently that this war will truly end all wars. May your life-affirming wisdom guide these fine young men and women. Keep them safe. We pray that they all return home soon and that this war will then be only a distant memory. We pray this morning for the souls of those who have not or will not return, especially for Sergeant James Burnside, a brave airman we lost too soon. May he and all the rest of our fallen brethren find that *peace that passeth all understanding.*"

Chaplain Shea glanced over his shoulder at Philip with a look of genuine empathy, and then recited the standard benediction, sending everyone out with the blessings of God.

Maybe there was a time for every purpose. Shea was a smart man. Philip hoped the chaplain was telling the truth. He feared a saying he had once overheard at the USO club was also true when it came to this war: "All God's religions . . . have not been able to put mankind back together again."

In spite of his doubts, he sent up a prayer for Burnsy and all the others. He hoped that they had found their peace. He wondered if God actually had a plan. One thing he knew for certain: Back in Nebo, Pastor Harrison had also told the truth. Sin did exist; he had witnessed it firsthand, and Chaplain Shea's sermon or prayers, though moving, did not answer any of his lingering questions, nor did it bring him any sense of personal peace.

After the service ended, Philip returned to his tent. There was more that Homer needed to know, more that he had to make certain someone understood. How could Burnsy be dead? How was that even possible? And he wanted his brother to know about the other enemies he faced along with his brothers in arms. And so, he wrote:

April 4, 1943
Dear Homer,

I have horrible news. Jim Burnside was killed during our latest mission while bombing a Japanese harbor in Kavieng. His death is almost more than I can bear. He was one of my best friends, a real life force. He will be greatly missed by all of us who have survived.

Fortunately, good news is circulating around the camp. The rumor mill says we are going home. That is, of course, too good to be true. I am still anticipating my orders for AvCad. Either way, I should be home soon. I don't want to burden you, but you once said we would always tell each other the truth. Here it is, unvarnished, so if I don't make it back, you will at least have some idea what we have endured over here.

The Japanese, although the enemy, are not the only threat to the survival of the men who serve in the Allied Forces in the South West Pacific. Incessant rain, mud, 100-degree heat, and humidity often reaching nearly 100 percent, combined with poisonous snakes, bugs as big as cigarette cartons, and mosquitos carrying dreaded diseases such as malaria, threaten the survival of the men stationed here. Some have been plagued with dengue fever, dysentery, and jungle rot, the latter often disintegrating leather boots and shredding the military-issued uniforms.

The men in the Pacific Theatre, and specifically in the Fifth Air Force, are not a top priority for the American generals in Washington, DC. President Roosevelt and his advisors determined that the war in Europe must be won first, and resources were allocated accordingly. Army Air Force pilots often fly heavy bombers that are literally held together with chewing gum and baling wire. Aircrews operating on a shoestring budget rise every day to meet the challenge of preparing our outdated Flying Fortresses for battle. Their expertise as mechanics and engineers is solely responsible for modifying the B-17s by adding .50 caliber machine guns to more effectively fight the Japanese Mitsubishi A6M. The A6M, or "Zero," as it is called by the Japanese pilots, refers to the last digit of the imperial year 2600 (1940), the year the fighter entered service in the Imperial Navy. The experienced Japanese fighter pilots and their fast, highly developed weaponry are ferocious adversaries for our large bombers.

The aircrews, even with all their ability to perform miracles and put airplanes in the air worthy of combat, are not able to fix the battle fatigue that affects so many of us. Neither are they able to overcome the cavalier attitude of some commissioned officers who approach their missions with reckless abandon in hopes of earning medals for valor or a promotion in rank. The officers' excuse is they only want to end the war as soon as possible. Well, we all want that. Even though most of the enlisted men are skeptical of some officers' true motives, we must admit winning the war would make the entire struggle worthwhile. The bottom line is the death toll is excessive. These facts and opinions are shared as enlisted men and officers alike take part in card and dice games. Their nightly "bull sessions" after attending an outdoor movie or drinking a beer or two, or three or four or more, give them an outlet to air their griev- ances, or "bitch" sessions, as most of the men call them, without retaliation from the brass.

There you have it, my brother. I hate sounding like a whining, whimpering baby, but what I have written here is the truth. I plan to fight on because in the end, I do believe our cause is a worthy one. There is only one thing of which I am certain: I will be home soon.

Your loving brother,
Philip

CHAPTER 58

Ordinary Days (Reprised) and Daydreams

PHILIP HAD NOT HEARD FROM EL in over two months, the Dear John letter being her last. He feared the worst—their relationship was, most likely, over. He wondered if she had received the letter he wrote in late March telling her about Betty. What would she make of it when she read it? He cast aside his pity party and decided instead to take a different approach. He would write a letter to her as a friend.

April 10, 1943
Dear El,

It's a cold, lazy Saturday April afternoon as I write. Rain, always the rain. I believe I mentioned my tentmates earlier. Chuck Winter and Ed Stevens are all propped up on their cots. Jim Burnside is gone. KIA. His empty cot is a constant reminder, causing a pain deep within all of us that is hard to describe. Word is there will soon be a replacement, but no one will ever replace Burnsy. He was truly one of a kind. As for Winter and Stevens, their minds are elsewhere, engrossed in magazines containing pictures of scantily clad women. I guess most of us welcome these few precious moments of tranquility. The terror that wraps itself around our throats and tightens our intestines during our bombing missions takes a brief interlude here in the tents. Soothing notes float through the air—calming something deep inside of me, momentarily alleviating the dread and fear that permeates my daily existence.

In the tents, we talk about drifting off to higher places, better places—to a homecoming football game where old friends and family members gathered on a brisk fall Saturday afternoon, to a quiet meadow with a girl and flowers and bees and a blanket and a basket full of sandwiches and lukewarm drinks, beverages that moistened parched mouths and made a gentle kiss a sweet delight. We talk about Thanksgiving dinners with all the trimmings, the unconditional love of a family, maybe even a graduation party where a family and guests gather around a piano and sing.

Ed asked me the other day what I thought about most when I thought about home.

I told him ordinary days, just like we once wrote to each other. Practicing the piano or the clarinet. Listening to music. Helping Mother pick raspberries or grapes from the vine in the backyard. The smell of a rhubarb pie. The taste of homemade ice cream at the church social. The laughter of my friends.

I asked him what he thought about. He told me, the mountains and streams that flowed down through the woods, streams of clear water a person can walk beside or cast a line, hoping to get lucky and catch a trout (not one like Steve) to fry up and eat right there by a campfire.

He talked about the peacefulness of the wilderness, especially in the early spring when the crocuses are in bloom. Made a man glad to be alive. He said it was perfect up there in those woods, then he laughed and said, "Like when I'm stuck down there in the ball turret." He has a macabre sense of humor. Maybe doing his job, a fella has to.

He actually got pretty profound, at least for Ed. He said he'd hike up into the mountains just to talk with God, especially when things got rough. Got him closer so God could hear him better.

When Winter, who was thumbing through his Movies *magazine heard Ed, he asked Ed if he still thought there was a God up there looking out for us. Winter told him, "The way I got it figured, the only protection we can count on is our .50 caliber machine guns."*

Ed responded, "I think He is with us, otherwise I don't think we would've made it this far."

Then I asked Ed, "What makes you think that God is looking out for us? There have been plenty of good men who have died out there."

He replied, "Can't disagree with that. However, I heard Godlove say that right there in the Good Book it says that the meek would inherit the earth, and if I ain't meek, then I don't know who is." Ed laughed at his own joke.

Winter ended the afternoon's conversation, "Yeh, well, if our number does come, I figure we won't inherit the earth. We'll inherit the Pacific Ocean instead, all in one big goddamned gulp."

What a crew, El. Even on a boring rainy afternoon, they provide plenty of entertainment. Hope all is well with you.

As Always,

Philip

P.S. Just told I've been awarded the Distinguished Flying Cross with cluster and Airman's medal. Not much consolation, but maybe they'll look good on a dusty shelf alongside all of the books in my study someday.

Philip prayed the rain would scrub the mission. Any day, his orders to report for AvCad should arrive. He had just completed his twenty-seventh combat mission. The same number of sorties in the European Theater would have earned him a ticket home by now. Unfortunately, his duty station was the South Pacific, where there was no limit on the number of missions an Army Air Forces airman might be assigned. But, recently, word had come down from Lieutenant

Emery at headquarters that twenty-eight missions was being considered the magic number.

Had he gone to Europe, he'd be home now, proudly displaying his medals, a Bronze Star and two Silver Stars. He would feign modesty when the folks of Nebo called him a hero. He'd regale the men sitting on the front porch of Boren's or around the potbelly stove at Franklin's Hardware Store with his own war stories. He would tell them of the bravery displayed every day by the men with whom he served. He wouldn't brag, simply tell the truth.

His tales would recount their heroics. He and his buddies had the medals to prove it. For months, they'd held the Japanese soldiers and sailors at bay. Now, he realized what Franklin, Newman, and Meacham had told him. The real heroes were the men who sacrificed all. He'd be sure to tell them about Burnsy, Levin, Fraser, Willard, Blakely, Stewart, Craig, Freeman, Major Bleasdale, and Captain Daniels. All heroes, all of them gone. But the wisest thing he'd learned on that front porch was there was no such thing as a good war—he could attest to that.

Long flights over the Pacific Ocean allowed him quiet moments to daydream. He imagined returning to graduate school or eating a juicy hamburger and drinking a chocolate milkshake at Boren's. Maybe he'd consider teaching music again, but this time at a college or a big university. He dreamed about exploring the new innovations in the field of electronics that some of his friends talked about. The possibilities seemed endless. A sergeant from New Jersey even told him about a new electronics company producing a machine that could bring moving pictures—with sound—right into a person's home.

He wanted to see faraway places with his own eyes—London, Paris, Rome, New York, Jerusalem. The places where Betty Hittman had traveled. He even had illusions of grander things. Maybe he would be famous, or maybe not. Maybe he was going crazy.

Perhaps Billy the Kid was right. Maybe his dreams *were* just delusions of grandeur. He couldn't deny he was a dreamer. He'd been adrift in those delusions for years, heading first to Chicago, then New York and, finally, to Broadway. Hell, he was still dreaming—becoming a B-17 pilot, winning the war. The last two items remained to be seen; the first three on his list now seemed even more distant, more unattainable. Being a concert pianist or a songwriter was hard enough, but throw in a war, and all things became exponentially even more impossible. Philip had once even gone so far as to counter Billy's warning with a literary reference quoting the poet Carl Sandburg.

"Nothing happens unless first a dream, Billy."

"Well, you got that part down, Nelly. I just hope one of these days you get a little better grip on reality."

He now understood reality in its worst sense, but also its best. The war was no dream, and he prayed neither was El's love. She was no delusion. At last, he understood the pure joy of truly loving another person and he hoped she did, too. He wanted to believe she would wait for him. Somehow, she would understand. She would forgive him, and their love story would be one for the ages.

With clarity, he turned to the last page of his diary and listed his friends, dead and alive, decorated or not. A fortunate few had already returned to the States to tell their war stories. How might his end? A bang? A whimper? Tonight's reality would consist of neither, only music and booze, a combination he hoped would douse all his fears—at least for the moment.

CHAPTER 59

Orders from Headquarters

THE RAIN SLAPPED THE CANVAS TENTS with a throbbing cadence. It splattered down, rivulets rushing to erode the dirt, accumulating into miniscule ponds of mud. At 2000 that evening, Philip plodded through them and headed toward the mission he loved the most. His sheet music tucked safely into his olive drab musette bag, he pushed through the dilapidated doors of the ramshackle building posing as the Allied Fighting Forces Club. Saturday night. The crowd trudged through the rain and muck to celebrate their existence, their survival. Philip's only purpose was to add music to the festivities.

The soldiers and nurses comingled at worn wooden tables and reminisced about days gone by, about boyfriends, girlfriends, and spouses left behind. They lamented the passing of parents and grandparents and reveled in tales of the glory days of high school or college. Consuming copious quantities of beer and liquor, the men and women chattered nonstop, also bemoaning the futility of war, a perpetual lament that nightly filtered up through the metal roof into the rainsoaked night sky.

Although weary, Philip took great delight in entertaining the troops. Most of what he played evoked feelings deep in his own memory, songs from a million years ago. He loved to play dance music and upbeat swing, songs the clientele remembered and could sing along to. The songs brought back memories to him of people and places, but mostly of her. In the end, he actually was a fool. Why couldn't he have been content with falling in love?

He slid onto the wooden piano bench just as Loretta Keno, the nurse he'd met while in the hospital, strolled up to the piano and snuggled next to him. "Hey, Lucky, how about playing 'Fools Rush In'?" She tucked her auburn hair behind her left ear. Her dark brown eyes projected her warmth and soulfulness. She brushed his arm flirtatiously. He had to admit, he enjoyed her attention, the touch of her soft skin next to his.

Philip struck the first few notes. Soldiers and nurses paired up and began dancing. Some gathered around the piano and sang as Philip played. He remembered the song well. Having Loretta next to him reminded him of their innocent indiscretion a few weeks earlier—a few drunken kisses. It was only one night. Two lonely people far from home and those they loved. Philip's love for El remained steadfast, despite his temporary foolhardy transgressions. He feared, once again, he may have given a young woman the wrong impression. As he played, he found the lyrics appropriate:

> "So, open up your heart
> And let this fool rush in."

They sang the last note as some shouted another request across the smoke-filled room. "How about 'Cheek to Cheek,' Lucky?"

He played—ebullient. Loretta sang along:

> "Heaven,
> I'm in Heaven . . ."

With the skill and aplomb of the master pianist he was, Philip produced one song after another: "You Are My Sunshine," "Don't Sit Under the Apple Tree," "I'll Never Smile Again," and "Blues in the Night."

Winter came to his pal's rescue. "Come on, Lucky, time for a break."

The crowd clapped as Philip made his exit to sit with Winter, Stevens, Loretta, and the new kid, Harley Thompson, who had replaced Burnsy in their tent. They all laughed and joked as Winter shared tales of their storied past. "Yeh, and you should have heard Lucky the night he played 'Rhapsody in Blue' at the Forbidden City nightclub in San Francisco," bragged Winter. "The whole damned place stood up and gave him a standing ovation."

"Of course, Burnsy got him the gig!" Stevens revealed.

"How do you know, Ed? You weren't there, were you?" Loretta asked.

"Hell, I've heard that story so many times, I feel like I actually *was* there," Stevens answered.

"There musta been at least five hundred people jammed into that ballroom," Winter said. "It was the damnedest thing I ever saw. Lucky was amazing. Of course, we were all pretty swacked that night, just like tonight, but I'm pretty sure he was amazing."

Stevens, Thompson, and Loretta continued to be amused by Winter's and Philip's tall tales as they guzzled beers and regaled the nurse and the rookies with their stories. Every once in a while, they would stop when talking about Burnsy. If they teared up, they would blame the booze or the smoke.

Lieutenant Stephen Lundeen, the officer in charge of personnel and legal affairs, appeared at the table. Conversation ceased. The grin on the lieutenant's face hinted he had good news. Speaking directly to Philip, he reported, "I just returned from headquarters in Brisbane. Lieutenant Emery cornered me there and asked if I was headed to Moresby. When I told him I was, he asked me to pass this little tidbit of confidential information on to you. Apparently, a personnel clerk you knew in basic, a sergeant named Tom Nadel, told Emery he'd seen your AvCad orders. He knew you'd been waiting on those orders for quite a while and asked Emery if he had any way to get word to you."

Lundeen paused. "So, here's the message from Nadel via Emery. Your paperwork ordering you to report to the States immediately to AvCad should be coming through here any day now."

"Hallelujah!" Winter shouted. "Y'all hear that? My pal's gonna be a pilot. Hot damn! Too bad there ain't no champagne around this hellhole. But let's have another round anyway. Looks like you might avoid the Brush-Off Club after all, Lucky."

Philip couldn't believe it. Was he actually going home? He had witnessed other soldiers receive their orders and then have them changed at the last minute. Could this really be happening? He envisioned his parents, his brothers, maybe the entire village welcoming him home. Rushing to Blessing Hospital, he would convince El she was making a huge mistake. Their love was real. He would ask her to marry him. That was a dream he could live with, a dream he knew would come true.

"Here's to our new pilot, 'Lucky' Zumwalt!" yelled Winter.

Word spread throughout the room as soldiers and nurses gathered around Philip, slapping his back and congratulating him.

Upon hearing the news, Major McCullar approached the table. "Well, Zumwalt, I couldn't be happier for you. Can't wait for you to get back here and join the Heavy Drivers' Club. Hell, I might even teach you how to skip bomb! With those golden hands of yours, you'll be one damned fine pilot. Hopefully, the war'll be over by the time you get trained, but I doubt it." McCullar laughed as only he could, a deep, masculine laugh that boomed throughout the club.

Loretta softly stroked Philip's arm and looked into his eyes. "You know what? You'll make a great pilot." She took his hand. "I'm so happy for you."

Philip smiled. Half drunk, he smiled and then did what he loved doing. He returned to the piano. As the liquor flowed, the singing grew louder and louder, but Philip didn't care. This was a night for celebration. He was going home.

He pounded the keys late into the night. The young men and

women danced like there was no tomorrow on the chance there might not be. The rhythm and the sounds sent the young people back to other places, another world, the one to which they prayed they would soon return. The rain continued, adding to the beat. The dancing would stop for a while as soldiers and nurses surrounded the piano and sang the songs they knew, songs that reminded all of home. For a few untethered moments, they didn't think about the war. There was no rank, no mission.

Zeralda's prophecy remained buried deep in the recesses of Philip's mind. He coaxed it forward. How was it she'd put it? *Your treasure will not be left in gold and silver coins, but in another form, one money cannot buy.* For now, only the piano and the music existed.

His reality became anesthetized by alcohol, and although an inescapable melancholy would sometimes filter through the crowded room, there was, thanks to Lucky Zumwalt, the joy of music. It filled all of them with hope, a possibility they would survive and soon be going home. He sang the last song along with the others. The liquor and beer had put them all in fine voice.

"... the world will always welcome lovers
As time goes by."

Philip banged out the final note. "That's all tonight, folks."

The patrons returned to tables and drinks, picking up where earlier conversations had left off. Philip headed for the exit of the ramshackle building with his sheet music tucked away in his haversack. The alcohol and the news he had received left him light-headed. Or to use El's favorite word, *euphoric.*

Loretta met him at the exit. Tall and willowy, she leaned against the doorpost. Her hair cascaded from under her utility cap down around the neck of her camouflage fatigues. Only a fool would mistake the gorgeous nurse for a combat infantryman. Their arms brushed as they left the club. Their brief interlude was one Philip would rather forget.

Loretta lingered, clearly yearning for one of the passionate kisses they had previously shared. Philip turned and stared straight ahead into the rain. Unwelcome, it accompanied the unbearable humidity and mud, the ubiquitous mud.

They stood facing each other, waiting for a break in the downpour to sprint to their tents.

Loretta, emboldened by the booze, whispered through her smile, "You know, Lucky, a kiss is still a kiss, a sigh is just a sigh."

Philip smiled back, generously. "It's 'a kiss is just a kiss,' Loretta."

Loretta laughed. "Okay. Guess I don't know the words very well, huh? But the world will always welcome lovers, you know. What the hell, hey, kiss or no kiss, I'm thrilled for you. How long until they process your orders?"

"I don't know, most likely a couple of days, but I don't care how long it takes. I'm going home." Philip's mouth turned from stone-faced resolve to a slight smile.

"Think it'll rain?" Loretta changed the subject again.

"Naw, not around here." He laughed.

"No, never." She played along with his sarcasm. "Walk me home?"

"Sure."

"I just love that last song you played tonight, 'As Time Goes By,' right? Have you seen *Casablanca*?"

"Answer number one, yes, that's the song. A great one. The one you don't know the words to."

"Ah, come on, Mr. Music Man, give me a break. I almost got 'em right. Did you see the movie or not?"

"Yeh, I saw the movie in Sydney. Fell in love with Ingrid Bergman and the song."

They realized the rain was not letting up, so they removed their combat boots and ran, giggling and splashing through the mud puddles saturating the pathways between tents.

Loretta slipped into hers. "Sleep tight, Bogie," she sighed as she lingered in the doorway.

Philip hesitated but succumbed to the invitation of her open arms. He hugged her, kissed her on the forehead, and sprinted away.

The monsoon was a dark, transparent curtain. Philip slogged through the muck. Loretta was, in his mind, as beautiful as the sultry, gorgeous Ingrid Bergman, but he had come to the decision that he could love only one woman, and that was El.

Arriving at his tent soaking wet, he dropped his pants, stripped off his shirt and T-shirt, and stood half naked in his boxers. He switched on the single light hanging over his desk. He unlocked his footlocker and pulled out some unfinished letters and his diary and prepared for his rumored departure. Meticulously, he lined the letters up in a row on his desk. As he sat down in the rickety chair, it creaked its welcome. He leaned back and stared at his footlocker.

Inside the olive drab box was contraband, not the sort one would consider illegal, but the kind the U.S. Army Air Forces would classify as dangerous. He recognized that he was, most likely, disobeying orders. He didn't care. If the Army wanted to take away a stripe or give him a written reprimand, so be it. The items in his footlocker would remain there until he took them home.

He wrote deep into the night. The end of winter in New Guinea. The weather couldn't make up its mind. The air was sticky and still. The rain compounded the humidity and temporarily grounded the planes scheduled to fly into harm's way. Fortress Rabaul was no dream. He dreaded each mission. His plane always took off around midnight. This sense of foreboding dominated daily existence, but tonight it was more pronounced. He placed two letters into unsealed envelopes, addressed them, and laid them aside. He'd add more later. A third letter was sealed, the one he left on his desk before he took off on each mission. A ritual.

He would make a diary entry tomorrow. He smiled, thinking of home and El. Tonight, he would return there in his dreams, back to better times. He swallowed his pride and began a fourth letter.

April 11, 1943
Dear El,

I am sitting here remembering the first night we met. I was hesitant to go to the Casino that night . . .

CHAPTER 60

Survive

IN THE MORNING, THE WAR AND THE JUNGLE still surrounded him. Putrid, inexplicable, unimaginable. Nursing a hangover, Philip was relieved it wasn't his Sunday to play the piano. He moved sluggishly from his cot to his desk and finished the letter to Homer. Afterward, in the momentary pseudo-comfort of his tent, he completed an entry in his diary.

He placed the smooth butt end of his fountain pen to his cheek. *Raining*. Appropriate. For now, he actually believed that he was safe for the first time in a long while. Here, he was sheltered from the rain by an olive drab slab of musty canvas erected and propped up at the edge of a rain forest. Port Moresby, New Guinea. A town and country he had never heard of before he landed there nearly a year ago. He wondered, *What idiot ever described this hellhole as paradise, anyway?* Since arriving in the South West Pacific, he had experienced moments he never imagined he nor any man was capable of enduring. Retreating to his cot, he read.

Afternoon settled in. He started a letter to Billy, set a record on the phonograph, and flipped through the pages of his second diary. With some degree of amusement, he read what he had written just a few months earlier: *Persist, since the attainable is no more than a rung on the ladder of life, on which a man may climb to grander views, though it will break beneath him if he lingers too long.*

Such a serious and philosophical fellow he was when he'd first arrived here. The singular operative word had become *survive*. Now it looked like he would. Go home, become a pilot, see the war to its conclusion. He would persist.

The fire in the stove warming the interior of the tent slowly burned down. He finished Billy's letter, sealed it, and placed it next to Homer's. Evening wore on.

Stevens was still absorbed in *The Last of the Mohicans* while Philip listened to the radio and Winter and Thompson read magazines. The soldiers tolerated Tokyo Rose's chatter so they could listen to Tommy Dorsey's band.

"Now, GIs, here's the Dorsey Band and Frankie Sinatra," Tokyo Rose announced. "I bet your girl's out dancing to this music with other guys back in the States. *Ha ha, suckers!*"

Philip found no humor in her insinuation.

Sinatra sang with the smooth tones that had made him famous right up to the song's conclusion:

> "... I only know there ain't no love at all,
> Without a song."

The flames turned to embers. Dorsey and Sinatra. Philip longed for some good dreams, not the nightmares that had haunted him these last few months. Maybe just one good dream of El. Was that too much to ask? Anything but blood, screams, whistling bullets, friends dying, the sounds of war, and the sight of one of his best friend's death.

He opened his diary, his third such journal. This one had a red cover—appropriate, he thought, given its content. He had recorded his latest missions in it. Within he listed the ever-expanding names of his deceased friends. He would never forget them, and then there was the entry that had occupied his mind since his first combat mission:

Nov. 8, 1942

Of all the subjects that soldiers choose for conversation, the most distasteful and least mentioned is that of death. For some psychological reason, no man will admit that death could possibly touch him personally. It is always a remote factor which occasionally involves someone he knows. The more frequently a man comes face to face with the Grim Reaper, the less likely he is to admit its existence. However, I now find that death is a possibility which I cannot overlook . . .

I have reached the following conclusions: If I live through everything, I shall have known experiences and sensations unattainable to the existence of the normal man. I shall have lived, feeling life with an intensity previously unknown, and whatever else it may be, that life will not be dull. If I am unfortunate and am killed, then I shall have died uniquely, and it will have been for a cause unequaled in human history. These are stirring times, when the liberties which have been won with such pain and toil are in mortal danger, and uncounted numbers of men have given their all for less. Am I better than they? I believe I can truthfully say that no one in this world has ever been willfully injured by me. My goal in life has been the boast that no person should be sorry to have known me. Perhaps that goal has not been met, but an attempt has been made. Never again will there be a time when I have fewer enemies than at the present. I could do worse. I certainly could do worse . . . . These men, these Americans—all of this, maybe, in the end, will be worth it.

Philip momentarily put the entire idea of death out of his mind and forged a new set of marching orders. Restless, he placed a fresh piece of paper on his desk and wrote:

A Tiny Speck
Powerful nations wave the sword
Weaker ones are forced to yield
What a future I can face—
Death upon a battlefield!
I am but a tiny speck
In a sea of human woe
Yet why should not my voice be heard
On who should be my friend or foe?
Tanks are rumbling o'er the land
Bombers fill the sky
Trampling down the rights of man
Humbling those who do not die.
Destroy the foes of liberty
Strike while yet we can
Burn out the filthy tyranny
And restore the rights of man.

Ensnared in a state of melancholy, he added a bit more to El's letter but left it unfinished. Placing the cap on his pen, he stacked his latest poem with the letters and placed them all carefully in his footlocker. Looking around the tent at his old friends and his new ones, he was grateful. In some ways, he was fortunate to have lived so fully, so completely, these last few months. He better understood death now, at least as much as any man on this side could. He had seen it firsthand. He had been naive in so many ways and sincerely hoped that El would welcome him back, his love and all. If she did, he had so much to tell her. If she would not, he would understand. But he longed for ordinary days with her.

His plan now was to get some sleep. He turned off the light. Short and to the point was his final diary entry for the day. His letters to Homer and Billy told more of the story, the boredom, the fear, and, yes, the miserable conditions. Homer and Billy would understand. Philip would never write such details to his parents. Three diaries and four letters sat atop the stacks of letters he had received from home. His footlocker also contained his sheet music and books along with his other personal effects. The diary on top of the stack had the word *Record* etched in gold-colored letters on its cover. The word glimmered in the fire's fading light. He had recorded what to him was important. Maybe his loved ones would one day appreciate that he had taken the time to write it all down. For now, he had grown weary and wondered if any of it mattered.

He closed the footlocker, slid under the mosquito bar, and thought about the poem he had just penned. Would any of what he had done or what he might do in the future have any impact on burning out the tyranny he had witnessed? Would the foes of liberty ever be completely destroyed, and would the rights of all be restored? Would any of it make a damned bit of difference? Would these sacrifices made by so many actually make his home safer? His parents? His brothers? El? Maybe he and his friends were just fooling themselves, caught up in the frenzy of war. Was he simply a pawn, a tiny speck in a sea of human woe?

He did, however, believe now, somewhere deep inside, that if he and his fellow companions on this journey were able to bring this war to an end, to defeat the enemy, that it would all be worth it. He had to believe that in order to keep going, in order to keep flying into the skies filled with almost certain death.

Maybe the rain would continue and tomorrow's mission would be scrubbed. He could use another day of peace and quiet, another day to read, to write in his diary, to write some more poetry, to listen to music, to dream of El, to live. He could make good use of another simple, ordinary day. Such a thought was a pipe dream, nothing unusual for him. The war had to be won, rain or not, but after tomorrow he knew one thing for certain: One more mission and he would be headed home.

CHAPTER 61

Blues in the Night

WINTER AND THOMPSON WERE ASLEEP, but Stevens was still using Philip's light to read. Philip pulled one of his diaries from his footlocker and read to himself an entry he had written earlier, an entry that haunted him:

February 16, 1943

Sometimes, I have trouble making myself believe that it has all happened. That I, the staid and conservative music instructor, should be engaged in a struggle where I attempt to kill and others attempt to kill me is incredible enough in itself, without the hairbreadth escapes which have occurred. I do not know definitely that I have killed, but I am morally certain of it . . .

I have been in the plane that killed many men, but only that one time do I know that I was the one who did the killing. Odd, that killing men can become such an impersonal matter!

Philip feared he would never get over the fact that he was a killer. He returned the diary to the footlocker and rolled over in his cot. "Good night, Ed," he whispered to his friend. "Turn the light out when you're done." The tent was quiet.

"Yeh, I'm almost finished with your book. Last chapter. That

Hawkeye is one tough hombre! But I don't think things are going to end well for Uncas. I mean to tell you, Magua is one nasty SOB and they're both hot for Cora. I gotta see how this all comes out in the end. Good night, Lucky. See ya in the morning."

Philip tried to fall asleep but couldn't. It wasn't Stevens's late-night reading that kept him awake. Instead, he was still thinking about home and El.

"Damn, Lucky, Uncas died, but he got that son of a bitch Magua. Helluva book. Do you remember how it ended? Pretty damned powerful. Listen." Stevens read, "'If ever I forget the lad who has so often fou't at my side in war, and slept at my side in peace, may He who made us all, whatever may be our color or our gifts, forget me!' That's you and me, Lucky. I'll never forget you and I hope you won't forget me either."

"Don't worry, Ed. There's not a chance in hell of that."

"I thought you didn't believe in hell," Stevens said.

"I don't. Now go to sleep and please, for God's sake, shut up."

"Uh, oh, sure thing, Lucky. Sorry. Good night."

"Good night, Ed."

April was a wet season in New Guinea. The rain always came, nearly every day. Some days, Philip's plane, *Blues in the Nite,* would fly a mission and some days it wouldn't. He lay staring up at the ceiling of the tent for a while, remembering the sweetness of another place, another time, humming one of the tunes he remembered so well, the one that took him back to her:

"It was fascination,
I know . . ."

"Hey, Lucky, I know that song." Stevens was still annoyingly awake and started to sing his own version in his raspy voice.

Philip had to smile. His new young friend was a piece of work.

He closed his eyes and could see El as the ball turret gunner completed his croaky version of the tune.

It *was* fascination turned to love, but the lyrics of the song his crew had named their plane after were also stuck in his brain:

"A woman's a two-face, a worrisome thing
Who'll leave ya to sing the blues in the night."

Drifting off to sleep, he hoped to dream only of her. He couldn't even imagine her being two-faced, but he did understand what singing the blues in the night really meant.

"Lucky, Lucky, wake up!" Stevens stood over him.

Sitting straight up in his cot, Philip stared through the mosquito netting at his tentmate. "Yeh. What do you need, Ed?"

"We're takin' off in an hour. The mission's on. You're flyin with McCullar. I was supposed to be on your plane, but Hansen just came through and told me he switched me to number seven, old 'Tail-End Charlie.' So, don't worry, I'll be covering your ass from behind."

When Philip didn't rise, Stevens kept up the patter. "Better throw on some clothes. I'm headed to the mess hall for some chow. Don't wanna kill any Nips on an empty stomach. Gonna eat some eggs and then drop some right on top of Rabaul." He laughed, amused once again at his own ghoulish sense of humor.

"Okay. Yeh, sure. I'm getting up." Philip laid his head back on the pillow, closed his eyes, and prayed this was his final mission.

CHAPTER 62

Of Regrets and Forgiveness

April 11, 1943
Blessing Hospital

EL WAS DOING HER BEST TO FOLLOW Dostoevsky's advice to love everything. Being away from Philip for so long made that difficult, and now she had created an even greater problem. When she wrote that letter back in January, she was only trying to be honest, to give both of them time to make certain their love for each other was real. She wanted Philip to have the opportunity to live life, enjoy it as much as he possibly could in that godforsaken place. But now she feared she had made a mistake. How long had she left him without word from her? She worried he would think she no longer loved him.

It was strange how everything seemed out of sync. She had experienced rhythm before he came along, for sure. He didn't teach her to dance, but he did teach her about many things—musical terms from *acciaccatura* to *xylophone*, how to sing out from her diaphragm with passion, and yes, he even taught her about the word *passion*, its Latin root, and what it really meant, at least in his opinion. He even taught her about the three Greek words that meant love. She felt that even now, in her work, in Philip's absence. Her work required love and passion.

The April breeze blew through the open windows. What was it

that one of Philip's favorite poets wrote? How could that silly man think that April was the cruelest month? It didn't seem cruel to her at all; it was divine, flowers and trees blooming with new life.

"Robinson, we need fresh sheets in Room 203. Hop to it!" Cadet Nurse Supervisor Ethyl Bennett was dispensing orders once again. Bennett was the consummate professional in El's mind. She never took a moment off, never missed a beat. It was clear that her students were important to her, but they were a distant second to the patients on the second floor of Blessing Hospital in Quincy, Illinois.

Bennett's command snapped El out of her daydream. A cacophony surrounded her: the flapping of pillows and sheets, the rattling of bedpans, and the clattering of clipboards. The treatment prescribed upon the charts attached to those clipboards was often the difference between life and death. Whispered moans or shrieking screams filtered out through the disinfected rooms into the polished hallways. Cadet Nurses hustled from room to room, heeding Nurse Bennett's orders. They were in high gear.

El pushed herself away from the intake desk and took a final sip of her lukewarm black coffee. She surveyed the hospital ward wing to which she was assigned. For three straight hours, she darted nonstop from room to room. The foul smells of antiseptic, bloody gauze, and receptacles filled with human waste drifted through the hallways, enough to nauseate the most experienced nurse. The stench did not deter her from her duty. She greeted each patient with a bounce in her step as she joined the other nurses hurrying around the floor tending to patients. Her smile and energy were soothing medicine to even the most tormented convalescent. Her feet already ached, but it didn't matter. Her responsibilities were minor compared to the soldiers at war, especially the one she knew most intimately.

The war had changed everything in her life and in the lives of those she loved. For now, she was content to address the needs of her patients. She accepted their suffering as she accepted her own; it was the reality in which she existed. She whistled along, completing her regimen of bathing patients, giving them back rubs, taking their vital signs, making their beds, and updating their charts.

It was a humid Saturday morning, but the sweet smells of mowed grass and budding lilac bushes wafted through the open windows of the hospital rooms. *The cruelest month of all—really?* She was looking forward to this lovely April evening. Throwing their cares away, she, her girlfriends, and a few of the young doctors had planned to take in *The Woman of the Year* at the Orpheum Theater. El loved Katharine Hepburn. She knew the routine: She would be paired up with Dr. Ernest Thoroughgood. She liked him; he was a fine man and she enjoyed his company, even though his German accent was sometimes difficult to decipher.

Yes, she liked him, but she wasn't in love with him. She had finally figured that out, and tonight, she decided, she would tell him as much. It was only fair to tell him that her heart still belonged to Philip. It would be awkward, but she knew it was the right thing to do. Then she would write Philip and tell him that *she* was the fool. And when he came home, she was certain they would be married.

A few minutes past ten-thirty, following a short coffee break, El set her cup down, extinguished her cigarette, and disappeared into the linen closet to grab fresh sheets. She paused, closed her eyes, and prayed. It was her daily prayer. To see him again. Her Philip. To feel his embrace, to see his smile. Her mind drifted back to Siloam Springs, the Majestic Hotel, to the discovery of ecstasy. She knew he would come home, keep his promise. They were destined to share a lifetime of new memories.

As she reached for a set of sheets, without warning, a feeling coursed through every inch of her body. It was a feeling unlike anything she had ever experienced before. Her legs grew weak, her heart began to race, the hair stood up on her arms. She felt flushed and struggled to stay upright and not faint.

Nurse Bennett walked by the closet and saw El doubled over, clearly in distress. "Are you all right, Robinson?" she asked.

"I don't know. I really don't know." El was overcome with emotion. Tears streamed from her eyes. "I fear something terrible has happened, but I have no idea what it might be."

Bennett helped El into the hallway and back to the nurse's station. El sat down. Bennett brought her a cold, damp washcloth and applied it to El's forehead.

"No need to borrow trouble, Elinor. Everything's going to be fine, my dear, just fine," said Bennett.

"I hope so," replied El with a shaky voice. But as the room spun around her, disconnecting her from reality, throwing all perception amiss, a frightening feeling rose deep inside her soul. For once, she feared her supervisor was dead wrong.

El recovered from her spell. Although still somewhat unnerved, she joined the others that evening at the Orpheum. Exiting the theater, El's best friend, Sally, blurted out an idea to the group. "Wasn't that just the best movie? How's about we all go and have a drink or two?"

Ernest looked at El for affirmation.

El declined. "No, thanks. I've got some studying to do."

The other nurses and doctors thought it was a splendid idea and headed up the street to the nearest bar. El asked Ernest to stay. He looked somewhat confused as he waited for her to speak.

"Ernest, this is not easy, but I need to clear the air between us. I fear I've sent out some misleading signals to you about our relationship. I think you're a fine man, but I'm in love with Philip, and I need to be faithful to him. I do hope you understand."

Ernest nodded, somber.

"I hope we can still be friends. Okay?" El asked.

"Yes. Okay. Friends. I understand. Good night, then," Ernest replied with lowered eyes and left quietly.

El wondered if he had actually understood what she had said. *He didn't even put up a fight,* she thought. Had she misread him? No matter. It was done. She returned to her room, sat down at the small desk across from her bed, and wrote:

My Dearest Philip,

Let me begin by telling you that I am the fool. I love you. I have always loved you. Please come home to me. Please forgive me. There is nothing more I can write. My tears are falling on this paper, but they are tears of joy knowing we will be together forever.

All my love,

El

CHAPTER 63

One More Mission

Port Moresby, New Guinea
Seven-Mile Aerodrome
April 12, 1943

AJOR MCCULLAR WAS AS EXPEDITIOUS and concise as usual in reviewing the takeoff checklist with his copilot, Lieutenant Andrews. Philip did the same with the radio operator checklist. In his mind, he knew, once he returned here or was sent to Europe after his training, he would be responsible for his own cockpit list.

McCullar began to taxi the B-17 E to the downwind end of the runway at 0130. The Forty-Third Bomb Group had been ordered to commence a major offensive, a night attack on Rabaul under the command of Lieutenant Colonel John A. Roberts.

As commanding officer of the Sixty-Fourth Squadron, McCullar and his *Blues in the Nite* crew headed up the squadron's main formation. The mission was deemed essential, so much so that two extra sergeants had volunteered as spare gunners. Philip had considered opting out of the mission and had even approached his squadron leader, but McCullar convinced him that he was needed on this most important mission.

Philip imagined his AvCad orders might be arriving in the morning and would be waiting for him on the personnel clerk's desk, but he didn't want to disappoint McCullar, or worse, have the major think he was a coward. After all, it was only one more mission. He figured there would be many more once he returned from training. Bringing his men home safely would be his main priority. He hoped someday men would extoll him as they did McCullar. When the men gathered at the USO or AFFC, anyone who flew with McCullar would boast for weeks that they had flown with the best bomber pilot in the South West Pacific.

"I was on McCullar's crew," they would brag over a beer. Automatically, the soldier gained the respect of all the other men at the table.

At 0137, McCullar throttled up to full power and released the brakes. Philip followed his ritual, sending a prayer into the celestial darkness. Halfway down the runway, nearing takeoff speed, a long streak of bluish-white sparks appeared below the number-three engine nacelle and in the right wheel assembly. The sparks turned to a nascent flame lasting five or six seconds and then inexplicably disappeared. A moment later, new flames stretched menacingly across the upper- and lower-wing surfaces. A stream of fire like an elongated fuse raced down the length of the aircraft. The plane was only a few hundred feet in the air when the tire on the left wheel separated from the landing gear.

McCullar wasn't certain what had happened. An animal of some sort had darted out in front of the plane. He had only lightly touched the brakes to avoid a collision. Seeing the right wing streaked with fire, the skilled pilot banked in an attempt to bring the ship back to the ground. The B-17 stalled. Staggering at a sixty-degree angle of bank, *Blues in the Nite* became an inferno. When the blaze reached the bomb bay, a cataclysmic explosion blasted open the aluminum fuselage, tearing the B-17 apart as if it were nothing but papier-mâché.

The force of the eruption propelled Philip through the side gunner's window. He hit the ground hard and lay in shock—singed, quiescent, semiconscious.

Scorching heat surged forth bold and brazen. The acrid stench of burning oil and flesh saturated the air. Raging and sizzling in triumph, the firestorm swallowed up the Flying Fortress and its crew until only the airplane's skeleton remained. Its charred belly sank into the mud flanking the runway. Effervescent infernos flickered in the darkness. They rose up into the shadowy sky, soaring, spectacular hues of orange, yellow, and blue. The verdurous jungle sat silently in the humid night awestruck by the instantaneous emergence of a blazing wall of fire. Sounds of shrieking sirens pierced the dark. Dim headlights rushed to the scene, illuminating the ethereal, silent aftermath of the crash.

Plodding through the mud, Nurse Loretta Keno was first to reach the surviving airman. She cradled his burned scalp and face while assisting the stretcher-bearers. She thought she recognized him. Brushing the soot from his face and then reading the airman's dog tag in the dim light, her suspicion was confirmed. Loretta's heart pounded as she read:

Zumwalt Philip A.
S/SG 16019084 USA
09

Oh my God, she thought. "You're gonna be okay, Philip," she whispered as she helped lift his limp body into the ambulance. "Just hang in there."

In triage, Loretta briefed Dr. Goldman. "A terrible crash, sir. No other survivors. This airman was thrown out of the plane. Burns are minimal, but I expect there may be massive internal injury."

She was doing her best to contain her emotions and remain professional. If Philip was breathing, it was so shallow it was unnoticeable. She held on to hope but was aware that Goldman might have preferred to dispense with the inspection of the lifeless body. However, they both knew it was his professional obligation to confirm the airman's death. Goldman placed his ear over Philip's mouth and turned back to Loretta.

"He's still breathing," the doctor reported in a hushed, urgent voice. "Let's get him to the operating room immediately."

"Start the plasma," Goldman instructed moments later.

Loretta inserted the needle, and life-giving fluid flowed through the tube into Philip's veins. The medical team worked with frenetic efficiency. Loretta stroked Philip's hair and gently wiped his forehead with a wet cloth. Aside from a few minor burns on his face, there was not a mark on his body. He was in shock due to the blast he had absorbed, the same blast that had thrown him out of the gunner's window, clear of the burning plane.

Loretta thought about the frivolous moments they'd shared. Lucky had made her laugh, especially when they'd had too much to drink. Throngs of soldiers and nurses had gathered at the club and freely engaged in revelry few would ever admit to in their hometowns. He was remarkable in so many ways; his fingers danced across the keys, and melodies sprung from the upright and filled the smoky room night after night. Voices had echoed through the camp late into the evening, filling the emptiness. Stumbling back to their tents and cots, the war-weary veterans had felt less of the pain that dominated their existence.

The medical team worked with precision. The surgeon's hands were steady as he operated. Opening Philip's torso, Goldman did his best to repair the ruptured organs and stem the internal bleeding caused by the blast injury. After applying the final suture closing

Philip's abdomen, he commanded the nurse, "Stay with him, Keno. There's nothing else I can do for this one. He's lost a significant amount of blood. Continue the blood transfusion."

The young doctor gently patted Philip's shoulder and headed for a vacated cot for some well-earned rest.

CHAPTER 64

Recovery

PRIVATE FIRST-CLASS EDWIN STEVENS CRAWLED OUT of his wrecked B-17. He stumbled to his feet. Surveying the airplane, he was relieved to discover his entire crew had survived the latest disaster on the runway. His plane had careened off the runway after sliding on wet pavement for several yards and landed nose down in the mud shortly after *Blues in the Nite* had crashed. Ed saw McCullar's plane go down. There was no doubt that his friend was dead. No human being could survive the crash he had just witnessed. A single ambulance and two jeeps arrived at the new crash scene. Ed and his surviving crew wandered around dazed, but grateful to be walking away from the wreckage that moments earlier was their plane.

A medic approached him. "You okay, soldier?"

"Me? Yeh, I'm fine. Any survivors in that one?" He pointed to the smoking shell of *Blues in the Nite* still burning at the end of the runway. He was certain what the answer to his question would be, but the medic's reply surprised him.

"Yeh, one fella. The piano player . . . Lucky, I think they called him. Hell, you'd have to be damned lucky to survive that. We heard the Fortress wing-clipped a wallaby. They found a dead one on the runway. Sarge said maybe the animal broke a fuel line, then a spark from somewhere blew the whole damn ship to hell."

"But Lucky survived? You sure of that?"

"That's what the sarge said. I guess you'd have to check with the medics."

"Yeh, can I catch a ride over there?"

"Sure, hop in."

Upon his arrival at the hospital tent, Ed spotted Loretta standing outside having a smoke. She took a long drag, saw Ed, and broke into tears. "Oh, Ed." She was sobbing now. "Oh, my God. Philip survived the crash. I don't know how."

Ed took Loretta in his arms. He wanted to leap with joy, but instead he held her and tried his best to comfort her. Once she stopped crying, they sat down on the bench outside the medical tent. "You got any more cigarettes?" he asked. She obliged, and he lit up.

"He's in recovery now. Marge Raffa is looking after him. I just had to take a break."

"Is he gonna make it?"

"I don't know," she said, regaining her composure. "It all depends on how severe his internal injuries are." She took another drag off her cigarette and exhaled the smoke into the damp air. "I don't know how it was possible for anyone to survive that crash. Did you see his plane? It's a miracle."

"If anyone could pull off a miracle, it'd be Lucky. Can I see him?"

"When he gets out of recovery."

"Oh, sure. He just needs some time, right?"

"Yes. He just needs a little more time."

Fifteen minutes passed. Each lit another cigarette.

"How do you ever get used to this?" Ed asked.

"We just don't talk much about it. They really don't give us specific training on how to comfort a man who's lost a limb or is about to die. Most of the time we just sit there with them, try to be present if we know they're close to death. Some of them simply ask us to hold their hands." Loretta's eyes lowered. If there were tears, Ed didn't detect them. "I feel so bad for them. So many are all alone—all they have are their memories. A few even pray to die. They just want the pain to end."

He wanted her to know he understood. "I remember the night my father died. I just sat in the chair beside his bed in the hospital. He was in great pain. I read a few verses of the Bible to him, thought it might make him feel better. I guess all I can do is hope that it did. Then he was gone. Just like that, he was gone."

"There's absolutely no way to prepare for death, is there?" she said. "It just happens. They're fine, maybe eyes open, talking about home. And then silence. Nothing. Young boys who still have so much to offer. Such a mystery, even to those of us who witness it every day. One minute they're muscular, breathing, talking, supple human beings, then suddenly they stop breathing and are gone. All the things that made that person a human being vanish right before your very eyes. I hate this war!"

"After my dad died, I just sat there, bawling like a little baby. I couldn't bring him back. All I could do was remember who he was, and that's still all I can do."

"I know. I remember some of them, some of their stories, the light in their eyes when they talked about home or a girl. When they die, we close their eyelids and clean them up the best we can."

The strain of her immense responsibility was evident in Loretta's weary face. She ran her fingers through her hair and tried not to think of Philip. "We wash their bodies. All that's left is what we studied in basic biology—skin, bones, blood. Then the heat and humidity take over. The stench of death, the smell of those rotting corpses. Then I wonder, where do their spirits go? What happened to their fight, their will to stay alive, to get back home? Philip's in there right now, and I'm certain that's what he's doing—fighting to get back home."

"I pray he does, Loretta."

She nodded, taking a deep breath, and wiped her tears. "I've never gotten used to it. It's strange, isn't it? Most of these men thought they were going to be heroes, win the war, and march down their home-town Main Street in a big parade, decked out in their fancy uniforms, basking in the glory of winning a war and saving mankind. But as they're dying, they're afraid. Some even whimper like a small child. They actually cry out for their mothers. It's so tragic, so sad. And after each one of them dies, a bit of me dies, too. But then it dawns on me. Just like all of you who are out there fighting, I have a job to do." She took a final drag from her cigarette and crushed it in the ash can next to the bench. "I pray Philip does make it home. He was a very special friend, you know."

"Yeh, I know. He's gonna make it. He's tough and lucky." Ed smiled through his tears.

"You're so right, Ed." She leaned down to comfort him. His head was buried in his hands. He didn't want her to see him crying. "He's lucky to have a friend like you." She kissed the top of his head and then disappeared into the tent.

Sitting on the primitive bench, Ed wondered if he was in shock. He wiped away his tears. Narrowly avoiding becoming a patient himself tonight, he was painfully aware that his meager prayer was a long shot. He had seen many an aviator and airman sent back into action due to the skill of the competent doctors and nurses in this place. They worked miracles every day. Maybe, just maybe, they could produce one more and put Philip back together again.

When Ed returned to the tent, he turned on the single lightbulb hanging over the makeshift desk his mentor had constructed. Opening Philip's footlocker, he discovered a stack of four letters neatly arranged and resting on the top of the books, papers, and diaries. Three letters were sealed in envelopes and addressed in Philip's impeccable hand-writing. One letter was not sealed, the one addressed to Elinor Robin-son. It beckoned Ed to pick it up. He didn't.

⊕

Nurse Raffa stood over Philip. His breathing was labored. She turned away to make a note on his chart.

"El." Philip was trying to say something. In the faintest whisper, in the fog of his anesthesia, he murmured again, "El."

Raffa grabbed a nearby medic. "Go find Lieutenant Keno and Dr. Goldman. Right now!" She pushed the corporal out the flapped doorway of the tent and returned to Philip's bedside.

CHAPTER 65

Coming Home

STEEL WHEELS ROLLED OVER STEEL TRACKS, fishplate fasteners, and creosote-soaked wood ties. Rhythmic. *Clack-clack! Clack-clack! Clickety-clack!* Hissing steam intermittently accompanied the syncopation of the rainstorm's pitter-patter against the windows of the stainless-steel train. Belching diesel smoke and spewing billowing exhaust from its underbelly, the California Zephyr whizzed across the heartland.

Philip stared out the rain-spattered window into the bleak morning dawn. Overlooking the reflection of his scarred face, he gazed out toward the beauty that rushed by. Crocuses of purple, yellow, and white, like clusters of Easter eggs, bloomed in the ditches of roads that stretched beside the rail tracks. Some roadsides were scorched, burned to extricate weeds. Innocent crocuses had most certainly fallen victim to such savagery. No matter. He was done with savagery for the time being.

After witnessing the splendor of the Rocky Mountains, he'd slept for hours. When he awoke, the wide-open prairies of Nebraska, Iowa, and Illinois stretched before him, images like mirages. New life sprang forth in the dark soil of the Midwest. Springtime brought hope, something he needed, especially now. It was April, and he was going home.

A few farmers toiled at daybreak behind horse-drawn plows. Others sat atop John Deere or International Harvester tractors, pulling their cultivators in the early morning drizzle. In the throes of modernity, they dug calculated rows in the moist morning dirt. If their God and the weather gods blessed them, the earth would sprout forth in autumn with an abundant crop of wheat, corn, beans, or hay. He remembered summer days on his grandfather's farm, sweat pouring from him as he labored in the fields, gathering hay and storing it in the barn loft. Farmers were good people, hardworking and industrious, although superstitious. Small towns and their deserted train stations sat unimpressed as the silver locomotive streaked through the countryside.

The *Zephyr* came to a halt in Chicago's Union Station, completing the first leg of Philip's journey, 2,532 miles. A few hours on the B&O *Abraham Lincoln* and he'd meet his family at St. Louis's Union Station. Would she be there? It would be just a short ride home to Nebo, at least short in comparison to the miles he had traveled.

It was impossible to erase her from his memory. His El. At least he hoped she was still his. He had survived. He imagined her racing around her assigned hospital rooms, making rounds in her Cadet Nurse uniform. He pulled the wallet from his back pocket and opened it to her picture. She sat on a bench in her white cap and white shoes, a long white apron covering her dark dress. Smiling. Her eyes sparkled, even in the black-and-white photo.

The future would be theirs. That was his dream, his hope. His olive drab U.S. Army Air Force jacket, displaying his silver, first lieutenant bars, and garrison cap rested on the seat next to him. He returned the wallet to his pocket and pulled a book from his briefcase. An Army officer approached. He could have been Ed Stevens's twin.

"Mind if I share a seat with you, lieutenant?"

"Not at all," Philip said. He collected his jacket and cap from the seat next to him. "Where you headed?"

The soldier replied, "Saint Louie. Got a three-day furlough; gonna get married!" The gold-colored butterbars on the soldier's epaulets indicated the second lieutenant's rank to Philip.

"Good for you."

"How about you, sir?"

"Saint Louie, too."

"I see you're a flyboy," the lieutenant said, pointing at Philip's aviator wings insignia.

"Yeh, just completed flight training in California."

"Where you headed?"

"Returning to the South West Pacific. Two-week pass."

"Looks like you might have seen some action."

Philip touched the scar on his face. "More than I wanted," he replied.

The lieutenant looked down at the book. "Is that *The Great Gatsby*?" The cover was unmistakable: two searing eyes, a pair of ruby-red lips set upon a blue background with a cityscape below. Between the eyes and lips was a nearly indecipherable hole.

"It was a gift from my girl. Actually saved my life." Philip ran his fingers over the hole, tender strokes with purpose, almost as if he was reading Braille. "So, you've heard of it?"

"Sure have. Read it in my American lit class in college before I enlisted."

"So you're a college man? Where?"

"Illinois Wesleyan University—English major there. *Gatsby*'s one of my favorite novels. Fitzgerald's a fine writer and Gatsby sure was an intriguing character."

"Maybe even a *great* character." They shared a laugh at Philip's weak excuse for a joke.

"Well, sir, here's to an orgastic future for both of us." They laughed again at the suggestion.

The two soldiers switched trains in Chicago. Walking through Union Station, Philip was surprised to see so many soldiers who looked a lot like some of the fellow combat veterans he'd known. It was obvious as they walked by that they weren't—no recognition, no greeting. Philip and the lieutenant boarded the *Abraham Lincoln*, found open seats next to each other, and continued their conversation.

"You live in Saint Louis?" Philip asked.

"No, sir. Quincy, Illinois."

"Ah, the Casino. Ever been there?"

"Oh, yes, sir. You been there? To the Casino, I mean?"

"Saw Dorsey and Sinatra. Quite a night." *How could he forget it? Their first dance.*

The lieutenant chattered on. He loved Sinatra, loved books, especially Hemingway, and couldn't wait to see his fiancé. It was going to be a simple wedding. Most of all, he had to be honest, he was scared to death about going to North Africa. Even though he was trained to do so, he wasn't certain he could really kill another person.

Philip was polite, nodded his head. *Oh, you can, but it's easier at 30,000 feet, even at 200 feet,* he thought. As the rain dissipated, he gazed out the window, marveling at the majesty of the morning sun rising in bright triumph over the Illinois prairie. *Will she be there? Will this scarred face repulse her?*

The *Abraham Lincoln* pulled into St. Louis Union Station and came to a gradual stop. Late afternoon, dusk, the dim lights descending from the overhang covering the station's platforms cast a gloomy haze over the cement walkways. A mass of humanity huddled together in wait for their loved ones. Steam from the engines billowed forth, engulfing the window where Philip peered out intently in search of El and his family. Soldiers shuffled with their duffel bags off and onto the trains. There were tears of sorrow and joy, hugs, brief kisses, prolonged kisses.

"Good luck, lieutenant! Kill some Japs for me." The young lieutenant Philip had shared a seat with grabbed his duffel and hustled ahead.

"Yeh, good luck to you, too! Give that new wife of yours a hug for me."

Philip descended the train's stairs, scanning the crowded platform through the haze. Then he saw her. It was as if she emerged from a cloud. El stood smiling, radiant in her favorite blue dress. He dropped his duffel bag, rushed toward her open arms, reaching, reaching, but the throng grew, pushing him farther back away from her. El reappeared and ran toward him. Stopping just short of Philip's reach, she smiled at him.

"El," he tried to yell out, but his voice seemed to vanish in the vapor. "El."

She fell into his outstretched arms and sobbed. She looked up at him. "You're here, you're really here. Oh, Philip, I knew you'd keep your promise."

"I did. I did, didn't I?" He looked up wistfully at the train station ceiling. "Thank you! Thank you, God! Thank you, God!"

The engine's steamy exhaust created a swirling mist at their feet. They wept as they stood locked in each other's embrace. The song "Cheek to Cheek" began to play over the train station speakers. It was as if Philip was living a dream. He swept El off her feet, and they danced just as the song suggested.

CHAPTER 66

Broken Places

April 12, 1943

LORETTA SAT UPRIGHT IN A CHAIR beside Philip's bed. She checked her watch; it was 0610. His labored breathing awakened her from a semi-sleep. She stood and looked down upon his peaceful, ashen face. He struggled to open his swollen eyes, trying to speak. His weakened voice, almost indecipherable, released a final, desperate gasp, followed by a single word, "El."

The moment Loretta took his hand in an effort to comfort him, she knew he was gone—a casualty, a statistic, a mere number. Serial number 16019084. Deceased.

When Dr. Goldman arrived, Loretta was still holding his hand but had gained control of her sobbing. In a crude medical tent on the edge of a wild, dense, and foreboding jungle, Goldman stood solemnly over Philip's still-warm body, pulled the sheet over his face, and pronounced him dead.

In that moment, generations died. The potential offspring of Philip and El became inconsequential, mute, deaf, blind, nonexistent. The world would never hear the songs he might have composed or read the poems or books he might have written. In that moment of time, Philip Zumwalt and *all* he had to offer was lost to the world.

His war was over.

Morning, just before daylight. Sergeant Nyman arrived at Ed Stevens's tent and woke him from a restless sleep. "Lieutenant Keno would like to see you as soon as possible."

Ed threw on his shorts and T-shirt and ran to the hospital tent. Loretta was sitting outside on the bench smoking. The moment she saw Ed, she broke into tears and rushed toward him.

"He's gone. He's gone. Oh, dear God, I can't believe he's really gone." Loretta's words were barely understandable through her sobs. "We couldn't save him." They held each other in the morning fog. "He fought so hard, right to the bitter end. So much to live for. I'm so sorry. The world has lost such a wonderful man." Loretta wept into Ed's chest.

He embraced and thanked her. "You know, you're an angel of mercy. You know that, don't you?"

"Thank you for saying that, Ed. We try, but if I was really an angel, Philip would still be alive. I'd never let a good man like him die like that." Loretta rose, wiped her tears, and walked away through the morning mist into the tent, where another day of suffering awaited her.

Ed returned to his tent. Once his tentmates awoke, he would tell them that Philip was gone. Quietly, he made his way to Philip's footlocker and opened it again. He picked up the four letters. He would mail two of them, the ones sealed and addressed to Philip's brother and best friend.

The third sealed envelope had an entirely different purpose. Ed opened the envelope addressed only *To the Fortunate Soul Who Has Been Put in Charge of Securing My Personal Effects*. He read:

To Whom It May Concern:
> *If you are reading this, I am grateful that someone has survived. You are one of the lucky ones, and I pray that your life will continue*

to be blessed with good fortune. I hope that I have ascended to the great Valhalla, the airman's rest. Please do not weep for me, for I did what I felt I had to do. I had always hoped that the fortune teller Zeralda's prophecy would prove false. She told me, "You will meet with unexpected dire circumstances at an uncommon hour, but do not fear. Your treasure will not be left in gold and silver coins, but in another form, one money cannot buy."

I have no idea what she meant by that, but since you are reading this letter, I must assume I met with some unexpected dire circumstances. All I ask is that you return my books, music, letters, poems, and diaries to my parents. Please tell them that I am sorry that they are left with only their grief and these simple reminders of my existence on this earth. I am certain that they will never understand what I went through and why I decided to do so. If my memory is their treasure, then I will be happy.

If possible, please let Elinor Robinson, a nurse at Blessing Hospital in Quincy, Illinois, know also that I am sorry that I did not keep my promise and that I loved her with my last breath. If it is my good fortune to go to Heaven, I will watch over her for all of her remaining days. I am certain that to you, who might be a stranger, this all may seem a bit dramatic, but I assure you this is only my attempt to make some degree of sense out of this madness. So, I sincerely hope that you will grant my final request and do as I have asked.

One last thing, one piece of advice: If you survive this war—love everything! When you return to the other end of the world, love everything!

Philip A. Zumwalt

A treasure, Ed thought. The treasure was Philip. His words, his kindness, his example—that was the treasure Philip Zumwalt had left to him and to all who knew Philip. Ed stared at the fourth letter, laying unsealed on the desk in front of him. The contents of that letter most likely contained Philip's final written words. This time, he picked it up without the slightest hesitation. It was addressed to *Miss Elinor Robinson, Blessing Hospital, Quincy, Illinois*. He removed the letter from the envelope and read:

April 11, 1943
Dear El,

I am sitting here, remembering the first night we met. I was hesitant to even go to the Casino that night. Funny how fate intersects in our lives, how forces collide, how society imposes its will, sometimes doing its best to keep apart even those who love each other as much as we do. Hemingway wrote the following in his novel A Farewell to Arms:

"The world breaks everyone and afterward many are strong in the broken places. But those that will not break it kills. It kills the very good and the very gentle and the very brave impartially. If you are none of these you can be sure it will kill you too but there will be no special hurry."

We may be broken now but, in the end, we will be stronger. I am coming home to you. I promise. I think about you every day. I know that this is a lot to ask, but I am going to ask it anyhow. Please wait for me, El. I've loved you from the first moment you stepped out of the shadows at the Casino. I loved you every moment of your senior year. I loved you at Siloam Springs, at the Opera House and the Majestic. I have never stopped loving you.

These are trying times, but as a friend once reminded me, "Even in the midst of tragedy, there is still hope. Even in the midst of war, there is still love." We must always hold on to hope, El. And we must always hold on to the love we have for each other.

I've received word that my orders for flight school are en route. That means I will be coming home soon. I hope you will be waiting for me with open arms. Don't worry about me, I will be home. They call me Lucky now. I am lucky because I found you lurking behind those curtains. Or did you find me?

When I get home, we will sit under that oak tree, have a picnic, stretch our arms out farther, toward each other, look into each other's eyes, and find ourselves lost in each other's embrace. One fine morning, the lark will sing out our song, a song that will never end, an eternal song of love and faithfulness. I have to go now, but I'll write more later upon my return from tonight's mission. You are remarkable and unforgettable.

Before I close, I must be honest with you. I have one more mission to complete, and I could never forgive myself if something does happen to me. If I do not return, El, I want you to remember what I wrote you in a previous letter. Do not be angry, be forgiving. I want you to move on with your life, be happy, and, above all, you too must try your best to love everything. I pray that your life with or without me will be one of joy. Find joy in the beauty of all things, just like the meaningful Dostoevsky quote you sent me. When you awaken, and in every moment you exist, take in the glorious surroundings of where you are at that precious moment in time. When you scurry from place to place in your daily affairs, take in the beauty of each and every person with whom you come in contact. Look for the good in all people. When you are blue, think of how blessed your life is, as it most certainly will be.

A part of me wants to hold on to you, to share joy with you, but I have become more of a realist and less of an idealist. My delusions of grandeur, as Billy called them, are not so grand anymore. All I want is to come home, come home to you. War does that to a person. I think in simpler terms now. I appreciate ordinary days more. I may or may not survive this madness. If I do, I pray you'll be waiting for me. If not, I pray you'll find someone who loves you like I do, who will wake up every morning in anticipation of just being with you, sharing morning coffee and discussing the day's plan—a person who will provide all the comforts you need to experience the joy you so richly deserve. And I hope you will love each other with all of your hearts.

As I said earlier, El, I am not Nostradamus. I'm not able to fore-tell either of our futures, but I pray we will be together, one way or another. Not to be maudlin, but if it is not in the cards for me, if my number is called, I hope that a part of me will live on in your heart . . .

Philip had not yet signed the letter. What more might he have had to say? Was there to be a postscript? Ed placed the letter in its enve-lope, sealed it, and again opened Philip's trunk.

Organized neatly in stacks were his three diaries, letters bound together with string, miscellaneous books, some sheet music, and his insurance papers. He placed the diaries, a stapled book of poetry, the sheet music, and all the letters in his own trunk.

The Great Gatsby sat on the top of the stack of books. Ed removed the book from the trunk and turned it over in his hands. Philip had told Ed the story of the night El gave him the book. It was his good luck charm. It had accompanied Philip on every mission. Had he for-gotten it? Ed opened the book. On the title page was an inscription:

To Philip,
*   "Tomorrow we will run faster, stretch out our arms farther . . .*
And one fine morning—"
*   One fine morning we will be together as one and then we will share the rest of our tomorrows together.*
*   Love,*
*   El*
*   Christmas 1941*

Ed tenderly placed Philip's letter to El into the middle of the book. He would mail it today. Philip would have wanted her to have it. He gathered the remainder of Philip's personal effects and carefully placed them in his own footlocker.

There were so many broken places, so many broken people. War did that; there was no escaping it. Perhaps by returning Philip's possessions his family might, at least, find some peace. Perhaps Philip's words would bring them some degree of comfort. Perhaps some of the broken places might be healed. That was Ed's prayer; that would be his mission. He would make certain that all Philip's possessions were returned to his family.

Brushing back his tears, he thought of Philip's final piece of advice. If he was lucky enough to survive, when he returned to the other end of the world, back to Mountain Lakes—to crocuses, to the woods, to trout-filled streams—he would live every day, every ordinary day, to its fullest. Without further ceremony, he closed his trunk and locked it.

PART FOUR

CHAPTER 67

Acciaccatura

March 12, 1948

ON AN ATYPICAL MARCH MORNING in Illinois, the sunlight slipped through the lace curtains of Elinor Thoroughgood's childhood bedroom, waking her from a restive sleep. She had taken a couple of days off from her duties at Blessing Hospital. Her husband, Earnest, was swamped at the hospital tending to a half-dozen new births. He had encouraged her to stay over and spend the night with her folks following the funeral.

Looking around her room, she was flooded with memories—her saxophone tucked in its case, the program for *The Life of Riley*, a framed picture of the mixed chorus singing at graduation, and a poster that one of her Quincy cousins had saved for her, advertising the Dorsey Band playing at the Casino.

El smiled, thinking of herself as a giddy high school senior, naive and precocious, trying so hard to be sophisticated and mature. She had been foolish about many things, but her love for Philip had been real. He had been so patient with her. Without a doubt, he had loved her and she had loved him.

She wrestled from under the sheets, wrapped herself in her chenille robe, and pulled the white oak chair out from the small wooden desk sitting under her bedroom window. Opening the middle drawer, she secured pen and paper and wrote:

Dear Philip,

You finally made it home. It took a great effort from your family and so many others. Petitions were sent to Springfield and Washington D.C. It took nearly five years of negotiating mountains of red tape, but two days ago, you arrived back in Nebo. Two young Army privates accompanied your coffin all the way from Ipswich, Australia, and then placed it in the care of Nebo's funeral director, Mr. G. H. Heck Hobbs.

Yesterday, Mr. Hobbs's assistants draped your coffin with the American flag and placed it in front of the stage in the high school gymnasium. The two privates, who looked young enough to still be high school students, stood guard over you. The gym was packed, filled with townsfolk seated in folding chairs. Dozens more stood in the rear. Mr. Homer Boren officiated the service. He was wonderful. His words were so kind and reassuring to all of us in attendance. He spoke so highly of you. Your friends who survived the war were there—Billy and Charlie. My parents and I sat with them and their wives, Pat and Karen, and Mrs. Staley. Essie and Randall Yarborough and Ina and Ronald Hague were also there. So were DeAnne Trout, Trudy Inness, and Dai Wilson, who had all lost their husbands in combat.

We gathered after the service at Hunter Cemetery. It was late afternoon; the sun was just beginning to set over the barren corn and bean fields. Mr. Boren offered a few final words and a prayer. A squad of local riflemen from the VFW fired their rifles in unison. The repeating din of the twenty-one-gun salute stretched to the Heavens and startled those who had never heard the deafening sound of simultaneous gunfire. A retired staff sergeant played a sorrowful version of military taps on his bugle as they lowered your casket into the grave. An Army Air Force officer knelt at your mother's knee and presented her with the flag, folded into a triangle.

I sobbed during the service and lingered at your graveside, softly weeping until my father led me away. I would have waited for you forever. Remember—a forever love.

There was a tap at El's door. "Elinor? Breakfast is ready, dear." Sandra's voice was soft and understanding.

"Thank you, Mother. I'll be down in a moment."

El pushed away from the desk and dressed, deciding she would finish the letter later. She pulled a small key from the desk drawer, folded the letter, and walked to her bed. Bending over, she dragged a wooden box from under her bed and deposited the letter inside. It rested on top of Philip's other letters. After locking the box with the key, she strung the key on a thin gold chain, hung it around her neck, and slid the box back underneath her bed.

After breakfast El put on her denim work jacket. "I'm going to take the dogs for a walk, Mother," she said.

"I'm sure they'll love it, dear."

El walked with Stella and Moose to Payson Central Park. She laid a blanket on the cold ground by the gigantic oak tree and sat in silence. The two labs settled down beside her. This was a sacred place for her—a still point. Sitting quietly, she remembered the last time she saw him and her last words to him. Her pulse raced as memory brought the moment back to her, clear and innocent. Through the open window and the frigid morning air, she had shouted out to him. Her voice rang with hope from the seventh floor of the Majestic Hotel. Closing her eyes, she saw him still, smiling bravely at the elevator and then shivering by the cab door, repeating the same playful salute he had given to her the first night they'd parted at the Casino's Blue Room.

Maybe it was the wind whistling through the branches of the old oak, or maybe it was her imagination, but in the gentle morning's breeze, she heard, "Until we meet again, my beautiful Elinor." A moment passed, and then the last words she would ever hear him speak swept, once again, through her mind: "I will always love you, too!"

El smiled to herself. *Ah, a grace note*, she thought. *It's there and then it's gone.* But those moments would always remain timeless in her mind. She looked up at the soft morning-blue sky and then back across the street where Mrs. Staley's yard was already preparing to bloom. Now, she better understood the rhythm of it all. Her heart was full.

Winter was over, spring just around the corner. She would try her best to love everything. She would do it for Philip, in his memory, but she would also do it for herself. Wiping away her tears, El smiled, sat up on her blanket, and took in the splendor of the park as the rest of this and all future mornings stretched out before her.

POSTLUDE

From "To Illinois Gold Star Mothers, Who Lost a
Child to War" by Kevin Stein, Illinois Poet Laureate

IN THE SUMMER OF 1948, RUBY ZUMWALT read her son's diaries for the final time. She cut open brown paper bags and wrapped up all the belongings Ed Stevens had so carefully sent. She tied string around the package and placed the parcel in the trunk at the foot of Philip's bed. She never again looked at the meticulous records kept by her eldest boy. The day Ruby died, Philip's brother Homer placed the diaries, a few newspaper articles, medals, and a book of poetry into a box, the same box that he presented to me on a Christmas morning.

That box now rests upon a shelf in a bookcase in my study. Surrounding the box are Philip's medals, symbols of his valor and sacrifice. On top of the box is a copy of *The Great Gatsby*. Inside the front cover there is an inscription written by a young, idealistic woman who was looking forward to all her tomorrows. A golden lavaliere bejeweled with two pearls reposes in my wife's jewelry case. These all, in their own way, constitute some of the talismans of this story. Although not exactly a reliquary, the box holds a place of honor in our family.

As for me, I have fulfilled a long-held obligation and kept my promise to try my best to "make something" of the story I was given.

The miniature black plastic recorder that I used years ago to record Homer's version of his brother's story sits on my desk. I place the last microcassette I had recorded on the machine's spindles and push the play button. It is Homer's voice. It is appropriate, for without Homer, this story would never have been told. In his final testament, I hear the love of a brother, a love that lingered through the decades, forged by blood and memory.

"Well, sir, all I can tell you is that he was a fine man. We all did what we had to do back then. All of us were involved in that war." His tone softens. "Most of them are gone now. Like I said, he was a fine man, and Elinor Robinson was a fine woman. I think I'll leave it at that."

Following Homer's funeral, while cleaning out his attic, I discovered a yellowed *Pike County Republican* newspaper in the bottom of an old trunk. On April 21, 1943, *The Republican* ran a front-page picture of Philip, chronicling his heroics and death. The reporter skillfully described the exploits of Major Ken McCullar and his men. The story also mentioned a photograph of another crew that had appeared in a nationwide newspaper circulation. That photo was of a new, four-motored B-17 bomber nicknamed *Chief Seattle*. The Flying Fortress had been financed by the good people of Seattle, hence the name. *The Republican* reported it thusly: *"Metropolitan newspapers later printed a picture of the big bomber, with members of its crew, including Zumwalt, taken just after the bomber had returned to its base after a bombing flight, unscathed except for a minor wing scar. 'I wish I could tell you the story of that picture,' wrote Zumwalt shortly after. But Philip's lips are sealed, and perhaps one of the great stories of the war is left untold."*

It is my hope that *The Republican* reporter would be pleased to know that a small part of Philip's story has, at last, been told. Words, however, can never fully recapture what Philip and his brothers and sisters in arms went through, not even their own words.

My wife and I are most fortunate to live close to our children and grandchildren. We so enjoy when they come to our lake home for dinner. On occasion, after dinner, my wife, our children, their spouses, our grandchildren, and I all claim our walking sticks and trudge up the hill to the state park trail that borders our property. We walk briskly into the dusk to my lookout place.

Here, at this end of the world, we sit on fallen logs, celebrating a moment of silence. We witness the gradual and graceful descent of the sun and gaze out through the trees that surround us, lining the shore of the lake's cove. The light-blue sky, laced with pink and white clouds, soars majestically above the water reflecting the splendor of this place, this still point. In those moments, I breathe deeply and take it in, the light, the beauty, the rhythm of it all, the promise of tomorrow. As I assemble there with those I love, in this place I love, I think of El and Philip and make another promise to myself: I will try my best to love everything.

In Memoriam

ELINOR ROBINSON (A PSEUDONYM) GRADUATED in 1943 from Blessing Hospital in Quincy, Illinois, and became a nurse. She considered enlisting in the U.S. Army Nurse Corps in hopes of being sent to the South Pacific Theater to join the man she loved. Her parents discouraged her enlistment; she honored their wish and did not volunteer.

Elinor married Dr. Ernest Thoroughgood (a pseudonym). Together they raised four children, two daughters and two sons. Although she never went to war, she became a respected nurse before retiring to become a full-time mother. Upon her untimely death, she was celebrated in her community for her extensive philanthropic and compassionate service to the local hospitals and her synagogue.

Major Ken McCullar died a hero in the eyes of his men, his nation, and his hometown. He was awarded the Purple Heart and Silver Star. Sometime in 1943, his family received notice that he had been awarded the Distinguished Service Cross. The Medal of Honor is the only higher military award that can be given to a member of the U.S. Army for extreme gallantry and risk of life in actual combat with an armed enemy force. The aerial combat technique called skip bombing perfected by McCullar and his crew was instrumental in the defeat of the Japanese navy in the South Pacific. For the remainder of the war, the Forty-Third Bombardment Group was known as Ken's Men.

American Legion Post 0118 in Batesville, Mississippi, is named the Kenneth McCullar Post.

Homer and Dell Zumwalt finally made their visit to Lucky and Gladys "Chic" Stevens in Mountain Lakes, New Jersey, in 1968, while Homer was on a business trip. They returned home and reported to their daughter that her uncle Philip was fortunate to have had Edwin "Lucky" Stevens as a friend. Until the day he died, Lucky Stevens, truly the Last of the Mohicans, meticulously assembled one of the most complete collections of World War II memorabilia in the United States of America. But to the Zumwalt family, he had delivered a portion of his collection that would always remain a family treasure. Lucky Stevens died in Mountain Lakes, New Jersey, on October 15, 1991.

Lonnie Zumwalt died of natural causes in 1978. Ruby came to live in Galesburg, Illinois, at the local nursing home in 1987. She passed away in 1989 in her rocking chair at the nursing home, shortly after finishing her lunch.

Ida Dell Kinnamon Zumwalt died in an automobile accident on February 15, 1998. Homer Lee Zumwalt died peacefully in his bed on April 25, 2010. Wayne Sidwell Zumwalt, the youngest of the Zumwalt brothers, died on August 23, 2010.

During the writing of this novel, there have been many joys, but there have also been some sorrows. I lost three of my dearest friends, Steve Fox, Steve Coffman, and Ed "Bo" Olds. Bo served as my primary aviation expert and literally walked me through the intricacies of flying a B-17. I miss each of those friends every day. I also lost my fraternity brother and Army buddy, Jim Boisclair. These unforgettable men are the basis of a few of the characters in the novel. Their untimely loss helped me to better understand what Philip wrote about following the death of his friends and crewmates.

My parents' generation still informs my life, and their legacy continues to resonate throughout my everyday existence. The optimism, hope, love, and faith that sustained them have endured. They encouraged us and instilled in us, their descendants, a lingering belief that the world can still be a good place where humankind can live in peace.

The unraveling of this story included the recollections of a few of that generation who were still alive when I began my research. I listened as they told their stories and heard the emotion in their voices as they remembered their friends who had died, voices now silent. These veterans, these survivors, shared pictures of themselves and their buddies, of their wives or girlfriends, of their parents, and of the places where they had been. With great pride, they produced their own medals and a variety of talismans for my inspection. Each of them, too, had a story to tell, and threads of those stories were woven into this one. Even in the midst of my research, as I walked the streets of Nebo, San Francisco, and Sydney, Australia, their voices spoke to me.

Writing this novel brought back memories of the telling of my own father's guarded stories about his time in war. I, too, lost an uncle in World War II. Just as Gail never knew Philip, I never knew my uncle Bobby, my father's younger brother. Bobby died on July 21, 1944, after he stepped on a land mine while storming a beachhead with his fellow Marines, reclaiming the island of Guam for the United States. He was nineteen years old.

My father survived the war. He mentioned to me a few times that his ship, the USS Narraguagas (AOG-32), was attacked by numerous kamikaze assaults during the Battle of Okinawa. I am certain that the horrors he encountered I could never begin to comprehend. Perhaps that is why he rarely shared them with me.

He died on July 7, 2007. My mother survived him for nearly ten years, living each day of her ninety-three years with the same spunk that got her through Cadet Nurse's training. She passed away on June 8, 2017. She read various early versions of this book and contributed immensely to my research of nursing and Cadet Nurse's training during World War II.

Author's Notes

ALTHOUGH PORTIONS OF THIS STORY were inspired by a true story and based upon actual historical events, this novel must be considered a work of fiction due to the fact that dialogue, certain incidents, and characters were created for the purpose of dramatization. If actual names were used, the fictional character depicted may not reflect the thoughts or actions of the actual person. Some names of the characters portrayed in this book have been changed or altered to protect the privacy of individuals and their surviving family members. Most of the excerpts from the diaries of Philip A. Zumwalt were extracted verbatim from the original documents.

Many of the letters came from my imagination, but some are authentic or based on diary entries. The diaries and artifacts that compelled me to write this story may be accessed in the Archives Room at Knox College's library in Galesburg, Illinois, the college where I ended my own teaching career. The library was named after H. M. Seymour, who donated the cream-colored limestone that effaces the library from a quarry on his farm in Payson, Illinois. He oversaw the construction of the library, which was dedicated on Knox College Founders Day, 1928.

H.M. Seymour and his wife, Lucy, had donated limestone from the same quarry and directed the construction of the Charles W. Seymour Memorial High School. The building erected to honor their fallen son was completed and dedicated on December 30, 1916. On that same day, three years later, Philip Arthur Zumwalt was born. On a warm afternoon in September, nearly twenty-five years following that dedication, Philip walked through the front doors of that high school and began his teaching career. The building still stands and now houses Payson Elementary School.

In the writing of this novel, I had access to many resources and a team of remarkable editors. One of those editors was Dawn Shamp who introduced me to the Table Rock Writers Workshop held in the mountains of Wildacres, North Carolina. It was there that I met Darnell Arnoult, my writing group, and a host of new friends who shared my passion for writing. That entire writing community inspired and challenged me to become a better writer. I benefited from the teachings of Abigail DeWitt, who instilled in me the daily habit of freewriting, and gained wise literary advice from Mary Struble Deery, Georgann Eubanks, Judy Goldman, Luther Kirk, and Lynsley Smith.

During my research, I interviewed many veterans of World War II, but two of them were most valuable: Reed Robertson was the navigator on a B-24 in the South West Pacific and gave me a realistic perspective of what an airman experienced in that theater of the war. He was one of the first Americans to set foot in the ruins of Hiroshima following the dropping of the bomb on that Japanese city. Gilbert "Gibb" Howard was a combat radio operator on a B-17. He flew twenty-plus missions over Europe. Both men were most honest as they related the horror of air combat to me.

As I wrote, I thought often of my own time in the military and the men who made it bearable, especially John Abraham, Jim Boisclair, Barry Klock, Ron Nadel, Tom McGreevy, Todd Tanger, and Bruce Winter. Also, to Mel Halfon, the best Army boss a soldier could ever have.

My research assistants at Knox College, Jordan Willits, Jeremy Ransom and Bridget Dooley made many useful contributions to the book, and Carly Robison's archiving of Philip's diaries and papers in the Knox College Library will enshrine his "treasure" for generations to come.

Further research assistance was granted by Knox librarian Anne Giffey and Jean Kay of the Historical Society of Quincy and Adams County. My exploration of Australia and New Guinea would have been far less complete without the expertise of our guide, Vic Martin, and his friend Jo Rush. Vicki Laing's tour of the Kingsclere Apartments in Sydney, Australia, provided me with a plethora of stories from that famous place.

The National Museum of the U.S. Air Force in Dayton, Ohio and the Smithsonian National Air and Space Museum have created separate havens for anyone interested in the history of aviation. It was in the Smithsonian where I accidently stumbled upon the exhibit detailing the story of the Vin Fiz. All such professionals are tireless in maintaining a portion of our American history and I was appreciative to have had the opportunity to gather information in those hallowed halls.

Encouragement from many of the faculty members, staff, and administration at Knox College was much appreciated during this journey.

H.M. Seymour Library at Knox College. *Photograph by Tom Foley*

Acknowledgments

I T WAS MY GOOD FORTUNE to have been given the essence of this book in the first place. I will always be grateful to Homer for trusting me to tell his brother's story.

My friend and mentor, Dr. Penelope Niven, was my first editor. Penny passed away in August 2014. A noted author in her own right and a member of the North Carolina Writer's Hall of Fame, she guided me through the early stages of this process and was a priceless resource. Her constant encouragement and wise counsel made it impossible for me to give up on this project, even when I wanted to do so. She left us too soon. Her daughter, the author Jennifer Niven, has continued to support me during the writing of this book.

Eternal thanks to the wonderful team that assumed the momentous task of continuing to edit this novel: Kathleen Barber, Joel Estes, Laurel Ferejohn, Pat Kane (winner of the award for having read the book the most times, other than my wife), Lori Lewis, Carol Killman Rosenberg, Dawn Shamp, Gail Zumwalt Swanson, Matthew Swanson, Stephanie Whetstone, and Lara Swanson Wilson.

I am indebted to The Book Couple—Carol Killman Rosenberg and Gary Rosenberg. Without their expertise and guidance in all aspects of book publishing, this novel would, most likely, never have come to fruition. Their professionalism and friendship during the completion of the novel is much appreciated.

My thanks to a loyal group of family and friends who have helped sustain me during this journey. Many agreed to become Beta readers and gave me valuable feedback throughout the many iterations of this book's becoming: Nancy and Steve Ballard, Kathleen Barber, Diana Beck, John Claude Bemis, Michael Boren, Judy Boynton, Donald Brannon, Stacy and Mike Campbell, Mike Clark, Patty Chamberlain, Steve Coffman, Mary and Kevin Deery, Abigail DeWitt, Nancy and Scott DeWitt, Diane and Joel Estes, Jack Feldman, Sandra and Don Fisk, Pam and Steve Fox, Susan and George "Sonny" Freeman, Bruce Gamble, Mary and Fletcher Gregory, Judy Goldman, Karen and Carl Hawkinson, Linda and Rich Hegg, Sheryl Hinman, Jeff Holt, Gilbert "Gibb" Howard, Jim Jacobs, Pat and Kelly Kane, Bernadine and Dale Kelley, Pat and Scott Kelley, Peg and Harley Knosher, Joyce Lemons, Phyllis and Gary Leonard, Sally and Steve Lundeen, Margie and Pat McEvoy, Trudy and Larry Meyers, Benita and David Moore, Owen Muelder, Roger Nelson, Jennifer Niven, Karen and Pete Nyman, Diane and Ed Olds, Betty Jo and Bill Ottoson, David Peterman, Reed Robertson, Mary and Rick Sayre, Barbara and Rich Schulze, Gayle and Jim Stewart, Susan and Brock Swanson, Susan and Jim Wandell, Jamie and Rick Yemm.

I am additionally indebted to Karen Jarchow, Debbie Marcum, and Jeri Stevens Kastner for granting me permission to tell a portion of their parents' stories.

I thank Poet Laureate of Illinois, Kevin Stein for graciously granting me permission to use a portion of his beautiful poem, "To Illinois Gold Star Mothers, Who Lost a Child to War."

Throughout this entire process, I have had the constant love and support of my family. My parents, Betty Ottoson Swanson and Fritz DeWayne Swanson, taught my sister and me what love and family truly mean. It is rare that an individual is able to say that his in-laws were like a second set of parents, but that is the case with Ida Dell Kinnamon Zumwalt and Homer Lee Zumwalt. I hope, in some measure, this novel reflects my love and respect for those amazing people, who in real life withstood and overcame the sorrows resulting from World War II. They all had and continue to have a profound influence upon my life.

Our children, Lara Ottoson Swanson Wilson, Lukas Zumwalt Swanson, and Matthew Kinnamon Swanson, are my great joy. Each contributed immensely, in their own way, to the completion of this novel.

I am grateful for my son-in-law, Fletcher Page Wilson, my daughter-in-law, Julie Anderson Swanson, and for our grandchildren, Fletcher Thomas "Fleet" Wilson, Grace Brooking Wilson, Foster Anderson Swanson, Banks Zumwalt Swanson, and Sam Eliot Swanson have all been there at various times to affirm me in the pursuit of my time-consuming dream.

My sister has supported me throughout the years and always has my back. So, to DeAnne Swanson Budde, her husband, Mike, her children and grandchildren, I say thanks.

In the end, I am most thankful to the love of my life, my wife and best friend, Gail Zumwalt Swanson. Her encouragement kept me going when I wanted to give up. Her editing skills were indispensable. She lived the story with me day to day and made certain that I was true to the character and legacy of her uncle Philip. Without her, this book would never have been written.

Resources

MY STUDY'S BOOKSHELVES ARE FILLED with books detailing World War II. During the writing of this novel, I continuously referred to them. Many of those books' authors' words and ideas informed me and influenced my thinking. To list them all would be exhaustive, but a few must be mentioned.

My understanding of the impact of Fortress Rabaul and the South West Pacific Theater on the Second World War would have been limited without the information contained within Bruce Gamble's fine historical trilogy on those subjects. His research on the *Blues in the Nite* crash was invaluable and matched Lucky Stevens's eye-witness account found in the letter he sent to Lonnie and Ruby Zumwalt. Whether a wallaby caused the crash remains a mystery.

Lisa See's wonderful novel, *China Dolls*, acquainted me with the glamorous world of San Francisco's Forbidden City Nightclub, and reading Anthony Doerr's beautiful novel, *All the Light We Cannot See*, introduced me to an engaging format that I attempted, to a limited extent, to emulate during the writing of this book.

While reading Sarah Blake's *The Guest Book*, I was exposed to James A. Baldwin's quotation, which I used as an epigraph to this novel. Sarah inspired me with her remarkable command of the English language. I discovered her work late in my writing process, but as a result, in my umpteenth revision, I paid particular attention to my sentence structure and vocabulary. I fear I will never approach the elegance of her writing, but she set a high bar to which I will continue to aspire.

Jon Meacham's *Franklin and Winston: An Intimate Portrait of an Epic Friendship* and Doris Kearns Goodwin's *No Ordinary Time: Franklin and Eleanor Roosevelt: The Home Front in World War II* were both extraordinarily helpful in better understanding the burden laid upon the principal leaders of the nations at war during World War II. Sidney Goldman's book, *New Guinea Diary: A Doctor's Tale from WWII*, gave me valuable insight into the difficult conditions that his father, Captain Perry Goldman, M.D., and other medical personnel endured while serving the medical needs of those stationed in the Pacific Theater during the war. And no book about World War II could be written without first reading all of Tom Brokaw's books written about *The Greatest Generation.*

Most notable, though, were a few books that were not about World War II. It was those books, the wonderful writings of Father Richard Rohr, that reminded me of the enduring concepts of faith and love.

About the Author

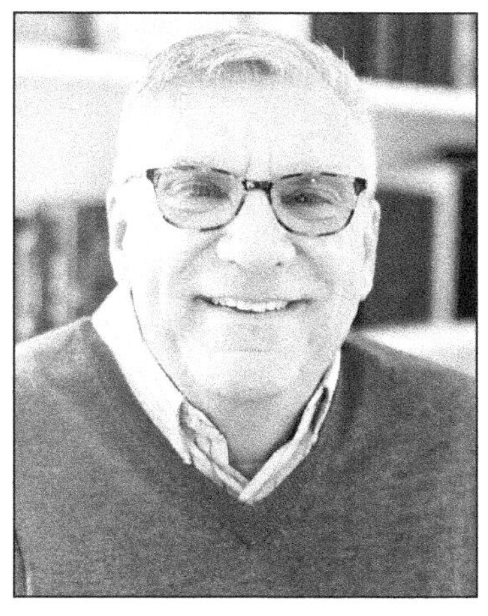

BARRY LEE SWANSON is an author, poet, U.S. Army veteran, and assistant professor emeritus from Knox College in Galesburg, Illinois. He received his B.A. in English literature from Illinois Wesleyan University and a master's degree in educational administration from Western Illinois University.

After a career in public education as an English teacher, coach, and school administrator, Swanson served as a full-time lecturer in the College of Education at the University of Illinois in Champaign-Urbana where he earned his Doctor of Education degree. He is past president of the Carl Sandburg Historic Site Association, and a founding member of the Galesburg Public Art Commission.

He is currently in the process of writing his second novel and publishing his complete poems.

Barry and his wife, Gail, reside on Lake Norman in North Carolina. They have three children and five grandchildren.

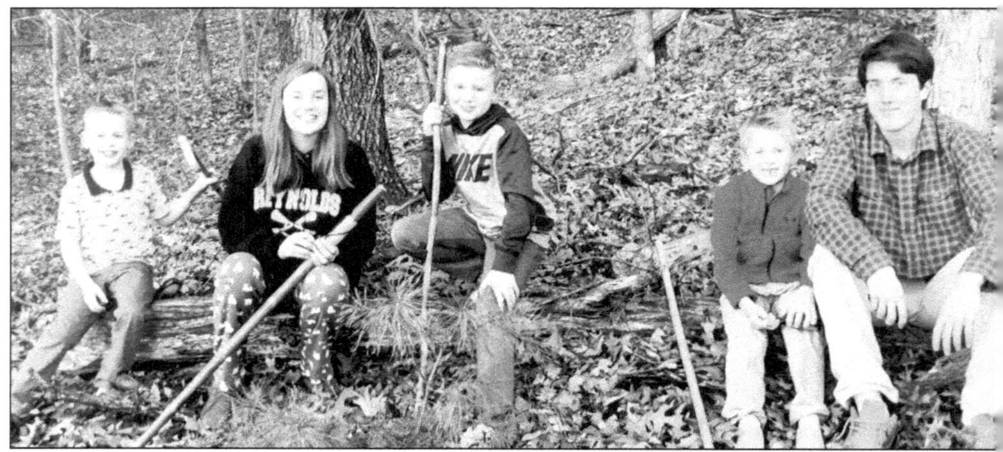

The author's grandchildren at Lookout Point
(*photo by Rebecca McNeely*)

Panorama

Of all the subjects about which men choose to write none is more colorful, more varied, more completely absorb[ing] than the lives of fellow human beings. As we travel along our own narrow little paths of existence we are constantly meeting those individuals whose true life stories surpass the wildest fiction. Many time[s] in my musing it has occured to me that I shou[ld] make an attempt to capture, in writing, the more unusual personalities with whom I come in cont[act]. Such an omnibus would make exciting reading. Lately I have met an unusual number of such [?] Men whose hectic history makes my own experience seem tame by comparison. They are the rebels [of] society, the seekers of romance & the restless searche[rs] for the rainbow's end. They have been privileged [to] see and experience adventures undreamed of a deca[de] ago. One of them accomplished a feat never befor[e] equaled ——— and almost unanimously they w[ould] aver that theirs is a humdrum life. Perhaps y[ou] could say that they are satisfied with life — that [because] they have known so much excitement, they can not [be] satisfied with ordinary existence. I cannot say. I know that their restlessness is contagious, and ea[ches?] endless vistas to beckon invitingly.

Philip A. Zumwalt